A Grim Journey

Scott Littleton

A GRIM JOURNEY

Copyright © 2021 Scott Littleton
All rights reserved.
scott.m.p.littleton@gmail.com
ISBN: 9798545463978

A GRIM JOURNEY

For mum and dad

A GRIM JOURNEY

Prologue

Slowly she pressed on, a single figure, all dark, quiet and grim. The stretch of flat land on which she strove, lay far into the distance, pocketed with rocks and boulders of every dull shade of grey: grey of a dark and dreary night, almost black, perhaps aspiring so; grey of the kind when hoping for a steady anchor in a storm; grey of simple times; grey of several times grey; a lonely grey.

This lonesome moor crept quietly from east to west in a tepid incline. To the north a brace of land stretching up to the foothills of the Lightlorne Mountain range. Down the steady incline to the east, from which the grim lady came, the lights of Stillham village glowed just steady in the distance, growing dimmer with every slow and forlorn step she took upon her quiet path.

South, alongside this quiet length of open land, a lake ran parallel in a long, thin, ellipsis. It dare seemed wider than a true throw of a stone, but its length ran off far to meet the horizon, keeping up a parallel to the moor. Perhaps it meant to keep it company, perhaps it worried so of its friend's wellbeing, perhaps it wished to be there in support of its cohort as it watched the grim lady move across its breast.

The grim lady, now progressing slowly across this apprehensive ground, appeared steeped in a subtle fog of a greyish black hue. It pressed in all around her and seemed to move along with her, an unlikely companion in her lonely stride through the quiet night. If ever could be ascribed such features to this enveloping mist, shy and awkward seemed the most apt.

As it moved along with her, always about her, surrounding her, the fog itself was apparently of its own mind. It appeared to sometimes briefly pause or stumble at a rock or small incline in the path of the grim lady. It was as if it was considering a cause of action, shy of moving onwards without first thinking through how it will approach any potential obstacle. Oddly enough once the lady herself reached the same obstacle she appeared to do the same thing as if mimicking the fogs worry, sharing the same anxieties.

As this figure and her ponderous miasma strained forward, the ground beneath them appeared to slowly adopt the greyish hue of its passing visitor. Quite gradually, even in the dark and dank of the evening, the grass, the stone, the gravel, the moss upon the stones, transitioned from their natural colour to approaching this familiar greyish black. It was as though the ground grew in a misery. Perhaps it wished to share some burden of the lady; so much weight seemed upon her – how unfair - or perhaps it could do no other than to give in to this strange and curious figure. Just as it seemed it may give over fully to the drab and gloom, the lady passed by and whatever colour originally betrothed, gradually restored itself.

This solemn figure with the mist pressed about her was of a height, perhaps five feet and two when pressed straight, but was slightly hunched over, not terribly so, but enough to suggest she bared some weight of a kind upon her.

The outline of this woman clearly showed that of a female traveller, but the enveloping mist and gloom around her seemed to withhold her somewhat from common sight. It was not that she was not visible, but rather she seemed to be at once pressed into the background: not pronounced in anyway, not seeking to be noticed, an entity shy of attention, wishing at most to be vaguely acknowledged by the world around them.

Just rarely a brief image of this figure would emerge to take a small glimpse of, before gently fading back into the background.

Upon her shoulders and most clearly seen in the fade was a cloak which pressed in all around her, resting just short of the ground beneath her feet. It was very dark, still grey, but of near ashen black in hue. A hood of the cloak covered most of her face.

Just enough of her would become visible to notice the woman bore features suggesting origins from the old Indian homelands. Her darker skin, the better to protect her from the light emitted by the burning star in the heavens in that land, seemed to have dulled down to a quite greyish tone. Her demeanour and the expression resting on her sullen face suggested a gloominous and grim outlook, but at the same time not one to be feared.

The apparel she wore all appeared as muted and grey as the aura and features of this woman. It was as if a stroke of fading grey paint had brushed slowly across the canvas for every step she took.

She was travelling with a staff, grasped in her hand just above halfway. It seemed to linger longer as she took each step before she pulled it up and forward. It looked whittled by hand rather than produced by any other effort. It was peppered with bumps and gnarls of the hopeful branches that once grew from its faithful trunk before it was cast into this new incarnation. Where she grasped it, the staff had a leather like material lashed round to allow a good grip and reduce the roughness upon the hand. It looked of the torn and ragged, but refused to come free, still duty bound until the last. The head of the staff was only just noteworthy with nothing more than a few extra notches and a wider taper than the shaft below. The wood looked of familiar oak but had not managed to evade the reducing effects that had befallen the rest of this Grim Lady. Much of its proud oaken stature seemed faded, now overcome with the familiar greyish hue. While it was still true enough for purpose it looked quiet and reserved as if only wishing to concentrate on the task at hand having shaken off any pretence of glamour.

Suddenly this Grim Lady stumbled, dropping to one knee and scraping it upon the rough ground. She pensively moved her left hand out in front of her to break her fall, grazing it as it dragged, but managed to stop any further slip with a lean upon her staff. Her expression formed one of pain, but also of acceptance; clearly a stagger or a fall was common enough an occurrence during her travel. Curiously, her stumble and near crash upon the ground did not appear to be caused by some outside source such as tripping on a rock or placing a foot on uneven peat beneath her boots. Her slight haunch and her grim demeanour suggested some less obvious and pervading cause, one not easily shaken off with a stagger, indeed maybe she

would just take hold of it whole without question.
      She strode ever onwards on her journey, her line a steady one, straight as can be and ever accompanied by that subtle fog, always orbiting her so, nervous and sullen, but ever faithful.

Chapter 1

"The events and feelings of the course of a day... They don't appear helpful. Helpful at all, in casting a shadow of strength to my emotional state of mind in the dawn of the following. A twist of the earth, experienced with happiness of a kind or, at the most merciful least, one which the sadness and despair inside me have not managed to overcome my exhausted and my undermanned defences, is no way to buffer oneself reliably against that which assails my mind and assails my soul before the next day." These words came slowly and not without some discomfort from Luther Dothmeer, sitting solemnly in his chair. He was hoping on this occasion that he may be afforded some respite by hearing a discrete reason as to why most mornings his mood was most sombre, sullen and quite plainly sad. A mood of despair.

Luther was a man in his early thirties, hailing from the Earstwhile Woodlands, a village of the East Borough, some miles away from where he was currently describing the troubles of his mind. Long chestnut hair hung down from his head looking somewhat scraggly and unkempt as if its owner were none too obliged to groom it too often. His skin was typical of one from The Boroughs, a pale flesh tone; the result of the local weather system producing mostly cloudy, cool days with the expectancy of rain a common thought of those who live there. What could be seen of his brow behind his hair suggested more wrinkles than expected for a man of his age. His eyes were of a piercing blue hue, quite striking and deep, but outwardly kind to those who looked upon them. Below this his features were all unremarkable aside from a quite bushy moustache which spread along the top of his mouth. Under his bottom lip, upon his chin and slightly further he wore a goatee like beard that dropped down to a subtle point.

He wore a pale, reserved, purple woollen cardigan featuring buttons down the breast that covered a thin black shirt top below. Hanging from a coat stand nearby was a long leather coat with hardened leather shoulders and elbows along with a not too thick fur lining, useful for the outdoors, providing warmth and some menial protection yet non-restrictive movement for the wearer.

On his waist sat a dark brown belt, grizzled from use over time. A leather pouch sat tied to the right. It contained a few items that proved useful when out in the woods such as a flint and tinder and a small amount of warding powder for use in dissuading unwanted beasties from entering a traveller's camp.

On the left of his belt sat a scabbard meant for holding the head of a small hand axe, a good tool in the woods and local area while doubling as strong words for anyone or anything that might wish to engage in a violent discussion with its wielder.

The scabbard currently sat empty as the axe itself lay on its side upon a knee-high table that stood beside the two seated men - no doubt an axe, however small could prove quite uncomfortable if sat upon. The trousers that were held up by the belt were of a black jean material, slightly worn at the knees. Upon his feet he had a pair of black leather boots.

"Do you have any notion as to why this is? Why does there appear to be a lack of cause and effect? Is there no prevailing evidence or inkling which perhaps may explain your demeanour?" A meaningful enough response from the wizened Deven. He hoped to provide some counsel towards Luther's worries but was unable to fully understand why he felt so sad and glum for such a prolonged period with no apparent reason for doing so.

Deven himself was a mage, a user of magic, a being that was proficiently learned in various mysteries of sorcery and physics. He had moved to the village of Overton shortly after the conflict between The Boroughs and the Conclave a good 20 years previous.

The mage sat talking with Luther inside the small library of his house which was set slightly afield of the village, somewhat secluded, but not as to suggest that the owner would be unwelcome of company. It was situated just in front of a youthful green wood consisting of ferns and acorn, trees of a good age. This wood encircled the side and rear of the house in a semi-circular fashion while affording room for a garden of a useful size. The wood didn't appear to express any sinister or fearful nature with a traveller feeling fairly confident in breaching its boundaries in search for herbs, plants or just a pleasant walk. Deven used the wood for that very purpose and was glad of it.

The house itself was single floored and constructed from brick and mortar with timber frame and slated roof. The front of the house faced the sun as it brought itself up each morning and looked to encourage the most growth of plant life across the outside of the house; the four simple windows facing this direction all proudly displaying various pots and plants hanging from their sills. The door to Deven's home was situated close to the left side, with a single window sitting to its left and the other three to the right. The door was wooden and painted blue with a brass knocker centred near the top. It looked as aged as the rest of the house and did not appear to have been repainted in any recent year. The rear of the house mirrored the front which could enable someone so inclined to run clear through the house in a single line if both doors were open. The back door was also identical to the front in both age and attention but lacked the knocker of the front – no doubt visitors were not often expected from rear of the house.

The roof was quite busy with moss and other woodland growth. A chimney stack sitting atop and looking in working order had attracted the nesting's of a couple of farrel birds, animals similar to owls common to The Boroughs. The difference being that farrel birds preferred diet was of berries and nuts from the heights of trees which necessitated the evolution of a more mammal like mouth rather than a usual beak. The birds often liked to nest near chimneys and were therefore commonly referred to as chimney birds or simply chimneys.

On the far right of the house, in line with the furthest window, the library sat. The walls were adorned with bookshelves, having sections devoted to fictional works and books useful for a user of magic, along with those filled with entries of history of the old world and accounts of the Magic

Event, which preceded the current age of Terra.

Deven sat in his usual light brown coloured armchair, clearly worn by years of use. His complexion was common for one growing up in the Boroughs with his light skin starting to wrinkle as middle age dictated. He had a fair head of light brown hair which was slightly swept back and some noticeable stubble upon his cheeks and chin. He was wearing a green hooded cardigan, well knitted, under which he wore t-shirt with a print of a local folk band upon it. He sat in the chair in a pair of somewhat worn blue trousers and upon his feat he wore some comforting slippers which were of a solid blue and leather sole which had seen much use.

His chair had a lever to the side which would when pushed caused the front to push out and provide rest for weary feet. Luther sat opposite in a similar chair, with a pale blue colour, featuring the same mechanism.

During their conversation Luther was having trouble keeping himself relaxed and calm. It was often a problem when in another's company or when out wandering. He would fidget so with a ring upon his finger, if perhaps twisting it round and round might untighten the apprehension within him. Another would have been the clipping and unclipping of the axe hanging from his side quite incessantly, but he was currently prevented from do so as it lay quietly on the table. Unable to engage in his favourite easing fidget, he made do with the twisting of the ring or periodically picking up the key ring that he had also placed upon the table, moving round the various items attached to it in a similar circular fashion. Luther until now refusing to do so, finally raised his eyes to meet Deven's.

"There are some evenings when I feel down or depressed and then wake up feeling the same the next morning. This, however demoralising, has some sense to it. I am sad and down before I go to sleep and wake up feeling quite the same. The sadness the day before has bled into the morning of the next. I guess that as I described, when I have a day when I am not completely overrun and experience gaps of happiness, it is by no means strong enough or a force enough to withstand or hold back anything that may seek to siege my fragile mood overnight."

"My common mood," he continued, "is that of being sad, of gloom, of a degree of hopelessness." Luther further elaborated on his experience. He pondered his thoughts as they came from his mouth. He wanted to know why he had these feelings. At least if he knew why, then perhaps he could discover a way to try and limit its effect upon him if not reduce it completely.

"Waking, as often as I do, feeling deep melancholy and despair, I wish I were able to combat it somehow. I wish that I could hold back the tide, that one day I could route its advance upon me… at least sometimes." Luther's demeanour had fallen with these words, as if they had pushed him from the precipice of a deep and empty well, that he wondered what lay at the bottom. The words had shown him the bottom. What lay there was his reality; he was a person of despair and did not know why that was or how he could ever change it. Perhaps all was hopeless.

There was a pause as Luther sloshed these thoughts around his head, trying to comprehend his feelings and berating himself for having them in the first place.

Deven also sat pondering somewhat. It seemed simple to him that someone could pull themselves together regardless of how they may be feeling. Surely, they could remove themselves from this state and carry on regardless, not allowing such things to have any meaningful effect on their personality.

"Many of us awake in the mornings not feeling our best," Deven motioned. "Perhaps you just require going forward and not let these things drag you down so much. You know that the world continues as always and that negative or saddening thoughts are just fleeting musings of the mind. A good night's sleep is always beneficial to your minds wellbeing."

Deven clearly meant well with his attempt of advice and reassurance, but to Luther it seemed that the mage may not have grasped just how this affected him that it wasn't such a thing that could easily be brushed off, that this was more a part of his very being.

The mage was indeed struggling with the gravity of Luther's affliction. He was trying not to think this a weakness of character in Luther. He believed he understood of course that there were reasons to be sorrowful; losing a loved one or some such similar event, would no doubt cause a sadness in someone, but this would pass in time. Being sad for no obvious reason, he thought, must surely just be a mind playing tricks and could be overcome with the right application of good thought and self-talking to.

"I don't think I can," Luther exclaimed. "It feels as though this sadness is woven around me, as though it can rise up from within me and overwhelm me with little to no indication beforehand. I certainly try my best."

Becoming worn out as the conversation went on, Luther said these words with less vigour than his previous admissions. Something that happened often, he seemed to feel tired much of the time, any social interaction or activity would drain him of energy at an accelerated rate. He assumed it must be connected to his emotional state and was yet a further reason to seek some kind of explanation for it all if he was even worthy of one. Why would someone as pathetic as he be even worth the trouble.

Deven asked Luther how long he had felt like this. "I can't really remember a time when I didn't feel like this in some way," Luther replied, his tone dropping further as he recalled how long he had felt this was. "As I look back, I recall times when I was sad and down and anxious, you know it feels more difficult to remember a time when I wasn't to some degree, afflicted." At first hearing these words Luther knew that Deven might assume this was the way of things when growing up as someone moved through their lives facing trial and tribulation. "I can understand you might think this to be perfectly normal, but I would like to press upon you as much as I can that this doesn't feel like the normal to and froes of mortal existence."

Deven paused for a moment in thought. He obviously didn't think Luther was lying to him. There would be no purpose in doing so and Luther was of good standing in the village; he was eager to learn the way of things, was known to be a curious and caring soul and was never seen to partake in any criminal endeavours. Deven didn't question the authenticity of Luther's description to him, it was more a question of understanding it.

The mage Deven, had seen suffering before during the defence of The Boroughs twenty years previous, a two-year long conflict between The Boroughs and the invading Conclave from the south. He had seen the death of friends, of souls too hopeful to be squandered, of bastard conflict, and resented those that sought it willingly.

He was a good man, he hoped. He had empathy for those around him, but he had a difficulty understanding why someone like this, with everything well in life to be feeling low and useless. Luther had not seen the times of the war, nor had he a negative or miserable upbringing, so why did he feel this way? It was frustrating to Deven and was a difficult exercise to restrain from suspecting Luther needed to just toughen himself to the wears of the world. Indeed, the world was tough, dangers abound, beasts and smiling angels were ready to reinforce this notion if you were not strong enough to resist it.

"Perhaps part of the reason for wishing to talk with me today is in hope that there may exist some way to help you with this problem, magically or otherwise," Deven said, breaking the silence. "I could knit a wound, remove an insidious growth or perhaps re-attach a severed limb, but magic concerning emotions and anything as close to your soul is quite dangerous indeed. I could as easily lobotomise you as make you feel happy for a brief period of time."

Luther knew these words to be true, he didn't really expect any sorceress help, but perhaps having been told somewhat formally that it wasn't an option would at least be one less thing to be anxious about. One avenue he could close off and not think about anymore.

"You know," Luther started, looking down. "It sometimes feels like this land, the world, this universe revels in my misery. It feels as if it is happy that I am sad."

Quite a ponderous silence followed. Deven was sure this was not the case. Someone's emotional wellbeing is not determined by the universe. Nor would it be its desire or source of happiness if certain people within it were unhappy and miserable. That couldn't be the way of things and Deven assured himself of this. It was a fact, he thought, there is no evidence to suggest any such thing. Indeed, how could you even go about looking for some confirmation anyway? Would a book written by some insightful fellow who had communed with the universe be enough? It would be quite simple to disregard such writing of those of a fantasist or a madman. So, what else? Conversing with the magical universe somehow? Some being? A god? Who knows and who would want to know, regardless?

"I am quite sure that there is no great power somewhere that has decided to make you sad, Luther," Deven explained. "Of course, there are beings whose magic's could tempt a person so or could make someone feel a particular way for a time, but I know of none that would come here to this place and focus all time and energy on arbitrarily making you sad whenever it could. Nor the universe, as some blanket being or state of energy, rules and wonders could afflict some curse upon you."

The look upon Luther's face was still one of a lingering drear, so Deven switched to a less informal tone, hoping to assure Luther as best he could, "It is nothing like that. Do not worry. I am sure that whatever this is that is affecting you and causes these days of unhappiness is just your current state of mind. Try not to think too much about it. I know at least from my own experience that dwelling upon such things is never a lot of use," Deven continued, "You are a good man, Luther, I sense no particularly evil energies coming for you. All is well, just push through my friend."

After concluding his talk with Deven, Luther thanked him for his time and hospitality, bid him farewell and left the house through the back door. He was hoping perhaps a walk through the wood behind the house may help him to think through the conversation with the mage and try to relax his mind somewhat. Interacting with people for any extended period of time usually caused quite a lethargy within Luther. It was tiring conversing, replying to someone, reinforcing that facade that he was not totally hopeless. To the outside he looked somewhat held together, but in reality, he was hard at work behind the scenes frantically working pulleys and levers, and wheels and cogs to both keep the scene going, preventing the true misery from seeping out.

Chapter 2

Luther entered the outskirts of the wood where the trees were not yet too huddled. Mindfully looking around and taking in the greenery before him he noticed a trail snaking out and leading towards Deven's house. Luther thought this had obviously been trodden by Deven himself on his ventures in and out of the wood. He started down the path, deciding to let it take him where it would.

He walked along the trail, noticing the trees around him; they all looked quite cheerful and happy to have a guest walking among them. Various fungi and moss took shelter by the boroughs of many of the trees. Luther imagined these were some of the reagents that Deven may have sought for his needs. He identified several for such purposes such as the Colinfo moss that had a blue hue to it – often used for soothing pain or soreness on the body or the Yoolin mushroom, distinguishable by its red stalk and creamy white cap, a useful ingredient when used in a tea to calm the nerves with a pleasant ember taste to it. Luther himself had made use of these fungi, bought from the herbalists in the village to calm his own nerves on occasion and was quite fond of its warming flavour.

He walked further, thinking of his conversation with Deven. Had he said the right things, he wondered? Was his description of his malady coherent? Did the good mage think there was something not too right with this person who had come to his house this day? His mind buzzed with these and other wonderings. Wonderings which as was often the case, averted his awareness from his surroundings.

Continuing the path with his head floating up above, somewhere atop of the canopy, unaware the trees had come together more tightly as he advanced ever deeper into the wood, Luther noticed a small clearing off to the right, perpendicular to the path the trail was taking. It was a curious sight as Luther had not noticed it at all, until he had seemingly arrived at the exact right spot on the trail in which to take the most direct line to it. In fact, he thought, the undergrowth seemed to have parted ever so slightly enough to be of note, allowing an unimpeded gentle walk through. This could be taken as slightly odd to not have noticed before, but it was not rare for Luther to have this dance with rumination; his mind often wondering about a too many things to be too watchful over his surroundings. He thought this just another of those times and thankfully did not see too much into it.

He decided this clearing might be a nice spot to sit down for a time and perhaps ponder some thoughts and enjoy the greenery. At least it seemed as good a place as any. It should be fine, he thought to himself. He turned and made his way slowly towards the clearing. The trees still seemed cheerful enough and the sky above had not taken a worrying turn.

Upon reaching the clearing, Luther saw before him a circular area of ground that was mostly clear of trees other than a single oak which sat almost exactly at its centre. In the absence of any other pillars of the earth besides this one great, old oak, the clearing had a growth of grass all around interspersed with varying sizes of rock, jutting out just above the greened carpet. The grass was quite short perhaps just half the foot of a grown man. Luther found this curious as he would normally expect such grass to grow with great purpose, free to do so from the lack of any surrounding trees that tended to block out the nurturing gaze of the sun above. The rocks were not particularly tall themselves; they appeared more as a slab of slate that was placed flat upon the ground with its thickness just protruding above the height of the surrounding grass. Luther imagined groups of people using these slabs as meeting points, on which to sit upon and converse or used as giant canvases on which to draw or carve all manner of woven words or roving runes. Perhaps recent rain had washed the chalk or charcoal away. Perhaps it had filled in the grooves, for he could see no sign of either upon them.

He ventured out from the cover of the encircling wood and proceeded to walk towards the great tree before him. Looking forward he could see what looked like a faint line of a path through the various flattened rocks that lay all about him.

A GRIM JOURNEY

There was clearly a line that wove its way around the flattened rocks, perhaps a good few meters wide, which opened up like the river to the ocean as it reached the great tree. It felt only natural to follow this path and besides, Luther thought, it would give him some time to examine the oddly flattened stones as he walked by.

As Luther gently strolled the path, left and right of him the rocks sat with their flat tops. He wondered to himself how really quite flat they were. It was as if a giant creature had taken each in turn, filed them flat and then pressed them back into the ground. The existence of these curious rocks, the absence of any trees in this clearing besides the great old one in the centre and both the path leading to this place from the wood and the subtle one he was currently treading upon, compelled Luther into believing that this place was surely created in some way and was not just a random series of improbable events. With these thoughts in mind, Luther kept moving until finally he came to the mouth of the path as it opened wide to meet the large tree looming welcomingly before him.

The great tree was broad and strong such as old Oaks tended to. It had numerous large branches coming from its trunk, spreading out its arms as if relishing the space, it had to itself. The diameter of this old lady of the wood appeared twice the width of Luther was tall, suggesting an age of quite ancient proportions. The wrinkled bark was of a brownish grey and had patches of common moss sitting comfortably about. The height of the trunk looking up from underneath seemed to rise up quite a stretch. Luther wondered if anyone had ever ventured to the top, it would surely be quite a view. At its base, the tree had great boughs that butted out, providing steadying strength to the mighty lady and creating welcoming alcoves for a weary traveller to take shelter. Luther took up this invitation and sat down with his back against the great body of the tree, his legs stretched out parallel to a long branch above him, grown almost perpendicular to her great trunk.

Luther sat quietly for a while. He tried to breath slowly and purposefully, to take in the quiet around him. He wondered if it was worth venturing to seek the audience of other wizened people or those who were learned not just in the classical magic arts, but of other more esoteric knowledge and understanding. There were many weird and magical things upon the planet; Terra was home to a many strange and weird entities and magic's. Perhaps information he sought was not readily known to those of his own race of humans.

Of course, he thought, he could just accept that he was a meandering fool and a silly bugger. Maybe everyone with a sense of awareness had daily struggles with worry and of sadness just as he. Maybe most beings were strong and useful enough to deal with these things themselves. He wished he was like these people. He envied those around him, so able to function; confident to engage with the world and feel worthy, unlike himself. Ugh, he thought to himself. He must stop thinking this way, or at the very least thinking so much at all.

Luther became too engrossed in his own incessant self-beating, that he had failed to notice the small object that had appeared near to where he was sitting. A strange little thing it was, the shape of a ball, slightly bigger than the head of a grown man. It was the colour of night, a much blackened black with no discernible limbs or tail protruding from the body. It was covered in quite long, fluffy hair similar to that of a long haired breed of dog. This small furry thing gave away no obvious clue as to its facing. There didn't appear to be anything resembling a head, a face or some way of ascertaining the orientation of the strange little thing. No eyes, nose, mouth or ears were obvious in anyway, merely a weird and peculiar ball of fur that was slowly rolling into Luther's peripheral vision.

Luther snapped to from his continuing doldrums to the sight of this strange fluff ball rolling towards him. He sat up with a start and got quickly to his feet. "Whoa, what on earth is this?" he said aloud. Never having seen such a thing before. He had his hand high up the haft of his axe, ready to unsheathe and defend himself if needed. "Excuse me," he said, "Who are you and what do you want?!" Luther was quite aware of how he may seem, asking a ball of black fur who it was, but, having enjoyed some degree of education, he knew that inhabiting the world were not just human beings; there were animals of magical nature, roving fiends, noble beasts and terrifying monsters that had all been encountered and throughout The

Boroughs of Old Briton and elsewhere across Terra.

The ball, rolling with a casual and plodding rhythm, moved ever closer to Luther. It did so without any audible answer to Luther's enquiry, but surprisingly, he felt less inclined to attempt a swipe at this funny looking ball and removed his hand from his axe. It approached the tip of his left boot, stopped, and then rolled to his right. It then veered away from Luther towards the inside of the bough where he had sat his back to and then stopped moving.

'What on earth is this peculiar thing that just rolled off my boot,' Luther wondered. He had made a calm attempt at communication with the creature as taught to him in his younger days but had not even noticed an acknowledgement from this spherical ball of yarn that it had heard him - if it even had the means to do so. It did not seem aggressive, it didn't seem angry, although Luther wondered how you could tell if a black ball of what appeared to only consist of ashen fur was even angry or not? It could be angry right now and he would have no idea.

Luther assumed that this entity was indeed an entity; it wasn't a ball of yarn or wool from a black sheep like animal that had been grasped by the wind and push across an expanse to arrive at this very spot.

The ball had begun moving again, out from the bough and away from the trunk of the old tree. This is not the action of a piece of fluffy detritus, Luther thought to himself, but of at the least a somewhat aware and functional being.

The only sense Luther had with regards to this strange little creep was that it didn't mean him harm. He was nursing the impression that perhaps the thing was not even very aware of him, again if it was capable of even doing so. He looked over to it and moved tentatively towards it. I really have no idea what this is, he thought.

It had stopped moving. If Luther could land on any meaningful description of what it was currently doing it would be that this dark fur ball was having a little rest next to the tree. Perhaps it had been rolling for a good while and was relaxing in the presence of this great tree, Luther thought. Perhaps it was enjoying itself, rolling through the wood and was intrigued as

Luther was by this strange clearing. Perhaps it was neither of those and it had no idea what it was doing and just happened to revolve its way along, happening to bang into this tree, tiring itself out.

Thinking it best not to wake the thing, Luther was suddenly aware that he had made a huge assumption, a troubling assumption. This thing in front of him, tucked into the base of the tree, was it actually here at all? Could this just be his imagination? Was he slipping further into psychosis? He had never before experienced such a vivid hallucination as this, having only seen passing things in peripheral; the mind and light playing tricks upon his mind.

He moved further towards the furry ball and without thought broached to touch it with his left hand. His fingers stretched out and he touched the fur. It felt warm, as if the creature whom it belonged to had taken rest near a roving fire, absorbing the brightness and heat, none too hot, just reassuring, making him feel safe. He moved his hand through the fur and slowly down. He thought at some point he would touch the body from which all this long fuzz had grown, but his hand never came across it. His hand had apparently moved all the way through the little creature and was now directly below it. Luther wondered, perhaps he had moved his arm at some strange angle and missed the body of this creature. He moved his hand back up through the furry mass, watching carefully to make sure he was on course to pass through the centre. Again, he failed to make contact with any solid part of it.

All the while, the small creature had not appeared to have moved or taken any notice of Luther's presence and seemed either content or otherwise preoccupied to be aware of anything going on around it. Luther, feeling brave and eager to confirm that he was indeed in the presence of a somewhat sentient ball of exactly fur and not in the midst of a wonderings of a lunatic, moved both hands in various directions through the darkened pelt hoping to find some part of the critter that could be described as a body. Up and down, left and right, round and round, spinning in circles and moving back and forth his hands went, trying to settle upon some kind of body or appendage of this little fellow. His motions though fairly firm were still not too quick of anger. He wished not to harm the thing but hoped to confirm its existence and hopefully his sanity along with it. Alas, though coming to a furious crescendo of flailing hand waving, the little thing was all just a ball of fur that was still quietly and perhaps serenely nestled in the bough of the tree.

Luther, having suddenly being aware what this might look like to any curious onlooker, quickly dropped his hands down to his sides and sat down. He paused there for a moment and stretched out his legs in front of him, the feet angled slightly away from each other and his hands resting either side of him on the ground beneath the great tree. He looked around on the borders of this clearing from which he could see from this side of the tree and could not make out any figures that may have stumbled upon his mad spree of frustrated arm waving. He took solace from this as he wished for the local community, known and unknown to him to think he was at least somewhat sane and not wondering the forests conjuring up hallucinations with a random waling of appendages.

He took in some deep breaths and stared at the strange little critter that had quite literally rolled into his day. It didn't appear to be breathing; there were no signs of a chest rising or sinking indicating any inhale of exhale of breath.

Luther, you madman, he thought, you are quite stupendously aware this small, unusual create has no body, why on earth would you now be watching for something to rise and fall that you know doesn't even exist. He let out a long sigh. This was all quite strange. Is this thing part of his imagination? If it was it was the most vivid and real object it had ever created and strangely enough, besides the embarrassing show he had just put on, he was wasn't feeling very upset or annoyed with himself that he might be going more insane, imagining sentient balls of fur sitting or perhaps standing in front of him in the bough of a tree. He would feel quite uncomfortable in any other unknown situation very different from his usual day, feeling his face go flush, his arms tingling with anxiety, but he wasn't feeling like that. He felt ok, he felt fine and perhaps a little relaxed even.

"Hello little guy, can you hear me? Do you hear my voice?" Luther decided to try and talk to it again, hoping for some kind of response. "I apologise, that was quite rude of me to stroke your fur like that. I was simply curious as I have never seen anything like yourself before. Can you understand what I say? Please give me some inclination as to whether you are aware of me." After a brief pause with that inclination not forthcoming, Luther realised that if it was aware of him, it wasn't going to let on.

Deciding that this creature wasn't going to take any notice of him and didn't feel like any kind of threat to him, Luther sat with his back against the trunk of the great old tree and closed his eyes for a little sleep before making his way back home. Normally it would not wise such to do so, being in the company of some strange little creature, but he felt no anxiety for it. He was feeling quite tired from conversing with Deven, his walk and encounter with this creature sat beside him that he thought a small rest might make him feel better and recharge his mental batteries for the day.

With Eyes slowing drawing closed like curtains, Luther tilted his head slightly, back against the bark of the old tree and drifted off into the realm of gentle sleep.

Chapter 3

"Stuck fast! Stuck fast I am! I can barely seem to move, what is going on?! It's gaining upon me yet with all my might and worth I cannot seem to press my legs into motion or gain traction upon the ground! I am being chased! Something is after me, but what! I cannot make out what evil this is!"

Luther opened his eyes with a start. He looked around him. For a moment he was unsure as to where he was or what was happening. He remembered he was sitting up against this old tree in the clearing and there was little occurring around him other than the stillness of the open glade and of course, some small little black furred creature nestled in the bough of the tree next to him.

He knew that he had had some kind of dream while he was asleep. He had the most certain feeling of it but could not recall what it was about. Slightly disturbing though, was how it had left him feeling. Quite often while asleep, Luther would awake abruptly, that same knowing feeling that he had found himself in some confusing and stressful dreamscape, wholly vivid at the time, but now hopelessly lost and all a blur. He sighed and hoped that perhaps one day he could recall some vague notion as to the subject of his dreams and if they were a contributing factor to his miserable feelings most mornings.

Looking up, Luther noticed the sky had grown darker at the onset of evening and the clouds had all huddled together above him, seemingly setting a hint it was probably best to make way for home. He reckoned he must have fallen asleep for a couple of hours here, alone in the glade. A dangerous thing to do for too long without a watchman or a subtle use of warding powder; there were more than little furry balls roaming the woods and dales of the land. Luther told himself to make sure not to drift off so long in the future or be deftly sure to make use of his powder before doing so. He looked over to the little creature and thought to himself that perhaps the small thing made a good stand in for a watchman. At the same time, he remembered how even with the most animated of gestures, it failed to notice or acknowledge him so the chances of it heeding anything stalking the woods was fairly slim.

Luther stood himself up, slowly rising to his feet. He moved his left forearm across his face from near the elbow to his wrist, wiping away the dribble that had accumulated in the corners of his mouth. He brushed down his trousers and tried to break free from this discombobulating feeling that had lingered from his long nap against the tree. The little furry ball was still in the same spot, tucked quietly as it was in the bough. He looked to the spot on the border of the glade where he had walked out of the wood and made way to it to find his way home. As he reached the edge of the clearing he turned to see if the little thing was still there and noted that it had yet to move itself from its little resting place. Turning back, Luther walked on into the wood back towards Deven's cottage.

He found again the small trail that led to the glade and followed it back to the main path he had taken from the mage's home earlier on. He walked on at a fairly brisk pace, eager to get home and find something to sate the rumble he now felt in his stomach.

The woodland in this area didn't feel particularly ominous or worrisome at a dusked hour. The trees were a little sullener and the colours were slightly dimmed as usual for this time of day, but Luther felt no impending danger or trouble walking the wood. He also felt less inclined to berate himself too much and managed to take in the surroundings and think of what he might eat when he got home; he thought that he might cook some bangers with some bread and perhaps have himself some chips to go along with it. He loved the smell of sausages sizzling over a fire and cherished the thought of getting to it when he got home.

After a good while of quiet contemplation on the joys of cooked food, Luther found himself exiting the woods to see the smoke billowing from Deven's chimney - a sure sign he was also thinking of dinner time. He walked to the right, away from Deven's house and back towards the small village of Overton and his own little abode.

The path leading past the mage's house into the village

was mostly dirt track, but for some rocks and pebbles scattered hither and of course the small black fur ball rolling along next to this worryful man as he made his way home.

Luther stopped. It felt like someone of something else was moving along beside him. Looking down and to his right he was surprised to see a small little creature of apparently nothing, but black fur. He realised that the critter he met back in the glade was sitting quietly perhaps, just close to where he was standing. How on earth did it get here from the glade? he wondered. Luther filled with anxiety. Did this thing appear, just now out of the blue or perhaps more accurately out his mind? Did the small creeper take some sort of liking to him and decided to follow him home? But if it did then why had he only just noticed it moving alongside him? This was after all just a simple dirt track with the small estate of Deven's to his left and grass fields to his right. He would surely have noticed this small woolly ball coming to him from either side, he thought. Unless it came barrelling from the woods behind him.

The worry that Luther felt the most was not that he had apparently made friends with a small lump of long fur having never read of such a creature before in his life. No, this was not his worry - and how he would love to have had that his worry. His anxiety was that this thing's existence at all and he had just conjured it up right now on the spot as a way for his mind to torment him so. He decided that the only logical thing to do would be to call in on a friend on the way home to verify if they too could see the little thing.

Luther continued following the track towards the village. It was odd, although he felt an anxiety because of the unknown origin of this creature, he didn't really feel overly panicked or worrisome about it. Normally by now he would be in full fight or flight mode, waiting for the inevitable explosion of his brain as it buckled under his self-induced spiral of worry only to finally recover and berate himself further. Silly Luther, you must stop doing this to yourself, he thought. This is indeed quite the odd event, but you are ok. Just go by the Duck Feather Inn, Nathanael's tavern, on the way home, under the pretence of popping in for a simple evening drink and let his mentioning of the creature put your mind at rest. Yes, this will put an end to it.

A GRIM JOURNEY

His mind was set.

Past Deven's home, the fields crept up on either side of the path as Luther strolled. He was moving ever closer towards the Overton Village square with the dirt track now featuring some cobblestones beneath the feet and some low hedgerows upon its sides. He could see several chimneys puffing some smoke out to the world from the fires below. People must be readying supper for the evening he thought. After a further short stride, he was upon the Village proper.

Overton in the Lonefield Borough was a typical village of The Boroughs of Old Briton. It consisted of a collection of characterful buildings which were the homes and workplaces of its various residents. It featured a central square and a local green set aside for festivals and other gatherings. To the right as the track heading north first broached the village, stood the Duck Feather Inn, the local tavern which, famous for its Husky Honey Mead had stood for as long as the village existed and was run by a retired member of the Mage Scribes Guild named Nathanael.

The Duck Feather Inn was sizeable for a village inn, exhibiting large, sturdy, stone walls creating a wide base footprint of the building. Above this was another floor, no doubt to hold the various rooms for patrons and housing for good Nathanael himself. Lastly perched on top of the inn was a dark reed thatched roof, snugly sat in place, featuring several stone chimney stacks which at this time were bellowing out smoke at a leisurely pace - a good sign of a busy establishment, Luther thought.

The stones, gallantly holding up the great mass of the building were all grey granite stone of different sizes, chiselled into rectangular shapes and set-in line courses upon each other. The four corners were constructed from the largest and squarest of them, the better to provide a most stoic base of strength to the tavern and brace the weight around it. Many of the stones on the outside edge of each wall featured little nooks and crannies which in turn housed small growths of dark blue, huddle moss, named so because it tended to grow around the dwellings of magic users, feeding from the nascent energy given off with the enactment of magical rights.

The side of the building facing Luther featured several windows, each with wooden shutters to be closed at night which were currently just halfway there. Nearly all windows of the place featured a wooden flower box hanging below the sill. Each in turn were stuffed full of various plants and herbs, with no particular rhythm of placement, but rather perhaps chaotically strewn about the place in a random fashion. The majority of the flowers and herbs were of bright and daring colours, not all useful for the whims of a retired mage brewer, but rather an aesthetic choice to please the patrons of the inn and providing an enjoying view from the outside.

Between the Duck Feather Inn and the path on which Luther was currently standing, there lay a perimeter wall of the similar granite stone surrounding the tavern in its entirety. Luther imagined this was created from the left-over stone when constructing the tavern itself. This perimeter wall was set only roughly up to his knee, most likely more of a visual boundary for the plot of land than any meaningful way to keep out intruders late at night; attempting to rob or attack a mages home would not work out too well for the intruder. This wall, similarly, to the walls of the inn itself, was pocketed with little nooks in which plant growth was clinging to. This time however rather than the dark blue hue of huddle moss glistening ever so in the evening light, creeping vines and moss of the common kind had set up home and embraced the companionship of one another.

Luther wondered who had visited the inn that night and how busy it might be. He was not particularly looking forward to entering the place if it was heaving with a mass of people due to his innate reluctance to be around large groups of people but thought it best, he spoke to Nathanael.

With no small amount of trepidation, he walked past the outer wall towards the entrance door of the old inn. The door itself was situated to the left-hand side of the building and was made of good and thick, old oak planks joined vertically creating a square bottom and sides while leading up to a shallow curved point at the top. Slightly below the apex of the curvature there was a small window no bigger than the size of a dinner mat fitted with glass. To the right and at just above roughly waist height, hung an iron door handle shaped like a loop on which to open and close the door. Above the entrance swayed a wooden sign attached to a metal arm protruding from the tavern. The sign featured a common river duck with its right wing stretched out, displaying an array of grey and white flight feathers, with the words 'Duck Feather Inn', written just below. Luther reached out tentatively with his right hand and clasped the door handle. He twisted it to the left, pulling up the lever on the inside of the door and breached the inn.

Chapter 4

As the door swung open, Luther was met with the diverse sights, sounds, and smells that were unique to a tavern of an evening. To the right and filling up the majority of the floor place within were numerous tables of different shapes and sizes, each in turn surrounded with their own chairs of different shapes and sizes. Upon many of these chairs sat people from various races of people of the land. The Duck Feather Inn had the most rustic feel to it and was one of the reasons why Luther, like so many others were drawn to its charm.

To his left he saw the familiar U-shaped bar with its dark wooden surface, bedecked with an eclectic range of mead, ale, tea and coffee. Behind the bar, currently speaking to a female elf perched forward ordering a drink, stood an older gentleman, perhaps sixty years or so in age, with short grey hair and a long wispy beard down to his belt line - surely, Luther thought, Nathanael's appearance did nothing for wizardly stereotypes.

Past the bar, in the corner, was a wooden staircase leading up to the second floor. It ran down the back wall of the inn to the left in parallel with the long edge of the bar. At roughly two thirds down it stopped, presented a landing, and then turned ninety degrees left and came down the rest of the way. It seemed quite an old structure and had no doubt been trodden by a great many people over the years.

To Luther's right near the wall housing the main door was a table, rectangular in shape and sat around by four people: two elves, a human and a flarfen. Luther pondered just how diverse the races and peoples of old Briton were. The elves arrived in Briton and the other lands of Terra during the Magic Event - though they would not put it that way - as Luther learned from his studies in his youth. The elves along with other fantastical races, creatures and importantly the essence of magic itself were living quite happily in their own version of Terra. Whatever caused the event several hundred years previously or exactly happened during it, Luther was never taught, but it seems the two universes or realities were fused together: the magical and whimsical nature of that universe becoming one with the more physical and mundane of Luther's.

The two elves currently sitting beside each other were both female and fairly equal in height. One had light brown hair and the other with a dark more bourbon brown. They were, as was quite typical for the elvish people, very elegant, pleasing to look at and with an air of nobility about them. Luther thought highly of both ladies as they were always so kind to him and made the fairly simple and yet reassuring gesture of giving him an honest smile whenever he entered their shop or saw them in passing.

The light brown-haired elf sitting on the left, opposite the male human, Steven was named Gwithen. She ran the local herb shop with her sister Lilly sat next to her. She was wearing a blue cotton top with a wraparound type of jacket and blue jeans below tied with a bark brown belt. Upon her feet she wore white canvas shoes. Both Lilly and Gwithen were especially sweet to Luther as they knew about his problems and were very empathetic to his struggle with sadness and anxiety.

Gwithen, Luther remembered, had lost her husband in the war with the Conclave two decades past. His story of bravery against quite overwhelming odds was known across the local area, earning him post humorously the Goat Trodden Crest – The highest military honour awarded in The Boroughs. Luther recalled the interesting name of this lofty honour was acquired due to all Goat Trodden Crests ever presented being crafted from an old dwarven shield found in a field one hundred years previous and had since been trodden into the ground by flocks of goats since that time. It was a rare and precious find which must have been dropped by a dwarven shield bearer during one of their rare ventures to the surface.

There was always a faint air of melancholy around Gwithen. Luther knew elves tended to mate for life. If one of the pair passed away before their time, the other would usually stay celibate in love and homage to their fallen partner. Luther felt sad for her losing her husband and always tried his best to smile to her even if he himself didn't feel particularly jolly.

Her sister, Lilly was the younger of the two. She was wearing a pale blue dress, tied at the waist with a thin white leather belt with boots of dark grey, velvety leather. Lilly was married to a human named Toby, who was the village blacksmith. He produced Luther's very axe by his side which he was incredibly pleased with and made great use of. Toby also produced other tools and weaponry for the local people and passing merchants. He wasn't anywhere to be seen in the tavern though so Luther presumed that he must still be finishing some work for the evening, making good use of the heat of his forge before extinguishing its flame.

Both Lilly and Toby had faced some intrigue from the local populace with their wed lock as Elves and humans, though capable of producing young together, was usually quite a rare thing in such couplings and was the case with the two of them. Therefore, people from either race wishing to have children commonly paired with members of their own.

The human sat beside the flarfen, opposite the two sisters, Luther recognised as Steven Lodson, a man in his early twenties who worked as a carpenter with his father Frank Lodson. They had performed work for Nathanael in this very tavern, reworking the bar after the wear and tear of several years had required him to retire the old one. Luther knew Steven as a fairly innocent individual. He seemed to have been spared any major trepidations in life; he had both parents still living who brought him up with love and care in this very village, he was doing well for himself, learning to be a tradesman of wood and timber and most luckily of all, he didn't appear to suffer from any ongoing sadness of reasons known or unknown. Luther's hope was that he never would. He didn't like to see other people unhappy if he could help it as he knew himself from his own dreary experience how quickly a demon it can become; laying waste to one's defences so hopefully constructed, but nearly always overcome by the inevitable grim tide. Washed away.

The flarfen himself sitting to the side of Steven was named Thraven. He and his family were local fisherman that lived by the Panifery River, which ran close to the village. The flarfen people were a race of river folk that were humanoid in stature with two arms, legs and hands, but with a tail which, at this moment was dangling down from the left-hand side of his chair. He was wearing a leather top with a dark red shirt underneath and woollen trousers of an almost black colour. As was usual the flarfen people - Luther had never encountered one wearing any - he was bare foot with his fury feet and claws crossed under the table. His hands were quite similar to those of a human except he had three fingers furred rather than four and bare, but with an all-important opposable thumb. His face was covered in dark brown fur like the other visible parts of his body with a stubbed jet-black nose and dark brown eyes. Whenever he opened his mouth wide Luther could make out several sharp fangs within, no doubt used to hold and rip apart fish which was a main staple of the Flarfen diet.

Luther saw that the four of them looked to be engaged in some kind of board game. They were discussing quite furiously the best way to proceed in their little adventure – no doubt they were playing a co-operative endeavour and were in deep discussion on what tactics they should be employing to overcome the challenge in front of them.

Beyond this group and their game, the other tables were filled with people who were either in discussion, laughing, joking or playing some other games of their own.

There was Kate and Gareth, who ran the local store where Luther would often pickup supplies and a little treat for himself whenever he was walking by as he often desired some chocolate to help lift his mood. Beyond them enjoying some fresh brewed coffee sat Carrey Bodshaw and her husband Reginald, both in their mid-forties that ran the 'Tailors and Tannery', just up the street from the inn.

In the northeast corner of the inn, near the back wall, there was a group of six people playing some sort of card game. They were all humans except an elf who Luther recognised as Mathlaw the huntsman. He supplied the Bodshaws with hides for the tannery and game for Kate and Gareth's Store.

Mathlaw was quite a solitary person, most likely in part due to his occupation or perhaps, thought Luther, it was the reason he was a huntsman - Luther did not know either way. Apart from his current social situation Mathlaw was usually out alone either hunting or making camp in the wild forest lands and plains around the Borough. He was notably more muscular than most elves Luther had encountered, but still exerted that elegance that his race was known for. The muscular elf was wearing a light brown cotton tunic over which he had a brown leather, studded breast plate, no doubt good protection for his type of work. The rest of him below the belt line was obscured by the table and his associates, but Luther could see his recurve hunting bow and quiver propped up against the wall beside him.

The group of people which Mathlaw was sitting with, Luther had seen recently around the village, but was yet to make their acquaintance. He thought to himself that right now with all of them together and with such a lot of people in the general vicinity that, approaching the group to introduce himself would most likely prove too anxious a proposition.

They all seemed of the rugged type with various hand weapons hanging down from their belts. Perhaps they were a group of adventurers who explored old sites around for treasure and a challenge, Luther wondered. Perhaps they had made friends with Mathlaw after encountering him out in the wilds or perhaps, they sought his council regarding a local area of interest they planned on visiting.

Up from this group, back towards Luther was a mixed group of five humans that Luther had no recollection of seeing before. Of the group three were male and two females. They were all dressed in fairly matching ware, tunics of thick material and jean trousers with different shades of brown boots with leather soles. There was a mix of short and long hair with all three men being clean shaven. Four of the group were eagerly listening to one of the women who seemed to be holding court; telling them a story perhaps, Luther thought, as he couldn't make out what she was saying over the din of chatter in the tavern. As he peered over them, wondering if he had ever seen them before, the orator looked up and met Luther's gaze with her own. He thought nothing of giving her a brief smile but was only returned with a slight furry of the brow and a turning back to her story. Luckily not looking too much into the meaning of this he then gazed across and saw the large table in the middle of the tavern.

The table situated in the middle of the ground floor of the tavern was a grand old oaken thing of a dull and dark brown, pocketed with dents and scratches - signs of a good many years in service. Luther likened the table to some of the myths of old he heard of a round table which gallant and noble knights might sit around as they discussed which nefarious evil, they would seek to bring down next.

Currently sat around it on four curved benches, was a group of six people joyously engaged in a pen and paper role playing game. Luther knew this immediately to be the local role-playing group of the village that met on this day every week down at the tavern. They were playing Granlog, where they each took the role of a hero trying to thwart the evil machinations of the evil Kranmak, the sorcerer king who had conquered the land of the fictional world of Drabenhelm.

The group was made up of four humans: two male and two female, a female elf and a male gnome. The Gnome, Golon, was a good friend of Luther's; they often played all types of board games, but usually in either of their own homes rather than too busy a place such as the tavern. Luther tended to come out of his shell a lot more when in such a quiet and relaxed setting. He remembered Golon asking him to join the merry band of heroes as he took them on a "grand old adventure," as he put it, but Luther didn't want to put people out by missing sessions due to his terrible melancholy suddenly making an appearance. Golon expressed to Luther that he didn't mind, but nevertheless Luther thought best not to.

The good gnome owned the friendly local board game and interesting items store quite wonderfully named 'Golon's Exciting Emporium of Wonderment and Adventure'. It was a pleasure of Luther's to look upon all the various games and items that bedecked the shelves of Golon's shop. Gnomes were known for their short stature with Golon being perhaps just two foot, six inches tall. He was wearing a bright blue shirt with extravagantly ruffled, puffy sleeves with matching blue ruffled trousers and darker blue velvet over vest. Upon his feet he wore black suede silver buckled shoes. The wonderfully dressed gnome bore little hair on his head, only some grey upon the sides and back, but with a wonderfully fancy, twirling grey moustache.

The lone elf in the group named Thelia, was well known to all in the village as she was the elected leader of the village council. A stern and meticulous woman she was indeed, never married as far as Luther knew, but he harboured suspicions of her intentions towards Nathanael. She tended to be stern with him the least and seemed happiest when he was in the vicinity. Whether Nathanael harboured similar feelings, Luther was less sure, but Nathanael was always pleased to see her on her not infrequent visits to the tavern. Guessing the age of the elves and the tendencies for their bodies to not show much sign of aging, it was difficult to hazard an attempt at the age of Thelia, but he thought she was likely at least in her sixties, if not older. Her hair was dark brown, and she sat at the table in a knee length dress of cotton and simple looking, black shoes.

There were several other tables strewn in and around these others and of course there was the great fire that was ablaze in the middle of the back wall of the tavern, but Luther failed to take notice of too many more of them and anxious to talk to Nathanael, he turned towards the bar.

Nathanael had finished serving the elf woman who was now sitting contented, reading a book and sipping on her mug of freshly brewed tea. He was now looking out across the inn, possibly now and again pausing on a certain lady at Golon's table, Luther noticed. Luther knew Nathanael was almost certainly aware of his presence and so he approached the bar and spoke out Nathanael's name, "Nathanael, hey, how are you?"

The old man turned to the sound of his name and said, "Hello good Luther, I am well sir! How are you today?"

Luther feeling warmed by Nathanael's stirring words replied, "Good to hear Nathanael, I am well too. Could I bother you for a cup of coffee - decaf? Perhaps of the local blend?" Before Luther had even finished these words, Nathanael had already swung round and begun pouring some coffee from a glass jug into a cup; no doubt he had quite the inkling of what Luther was going to order and was indeed correct.

"Thank you, Nathanael. That is a good cup of coffee," Luther asserted. "How is business today? You look quite busy."

Nathanael took another sweeping look across his tavern and turning back he said, "Yes, it is quite busy today. Besides the usual lot, we have a few tables of fresh faces and of course that group of people over at the back with Mathlaw. How was your visit to Deven's? Could he provide you with any insight?"

It was Nathanael who suggested he visit Deven. He thought perhaps the younger and still practicing mage might have some new insight which could help Luther since he himself had been outside the bustling world of magical and physical research and discovery for a while now.

Looking down, Luther told Nathanael that no, Deven was unfortunately not able to provide him with any explanation or remedy either spell or otherwise that could help with his problem. Although he did mention that afterwards he had a nice walk and a nap in the woods by Deven's, so it was not all for nought.

"That woodland might be quite nice and calm, but you know better than to fall asleep like that without warding powder or watchmen," Nathanael stated, though not with too serious a tone.

"Yes, silly of me really, but I just closed my eyes and drifted off. I think my discussion with Deven, bringing up all the things that describe a mad man, tired me out."

Nathanael gave Luther a raised eyebrow and said, "Now you know you are not a crazy person Luther. You just have some interesting quirks and a caring of others. Well done on coming here when so busy as well."

"It was nice," said Luther, thankful for the reassurance. "After the walk and nap afterwards, I feel a bit different at least, like something changed a little. And yes, I did manage to come in on such a busy night, but not without much worry!" As he said these words, he looked about him; he couldn't see the little creature that had followed him home anywhere in the tavern. He had almost forgotten about it until this moment. Where had it gone, he wondered? Why had it disappeared now that people were around who could verify its existence? Was it hiding somewhere, under a chair or a table somewhere? He lent back slightly and looked around under the stools beside him at the bar, but to no avail.

"You ok Luther? Did you lose something?" Nathanael said, interrupting the cogs spinning in Luther's mind.

"No sorry, I thought... I thought I dropped something, but it's ok." It seemed to Luther that the little critter had either wondered off somewhere, was waiting outside or of course - most likely - didn't exist in the first place. He should have made sure the peculiar little thing had come through the door alongside him but was in such a hurry to placate his anxiety he had failed to perform such a simple task and condemned his little plan to failure before it had even begun. Where did it go? This is very trying, he thought, still half looking around.

"Luther? Are you alright?" Nathanael enquired again, slightly perplexed as to why Luther was quite hurriedly looking about himself.

"Yes, sorry Nathanael I could have sworn that I saw something drop from my belt, but it seems I was just imagining it," Luther quickly replied. It was obvious then to Luther that Nathanael hadn't noticed anything even if it was here previously and hidden away shortly afterwards.

"Ah, right, if I find anything at closing time, I will let you know."

Luther knew he wouldn't be finding anything but thanked Nathanael all the same. Just then another patron standing at the bar hailed the old mage for a drink and Nathanael turned away, leaving Luther to stare down into his coffee cup and wonder whether the little thing was just a figment of his imagination.

After finishing the last of his coffee while perched on a stool at the bar, Luther looked up and around the tavern again. He had kept his gaze mostly to himself by this point, attempting to keep his anxiety in check all the while not being overly interested in attracting anyone else's attention. It seemed most people were busy in their own little social gatherings to take much notice of him, and he was glad. He got up from his stool and gave a reserved wave to Nathanael who was busy with another customer. Nathanael replied with a quick yet friendly wave of his own after which Luther made a turn for the door and soon enough was standing outside again.

After closing the tavern door behind him, Luther looked around to see if he could see the little creature that had followed him from the wood. He was aware that looking for a dark little furry thing in the evening light was never going to be the most successful endeavour, but felt compelled to check, nevertheless.

Out in front of him past the perimeter wall was the path leading back out towards Deven's home to the left and further into the village on the right. Straight in front of him perhaps one hundred feet away was the village hall, used for village meetings and groups and such. It was of a similar stone to the tavern itself, but only consisted of a single story; a ground floor with a wood framed and thatched roof of similar material to the tavern. He couldn't make out any little creatures sitting around out here. 'Did it even sit? Was it sitting before?' He decided to cut his losses and make for home.

Luther turned right from the border of the inn and walked through the village towards his home. By this time, it was well into the evening with the shops closed for the night. Most buildings of whose owners Luther had not seen at the tavern that night, were glowing from the warm embrace of a good fire and their chimneys piped a good bellow out into the night.

He walked past the guard house which lay at the centre of the village. It was built from the ever-present grey granite with two floors and a turret sitting on the east end of the slated roof. In the centre of the building was an archway of perhaps ten feet wide that went up to meet the brick of the floor above. Sitting within this archway was a pair of dark wooden doors, each forming half of the arch each and lined with steel braces along each edge. This was no doubt a useful object in impeding the escape of any prisoner from the guard house, but perhaps more accurately any large and angry beasty being kept at bay from the outside should the townsfolk take refuge inside. Luther remembered several years previous when a bounding plains Troll rumbled through town in quite the angry fit. Most folk had made for the guard house while Nathanael kept it busy

A GRIM JOURNEY

with a spirited lightshow. The building was only vacated once Deven arrived and had encouraged it to leave with the aid of several persuasive balls of fire. Either side of the Doors were thin watch holes which allowed for observation of the outside of the building in relative safety; they were thin enough to peer out, but not wide enough to enable someone or something to climb through. There were large wooden covers on the inside that hung down from each which could be pulled up and fastened from above, blocking up the holes as necessary.

Luther's house lay on the northern most reach of the village; noticeably set apart from the rest of the buildings somewhat like Deven's, but not as long a walk. The route took him past the stables which was closed for the evening and all the horses likely asleep. His house was a small cottage made from stone not cut to shape like most buildings in the village, but still held together well with a good tangle of concrete. Atop the dark thatched roof was a very solid looking chimney of square cut granite; Luther had replaced the chimney himself after the previous stack had become dislodged and broken by some overly aggressive winds two winters previous. He was determined to make a more robust and stoic chimney that would stand up the elements with more vigour than the last and appeared to have been successful in the endeavour.

The cottage was fairly typical in layout and design; it had a door in the middle facing the path from the village with a window either side. On the rear, the back door was off centre and to the left as you faced out. To its right was a small window, to its left, a larger one. There were trees dotted around the outside; some lining the path leading up towards the cottage and some strewn hither about the cottage itself. Most notably was an old lady of the wood - a grand weeping willow – who sat just to the left of the cottage in the front garden. It looked quite ever so old with a thick and mottled trunk with numerous large branches of swaying melancholy as only the willow can infer. Luther was fond of this old lady in his garden; she gave him some comfort and peace watching as she calmly swayed in the wind.

Beyond the cottage was roving green land on either with woodlands in the distance and a track running past

Luther's house, heading north from the village. There were several small stretches of water as the land itself formed into shallow hills leading away to the horizon. The banks of the Panifery River could be seen to the east along with the outlines of several flarfen homes.

Living on the outskirts of a village as Luther did was not as safe as being within a stone's throw of the centre, but he preferred the relative quiet from being in a lightly secluded location. There was a duality in Luther; on one hand he wanted nearby the amenities and companionship of the village, but on the other he wanted these same things just far enough away that he could feel quiet and alone. Being himself secluded and yet within reach of assurance and hopefully some help, not only for himself, but in case it was requested of him, was important to Luther and he hoped it would stay that way.

He stood looking at his home and thought how he was loathed to have guests inside. Not because he didn't like company. He was not fond of guests because he felt a sense of unease and anxiety of people being present in his home. His safe place. What if they mocked him? He would have nowhere to run and hide. What if they didn't like the way it was furbished or decorated? What if he wished to just run away and be by himself? These thoughts and fears washed over Luther at the idea of it. This was not to say he would turn away someone who might come calling. He would try to make effort as be he could and indeed when good friends came to visit, after a while the anxiety and foreboding feelings would subside. Luther knew how silly he could be with his over working mind, but he struggled fighting the whirlpool as it span round, so great effort was needed to pull himself out of his negative thinking.

Luther stepped forward and put his key into the lock of his front door; a solid wooden door of rectangular shape with four steel braces: one both at the top and bottom with two holding the middle. He turned the key to the left and, giving the circular blackened steel door knob a twist, pushed on through into the cottage.

He took a long sigh of relief to be back at home and with a smile took off his long coat and hung it from a steel peg on the wall to his left. He then walked in that direction into his kitchen where he removed his axe from its sheath and placed it on an oval wooden table sitting just to the side next to the larger rear facing window. He turned to his right and threw some fuel into the wood fire stove sitting in an inlet along the back wall of the cottage. He had the thought of cooked sausages on his mind and wished to get them going as soon as possible.

After finishing his dinner of sausages and chips at the kitchen table, he got up and walked through to his small living room. The wooden flooring of the cottage creaked ever so slightly whenever his feet pressed upon a fidgety plank. His living room was situated in the back right of the cottage with the smaller back window looking out. There was a long brown sofa running up along the right-side wall with a matching brown armchair just before it, half facing the fireplace to the left and half facing the small window looking out. To his right was a bookshelf against a wall housing the doorway in which, he was currently standing. It was filled with books such as 'The Herbalists Guide to Flora and Fungi', 'The History of The Boroughs of Old Briton', and 'Trials of the Ragged Knights'. He grabbed a book named 'Known Creatures of The Boroughs', from a middle shelf and sat down to read, half in vain, hoping to read an entry he may have previously missed on small black little creatures rolling around the woods.

He sat down in his armchair and began reading. After a brief period of thumbing through the pages of his book, Luther had dosed off with the warm heat of the fire nursing him off to sleep. The small little ball of dark fur currently sat nestled between two of the cushions of the sofa may well have joined him in the realm of slumber - it was difficult to tell.

Chapter 5

"Hear me good people! Hear me! I know things have not been well of late. That you have suffered from poor crops, poor trade and not enough coin in your pocket. Allow me to provide some insight as to why life is proving so trying and cruel!" The man saying these words was stood atop a stage in what looked to be a town hall. He was addressing a large crowd of concerned looking townspeople.

The orator in the hall was dressed impeccably; a dark red suit with a matching red waist coat and tie hanging from a cream silk shirt. The suit appeared to be made from a very fine material as if the wearer expected to be clad in nothing less. His shoes were faultlessly made from a fine leather which reflected the light from the large torches hanging in lines on either side of the hall. The man was clean shaven, by cutthroat almost certainly and had short and neat dark brown hair upon his brow; the keen observer could make out the man was thinning on top but had made good use of a comb to cover this as much as possible. The outward physical language, he was displaying, was one of strength and confidence, as if this was not the first time he had addressed a huddled mass from such a platform. He was quite captivating and the people in attendance were listening intently, hanging on every word.

The crowd of people here, listening to the words of this man, were to the last person female or male, human. Within constraint of the human race there sat people representing all walks of life: there were farmers, shop keeps, wealthy tradesman, off duty guardsman, down and outs and even the local mage.

"Let me tell you indeed my friends!" The well-dressed orator continued, looking deep into the eyes of members of the crowd in turn. "There are those amongst us in this very town whose presence causes harm to our collective good. Look around you and see the lack of their attendance here today and you will see what I mean." He waved his arm in an outstretched circular motion across the crowd. "My friends, you all saw the truth and wisdom of those that requested your presence here. You all see the most glaring reason for the problems we face as a town." His face turned sterner at these words, and he paused longer in the eyes of different members of the crowd.

"There are some around here that are not interested in helping us to prosper. Some horde wealth, some are lazy, some conspire to undermine us, and some are hoodlums and unsavoury types that wish only to cause harm and misery to those good people here today." The crowd looked around at each other and begun muttering amongst themselves as if contemplating the meaning of what the orator was saying. It appeared the people here were mostly in agreement with what was being suggested, but there were a few quizzical looking faces and several who were none too happy to be hearing such things.

"Why have no elves come here today?" he continued, "Why do we not see any of the gnomish folk amongst us? Why not the flarfen members of this town? Do they not think us worthy of their time? Are the people here today the only ones that care for their fellow denizens of The Boroughs?" At these words the members of the crowd had turned to one another once again, many agreeing with this sentiment with some saying it loudly enough to be heard across the hall. "I am not saying that anyone absent here today is evil," he continued, "No of course not. I am merely saying that perhaps certain people don't seem interested in the prosperity of our town and this good land of ours. Some people are more interested in furthering their own agendas, of controlling us for their own good to the detriment of good people such as yourselves here today." He paused again as the murmuring rose up from the crowd. "I see here on the faces of many here today, the look of knowing that can only come from well learned and caring folk when they hear the truth from humble lips!" At these words many in the crowd nodded and smiled, their ego having been sufficiently massaged.

"So, it is all well and good to proclaim the case and to enlighten respectable people such as yourselves with the truth

A GRIM JOURNEY

that you no doubt would have come to yourselves with the good intelligence you were born to! But what, what my good people should be done to remedy this situation?" The well-dressed man was now the most serious and stern of voice, the crowd hanging on his every word. "My good friends let me tell you. It is a simple and just medicine to administer. We merely just remove the tumorous influence in our midst. We stop them from enacting their machinations of malice. Upset their plans to undermine the hard-working people of this town!" With every word uttered from his lips he grew more beguiling to the crowd, breaking down walls of mistrust and swaying those present to the merits of pleas. He looked across the crowd at the many shouting in agreement, nodding their heads and smiling all around.

The braying and cheering from the boisterous gathering in the town hall was enough to obscure the opening of the doors at the rear side and the exiting of several people from the building. These people, a good small sample representation of those present, all seemed joined in their concerned looks and shaking of their heads. It seemed that not all were convinced by this well-dressed man's silvery words.

"They don't actually believe that the problems we face are because of the flarfens?" one middle aged woman said to her female friend as they walked out. "I have never had anything but good words with Corrin and his family," she continued.

Another group of four men, all of them roughly in their twenties were shaking their heads with a deep look of concern and confusion.

"That man spits lies and falsehoods. None of that made any sense," one of the men said, with the other three nodding in agreement.

"You are right, he is preying on the worries of people round here. Everyone faces the same problems in life, not just the human folk," one said in response.

Back inside the hall, the well-dressed man and now leader of the riotous crowd, was gearing up for the final crescendo of his performance. It seemed this was not the first time he was to give it and knew exactly what to say to get the reaction he desired.

"My friends, now that we know what to do in essence, here is how we go about it in practicality. We will subvert the intentions of those who wish us ill by the application of active resistance. We will refuse dealings with them. We will not buy their produce. We will make our own gatherings without them. We will forbid our younglings - whom we owe our truest of protection - from mingling with them. We will not only cast them from our lives, no, no, no! We will take back from them what is rightfully ours! We will show them that we know how they mean to keep us weak but shall not let them!" He raised both arms with clenched fists while looking up to the ceiling which incited the now baying crowd to into a rapturous applause and cheer that filled the room with a din that could be heard from those who were now moving away from the town hall with dismay.

The orator, having finished his grand speech, stepped from the podium on the stage and came down into the crowd. Left and right of him people were all smiles and joy as they surged forward to shake his hand and be granted some small sliver of his attention.

"You are so right Fabian, thank you for spreading the word!" cried out a richly dressed man from behind the front row of eager townspeople.

"It's about time someone said it!" exclaimed a woman on his left as he shook her hand with a gleaming smile.

"I can't wait 'till we let 'em know that we're onto them!" shouted an older man who looked to be visually down on his luck; wearing scruffy clothes, a rag tag, pair of shoes with well featured holes and a dishevelled look upon his brow. The orator, Fabian, took each of these pleasantries in turn, acknowledging them all with a wry smile of a cat who had found a delicious bounty of cream.

As he moved through the crowd towards the exit of the hall it became apparent that he was being flanked by two fairly large and ample men that were keeping watch upon him; their arms stretched out to both brace the crowd and dissuade too much forward motion towards their charge. Along with keeping him from obstruction and harm, the sight of these two large men added to the whole pomp of the occasion. The people would mind the importance of the man that was passing amongst them.

Both were quite similar in appearance; roughly the same height of perhaps six feet and four inches tall. Their build – of which was a quite a mass of muscle - was strong and menacing. Both had similar short, cropped hair and clean shaven upon their round and tough looking faces. They both wore black trousers with dark red gambesons; the padded jacket reaching down halfway from the waist to the knee. Around their waists the large brute to Fabian's right wore a black, gold buckled belt while the brute to his left wore one with a silver buckle with both large and overbearing fellows wearing black boots which seemed very capable of stomping upon careless toes or other appendages, dare they step out of line. They kept a parallel line with Fabian, staying either side of him, never allowing some the cheek of straying in too close or sternly pushing back anyone trying hard to invade his personal space or blocking his path out of the hall.

With the crowd still eager for his attention, the huddle of people slowly and loudly moved through the main doors of the hall which were situated centrally, at the back of the building. The two large wooden doors were easily pressed open, one by each of Fabian's large cohorts and within moments the throng of people were now outside in the darkened night of the evening.

Waiting on the path outside of the village was an impressive looking coach lit from above by a streetlamp - being perhaps just lit by the watchman. It was a large, closed top carriage which looked to easily carry six people within. The outside was decorated with gold filigree along the top of all sides of the coach, along with particularly detailed designs around the windows and doors of the vehicle. The spokes of the four large wooden wheels holding the carriage box were plated, again in gold; clearly the owner of this carriage was wishing to give off an impression of unreserved wealth and power with the decorations on the outside bordering on garish and overstatement. It was drawn by three white horses which struck out in great contrast to the dark wood of the carriage itself.

A GRIM JOURNEY

They were impeccably groomed with their white manes and tails both braided tightly, and their coats brushed and gleaming in the light from the streetlamp above them. Their shoes looked shiny new with not a sign of any wear and tear upon them. Around their heads they wore black leather bridles and shutters for their eyes, all yet again punctuated with gold buckles and trappings in fitting with the rest of the coach. All three of the handsome horses were standing patiently for their passengers before making the off with steam slowly puffing from their nostrils having arrived not long before with great haste.

Sitting atop the carriage in the coachman's position was a wiry looking man in a fitted black suit with waistcoat and white tie. He was wearing a black top hat on top of a short head of hair and a clean-shaven face. He was presently sat back in a relaxed way with his legs crossed, looking at the crowd. As he was doing so, his crossed leg was bouncing jovially so, with his pointed shining black shoes prostrating to the sky overhead. He had a knowing smile upon his face at the scene playing out in front of him, with the large crowd of people surrounding the man making his way to the coach.

As Fabian arrived near the door of the carriage the wiry coachman atop clicked his fingers and the door swung open, ready to take in passengers. One of the large individuals flanking Fabian was the first to enter the coach. Fabian was the next to pass in, but before doing so, and standing on the steel step of the carriage, turned and addressed the crowd one last time, "Thank you, my friends, for allowing me to come and talk to you this evening! I am so humbled to be invited to your charming town! We will turn the page and start a new chapter of prosperity with our eyes open to those who oppose the good and free people of this land! Goodbye my dear friends!" A great final roar erupted from the herd of people seeing off this impeccably well-dressed man and with it he turned and entered the coach, quickly followed by the second large gentleman who promptly closed the carriage door behind him. Once all passengers were aboard the wiry fellow sat up slightly and waved his hands in a motion along with some words under his breath which caused the three horses to break into a trot, pulling away from the hall followed by a canter as it made its way along the track and out of the town.

Inside the coach Fabian, the well-dressed Man, sat across from his two stocky guards and next to a woman that was evidently already inside and waiting for him when it pulled up outside the hall. She was not to be seen from the exterior and would not be noted at all unless one stuck their head inside the window of the carriage intent for a good look around. She appeared to be masked by some aura, some obscuring cloak of deception that kept her hidden from all those peering in. Her features were beautifully feminine, with pearl white skin free of any blemish. She wore all black, from top to bottom: a black turtleneck jumper, black leather skirt and black tights with black leather boots up to her knees bearing heels several inches tall. Finally, above all she wore a long black leather coat with pockets either side which she currently had her hands in, holding its hem over her crossed legs.

"It appears you have yet again worked your charm over the people of this little town. They look thoroughly enthralled." The hidden lady said, without as much turning her head towards the well-dressed man at her side.

"I will take that as I may for, I know you would be hard pressed to even contemplate an honest congratulatory word, Vespera," Fabian replied, similarly staring forward as if the two of them were playing a subtle game between them of who may flinch first and physically address the other. "I would dare say it is not too difficult to ignite the spark of mistrust and turn it towards an easy prey. The people of this town were ready to be crafted into what I will of them," he said, with a false sense of modesty.

"Quite. But I did notice some people leaving the gathering jus now. Perhaps not everyone was convinced of your honeyed words?" She appeared to relish the chance at making even the slightest of jabs at the man sitting to her right.

"There will always been stragglers my dear. They are the exception that proves the rule, for people's thoughts and impressions are easily malleable given enough attention to their egos and a simple scapegoat on which to hang from its neck, the cause of their problems," he responded. "It is a simple matter for me to manipulate the minds of the plain masses of the land. They are easy prey and really, take so little to persuade. People rarely wish to look in on themselves or their own or most importantly those above their station when it would be much easier to rest the blame of their useless flailing attempts at life on those they see as below them, different to them or simply not within ear shot." Fabian had slipped somewhat back into his orator way of addressing the crowd when he said these words and noticing so, he composed himself back into the seat of the coach with a pleased smile on his face. "There are always those who resist the charms of a charming man, they are the hopelessly righteous. They have those silly notions of truth and justice and will always need to be dealt with. It is not because I could not fill their minds with the sweet words they would so easily absorb, but rather, they are so full up with learned ways and notions that there is no longer space and desire to be filled with that which I tell them is true." The two bodyguards opposite the couple were smiling at the words of their master and both admired as much as the crowds in which he bent to his will.

"Tell me what you have discovered on your travels of late. Are there other towns out there ripe and ready to be plucked up and taken to the bosom of a simple and humble servant of the people such as myself?" His eyes twinkled and a sneer of a smile came across his face which was met with the same from his two footmen.

The hidden lady, next to Fabian disregarded their little exchange and turned to him saying, "I have found several of which times are troubling. Several whose ire could be turned upon their fellows and those different from themselves."

As he no longer wished to keep up their little game or even because he felt she had yielded to him, Fabian turned to her and said, "That is very good. You have done well. You must tell me about these places so that we can plan accordingly. We should look to see how well we can exploit the local populace." He turned back and looked out of the window of the carriage. "I will have control of this borough and all The Boroughs with time. Indeed, I am happy to take my time. The people of this land are, like so many, easily swayed to believe their misconceptions. Fools they are." He looked out across the fields moving by as if lost in his own sense of assured self-importance.

"Oh, there was one little place," Vespera added, interrupting his thoughts.

"Yes?" he said, turning back to her.

"Yes, a small town called Overton in the Lonefield Borough to the northwest. I believe they might give us some cause for concern when you make your way out there eventually."

"What might be the problem then dear Vespera? You have doubts in my abilities?"

She replied promptly, with a note of sarcasm, "No, I have no cause to doubt the awesome power of your persuasion, but this town has not fallen on to hard times or is mistrusting of their different groups. They even have a council whose lead seems to be quite head strong and resistant to persuasion. You will surely have to exert your most beguiling techniques when we reach that quaint little village."

Fabian had raised an eyebrow upon hearing this. He thought it difficult to believe in someone not taking advantage of the power of their station to better their position in life, regardless of the impact of those under their care. He slipped back into his self-aggrandising tone, "I believe they simply need to be made aware of the looming problem they face. They need only a humble gentleman such as myself, to lift the blind across their eyes and let them see that even if their lives be sound and well, could be even better if they, but understand the motives of some of those among them! Ha! I do relish a challenge so that I may enjoy the triumph ever more sweetly once I have conquered it!" Waving his hand out of the carriage he said casually "Now, tell the Coachman, take us home. I desire to be back to a setting that isn't so drab and unappealing."

Chapter 6

I am being stalked! Stalked by some abhorrent fiend of whom, I have no idea of their identity! What is this great hall around me? How did I get here and how have I got into this chase that I find myself in, so out of the blue? I am moving, yes! I am moving, but so ever slowly. It comes forward at great pace, but yet to grasp me!

This thing that is following me, I cannot seem to clearly make out or describe it. I know it is there and I know that it yearns to have me in its clutches. It wishes to take me whole and devour me, yet I cannot describe anything about it. Only blur and mist and misdirection are apparent. Oh, why can I not for the love of things visualise this bastard villain that strives for my soul.

This place, this hall, what is this place? It appears to be some large gathering chamber or dining hall, with three arched sections; great dark stone arches that leer over one all and most definitely myself. Great benches align deep into this cavernous hall and I here in my wretched, dragged step, I cannot get away and yet it comes for me! There are other things at these benches, but again they are but whispers and deceit. I do not know what they are either, but they appear less to my pursuer yet revelling at its chase… of me! Why can I not get to a pace! Move my incompetent body! Move or you shall never again see the light of day as I am obliterated from existence by this dark and foul thing that hunts me!

Luther shot up, his face all a blur with confusion and an unearthly sense of dread. Where was he? Ah in my bed,' he thought. I was dreaming again those strange dreams, but of what exactly as always, I cannot recall. I know that something was happening, and definitely most vivid, but what, damn it, I cannot remember! Luther, having again being incapable of recalling what he was just previously dreaming about and, after noticing the time on his clock of four am, laid back down in his bed, pulled the covers over himself and closed his eyes in an attempt to go back to sleep.

Luther awoke again and this time with no frightful sense at having previously been tormented by some rogue dream or beset by the anguish of despair. It was the natural kind of coming too that most people would experience in a morning rather than the sudden jerk back into the land of the waking.

He looked around him and saw on his clockwork clock sitting on his bedside that it was nine thirty in the morning. It had been two weeks since his meeting at Deven's house and his making of acquaintance with a small dark furred object. He had not seen it since that night and was becoming to think that it was just his imagination creating strange things from himself becoming overanxious after delving deeply into his problems with Deven. He thought it well that he hadn't asked Nathanael directly that evening as it seemed to have resolved itself anyway and it would be one less thing for people to worry about him.

He didn't have that familiar feeling of a just recent dream, but he did have one of a sadness and dreary state. He laid there for a few minutes marshalling the energy to pull himself out of his bed. He had a melancholy seeping through him, and it would take an effort to overcome.

After perhaps half an hour, he finally managed to sit up and swung his legs anticlockwise out of the bed until he was now sitting on the edge of it. In front of him was a wall of his bedroom with a poster hanging from some string on a screw. It was a picture of the main character from a book called 'The Torrid Affairs of Magical Mystery'; a collection of stories concerning the great detective Randolph Montgomery Henceforth and his never give up attitude in solving the devious crimes of the wicked. He purchased it at Golon's shop with the hope that seeing it of a morning would help to cheer him up and bring a smile.

Randolph Montgomery Henceforth was quite an eccentric character after all, and this poster displayed this nature greatly: It was of Randolph running towards the viewer, down an alley in a built-up area of a town, no doubt after some scoundrel he was wishing to bring to justice. He was wearing a long coat with a furred collar over a brown corduroy three-piece suit and dark brown leather boots over his ankles. The look upon his face was that of stern determination which was offset by the 'handle-bar' style moustache on his face which was quite fun and comical to look at, but endearing, nonetheless.

Luther was fond of keeping such things as this poster around the place. Whenever he awoke - as was today - or entered a room in the house, he might catch a poster or his bookcase of fantastical books of fiction or his board games and raise a smile; reminding him of the wonderful and innocent things in the world was of great comfort of Luther. They acted quite like light houses in the night; bright lights of cheer, of reminisce, of friendship and joy that could help steer Luther back from the rocks that could easily set his mood aground and stuck in a misery for too long a time.

He had to admit to himself that although he felt his usual sadness, this morning at least, he wasn't feeling as sad or upset as he might normally feel. He told himself to take this as a good sign and not to and dwell on it; waking with a good feeling could sometimes cause him to worry that he would somehow pay for his joy or feeling of goodwill with some later event of misfortune or sadness.

He was quite surprised by this fact. He knew today he would be undertaking something out of his usual routine of things. Anything outside of his usual routine would cause him great discomfort and concern so feeling as he did this morning was most unusual.

He stood himself up and went over to the sink in his bathroom. He looked himself in the mirror on the wall above the sink and rubbed the sleep from his eyes with some water from the tap.

"You're feeling alright today, Luther," he said aloud to himself in the mirror. "It's going to continue for the rest of the day, so think positive." He proceeded to have a good wash of his face and made himself ready for the day.

Luther had spoken with Golon about his visit to Deven's and, after hearing Luther tell of their meeting. He told him how Deven was unfortunately unable to provide Luther with much help. After hearing this, Golon talked of an old acquaintance he had which might be able to provide insight into the issues he was dealing with.

"I was at first quite reluctant to mention this, dear fellow," Golon said at the time. "My old friend Celeste Ignophenen may be able to help with what ails you, but more so, give some insight into *why* it ails you," he said.

Luther at the time wondered why Golon had not mentioned his friend earlier and enquired so. Golon replied that it was not because he didn't wish to help his friend Luther, in fact he wished to help in any way he could, but Celeste Ignophenen was not an easy person to locate, let alone get to. If there were possible ways to help Luther closer at hand, then Golon was happy to let him pursue those before mentioning her name.

Luther understood Golon's good intentions and thanked him for his help. He asked why this person was difficult to locate with Golon replying that she was not one to keep to the same place for too long, being quite the wandering nomad. She was known to travel these parts only rarely and often times was seen on the edges of The Boroughs and the Lightlorne Mountain range to the west.

Luther expressed his intention to try and find her as he was earnest in his desire for answers and salvation from his misery. He pressed Golon for her last known whereabouts, who mentioned that the last he had heard, she was visiting the frontier town Bramstone to the southwest, seeking some information they held in the great Library there. With this Luther's mind was set, he would set out to Bramstone as soon as possible and enquire of her whereabouts.

Golon described her as a human female, quite prim and proper in her demeanour, from the northern Boroughs originally, with pale skin and fairly dark hair. He mentioned that she travelled with a familiar of sorts in the form of a warble bear – a small magically imbued bear that had the ability to teleport short distances. Golon explained that she sometimes had to make use of its special ability when attempting to acquire certain artefacts for her study, though he didn't go into any great detail.

A GRIM JOURNEY

Luther made up a travelling pack for his trip consisting of the usual things he would bring with him when faced with any particularly long journey – though not a common occurrence: a small pouch of warding powder, a box of matches in a dry tin, a good blanket and pillow, tin opener, some clothes and a length of tarpaulin should he need to create some shelter from the rain or too much sun.

He planned on stopping off at the store in the village to obtain some small food supplies after a visit to the stables. He had thought for some time to get himself a horse but had always faltered before doing so as it would mean he had little excuse not to travel abroad from the village more often; though he enjoyed travelling the woods surrounding Overton village, he was not often interested in travelling further afield. Luckily, he was not needed to for his work didn't require the need; he had a knack for finding the required components for warding powder which he sold to the herbalists, Deven, other passing mages or traders and Nathanael, on occasion. He didn't make vast sums of money for his troubles, but he made enough to have a sensible and comfortable living which was all that he required. It also gave him cause to leave the house; a driving factor in him not living completely like a hermit which he may well have done if not for the need to make a living.

Chapter 7

Once Luther had his pack ready and locked up his house it was roughly noon by the time he made off into the village. His first stop was to the stables which were situated just on the north edge of Overton village as Luther entered it, bearing straight from his home. The Stable barn was constructed of a light, yellowish wood forming an arched building featuring two groups of four stables facing each other with a middle through way sitting between them. All were occupied except the two right at the back on either side of the throughway, against the rear wall. The front of each stable had a wooden fence across it facing the middle through way and contained a hinged door which came up roughly over four feet in height to allow the horses to have their heads out to see each other and be seen by any potential buyers. The barn seemed well lit from not only the front facing and large, sturdy doors swung open, but with shutters of windows all along the tops of the side walls now open allowing for light to come into the stables from many angles.

To the right of the barn was a paddock ground which was used for exercising the horses and no doubt, Luther thought, to show customers how well they could move. It was roughly eighty feet across and forty at its width which allowed for some stretching of the legs indeed, but not a full gallop.

On north side of the barn was a small stone bricked building which was home to the stable master Owen. It was a modest house with two floors and a thatched angled roof featured a central chimney that was currently all quiet and asleep.

Luther, not noticing him anywhere around, approached the front of the house and used the central knocker of the dark wooden door in an attempt to gain his attention.

After a brief pause the front door opened revealing Owen the stable master. With a large grin the man said, "Hello there young Luther!"

A GRIM JOURNEY

Owen was a man of perhaps seventy years old and had run these stables for as long as Luther had been a resident of the village. His wispy white hair grew around the sides of his head with a lack of any on top. His face was quite worn with wrinkled eyes full of friendliness. He wore a dark tunic top over which he was the most laid back of cardigans that was awash with frayed wool and clinging bits of straw. His dark blue trousers were quite similar, featuring several small holes and patches of dust from moving bales of hay around the yard. On his feet he wore a good hard pair of brown boots which towed the line of worn in through good work with scuffs and stains aplenty.

"Hello Owen, how are you? How is your sister?" Luther said to the jovial stable master.

"I am very well my young sir, very well! Mary is well! How are you my dear lad?!"

"I am well as can be," replied Luther.

"Good, good! And how can I help you? I assume you come with regards to a horse?"

"Yes indeed," replied Luther. I am to make way to Bramstone in the southwest and will need a good mount to get me there."

Owen's eyes lit up and grew a wider smile, "Ah right! Quite the journey indeed." Owen knew well not to pry too far into the reasons behind someone's journeys and expeditions when purchasing a horse so didn't press any further. "I currently have six horses stabled, all good and strong and capable. Shall we go and have a look and see if there is one that appeals to you?" He had already closed the door behind him and began walking over to the stables before Luther had even replied so he just followed the man to inspect the horses.

The three left horses from the nearest to Luther were brown, black and white blotched and brown with white blotches. To the right from Luther was a nearly all brown horse with some white patches here and there, a dark brown horse and finally a black horse with white patches of fur above and below its eyes situated the furthest from where they were standing.

"All right, let's go in and have a look, shall we?"

Owen stepped into the middle through way of the stables and beckoned Luther to follow. "They all have good energy in them and are quite friendly." Owen walked over to the dark brown horse stating, "This here's cookie, he's a good strong and faithful horse" Luther came over and put his hand on Cookie's mane, stroking it slowly.

"He does seem a good one. What of the one behind you, the black one with the white patches around the eyes?" he said to the stable master.

Owen turned round and looked at the dark horse sticking its head out of its stable as if greeting potential buyers was a common occurrence in its life.

"Ah that is Guinevere, she's a good lass, a little older than the others and quieter to boot, but she won't let you down. Oh no sir."

Luther gave cookie a smile and a good pat before walking over to Guinevere. He stood with his hand on her head above the nose from the side so she could see him. He stood there a few moments looking at her and said, "Yes I believe this is the one I would like if you don't mind Owen."

"Of course, Luther, no problem at all. She is a loyal one is old Gwen, mark my words!"

"Thank you, Owen, I will also need a saddle and other sundries as required as I will be setting off right after I visit a few other establishments," Luther said, turning towards him.

"Righto Luther, I will get her ready for you when you come back. We can settle up then also," Owen said, smiling while removing the latch on Guinevere's stable.

"Thank you, Owen, I will be back shortly."

Luther walked further into the village, proceeding south, past the guardhouse and square, towards the local store. It was a simple grey bricked granite building with an angled roof of slate tiles. The front facing had a rectangular wooden door. Across the slates of wood were several bracing strips of steel and a solid looking door handle on the middle right. Directly above the door was a weather worn rectangular wooden sign hanging from a black steel arm. It simply read: 'Local Store'. The door was situated to the left of the building with two windows to its right. Both windows were situated in strong looking bays with steel braced shutters which were currently swung open; they must be open for business.

    Luther reached forward, opened the door, and entered into the shop. He was greeted by room cut in half by a long counter, stretching from wall to wall. The floor was all oak floorboards that were well worn from the coming and going of customers with a particularly worn patch just in front of the counter in the middle of this side of the room. On Luther's side sat two large wooden barrels butted up against the left wall, one filled with roasted coffee beans and the other filled with grain. On the right wall, either side of another window bay hung different sized and shaped satchels. Behind the counter stood a lady attending to a display of little animals crafted from wood. Behind her, along the back and side walls on her side of the counter were a wealth of shelves, each a raft of all sorts of items for purchase. There was food stuffs of all different kinds: raw vegetables, potatoes, fruits, tins of various things, boxes of cereal and baking and cooking items of all kinds. There were also household items like cutlery, cooking pots and pans, matches, plates, string, clothes pegs and all other manner of things one might expect to see in a general store, all arranged neatly in their places.

    The lady behind the counter looked up as Luther entered the shop and with a smile said, "Hello Luther, how are you today?"

    "Good morning Kate," Luther replied, with his own, but slightly apprehensive smile. "I am well, thank you. How are you? Is Gareth letting you do all the work today?"

    Kate turned and looked towards a doorway in the centre of the array of shelves behind her, saying with a louder voice, "No, he managed to get himself out of bed! Taking too long to put away this morning's delivery!"

    Luther returned her smile and looked at the doorway expectantly. He was worried of conversing with two people at the same time and worried he might blurt out some incomprehensive nonsense, but it was always nice to say hello to Gareth.

    Just then a gruff looking man walked through the doorway. He was wearing a dark brown t-shirt under a chequered shirt with the sleeves rolled up revealing some hard-working strong arms. His also wore some blue jeans which were worn at the knees and dusty, most likely from taking in the day's delivery. Over all this, he wore a tan apron with pockets either side. The head of the man had medium length brown hair, swept back and tied in a ponytail, a strong looking nose, and stubble sweeping round his face.

"Thanks, my dearest. You know I only live to serve you." Gareth bowed down and swung his right arm in a great swinging action. They both looked at each other and laughed.

"You, silly bugger," Kate said, still smiling. "Look who is here, Gareth."

Gareth, having already noticed Luther turned and said, "Hello Luther, how are you today? What are you in for?"

Luther replied, "Good day Gareth, I am well and looks like you both are as well. I am off for a little trip to Bramstone in the southwest and was looking for some supplies for the journey."

"Ah right, quite a journey! You best let Kate know what you need then, she will get you sorted, no problems." He gave Luther a smile and disappeared back through the doorway.

Luther listed to Kate the items he needed for his journey. She went to and fro across the shelves behind her, every now and then popping out through the doorway to retrieve something from out back. Once all he asked for had been retrieved and placed on the counter Luther paid Kate and placed the items into his pack.

"We will be needing some more warding powder soon," Kate said, with a smile as Luther handed her some silver pieces in payment for his goods.

"I will hopefully not be too long Kate, but I brought a batch with me if you would like it now, in case I am longer than expected?"

"Yes, that's probably a good idea Luther, I guess I should have asked earlier and just deducted what you owed for the items from your payment, but never mind."

Luther quickly replied "Oh don't worry Kate, I should probably have mentioned it when I said I was off away for a while. Silly me." He handed over a velvet pouch he had in his pack, filled with fresh warding powder, took the payment of gold pieces from Kate and bidding her farewell, turned and exited the shop.

The next stop on his rounds was to the herbalist store to get a few items from Gwithen and Lilly. He also wished to let them know he would be away for a while should they have any worry about him.

He walked north-east, across the square, this time behind the guardhouse to the Herbalists. It was a round-about course that Luther was taking through the village. Rather than a linear fashion through each stop in turn. Luther visited each place as his whim directed him.

The herbalist shop was a timber framed and walled building rather than the stone that was a common in the village with a thatched roof that was quite moss grown and scaled by several vines, criss-crossing across its breadth. Its chimney was made from stone by necessity but was also bedraggled with wild growth in a similar fashion the roof. The front of the building had a door sitting centrally with arched windows either side of it. Below each window there were flower boxes bursting with flora of all different colours. Around the window frames more vines from and flowers had gathered from some large plant pots situated on the ground below. The house very much felt to Luther like a living being itself rather than a building created from innate objects. It reflected its purpose and the ways of the people who resided within it. Luther opened the wooden front door which had a small flower box situated roughly halfway up from the floor and entered the shop.

Quite like Kate and Gareth's, the herbalist store had a counter across the width with shelves and alcoves behind, but this time full of all sorts of herbs and plants, most of which were used in some manner as the basis for a tonic or potion. There were small herbs in pots: the Claranetus herb, used to create a cream for the use of cuts and bruises; Wolf-whistle, a dark grey leaved herb used to create a potion which enhanced one's senses in the dark; the Bilge-mushroom used for headaches and other pains along with an assortment of other wonderful flora with a myriad of uses. There were also larger plants sat in bays on the floor behind the counter including some of the vines which had crept all around the house along with rose bushes, small shrubs and flowers such as bluebells and daffodils.

On Luther's side of the counter and to his right, was a wicker table and two chairs alongside a wicker pot containing some flowering bulbs, resting quietly. In the corner behind the table were more potted plants which was mirrored to Luther's left. Both standing behind the counter was Gwithen and Lilly who were separately tending some plants they were repotting, having outgrown their old lodgings.

"Hello Gwithen, Hello Lilly," Luther said, looking at them both.

Each sister looked up and smiled. "Hello Luther!" said Lilly, followed quickly by Gwithen.

Luther felt at ease, as he always did around the two sisters. It was nice to be so, he thought, and wished it was something that he felt more often.

"I thought to pop in for a few provisions and to say I will be off for a while on a trip to Bramstone, to the southwest… and of course to say hello to you both."

The ladies both looked at each other "That is really great Luther, we know you don't like to go too far afield very much so this must be a big undertaking for you," Gwithen said, with yet another reassuring smile.

"Yes indeed," continued Lilly. "Well done for doing so! Going for any particular reason or just felt like a trip?"

Luther felt comfortable enough to divulge the meaning of his trip, "Yes there is a reason. I would struggle dearly to go on a long journey such as this without good reason I think, as you both know of course. Thank you for the encouragement." He explained the purpose of his trip, of his meeting with Deven, Golon's suggestion of seeking out his old friend Celeste Ignophenen and that she was last seen in the area of the fortress town of Bramstone.

"You might be off for a little while then Luther," Gwithen suggested, "Hopefully they are in Bramstone, but what if they had moved on. Will you seek them further?"

Luther hadn't really thought about this too much and stood there for a moment thinking. "I suppose I should do really. If I go that far I should keep going until I find her. Hopefully, she isn't too far afield, but I am quite resolved to find her."

"You definitely do seem so Luther," Lilly motioned, "I think you are doing the right thing."

Luther smiled and felt slightly less daunted by the trip in front of him. Although perhaps to some well-adjusted members of the borough, his trip might not be too trifling, but to Luther and his worrisome mind it was quite the undertaking. He purchased some Claranetus and Wolf-whistle herbs, ground down by mortise and pestle and then placed in little herb bags. He added them to his pack and after bidding the sisters farewell, he exited the shop.

Next on Luther's trip around the village was a visit to Golon's shop. He wished to tell him he was indeed still going to make the journey to Bramstone today and to thank him for the suggestion of seeking out his old friend. 'Golon's Exciting Emporium of Wonderment', was on the north side of the square, back towards the stables, across the square to Luther's left. While gripping the haft of his axe, he stood still a moment and thought perhaps it best he got it sharpened by Toby at the blacksmiths. So, instead, he turned south, walking down to the forge.

Toby, the village blacksmith, and husband to Lilly, was standing at his forge, working a piece of steel. Luther knew not what it might become but noted the potential it was bathed in; yet to be bent into shape to fill one particular role or another. It could become anything at this point, so full of possibility and naïve to what to the reality of the future. In a sense Luther wished he could still be like this, still unaware of the possible outcomes in life, not yet burdened with the forthcomings of being a certain way, a certain mind set, hampered by and dragged down by an existence. He tried to move his mind on - best not to dwell on such things.

The forge was situated outside the attached abode at which Toby and Lilly lived. It was covered by a slate roof with two red brick walls holding it up, a wall at the rear with a doorway to the back left leading into the house with a fourth wall facing the square missing. Luther imagined this was to allow the heat of the forge and hard work to be released easily into the outside world. The actual fiery forge itself was situated up against the left wall with its chimney leading up out of the roof with the large bellows currently sitting idle.

Further across towards the centre of the room was a large anvil at which Toby was currently working and behind him to the left wall was a variety of tools and weapons which Toby had previously worked, along with some long blanks, waiting to be fashioned into what they may.

Toby himself was over six feet tall and braced with a muscular frame of strong arms and stout legs. This was not an uncommon build of a blacksmith, be they male or female; the hard work of the forge tended to make a smith muscular out of sheer force and repetition. Toby had short black hair and a thick moustache with the skin of his face featuring several beads of sweat dripping down as he hammered down blows onto his work. He had on just a thin, light grey t-shirt top thick dark blue, jean trousers and steel capped boots below a thick brown leather apron down to his knees. In his hands he wore leather gloves, the better to grasp his tools and shield his hands from the wear and tear and heat of the forge.

"Hey, Toby!" Luther shouted in between hammer strikes, hoping to get Toby's attention above the din of clanging metal.

Toby stopped and looked round to see if there was actually someone shouting his name or just him hearing things, to see Luther standing behind him with a smile. "Aha! Hey Luther, sorry it's quite loud and difficult to hear, especially with these in." He pointed to his ears to show they had plugs inserted into them. "Got to be careful of the ears, I don't want to get tinnitus or lose my hearing altogether," he shouted, somewhat unaware of the volume of his voice. Luther realised even though he had the good smith's attention, he may still have to shout back at him.

"Is it ok to get my axe sharpened up? I am off on a bit of a journey out of town and would be more put at ease knowing she was in good condition," Luther shouted. He undid the sheath from his belt and pulled out his hand axe.

"Yeah, that's no problem Luther, I can do it for you

now quick." He gripped the piece of steel he was working – it looked to be taking the shape of a spade head – and pushed it back into the forge. He then took the axe from Luther and walked over to a sharpening belt set up towards the back of the shed. It was a leather like belt around a series of wheels which was run by a little steam powered contraption. The fuel for the steam to power the turning of the belts was not coal, but an interesting magically infused ore which burnt solidly for a long period of time, producing barely any smoke. Toby held the head of the axe with his left hand and the middle of the handle with his right and while pressing down on a pedal attached to the machine, moved the blade into contact with the spinning belt. After a few seconds he turned over the axe and did the same with the other side of its edge. After a minute or so of turning back and forth, Toby released the pedal with his foot and the machine came to a halt.

"There we go Luther, she's back to peak condition," Toby said, casting an eye up and down the edge of the axe.

"Thanks Toby, what do I owe you?" Luther asked.

"Ah no worries, it's just a two-minute job. Here you go."

"Oh, ok, thank you Toby." Luther took the axe from Toby and placed it back in its sheath.

"You speaking to Lilly and Gwithen before you go?" Toby enquired, "I imagine they might wonder where you are otherwise." He gave a smile while heading back to his forge ready to continue work.

"Yes, I just came from there actually. All is well," Luther shouted.

"Ok, well, have a good journey Luther and we'll see you when you get back." Luther thanked Toby and walked out of the shed across the top of the green square, towards Golan's. The clangs of hammered steel beginning once again.

The central square of the village was a grassy green that was well kept by the local grounds man. It was used for games of sport and the annual summer and winter fetes amongst other sporadic events that cropped up from time to time. While Luther was crossing it, he noticed a figure walking towards him along the trodden track, heading west, across the green. It was Reginald, who ran the Tailors and Tannery store with his wife Carrey. Reginald had short black hair and a goatee beard. Also, on the dark brown skin of his face he bore a scar across his left cheek. Luther remembered him telling the story of its creation; he had received this scar during his younger years during a particularly vicious battle in the war with the covenant to the south some twenty years previous. He had parried a spear thrust from a covenant soldier, but it still managed to slice across the left side of his face, luckily only leaving him the scar and no other permanent injuries.

Luther waved at Reginald once they had come close enough for him to notice it for sure; Luther was apprehensive should Reginald not realise it was him as he didn't want to look like a lunatic just flailing his arms about. Reginald noticed and waved back.

Once the two of them had met, Reginald stuck out his right arm for a handshake. Luther reached out his hand in response and was grasped tightly. Reginald had strong grizzled hands, both from his days as a soldier and from his work at the tannery with his wife. He was wearing a thick shirt and jeans with a brown belt along with brown boots that looked worn from good use.

"Hey Reg, how are you?" Luther motioned, while still in the midst of a good handshake.

"Heya, Luther!" Reginald brought his left hand up and affectionately patted Luther's right shoulder as they finished their handshake. He continued, "How are you, my boy?!"

Luther replied, "I am well Reg. In fact, well enough that I am off on a bit of a trip to Bramstone, to the southwest."

"Blimey, that's a bit of a stretch, I assume you are going by horseback or carriage or the like? Might be a bit of a long walk otherwise!"

Luther smiled at the old soldier. Reginald was a good man and Luther respected him greatly. "Yes, I acquired a horse from Owen just now and I am in the midst of making a few rounds before I head back and be on my way. How are you and Carrey? All well?"

Reginald replied "Oh yes she is all fine and well. I just popped out to visit Golon and take some measurements for a new suit. You know how he likes to have new items made for any occasion!" Reginald said these words while patting Luther gently again on his shoulder.

"Ha, yes, too right he does - always impeccably dressed! Well, it's good to see you Reg, as always, but I best get on with my rounds. Please send my regards to Carrey." Reginald said he would and with another shake of hands the two men parted back on their ways across the square.

Luther made across the square. Walking the path were several other villagers walking up and down it, each on their own set of rounds no doubt. Luther gave a nod and a smile as he passed them.

Although the "Golon's Exciting Emporium of Wonderment and adventure," did indeed have a sign hanging outside, it really didn't require it. The front of the store was adorned with all manner of weird and wonderful items: there was a wooden painted star with a tail that was glinting and shining perpetually even in the light of day - no doubt by some magical enchantment; there was the bust of a dragon, joyously breathing a gout of flame across the top of the store front which seemed so very real to Luther. Obviously, a magical decoration rather than actual dragon fire, which would no doubt burn the building to a crisp.

On either side of the store front, on the other side of the glass were two identical looking staircases with small figures duelling with swords up and down. They seemed models come to life with their wooden joints giving away the charade of real life - if somewhat very small - men fighting one another to and fro, between towers. In the centre of the store front were two strong looking wooden doors; quite large and more than required for even the tallest gnome, but this was to allow races of all sizes entry into Golon's store. As Luther approached, both swung open. He stepped through.

Inside, the shop was just as characterful and interesting. There were all sorts of display tables with games opened up showing all the different materials, models and manuals inside. Along the walls were stacks of board games, fun outfits, models created from a type of pewter, paints, special party glitter and fireworks, just to name a few. Rather than simple and perhaps dull signs denoting the sections of the store, instead were little wooden figures such as a gallant knight charging with a lance whose banner displayed the name or an enchantress sending forth a whimsical display of magical force spelling out the section instead.

In the middle of the shop was a circular counter, its top and front made from a dark mahogany with a section to Luther's left cut and lined with hinges for access behind it. The front section of this flap was cut out completely so if you were small enough you could simply walk under the hinged door as easily as opening it up and walking through. And indeed, this was the case when Luther approached the counter, Golon, who must have been arranging a display in Luther's peripheral, moved swiftly and elegantly behind the counter without an inch of movement from the flap.

"Hello! Hello Luther! How are you? You are setting off on your trip today I assume?" Golon exclaimed as he stood atop what looked like a wooden stool with several steps protruding below; this allowed the gnome to ascend in a simple manner and - just as he did this time - with quite a flourish in his step.

He was impeccably dressed, as usual, thought Luther, wearing a purple silk shirt with a ruffled collar, matching-coloured pantaloons that came down to just below his knees with white socks covering the rest away, all topped off with some dark blue suede shoes with fancy silver buckles.

"Hey Golon, I am doing ok." Golon gave Luther a knowing look of encouragement. "Yes, sorry. I mean I am doing well and thinking as positive as I can muster, I am off today yes. Yours is my last stop before I head back to Owen at the stables and set off."

Golon gave smile to Luther and put his hands on the silk of his shirt, on his hips and rocked slightly on his heels. "This is great news Luther. Wonderful news. I am sure you will find her soon enough and I am sure she will at least provide you with enough insight to make the journey worthwhile. Now, let me show you the new cuddly toys I just got in. I think you will find them most splendid!" No sooner had the words escaped his lips had Golon strutted down the steps of his stool and hastened over to part of the back wall where his new arrivals were being displayed. "These came in just this morning Luther; I am quite pleased with them. They are producing some quite wonderful stuff over at Thatched Heath in the Northern Boroughs." He stood, looking up at Luther while twirling his extravagant moustache.

Luther stepped forward and glanced over the stuffed animals on the shelves in front of him. In the middle of each shelf were what looked like quite real, puffy clouds, housing the words 'Stuffed Toys', blinking with the colour of lightning as if the clouds were holding on to a thunderstorm, ready to let loose an exciting downpour.

There were all manner of different stuffed toys adorning the shelves in front of Luther which he scanned with his eyes: there were elephants, bears, seals, lions and other animals native to old world Terra alongside the more magical kind such as dragons, trolls, werewolves, minotaur's and some small black fur ball looking thing… Luther's eyes widened, he could feel the hairs on the back of his neck rise up as he was overcome with anxious worry. Was the thing back, he thought? No, no it couldn't be back, it was just a silly machination of his over working mind, he said to himself. He looked back to what he thought he had seen. Was that the black critter that he had seen in the woods and walking behind him several weeks previously? Oh no, that wasn't anything he assured himself. Having looked back and seen that in actual fact it was the belly of a black bear, Luther's heightened state relaxed. He just hadn't noticed the rest of him in haste to see all that was on display.

"You ok Luther?" Golon said, with an air of concern.

"Yes, sorry, I am fine. I was just thinking about something I forgot to do before heading off. All fine," Luther replied. He was relieved that the strange little thing hadn't reappeared in his life, but at the same time didn't really want to divulge to his friend that he may have been hallucinating small furry creatures without any discernible limbs that rolled around beside him.

"These are all very nice Golon," Luther said, changing the subject of their discourse and hopefully, that of his mind. "I am sure they will sell in no time at all."

Golon had a smile on his face, as if this were exactly what he was looking to hear and said, "Yes I believe so! Exceptionally good stuff! Now tell me, are you ready for the off?" Golon moved back to the counter and up the stool again, so he was standing closer to Luther's height.

"Yes, all ready. Yours is the last stop before I head back to the stables and set off on my new horse." Luther followed Golon back across to the counter and was now rubbing his fingers around on the counter in a nervous sort of way; running his nails along grooves when he found them or making figures of eight with a nascent energy as was his way when anxious.

Golon, knowing his friend well, spoke up and said, "Don't worry Luther, you will be fine. You are capable of such a trip. By sticking to the road and being on horseback, I am sure you will be there in no time. I am quite sure there will be plenty of taverns to stop by on the way. It will be a rewarding trip and good for you, my friend."

Luther was looking down at the counter, watching his fingers move over it, lost in his thoughts, but lifting his brow when hearing those last few words. "Yes, it will. You know what I am like though, I worry for everything. I wish I had your optimism and positive attitude - I admire it greatly."

Still standing on the stool Golon said, "Ah, I have just been around for a while now and I know my lot in life is to try and bring some joy to people both through my own exuberance and of course my shop here. You are a good person Luther, and you are better than you think you are. Trust me. Most people round here know that to be true."

Luther was moving his gaze around the shelves and displays behind Golon, avoiding eye contact, but now focused on the gnome. "I know, ugh, I just don't like to stray too much from the safe things in my life. Difference and change cause me great worry. Doing things outside of the norm brings uncertainties and anxiety. It is of course probably a good thing. My silly brain gets the best of me at times." He started knocking gently on the countertop with his closed left fist. "Thanks, Golon. I best be off then. Don't want to leave my new horse waiting."

Luther made to turn away and leave the shop when Golon interspersed; "Oh before you go, here, take this. It's a ball of fireworks. Just chuck it up in the air at least twenty feet and it will do the rest. It might keep you amused should you found yourself camping outside or simply just as a distraction." The gnome pulled out a ball about the size of a large marble but handed it to Luther.

"Thanks, Golon. That's really kind of you."

"No problem at all my friend. Tell Celeste I said hi."

Luther nodded and put the ball into a side pocket in his pack and walked out of the shop. Standing outside, Luther felt a little better about his trip with the anxiety subsiding somewhat. Perhaps it was the encouragement from Golon or maybe, mistakenly seeing the black ball of fur and confirming it was just his imagination, gave him some strength and reassurance. Having cause to believe things might end up ok made Luther feel good and hoped such instances were more common.

He turned to his right and walked the path back towards the stables. As he made his way, he could see Owen in the distance with a black horse sporting a saddle. As he got closer, he gave a wave to the stable master who responded in kind and then greeted him as he walked up to the stables.

"Here she is Luther, all saddled up and ready to go. She has a few saddle bags as well at no extra cost!"

"Thank you, Owen she looks, great." Luther decided to make use of the saddle bags and pulled various items from his pack and placed them inside. He then tied his pack on.

"Right," Luther said. "How much do I owe you Owen?"

"That will be thirty gold pieces please Luther."

"Ok" replied Luther. He pulled out a different bag of coin from pack. He had packed some more with him, knowing he was to buy a horse today. He pulled out thirty gold pieces and handed them to Owen. "Thank you very much Owen."

"Thank you, sir!" replied the stable master.

Luther shook Owens's hand gratefully before putting his left foot on the left side stirrup and mounted the horse onto the saddle. It felt quite comfortable. He hadn't ridden a horse for some time, but the ways were coming back to him even as he sat there which made him glad. "See you soon Owen and thanks again."

"Thank you, Luther. Good luck on your journey."

Luther gently encouraged Guinevere into a light canter and rode away from the stables. He saw the path heading to the southwest and set off in that direction. Right, I am actually doing this, he thought to himself. Crikey, no turning back now. He knew he was doing the right thing and the drive to find some truth of allowed him to put aside his immediate anxieties and pressed on.

Chapter 8

The road leading away from Overton and to the southwest was similar to that leading from Deven's to the main part of the village; mostly just a clear track with some grass and stone in amongst it. It was suitable for horse or coach travel in any case.

The fields to the right were filled with crops and to the left were untamed stretches of tall grass, peppered with gatherings of trees, spreading their reach all about them.

Luther was feeling at the least, content to travel this way and see where it led him to. He knew as much that it was going in the right direction, and he would hopefully come across an inn or signposts which would give him further information in regard to where he was heading.

Guinevere was walking at a casual pace and Luther was happy for her to do so; travelling too quickly, seeing everything he recognised pass by too fast with just the unknown left, was probably not the best idea, he thought.

Several hours since heading off, the fields on both sides gave way to trees, slowly gathering more and more as they pushed on, to a point where Luther found himself on the edge of a forest. The columns all around him were tall, mostly ferns with a spattering of birch and oak among them. Luther felt the grasp of the wood; the smell of the leaves on the tips of the branches from the columns rising high; the canopy above creating a darker under croft with it yet still in the light of day; the soft blankets of moss together in patches all around the base of the trees, hugging rocks and stones. He definitely enjoyed being in the presence of a forest, even one so dense with trees as this, blocking out much of the sun above. It was known as the Dell Wood, a large expanse of forest that crept across several boroughs with many a thing, but large and small residing within.

Something of the trees were a calming effect on Luther. They were steady and true, quiet and serene; just existing and minding themselves. Not interested in worry, simply happy to be. Luther admired them and enjoyed their company. The woodlands of the world had an air of magic around them, indeed literally, as they were home to all manner of beasties both magical and traditional, dangerous, and benign, not all of which were known and recorded by the guild of Mage Scribes. Luther respected and revered the woodlands; their mysterious nature and embodiment of nature's intent encouraged a reverence and respect from him, and he was glad to be in its presence.

The Dell Wood was large and incredibly old. Some of the trees, Luther was told, were several hundred years of age with the wood itself stretching quite a good, few miles in either direction; He would be travelling through it for several days before reaching clear skies again. There was talk of trees even older than this, of a great size with distinct colourings, of great mass gatherings of huddle moss together in awe of them. From cartography he had seen in Overton, there must have been a dozen or so taverns and inns within its reaches along with a few settlements and no small number of points of interest. Although Luther felt a sense of urgency in his travels, he wished to visit at least a few of them and enjoy his time in this old forest as best he could. He may of course become too filled with worry or become saddened and have to lay up for a time somewhere, but he was hopeful he wouldn't become too afflicted during his travels and even if he did, he told himself, it doesn't matter. You must be like the old ones all around you. They are just being and letting the wind pass over them like all the worries and sad thoughts should wash over you and not be allowed to linger.

Luther travelled at a relaxed pace with Guinevere walking the track quite happily. He had been in the woods several more hours now and had yet to see anyone else as they wound their way through the sea of trees and plant life. Just as he was pondering when he might encounter another traveller or resident of the wood, he saw a figure riding a horse, walking the track as it came round the corner to Luther's left.

The mount which the figure was astride was perhaps more the size of a pony than a full-sized horse and was a shade of tanned brown from what Luther could make out at this distance. The person riding the horse was wearing a trench coat of beige and a matching weather worn hat with a wide rim. This figure didn't seem tall enough to be a human and fit more the silhouette of a flarfen and, as they approached closer, Luther saw that it was indeed one of the river folk. It was not unheard of to see a Flarfen on horseback, but it was a fairly rare sight and Luther had never encountered one before.

"Hello there," Luther said, in a relaxed tone as the two travellers pulled by one another.

"Good day, good day!" said the flarfen.

Luther saw now that it was a female with whom he was addressing. He could make out that she was wearing a light tunic top below the long coat and thin dark brown trousers - really the folk of the river didn't need to wear too much clothing as their thick fur kept them quite warm regardless.

Luther said, "Good day madam, I am Luther, from Overton Village." He gave a meek smile while trying to come across as well as he could.

"Hello Luther!" said the flarfen. "I know Overton fairly well. I have friends over by the Panifery river close by. My name is Foilee, traveling purveyor of oddities and fancifuls." She rose up slightly in her saddle and pushed out her chest as if this was a well-rehearsed line which she was fond of recalling.

"Oddities and fancifuls?" Luther questioned.

"Yes indeed," she said. "You would be quite surprised by what interesting items can be discovered laying contently at the bottom of a river or lake, ready to be grasped by a searching hand. We Flarfen spend many a time floating about in the watery ways that we come across lots of them. Of the fisherman of the local rivers, I give a good price for their finds of which I then sell on during my journeys. There is gold to be made for the entrepreneurial Flarfen. Most would rather stay within a reassuring distance to the water than travel far and wide plying their wares." She sat back quite proud of her lot; she clearly relished her profession as a traveling trader, a profession not common at all amongst her people - perhaps only for the stronger willed and ambitious, Luther thought.

"I must say, if I may, I have never before met a travelling merchant of your good people before, so I trust your words indeed Foilee," Luther said truthfully. He had, from Foilee, the impression of a good-natured person and had relaxed somewhat with the language of his body following suit.

Foilee clapped her right hand on her left hand which was holding the reins to her pony and exclaimed, "How about yourself Luther of Overton, what brings you through the Dell Wood this fine day?"

Luther didn't feel the need to be too bashful with the intent of his journey and so explained that he was on his way to Bramstone in search of a woman there which may have knowledge of a subject dear to him.

"You have a ways to go yet Luther, but I am sure you know that," she said, with smile and another pat of her hands on the reins.

Luther smiled and said, "Yes, but I am hopeful that I will have a pleasant time along the way, so the journey will not seem in any way too arduous or taxing. That is the plan at least."

Foilee replied, "I am sure it will be. The wood is a nice journey, especially if you don't wander too far from the path."

This pricked the ears of Luther and he had to enquire why, "Oh? If I strayed from the path through the wood is there things out there that might not be happy I did so?" Luther's heart raced a little and his anxiety perked up a bit.

"Well, most likely all would be fine, but this is a wild wood and not all of it is happy enough to be encroached upon; you don't want to be disturbing a grouchy troll or some such if you can help it."

Luther thought for a brief moment. He didn't have much intention of straying from the path at all and definitely didn't get on the wrong side of a troll. "I will endeavour to not stray from the path if I can help it. Thank you for the advice, Foilee."

"That's no problem at all!" she exclaimed, saying further, "I had best be on my way, I need to make the next Flarfen Village before dusk. Before I go, I don't suppose you would be interested in any of the oddities in my collection? I have to ask, what sort of a trader I would be otherwise?!"

Luther chuckled lightly and said, "Yes, of course, please, let me see." Foilee turned to her left and then to her right, both times untying the knots on her saddle bags which then draped open to display her various wares. There were an assortment of rings, necklaces, bracelets and other jewellery along with smoking pipes, fishing lures, several small blades, a couple of lockets and what looked like a stone carving of a warble bear. Luther, not wanting to be rude on his first meeting of a travelling Flarfen trader and especially one so nice, thought he ought to purchase something.

"Oh, that carving looks quite nice Foilee, how much would you like for it?"

Foilee looked over to it and said, "Oh just a single five silver piece for that one." Luther handed over a five-silver piece and Foilee leant back, untied the carving from its place on the laid-out saddle bag and handed it to him. Luther took the carving and after a moment looking at the little statue of the bear, placed it carefully into his own saddle bag for safe keeping.

"Well, thank you very much for the patronage, Luther and most importantly, very nice to meet you!" She closed up her wears patted her hand again. Tipping the top of her hat, she gently encouraged her pony to move on.

"Very nice to meet you as well Foilee. I wish you good journey." He then asked Guinevere in the same way and the two travellers parted.

Luther felt quite good having had a nice encounter on his way through the wood. It made him feel better about his journey even if it was accompanied by a word of warning. He didn't have much intention of straying from the road that wove through the forest, so he felt comfortable enough not to worry about it too much.

Guinevere had been carrying her charge for another half an hour when Luther saw what looked to be a tavern on the left-hand side of the path some two hundred feet away. He thought he might stop a bit and let her catch her breath and have something to drink so, as it came up, he motioned her towards it.

The tavern was a small building made from timber with a thatched roof atop. It consisted of just a single floor with the entrance situated to the side facing Luther rather than towards the path, passing by. From the wall faces Luther could see they all had windows with wooden shutters with heavy duty steel bracing to them. He imagined that this was due to where the inn was situated and, although the wood was mostly peaceful, it was still a wild wood as Foilee had mentioned, which meant you might get the occasional beastie wandering by. Securing the premises if needed, was a must.

Luther unseated himself from his reassuring saddle atop Guinevere and tied her reins to the post standing to the left of the building that had a watering trough stationed next to it. He gave her a stroke of her mane and a patted on her neck before turning to the inn door. Above it, as was common with taverns, hung a sign which read, 'The Pathway Inn', with an image of a path winding through a wood. Quite apt, Luther thought. The door to the inn looked very sturdy, constructed of thick wood. He opened the door using the handle on the left and stepped into the tavern.

The inside of the Tavern was quite small, featuring a bar with several stools, six tables spread around and a fireplace on the right-side wall. Only two of the tables were currently occupied: one by a human man, drinking a pint of beer while reading a paper and at the other a male and female, human both conversing over a pot of tea. Behind the well-worn bar stood a man wiping some glasses - the contrived image of a bar man in no danger of being extinguished. He looked up at Luther as he entered the tavern and gave him a nod before turning back to wiping his glasses.

The patrons of the inn didn't seem to take much notice of him, either engrossed in their newspaper or their conversation respectively. Luther walked to the bar and asked for cup of coffee from the bar man who put down his glass and his cloth and went and prepared it for him.

When he returned with a cup of coffee and a little jug of milk he said to Luther "There you go sir, that'll be two silver please."

A GRIM JOURNEY

Luther paid the man and sat and drank his coffee quietly. He didn't actually feel up to engaging in any long conversation with the bar man who thankfully seemed quite happy to go back to wiping his glasses. Luther sat and thought about the trip so far, how it hadn't been too taxing on his mental state and perhaps if it kept this way then he should be able to get through it quite ok.

Before long, Luther had finished with his coffee. He thanked the barman for his service who replied with another simple nod, got up from his stool and wandered back outside to Guinevere. She was standing quite happily, having had a good drink from the water trough.

"Hey Gwen, I hope you had a nice rest and a good drink. I would like to get a few more hours in before we settle down for the night if we can. It'll be dark by then, but we should be fine." he said, while patting her gently on the neck and looking into her eyes. He knew it might seem strange, but he had the thought that perhaps Guinevere understood him to some degree. Maybe in his manner and his body language she gathered his meaning or maybe he just thought about it too much. It was nice to think he had a friend by his side on this trip and she seemed like a good sort that he was glad to have with him. Luther untied her from the post and with a foot held strong in her left stirrup, sat astride her once again. He gently prompted her to move off from the inn and they resumed their journey through the Dell Wood.

They moved at a strolling pace for over an hour more by which time the sun had begun to set and dusk was setting in. A thought came to him, he hadn't enquired at the inn concerning where he was exactly, and whether he was heading in the right direction, namely, towards Bramstone. It was a little bit of a worry, but from the maps he had checked before leaving Overton, he was happy enough that he was heading in the right direction.

They were still entirely in the Dell Wood with trees abound wherever Luther looked, and the wood seemed intently darker and gloomier than earlier in the day. The little light coming through the gaps in the reaches of the trees above was just barely enough for Luther to see a useful distance in front of him.

After a further half hour of a slow and lazy pace, Luther thought it best to pull aside somewhere and make camp for the evening; he was starting to doze himself and didn't want to push Guinevere too hard. He pulled Guinevere over to the right, off the path about fifty yards and found a small patch that was enough to make a slight fire and pitch his tent if need be. He tied up Guinevere to a branch of a nearby fir tree and pulled out a metal bowl and a canteen of water from his pack. He filled the metal bowl with water and managed to wedge it between several limbs of the same tree. She seemed quite happy to have a drink and had enough slack on the rope should she wish to move around, reach down to graze or lay down for a rest.

He searched around the immediate area and with not too much effort, gathered enough dead wood to create a decent fire for the two of them and got to lighting it. He arranged the small parts of kindling into a coned like shape with them leaning upon each other in the middle space between them. He then took a particularly dry looking piece of log and with his axe, scraped off some thin shavings which he then placed between the kindling. With some encouragement from a lit match, the shavings were alight and after little time at all the kindling was aflame and he had a warming fire on the go.

Luther pulled a can of beans from one of Guinevere's saddle bags along with a metal cup, metal pot and a small metal platform which looked to be used for seating such a pot upon it. It was hinged to allow it to be folded up - all the better for carryings sake. The legs of this apparatus had burn marks all across it suggesting it had seen a sizeable amount of use. He unfolded the platform so that four legs were spread and placed it so that the platform part was directly above the fire. He then opened a tin with his axe, the contents of baked beans pouring into the metal pot and while holding the handle, Luther placed it on top of the metal platform. He poured some water into metal cup which he drank down before refilling again and placing it next to the pot on the little metal platform. He planned to have a cup of decaffeinated coffee of the instant kind, which he then pulled from his pack still attached to the saddle bags. Having a normal cup of coffee at this time would no doubt keep him awake and Luther tried to keep himself not too full up with caffeine in the first place as it could at times prove fuel for the fire of anxiety that was ever present in the back of his mind.

Once Luther had finished his beans, with cup of coffee in hand, sitting with his back up against the tree to which Guinevere was tied, he rested his head against the bark of the woodland lady and tried to have a mindful take on the sights and sounds around them.

The clearing in which he was camped was small with the encroaching trees all around him casting shadows wide across the view of the fire. Some of them had common moss growing around their boughs, some had fungus strewn around their bases: he could make out the familiar Yoolin variety, a few Bilge mushrooms here and there, the odd cluster of Medusa and one or two Shaggy Parasols. He could make out the sounds of a few night-time birds in the distance as well as a few insects here and there, but mostly the wood was quite quiet; they were mostly tired from the day and ready to sleep until tomorrow.

Luther finished the last few drops of his coffee, stood up next to Guinevere and was about to pull out some blankets when something caught his eye across the fire. It had become quite dim by this point as Luther was readying to let it burn out but was still quite happily illuminating the immediate area. He wasn't quite sure what he saw, especially as the fire was drawing all sorts of long and miss-leading shadows from Guinevere, himself and the trees surrounding them. He was also tired from the long day and knew he couldn't trust his own mind too much in this state so he turned and looked across the fire to see what he could see; only the usual kinds of fleeting shadows flickering from the fire or the embers flitting little flickers across its brow. And then he blinked… and he saw something he hadn't seen there before, a small little black ball of fur possibly sitting or possibly not sitting across from him, on the other side of the fire. Luther immediately felt himself go flush as a panic raced over him. Was that the little black ball from several weeks passed? Why had this thing returned? Had his trepidation concerning the trip tied with his lethargy from the days travel created phantoms in his sight or was the light of the fire producing an odd shadow that was currently causing him distress? He had to know.

Luther looked all around him. Was there anything about, projecting the shadow he wondered? The only object he thought may be capable of this was either his mug or the pot sitting by the fire; they were round enough and with ample projection could form a shadow large enough to fit the subject. The mug was on Luther's side of the fire though, which had a shadow cast off away from the fire so this couldn't be the culprit. His cooking pot on the other hand was sitting on the other side of the fire and he could not make out from here where it's shadow lie. He moved slowly, around the fire and towards the pot with his eyes transfixed on the little black, furry critter that was possibly perched just on the edge of the light from it. He moved the pot with his right foot and nudged it a short distance over to his left. It was projecting a shadow he could clearly see, but it was facing away from the dark, round little creep that hadn't budged from its spot. Luther thought he may have to admit that it seemed the little creature had reappeared in his life.

Oh dear, he thought. I thought I was rid of this thing. It seems I am going quite mad.

Despite his obvious alarm and nursing a creeping sweat upon his brow, he felt the urge to come and sit next to it, so without much thought, he did so.

He sat, facing the fire across from Guinevere with the fur-ball, still unmoving, sitting to his left. Without a thought he found his left arm move and wave across, through the little thing. He wasn't quite sure what this accomplished; he had previously confirmed it was at least incorporeal and if it was just a shadow projected by some strange circumstance or a figment of his imagination then his hand passing through would be the expected outcome. Oh well, he thought.

Strangely, as before when he had encountered it that day after his meeting with Deven, he wasn't feeling as anxious as he would expect to be in such a situation. The fact he was just sitting next to it rather than keeping clear and trying to ignore it was quite refreshing to his mind which may normally have great cause for concern. He was surprised at how he was feeling. He was not under usual circumstances, in a fit of anxiety and worry, but clearly, he was either hallucinating or he had continued to encounter some new creature that had not ever been encountered before.

He was overcome with this urge to look at it, to study it perhaps. It was definitely an oddity; how did this thing exist while apparently not being of any physical nature. He could see it, it looked like it should have depth and some kind of mass, but it didn't. So very odd he thought to himself.

Luther sat there quietly for a few minutes, sitting next to the small little critter that shouldn't exist. Rather than an escalation of distress - which he was expecting - Luther felt himself becoming calmer. He didn't feel as flushed or his heart racing a mile a minute. He was quite unsure of the reason for this happening, but he was feeling a sense of calm which he wasn't interested in changing. He sat there unmoving for a while longer. Sitting in a malaise of confusion, worry, contentment and calm, all at the same time, swirling the twists and turns in his brain.

After a few more minutes with Luther feeling relatively relaxed, despite what might be the obvious sign of madness perhaps sitting next to him, it gently started to move. Gradually the little ball of fur began revolving, moving itself slowly away from the fire, towards the darkness of the woods behind them. Luther was not overly startled by this, rather he half expected it to move, either because he guessed his mind would begin a further stage of delusion or maybe he was accepting the situation in front of him and was ready to let things unfold as they would.

It was moving now towards the edge of the firelight and with it, Luther found himself standing up and following. Before it crossed the boundary of light marking the edge of the fire's gaze, Luther quickly grabbed a stick he had been using to stoke it and went over to his pack and grabbed the pouch of fire dust he had purchased from the store back in Overton. He pulled a pinch of it from the pouch and sprinkled it on the end of the stick which had been shoved into the embers of the fire.

A GRIM JOURNEY

With a swift motion Luther jabbed the end back into the fire and quickly removed it. The tip of the stick was now radiating a tremendous glow that extended the boundary of light even further away from him. He then gave slow chase to the little black fur ball that was still slowing moving away.

Chapter 9

Within the blackness of a great quiet wood, on a quiet night, a quiet man with torch in hand, was treading just so quietly as he followed closely behind a rolling little ball of fur. A ball of fur he was not entirely convinced even existed, but was nevertheless compelled to pursue, deeper into the forest, come what may.

The quiet man Luther, his makeshift torch in one hand and the head of his hand exe embraced gently by the other, was feeling both concerned and relaxed in equal measure.

Where was this thing going if it was even a thing at all, he wondered? Was he following a small little creature as real as the tall trees of this quiet wood, on this quiet night, as it made its way to wherever it was heading or, was he just wandering off like a madman, embracing his insanity, never to be heard of again? Despite the oddity of the situation, he felt a need to keep attending the creature, at least until it came to a stop or possibly disappeared somehow like it had before - whichever came first.

The critter rolled on for what like several minutes, in a fairly straight line, surprisingly clear of any obstacles. This posed as interesting to Luther because it was if a mathematician had looked at the layout of the wood and with a ruler drawn a straight line through it which avoided collision of any trees, logs, bushes or other objects that may cause the two travellers to take a sidestep or more to avoid walking into them.

This was of course until Luther found himself stopping just short of the trunk of a large and round tree. She was a mature lady of the wood that was difficult to really miss even with his attention so intently focused on the little black, furry beastie as it went on its way; trying to ascertain and maybe settle the dispute in his mind as to the legitimacy of this thing's existence. Luckily, he had come to a halt in his trailing of the small furry creep just before clattering into the dear old one in front of him.

A GRIM JOURNEY

Now that he had stopped before this lady of the forest, there were two things at the top of Luther's worrisome mind. The first being what a grand dame she was; broad around the trunk, several times the width of himself with ragged knots about her wrinkled skin and a trunk with branches only making manifest nearer the top of her great height. Luther noted that the lack of arms about her lower half was most likely a symptom of the absence of a meaningful amount of sunlight down below the greater canopy; the good lady most likely felt more inclined to spread her arms high to reach as much light as she could. The other thing pressing on Luther's mind was that the little fur thing didn't appear to have stepped aside and made way around the great tree. Luther walked anti-clockwise around her to the opposite side from which he had almost bumped into.

The little thing seemed to have vanished. There was no sign of it. He held his torch aloft and span around in desperate search, looking to see if he could make out where it had gone - if it had gone anywhere at all.

The radiance from the torch illuminated the immediate vicinity: the body of the grizzled old lady was clear in his view; the wrinkles of her skin very prominent in the light; his own body, his purple buttoned cardigan over his black long-sleeved shirt and the leather of his dark boots glaring here and there along its surface; the undergrowth of the Dell Wood with its mushroom and moss and vines and bushes and other woodland things. With all these in sight there was one thing that was missing, the folly of his pursuit, the reason he was now standing in front of an old lady of the wood, off the beaten path, in the middle of the night in the Dell Wood.

He waved his torch arm right and left, but all he could see was the faces of the trees looking back at him or the other smaller plant life and detritus on the woodland floor. There was no sign of the small little creeper that he was following only moments ago.

Luther decided to cut his losses and wander back to his camp site. He remembered the direction he came from and could make out the feint light of the fire in the distance. He had just started his way back when, all of a sudden, he heard a strange noise to his left, as if someone was sobbing or groaning. Unlike his struggle with the validity of the black fur ball, this sound seemed quite real. He stopped his movements and listened intently to see if he recognised the noise and what may be creating it. The groan happened again. Luther heard a long guttural groan; a very deep base of a tone laced with melancholy. And again, the groan happened, a deep and long note of sadness echoing through the forest. There was little doubt in Luther's mind as was making the noise; it was a Troll.

Trolls were very much solid, tangible, and real things in The Boroughs of Britain and other lands of Terra. It was terribly difficult to miss them in fact. They were large hulking beings eighteen foot tall on average and nearly as wide. Their legs were short compared to their height but had long arms which gave them a great reach; much to the surprise of any being wishing to upset a troll and then make good their escape. Though, Luther thought. Why anyone would want to do that outside of a keen sense of suicidal oblivion of course was not something a rational person would do.

The skin of a Troll was quite rough with patches of hard callouses and of a colour which could change with their mood or surroundings. If a troll was quite angry its skin may flash a bright red, if it was tired and sleepy it may go a dull grey and when it was sad it had been observed to go a dark blue or even black when in mourning. For Trolls were emotional creatures. They were quite capable of conforming to the stereotype of a raging beastie; traipsing through a village causing chaos but were equally happy to sit around with their family, talking to one another in their low guttural tones quite content and happy in life. The troll that Luther had stumbled across felt to him to be in a great distress and would no doubt be a in some dark colour matching the darkness around them - not a particularly good thing if you were trying to avoid upsetting a large monster, capable of pulling some poor fellow's limbs off with relative ease, should you give it cause to.

Again, the groan pressed out across the wood. Luther thought of what to do. The easiest thing would be to make way back to his little camp and try to ignore the fact there was an upset troll close by. The other, more mortally dangerous thing to do would be trying to find the location of the groans and see if he could ascertain why, it seemed so upset and perhaps somehow, provide comfort while avoiding being pummelled or squished in short order. Luther's mind was certainly for the former, but within him he felt an affinity with this creature's pain; he knew very well the affliction of sadness and misery and how it wrenched brashly at a being's soul. He decided, however foolishly and against his better judgement to make his way carefully and quietly towards where he believed the groans were coming from. He held his torch high so that perhaps the troll would see him coming from afar and if in an aggressive mood, would let him know before he got within arm's reach.

He stooped very slightly as someone does when trying to skulk or gently tread upon the ground and moved slowly towards the troll's crying pain. It groaned again of that same guttural tone which caused a momentary pause in Luther's motion; from a mixture of fear and the need to confirm the direction in which it came from. He carried on, with torch held high and careful steps, tepidly treading through the undergrowth.

As he crept forward, he heard the groan again, but this time louder than before. It seemed he was moving in the right direction which Luther weighed in his mind was either a good or a terribly bad thing; the closer he got the more perilous his position became. He continued further on his bearing onwards the misery floating upon the night air and with every step the groan became clearer and clearer.

He couldn't make out a great deal past the light of his torch; roughly ten feet in either direction. He could see trees all around as usual by now along with the shadows of different flora in the under croft of the woodland floor, but no sign of a troll.

He kept moving, closer and closer to the origin of the wailing groan, until he thought he could make out a further sound in their air, the breathing of a fairly large creature in his immediate vicinity. Luther span himself with a sudden urgency, expecting to be confronted by the outline of a beastie close by. But all he could see was dark black shadows of trees. One of the shadows of these trees had a girth slightly larger than the others and its branches appeared to be swaying as if caught in the wind. Oddly, Luther could not feel any breeze on his brow or the movement of any other trees next to this one. This all seemed quite strange, and Luther began to worry even more than he already was.

    What is going on here, he wondered? Before his anxious thoughts could begin sloshing around his anxious brain in their usual way, he noticed that one of the branches of this tree seemed to be moving in his direction. It came closer and closer and within a brief moment the branch was upon him. It wrapped itself around his waist.

    What sort of tree is this?! He thought, swiftly followed by a shout of "whoa!"

    Luther placed his left hand upon the branch that now literally had him in its grasp. This bark was quite rough and had patches extra hardened, like callouses on skin. The end of this branch seemed to fork out into several smaller ones. He thought this to be very strange indeed which he thought even stranger when all of a sudden, he was being lifted up in the air and reeled in back towards the trunk of the tree.

    Oh dear, he thought. A sudden realisation coming over him. This wasn't some magical animate tree with arms outstretched grasping hold of him no, Luther had found the Troll.

    With this realisation Luther was quickly overcome with a deep sense of fear: was he about to become dinner for an angry troll or just squished asunder for startling the creature. He was certainly about to find out.

    He began to berate himself, how on earth did you not realise you were right next to a troll, you stupid fool. It's not exactly like they are hard to miss.

    The branch of which Luther now understood to be the long arm of the great creature, with the protrusions clearly the thick fingers on the ends of its wide hand holding tightly upon him, had pulled him to the trunk and up into the air. Both of his own hands were still free which allowed Luther to pull his torch in front of him.

    The light of it moved quickly as he swiftly moved his arm to illuminate that in front of him. Perhaps only a few feet away from him was the face of an unhappy looking Troll. He could make out two large eyes which were reflecting a dark red in the light of Luther's torch. They appeared to be quite sodden from the shedding of several tears. The eyes were quite large indeed, greater than the size of two hands clasped together. They were similar to those of other races of Terra, with the whites on either side of pupils, but were in this case of the darkening red. They bulged in their sockets as the troll brought them to bear upon him. The face had a large nose in the centre as was common for trolls and Luther briefly imagined that the great thing must had smelled him from quite far off as he blundered his way towards it.

The troll had large ears drooping down from the side of its face somewhat like those of an elephant, but unlike the smelling prowess of its nose, it was believed they were actually quite hard of hearing. The skin of the face was fairly rough looking and quite notably was a dark blue, almost black. There looked to be growths of living matter upon her face, along with what else he could see of her, namely her arms and neck as though it was an extension of the land itself. Some of it seemed to be moss that was happy to make its home clinging on to her. Perhaps some form of symbiotic relationship or one that caused no bother to the great creature.

It dawned on Luther that this was why he couldn't see her in the dark; it had appeared as if a tree amongst the many others in the Dell Wood. How could he have possibly made her out in such a light with such colouring and features about her? He clung onto this thought at least, for it made him feel a little better at stumbling nose first into great peril.

He was unsure as what was about to happen to him. The beast had a good grip upon him, but not crushingly so. Perhaps it didn't intend to destroy him right away.

Luckily Luther was not allowed to bring his terror up to full height as the troll suddenly spoke, "I am not going to eat you dearie. Don't worry." These words were deep and slow, seemingly emanating from down in the depths of the stomach.

He managed to hold himself together enough to say "Thank you, I do not wish to be eaten or have my life cut short this evening. I am Luther."

A GRIM JOURNEY

The troll gave what looked to be a gentle smile on her saddened face and replied, "No I won't be doing that no." She gave a big loud sniff which shook Luther's ears. She continued, "I am Agatha, oh yes Agatha, yes."

And so, Luther realised he was in the grasp of a lady Troll. A lady troll that seemed to be quite unhappy. Luther hoped she would not squish him in hand to attempt to lift that unhappiness. He supposed he was about to find out.

"Agatha, I am glad to meet you. I am sorry to have stumbled upon you like this. I heard your cries of anguish and came to see if you required any help. I mean no harm."

Agatha the troll, looked him in the eyes with a surprise in her own. "One of the little things coming to see how an elder be and wishing to help? Not heard of that before. The earth rumbles of mistrust only. Yes." Her grip tightened just slightly around him, indicating a sense of mistrust towards Luther's intentions.

"I mean it Agatha. You see I too have a penchant for the sadness, in fact I am unhappy quite often. Because of this I heard your cries of and wished perhaps if there was something I could do to alleviate your pain, knowing as I do, how much it is to hurt."

She narrowed and then relaxed her eyes. "Oh, yes? Oh, I am not too sure what half your words mean dearie, but I think you saying you know my pain? You don't want my pain oh no."

Luther kept eye contact with Agatha. "I am sure I don't, I am also quite sure you would not want mine either. We wish nothing of our own misery on others, hoping to spare them of it, knowing how it rends our hearts so."

The great troll, Agatha, suddenly, but with a gentleness, moved her right arm clutching Luther and placed him back onto the ground. She let go and moved her arm back to her side, resting. He could see now that she was sitting down crossed legged, wearing what looked to be a simple dress with some dark chequered pantaloons underneath and bare feet. The clothing looked like it had been stitched from a tent or other large piece of material. Perhaps Agatha had come across such a thing on her travels with the occupants apparently no longer of need of it as they ran, screaming for their lives,

"Agatha," Luther said, as calm as he could while still mindful of his own personal safety even with the assurances of the good lady. "Could I ask why you are sat here upset as you are in this wood?"

Agatha was looking down at the ground but moved her head to look at Luther. He met the eyes of the great troll. "Oh Dearie, I am sad. Oh yes, I am sad yes, because I am alone. My mate, he has died some moons ago and now I am all alone. I miss him dearie, oh yes."

Luther kept eye contact with her. "Oh, I am so sorry to hear of your loss Agatha, it is such a tragic thing to lose someone you love," he said, compassionately.

She snivelled and wiped her eyes with her large left hand. "He is not lost dearie no. He died you see," replied the elder troll, misunderstanding his intention. "Oh yes, I miss him so, my Theodore. He was old, yes, as me, and it was his time to go back to the earth, but I still miss him so, oh yes." Her eyes welled up again and had another sniffle.

Luther felt sorrow for the old troll; she had lost her love and now seemed astray in the world, not quite sure what to do with herself. He knew something of loneliness though not from the loss of a loved one, but of a self-inflicted one. He did not want to inflict himself on another. He felt it unfair to burden another person with his incessant unhappiness. He would not want them to feel like he dragged them down, that they missed out on things or felt pressed to look after him or be away from him as he withdrew into himself, battling that which had him in its grasp of dark depression.

"Do you live here in the Dell Wood Agatha or just passing by?" Luther said, with a gentle tone.

"Oh, I don't really have a home anymore dearie, oh no. We used to have a cave that Theodore and me called lived, but I don't want to live there anymore without him, oh no, no." She was now gazing again off into the forest and not looking down at the little human standing in front of her. "I just go wandering to see what things are, so I don't think about my Theodore. I end up sitting and sad, oh yes, yes."

Luther, without thinking about the possibly fatal

outcome of doing so, raised his left hand and put it on her arm as it still hung down beside her with her hands laying half open on the ground. "It must be very tough for you Agatha. I am sorry your mate passed. As I said, I know of a sad heart." He paused briefly after avoiding the use of overly long words so as not to confuse or offend her by mistake. She turned her head again to look at him and he continued, "Yes, I am full of sadness for as long as I can remember. Unlike yourself, good Agatha, I do not know why. But know this, I understand your pain and misery even if it be a bit different shade of my own." He gave her a reassuring smile and was feeling at least a little confident as she hadn't become enraged at his tender gesture.

"Thank you, little Luther. I like having someone to talk to again. You little ones normally all run away from Agatha, but you sit and talk to me, oh yes. We Trolls are not all stomp and smash dearie. We just want to live quietly. Theodore and Agatha live quietly. We don't like to eat many meaty things anyway, we likes to eat roots and v-e-g-e-ta-bles, oh yes. I like to eat the autumn pumpkins, they are nice, oh yes, yes."

Luther felt more at ease still, discovering that a 'monstrous man-eating troll' as was often touted by many a drunkard of The Boroughs, was actually a quiet and thoughtful creature. At least this one was and this being the only Troll Luther had ever talked to, he was hard pushed to think otherwise. That was not to say that he wouldn't keep a distance from a troll in the future, hopefully better than he did this night, but he would keep a more open mind going forward and stave off the need to make flight. At least at first.

"It is no problem, Agatha. I just hope that you feel if just a little less melancholy - I mean sad, sorry. We do the best we can, don't we?" He raised his hand and pulled it away from hers; he seemed to be doing well in his conversing with the great lady and didn't want to ruin it by lingering to long with his gesture.

"Oh yes we do the best we can, oh yes. And what are you doing here Little Luther. It is dark in the woods here and the path is over there." She raised her giant right hand again and pointed back towards the path some several hundred yards away.

"Yes, I..." Luther was reticent to describe the real reason he found himself off the beaten path and in the middle of the dark wood - even if it was a Troll that may well feel less inclined to look down upon him like a crazy man than one of the smaller races - he decided to construct a tale less likely to paint him in the light of lunacy.

"I have a little camp where you just pointed, you see that glowing light there?" He bent slightly and pointed over to the light of his fire which was still dimly lit in the distance. He continued, "I was falling asleep by the fire when I thought I saw something moving amongst the trees. I got up and followed to see what it was. I lost where it went, but then I heard you being sad and thought to see if I could help." This seemed like pretty much the gist of what happened anyway, just leaving out the bit where the thing he was following may have been just a creation of his malfunctioning mind.

"Oh, you must be careful dearie, wandering around in the wood at night, oh yes! You might find yourself in trouble!" The old Troll said this with little awareness that she herself could be construed as 'trouble,' Luther thought.

"Yes, you are right Agatha, but I couldn't leave without knowing if there was anything I could do to help someone with such sorrowful a tone as yourself, I mean, I didn't want you to be sad." He tried to keep the gaze of the old lady as he said these words and raised the best smile he could, hoping she understood how genuine he was being. This seemed to be the case; she raised her right arm and with her expansive hand and gave him a pat on the back. What perhaps to her was a gentle pat anyway, to Luther it was more a sudden force that caused him to brace himself abruptly, lest it knock him straight over.

"There isn't much you can do dearie, no, but thank you for coming and seeing how I am. Most people would not come so close to an old troll like me in the woods even if I didn't want to squish them, oh yes. I feel not so sad now having had someone to talk to, oh yes. I will go and find something to eat, oh yes. Maybe I can find some nice roots to eat hereabouts."

The great old troll stretched out both arms either side

of her and hoisted herself to her feet. Luther took a few steps back as not to be accidently squashed. Now raised to her full height she was even more imposing to Luther, and he wondered how he could ever have mistaken her for the shadow of a tree. She looked away further into the wood and Luther followed suit, but he could not make out anything past the radius of light from his torch; perhaps she could see better in the darkness than he could.

"Ok dearie, I had better go off. One thing I still like is me food and I will go find some, oh yes. Nice to meet you Little Luther, I may be an old Troll, but I don't forget Kindness." She turned away and walked off into the night, her huge feet on her stumpy legs thudding on the ground as she went.

Luther stood and watched her go and for a while still heard and felt her steps as she snapped and cracked dead wood and plants under foot. And when all sign of her had gone, he still stood there, in a stunned malaise, not completely registering what just happened. It was all quite a lot to take in; he had seemingly had some kind of lethargy induced hallucination of a ball of fur, rolling through the forest before stumbling across a great troll and somehow surviving the encounter unscathed.

The point was not lost on Luther that maybe this creature had meant to lead him somewhere into the woods. Perhaps it meant to draw him towards Agatha; perhaps it meant for him to come discover her sad in the woods, misery taking her with her wrenchful groans. Ultimately it may well all be a coincidence, he thought; the madness within him coinciding with the discovery of a creature upset and in need or some comfort. It was definitely something to think about, but perhaps, thought Luther, it was best left until tomorrow. He was quite very tired now, and it was the middle of the night, best to go to sleep.

He snapped too and turned round, back towards the light of his campfire in the distance. It was now glowing at its dimmest, likely to smoulder for a while before exhausting all its energy; it's impetus to further burn bright all but spent. He began walking back towards it at a brisk pace, suddenly remembering that he had not placed any warding powder about the perimeter of his little camp. He may have been lucky with one beastie tonight, but he thought likely his luck might not hold should something else come wandering by with evil intent.

It took only a few minutes for him to reach the campfire. It was now very low, but still radiating enough light for him to see Guinevere half asleep next to the tree where he had tied her reins.

His pack and his cooking utensils he had used earlier along with other items he had pulled from his saddle bags, were all as they were before he went off on his little ramble. At least it was where it probably was. He couldn't really recall if he was honest with himself, but he failed to notice anything obviously missing and so was happy enough that all was well.

He went to his pack and pulled the small pouch of warding powder that he brought with him on the trip. There were various schools of thought for the placement of warding powder: some thought a liberal pouring around the perimeter of the camp was the most impactful; others swore that sprinkles at regular intervals such as every few yards, was the better method while others still suggested the efficient use was to place a good amount at key points of a triangle, square or other such shape. Luther was of the school of the latter practice. He only ever had positive results by the application of dust in the corners of a small square around his immediate vicinity. At least6 he hadn't ever awoken to the discovery of an angry monster or mischievous creature, seeking to cause trouble. For this was how warding powder kept a traveller safe; anything within a certain distance that attempted to come closer would begin to feel quite nauseated and sloth like. This effect would become more intense the closer one came. The effect only took hold of a being with ill intent on their minds such as robbing those in a campsite or in the case of a roaming monster, the devouring of all those present.

For warding powder to have any effect, along with its correct application round a campsite, it must be placed by the person who wishes to be warded. The act of touching the powder itself seals the magical pact created by the enchantment placed upon it by a mage or a shaman or similarly capable magic user. With the magical pact thus sealed the person being warded must remain in the centre of whatever shape or perimeter has been created. Further to this, that same person should place all the powder around the camp to create the strongest barrier of protection. If they were to leave the area, the warding would no longer occur, and any other members of that person's party would be open to harassment from anything walking by.

      Luther sprinkled powder at four points around the campfire and the tree to which Guinevere was tied. He then pulled out some blankets and put them down close to the fire, inside the perimeter.

      "It's been an interesting day Gwen," he said, patting her neck. "I hope I haven't driven you too hard today. Have a good rest and we make our way on tomorrow." Luther laid down under his blankets and quickly fell asleep.

Grim Passing

The grip on her staff was strong as she grimaced, raising herself from another stumble. The grim lady moved slowly, with little regular cadence in her footsteps. The walls of the canyon struck up on either side of her as she walked through it; a lonely figure, contrasting with the great sides of the gorge that dwarfed her presence.

The valley was formed of a very dark stone which, even if it were in the light of day would be little less disheartening and grim. The moonlight was absorbed almost completely by the stone but was just enough for the minimal illumination of some of the sharp edges jutting out. The frame of this gorge seemed dreary and bashful with the grim ladies passing, as if in solidarity with her gloominess and her sombre demeanour.

The floor of the valley consisted of stones and boulders with flat tops, laying amongst the earth, as if they had been worn smooth by a river, the same river that perhaps cut this valley through the dark and dismal rock.

Unlike the walls of this hall of stone, there was some smattering of plants amongst the boulders as they laid quietly around the grim lady. There was still quite an absence of any larger flora such as a lady of the wood, but there seemed enough good soil between the rocks for something to grow, even in this dark and lonely chasm. Perhaps there was some silt with life giving nutrients still present in the ground, left behind by a once roving river or the small raggedy plants and bushes growing in this solemn place were hardy enough to eke out a living with the smallest of sustenance.

The subtle fog still converged around her, still all-encompassing of her form and still as reserved and pensive as the grim lady herself. Even as she stumbled again, it moved with her, as if mimicking that movement or perhaps trying to tend to her as she fell to one knee. She had raised herself up

A GRIM JOURNEY

again with it always hovering around her and carried on as before.

She had travelled now, onwards from that lonesome moor in the foothills of the Lightlorne Mountains. Her path had seemingly taken her further inwards, towards the mountain range itself. The canyon that she now travelled featured a more noticeable incline which may have accounted for her stumbling more often or perhaps she did so because of what laid on her, little aware of the features of the world around her.

She looked to be focused on her journey; she didn't stop for rest or sustenance and carried no bag or pack in which to carry such that she might do so. Her pace was slow and lacking rhythm, but somewhat relentless, never stopping for a breath after even yet another stumble down. She simply pulled herself back up with the encouragement of the mist at her side, and dutifully resumed her march through the valley.

Curiously, even in this barren stretch of land, reaching further into the mountain range, there were small dwellings, pocketing the top of the canyon edges, looking down on the figure below. This ragtag tangle of buildings was an eclectic mix: some were entirely made of wood, each plank unique in its various notches, hue and tree of origin; some were a close to a mottle and daub construction; others were built with misshapen stone held together with some form of cement and a kind of thatching for a roof, made from various types of plant materials. The residents of these dwellings appeared to make do with whatever materials they could gather rather than any particular planned approach to house building.

From down in the canyon, one could make out the outlines of figures, perhaps human or some other race amongst the structures. Clearly these were still inhabited, but by whom, it wasn't obvious to the naked eye. If they were aware of the gloominous lady slowly walking along the floor of the canyon, they did not appear to be showing it. Perhaps they were too focused on their daily existence in this grim place or perhaps the lady, with her aura amongst her, masking and supressing her existence, was not easily visible to them.

Still, as she walked, the earth and features of the gorge around her, though already lacking the desire to exhibit anything greater than dark, muted shades of black, brown, or green, seemed to become even more so as they grim lady walked past. Everything took on a grey hue to it as they became aware of her proximity to them, thankfully regressing to their original shade once she had moved on.

The grim lady still had the cloak wrapped around her. Still with the hood up, covering her face, but showing enough to see the quiet demeanour upon her brow. Her dark skin still wizened by that pale grey with her hands displaying bruises and cuts from her many falls upon the ground. Her clothes all greyed by whatever emanated from her, were as before as she walked up that lonely moor. There was no sign that she had stopped in the relentless journey; even for all the falls and bruises or thirst and hunger or the brief respite of sleep, she carried on to whatever destination she was drawn to.

It was as though she carried with her some burden, a burden of such over-bearing weight that she was compelled to continue on regardless of her own well-being. And so, she did so.

Chapter 10

A well-dressed gentleman sat back in a tall armchair made of red leather. It had gold studding along the seams and featured gold filigree embroidered on the back in an outline of a fox with the head draped in a silk lined cushion. The well-dressed man was wearing a dark blue suit with matching waist coat all made from a fine blue velvet. Upon his breast he wore a white shirt, with a blue, silk tie to match the rest of his ensemble. All upon him looked impeccably pressed, with not a crease or blemish to be seen. He sat with his left leg crossed over his right, pulling back his trousers to reveal his platted socks leading into his almost sparklingly shiny, dark leather shoes.

Fabian, the well-dressed man, held a glass in his left hand, with a large round rim and deep belly filled with several fingers of dark brown liquid. His right hand rested on the arm of the chair, feeling the leather.

In front of this man, well-dressed from head to toe, was a fireplace, extravagantly large, almost to the height of the high back chair the man was sitting in. The mantle was made of a dark shade of marble with intricate patterns carved into every part of it; not a section left plain and dull. There were swirls, patterns and flourishes with animals and birds cut between. It was exorbitant and lavishly designed.

The carved stone exterior encased a large roaring fire that was alive with energy and light. Several logs lay at its base, some more blackened and glowing than others with a pile of unused logs sitting in a brass basket to the side of the fireplace. A metal stoker, spade and tongs hung from a wrought iron stand to the opposite side of the fireplace, ready to be used should the need require. The fire illuminated the area where the well-dressed man, Fabian, was sat confidently in his chair. Chair and person were dramatically lit by the fire. He was the focus of the light from the roaring flame, holding his whiskey glass, waiting for someone to join him.

The room itself was in a majority of darkness; the fireplace providing the only light source with no other lit candles or lamps present. The walls close to the fire ran high, maybe fifteen feet with a mahogany wood dado rail, intricately patterned with leaves and flower like those from a rose bush. These walls though coloured with a simple beige were adorned with numerous paintings. There was a portrait of Fabian sitting similarly to how he was currently; in a chair looking aloof and confident. Several other portraits of other men and women were hanging, perhaps relations of some kind, though smaller in stature than that featuring Fabian himself. There was a wide landscape painting of a battle scene of several men fighting some beast of which was unclear as half of it was covered in the darkness as the light from the fireplace failed before alighting it proper.

To the well-dressed man's right sat another, green leather chair, quite lavish itself, but missing the same fanciful trappings of his own. Between this chair and Fabian's was a small round table, made from a dark wood, most likely mahogany. It sat roughly one and half foot square and several high with thin spindly legs from each corner that crept down to the floor and ended with feet slightly splayed out as they touched the ground. The top rim of the table was raised around the edges, housing a sheet of clear glass whose transparency allowed a fanciful artwork to show through from below. The artistic piece displayed a scene of a king's court; the monarch sat atop his throne, attended by various courtiers and sycophants all decadently dressed from head to toe. On the glass surface sat two coasters, seemingly one for each chair. The coaster on Fabian's side was empty as he had his glass of liquor in his hand, but the other side was occupied with the same dark whisky filling its bowels.

Sitting between and just behind the two glasses was a clear glass decanter of liquid the same colour as that in the glasses. It was portly in its appearance with a spherical body featuring concave impressions. A belt of gold filigree patterns, quite fanciful, perhaps an inch wide, sat around its waist with the whisky within coming up just to the bottom line. Upon its breast, as it rose up towards to the lips of the container was a symbol in one of the impressions. It was in the outline of a fox in silhouette, like that on the chair currently occupied. The neck rose up just an inch or two, itself featuring a gold filigree tie thinner than the waist, but no less luxurious.

The full glass next to the empty chair suggested that Fabian, the well-dressed man was expecting a guest to be seated in it imminently. This was soon proven to be the case as a door knocked in the darkness behind him and with a word of 'come' from Fabian's lips, an older gentleman in the black uniform of a butler came walking in. Only when he had crossed over from the dark side of the room, bereft of the light from the fire, did his appearance become clear. He was quite tall and slim with the worn features of a man past middle age with a distinct aloofness about him. The man was well groomed; clean shaven with slicked short black hair, a tie perfectly tied and sitting snuggly right to the throat with a black waistcoat under blazer and trousers, both pressed and straight as one could make them. On his feet he wore black shoes polished to impeccable level of shine.

"Sir, Mr Tropward has arrived to meet with you," the butler said as he came to a stop next to Fabian's chair. He paused and waited for a reply.

"Yes Jacob, send him in," said Fabian.

The butler, Jacob, walked back to the entrance of the room and opened the door. He looked to be speaking to someone standing on the threshold, but it was unclear as to who due to the near complete darkness of that side of the room. The butler stood aside, letting the person pass through.

"Mr John Tropward, sir," said the butler, leaving the room just as the guest walked through the door, closing it behind him.

"Come Tropward, take a seat and join me for a glass," Fabian said, in a gratefully dismissing tone without standing or turning round to meet the man.

Out of the darkness and into the light of Fabian's Fireplace came Mr John Tropward, a man in his mid-fifties, short in stature with a pronounced belly hanging over the top of his belt which seemed under no small amount of duress from the man's overflowing girth. He wore a dark tan suit that failed to match up to Fabian or his butler's tailoring; it featured creases in areas all across it with the odd dark stain mixed in for good measure. His shirt was tanned of a lighter shade which looked never to have made acquaintance with an iron, along with a matching tie which appeared hastily tied and pulled lose over the course of the day. He was at least clean shaven, with his puffing cheeks gone red seemingly from the effort of walking to this meeting.

He moved round the back of the empty chair to its front and looked at Fabian with eyes that suggested both lethargy and concern. He was met with a sly smile from his host and a raised right hand which motioned towards the chair, inviting the guest to sit down. Tropward turned and sank back into the chair with quite an undignified slump which no doubt tested the strength of the unfortunate recipient of the man's weight and inelegance; the cushioning of the seat gave a great exhale as his body pressed down into it which drew a raised eyebrow and a slight wince from Fabian as he did so.

"Well, are we, Mr Tropward?" the well-dressed man motioned aloofly to his guest who had now made himself comfortable in his chair.

"I am well yes," Tropward replied, who had pulled a handkerchief from an inside pocket of his jacket and begun dabbing his forehead. "And you, Fabian? How well are you? Have you managed to deal with the little problem at Thoroughbridge?"

The well-dressed man took a long, drawn-out sip of his drink and placed the glass down on the table. His face grew a little stern and turned to face the man opposite with his eyes. "Straight to business, as always Tropward. Not even capable of a finger or two of fine whiskey before getting down to the nitty, gritty. Fine." He turned his head and gazed into the fire. "Yes, the necessary plans are underway to return things back to how it should. A fair gaggle of the human population of Thoroughbridge will be assembled in the town hall of that good town and I will have them within my grasp before the night is up. This you can trust." He had picked up his glass again and was swirling it slowly, half absently - not wholly interested in his guests retort."

Tropward picked up his own glass, similarly, lacking interest in meeting with his host's gaze. "Good," he said. "We can't have the local populace of any of our interests sitting back, happy in their lives. The villagers and townspeople of The Boroughs must be swayed to our beliefs and eager to accept the truth will give to them. I am asked to impress upon you that should you fail in the delivering that which you have promised, that our generous additions to your lavish lifestyle will have to be called into question. How could our mutual friends consider compensating yourself when that which they were promised has not been delivered?"

Fabian, a man so immaculately dressed- a polar opposite in outward appearance to his guest, squashed into the chair next to him - was not fond of Tropward at the best of times, but here his contempt of him was stronger than ever. He spoke an air of almost shock and disgust that this man would talk to him, Fabian, with such a tone. "Don't worry yourself Tropward. You fall short in your appreciation for my abilities as an orator and a leader of men. They will know their place soon enough. I will provide them with ample mistrust that the real causes of their woes will be but a whisper in the wind; gently blown away by the suggestion of the folly of others."

"I hope this to be the case, Fabian," said Mr Tropward, now peering into the fire. "The plans for The Boroughs involve the subjugation of its citizens. Until that is the case, we will be unable to move forward with our intentions. I am sure you are well aware of this of course. I am here merely to remind you of this fact."

"Yes, of course I understand," Fabian said. He looked at Mr Tropward momentarily in some attempt to catch his gaze, but the man was still looking into the roaring fire that played in front of them. He noticed how uncomfortable this person looked in the seat adjacent to his own. He seemed short of breath, still, and flustered, as though great effort had been made to be here on this night. Effort that he was not too happy about making.

Although Fabian thought little of Mr Tropward, he was mindful enough not to taunt the man or show his disgust with him in too overtly a way; he needed their mutual benefactors for the moment at least, and so abstained from a lashing with his tongue in the uncomfortable man's direction.

"All will be well," spoke Fabian, across to the uncomfortable man, "I have not failed yet and will not fail going forward. That being said, I am not omnipresent and therefore cannot be everywhere at once. There were other towns that needed attention and still more after yours." The tone of Fabian's voice was sleeked in disdain, but his partner in the conversation seemed pre-occupied with his drink, the fire and puffing from the long walk to the room, to take too much notice.

The uncomfortable gentleman drank down the last of the liquid in his glass. Within a second of the last gulp, two sizeable men emerged from the shadows at either side of the room. These two large and overbearing men, both wearing dark red gambesons, equal in height at over six feet tall, walked over to the chair Mr Tropward was sitting in and stood silently, menacingly, with their hands crossed in front of their stomachs, awaiting instruction.

"If there is nothing else you wish to converse about Tropward then I bid you farewell. Go in confidence that all will be taken care of." He turned his face towards Mr Tropward again and gave him a slight nod as if dismissing a subordinate. The two large gentlemen let their hands fall to their sides and looked to be waiting for the guest to stand up from his chair, which he did so; pulling his awkward weight up from his seat with a great strain and immediately patting his brow with the same handkerchief as before. He placed his empty glass back down on the tabletop.

"That is fine whisky Fabian, you will have to tell me one day where you get it from. I am expected elsewhere this evening so I shall indeed be off. Do not forget the importance of proceedings. I am in no doubt of your abilities and expect nothing short of full compliance from those that doubt." Mr Tropward, aware of the arrogance and condescension, attempted to reassert his own position with these words, but didn't quite hit the mark. Fabian gave him a confirming nod and smile and looked back towards the fire.

A GRIM JOURNEY

Mr Tropward, the uncomfortable man, turned away and walked off back into the dark of the room, towards the exit, flanked on either side by the two large gentlemen, escorting him all the way. He knocked on the door upon arriving which was quickly opened by Fabian's butler who then closed it after Tropward passed through, leaving the two burley gentleman to head back to their stations in the dark on either side of the room, ready to be called when needed.

The well-dressed man poured himself some more whisky and after a few minutes called for his butler to attend him. The door opened and Jacob re-entered the room at his employer's call.

"I take it Mr Tropward was seen off with haste?" Fabian enquired.

"Yes sir, he seemed in a hurry himself and didn't linger more than was needed," replied Jacob.

"Good, good, will you tell Vespera to come in? I must speak with her."

"Very good sir," Jacob replied. "I will call for her." He turned around and exited the room once again. Just a few moments later without announcement, Vespera, the hidden lady, emerged from the shadows in the back of the room. Although the firelight embrace was enough to illuminate her fully there was still an aura of darkness around her as if she were cloaked somehow by some miasma, enough to break up her outline and soften the effect of the light upon her.

"Have a seat dear Vespera," said the well-dressed man. "Shall I pour you a glass?" The lady moved around the front of the seat to sit in the chair. She glided down and gently rested upon the seat of it, leaning back and crossing her legs upon doing so.

She was wearing thigh high leather boots over leather trousers, both a very dark red, almost black. Around her torso she wore a silk, fitted shirt with an engraving of a fox on one of its pockets. Over this she wore a black leather waist jacket and atop this a long dark crimson jacket which ran down to her knees. Her dark hair was tied back tight into a ponytail. She had slender facial features and an enticing beauty. She wore some makeup about her cheeks and eyes and bright red of the lipstick upon her lips. "I shall have a small drop yes," she responded. She was not at all concerned with leaving her host waiting for her reply while she first made herself comfortable.

He shouted for Jacob with the words "A fresh glass Jacob!" after which moments later the butler came walking in with a new glass resting on top of a small tray.

"A new glass sir," said the Butler, taking Tropward's used glass and replacing it with a fresh one. He picked up the decanter and poured several mouthfuls of whisky. He then turned and walked back into the darkness and out of the room.

"If I weren't obviously aware of your meeting previously with that Mr Tropward," said Vespera, "I would have no doubt deduced from the distortions he made upon this chair and his lingering odour of sweat and discomfort that he had been present just moments ago - quite the mess of an individual."

"Yes indeed," Fabian replied. "A mess, but a useful mess, nonetheless. He keeps a healthy buffer between us and the rest of those greedy fools. I barely have the patience for him, let alone the rest of his ilk."

"Indeed," she responded.

"So," he said, "Do you have news of the fruits of our labour?" While waiting for her reply he took up and sipped from his glass while stealing only a slight glance at his new companion.

"There is news to report, yes," she said. "The town Tensford, which you whipped up into a delirium a few weeks ago is well on its way. Several local townspeople – undesirables - are being shunned and ostracised by the local human populace. I believe there was some angry confrontations and threats of reprisal on a number of occasions. They are quite pre-occupied with their pointless aggression and anger at those who differ from themselves to take notice of what our benefactors are enacting on the council. It appears simple to facilitate otherwise detrimental endeavours when to whose detriment it is, is bathed in lies and deceit."

The well-dressed man, sat in his chair, suddenly turned to her and said, "Oh you believe all I say is lies and deceit?"

She turned to meet his eyes with her own, Perhaps the game of one-upmanship had started anew. "No, not all, of course, dear Fabian. Only to those who wish to hear them."

"It seems there are many," He replied.

"Yes, there are indeed. And to them there is no hint of deception in my words, only confirmation of their own base beliefs and conceptions. I merely provide ignition for the kindling already present inside them."

She turned away and looked into the fire. "Quite. The Tensford council is petitioning the borough parliament to allow martial law to contain the troubles and of course allow for mercenary troops to be hired to maintain control. Mercenary companies provided by our good selves of course."

"This is good news Vespera, I did not think proceedings would move so quickly with that town. It seems they were on the precipice and only required a little prod in the right direction. What of the other towns in the Drearom Borough?" he enquired, sipping his glass, eagerly awaiting the news.

"Stutton in the north, the first town to be graced by your presence is now under martial law after a successful petition to the Drearom Parliament. The first company of our own Bracks Militia have answered the call and taken this burden upon themselves," she said.

"To the east of Tensford, the Town of Chatsmead - where we staged our second gathering - is coming along a little slower. As you no doubt remember that place was largely a human town, so convincing their poor selves of the evils secretly cast against them by the other races, was not going to be an easy task."

Fabian's ears pricked as if he was again surprised to have his abilities questioned again so quickly. "Again Vespera, you doubt the power and ability of my persuasion?"

She stood up from her chair with glass in hand and walked to the edge of the fireplace. "Would I ever do such a thing"? Her lips pursed in a subtle smile. "No, I merely report - which is what you asked of me - that the seeds sowed may take just a little longer to germinate. They are coming round to the idea and with the stoking of the fire by some well-placed agents of ours, it will only be a matter of time."

He looked up at her and smiled a thin smile. "Good, good. It seems to me things are falling into place as they should. Once the major towns of the Drearom Borough are within my grasp, their peoples in awe of me and under my grasp, we will make way to take control of its parliament and install those in my favour. Too many people have it too good without paying their due respects to me, not just those simpleton townspeople, no, people such as our associate Mr Tropward. He dares air idle threats in my presence. He has no right to question me! The fat oaf! Wealth and status are wasted on such a feeble-minded fool and least not a good glass of whisky. He will play his part for now along with those other inept fools he represents. Their vision so easily blinded by the thought of losing their lot in life and just as easily as the common people they are moulded into the form I wish them to take."

Chapter 11

This is becoming ridiculous! Why am I struck dumb by some unknown hand? Why am I unable to even raise my limbs and move at a pace other than wanton slow-motion?! It is as if I am but a sloth on his laziest of days - barely moving at all! But here I am, failing miserably at running for my life from some unknown foe that stalks me so. In this hall, where is this? Some great hall of a castle? Some underground lair carved from the bedrock? I do not know. There are no windows that I can see, just torches lining the walls of this place and these tables around me.

Argh! I must overcome this affliction upon my body! I must not let my assailant catch me, who knows what horrors might await! And yet I have not seen him. Are they him? Perhaps they are her? Both? Neither? Is this thing chasing me a mortal being of reason or some monster, relentless in its mission to destroy me? I must move faster; I fail to make even the slightest of progress in escaping this place!

Eyes open, brown branches and green leaves. Where am I? thought Luther. What was just happening? Was I dreaming? I think I was, yes. Luther had awoke, up against a pillar in the forest. The forest where he had made camp and fallen asleep the night before. He begun to ground himself back into the reality around him. He assumed he was dreaming and - as was fairly common occurrence - had awoke with a start, confused and wondering what was going on and where he was. He looked over to his right to see Guinevere, staring at him. He wondered what she must be thinking; this person, her companion, startled and awake after some strange dream, like some poor soul, overcome by their own existence. Luther hoped she didn't think less of him or at least wasn't too worried about his odd quirks. Maybe he thought too much, and she didn't care either way.

It came back to him, where he was and what he was doing. He had had a strange evening last night, which one could easily mistake for a dream in itself; wandering the wood, following a little creature that may not even exist and meeting another that very much did. He remembered he was on his way to Bramstone, a frontier town in the southwest of The Boroughs. Finally, some answers and perhaps, some relief to his condition might be found if he could locate Celeste Ignophenen, an old friend of Golon's back in Overton.

He looked around his little camp and saw the smoking fire; all its energy spent with just a few smouldering small embers present in its black and grey remains. As was unfortunately common for him when waking up from a night's sleep, Luther was not feeling particularly joyful this morning, in the forest of the Dell Wood. He was overcome with a melancholy, a sadness of which he couldn't ascertain its cause, this cause which he would someday soon be acquainted with – he hoped.

He felt a detachment from the world around him, as if he were floating above it somewhere, out in the ether of it all, lost in some gloominous void with little to tether him back into the common reality that others lived.

He wished for something that may provide anchorage, to allow him some way to keep himself part of this world and not blown away in the wind by this affliction of his mind. It was so difficult, so overwhelming, this grip on his being that had no wish for him to remain stayed in a normal reality. It was a feeling of nothingness. That nothing mattered, regardless of if it had the day before or how important to him it may seem. Things that were close to his heart, things that perhaps made Luther happy, were all meaningless to him now. The only thing he thought to do at this moment was just sit up and pour himself some water. Perhaps if he sat for a while, this dark cloud might pass over him or at least abate from the cast of shadow of sadness upon him long enough that he may try and function and continue on journey.

Luther sat with his back up against the tree for what he felt was roughly an hour. He did not own a watch but was usually quite good at keeping time by the passing of the day. Moreover, he didn't actually care what the time was; the depression that overcame him supressed all thoughts of urgency or plans he had in progress. He just sat there almost as if in a waking coma, unable and unwilling to move and resume his quest to find some understanding of himself.

Sitting there as he was, looking around him: the remains of the fire; the trees bordering his little camp; what he could see of the sky above or Guinevere standing there quietly, he began to feel a small resurgence of hope. It was just a thin, wispy thread, but perhaps enough to grasp hold of his soul and pull him back to earth. Back to maybe entertaining the thought of existence, of something resembling normality.

He decided to do just a simple task at first, then he could perhaps string further tasks together and hopefully by the end of it he might find himself back on the road again. He got up and onto his feet and gave a long, drawn-out stretch. He felt the vibration of the tendons in his arms as he stretched them out and, in his legs, as he stood up straight. He felt the rush of blood flow to his head which took him a moment to clear, but he was up and ready enough to make some attempt at the day.

He dusted himself down and walked over to Guinevere. He thought she looked happy enough this morning. He filled a little more water into the bowl nestled in the tree which she reached over to and started drinking. He gently stroked her neck with his hand followed by the occasional pat. It made Luther glad to have her with him on his journey. She provided comfort with her presence and hopefully wasn't interested in judging his struggle to cope with his internal strife as he did. He wondered how he would be without her; beyond the obviously slower progress he would have made on foot. Travelling alone, with no companion to talk to, even if they were incapable of talking back or provide any verbal reassurance, felt so much better to him than travelling completely by himself. Perhaps it was better even, he thought.

He turned round and set about clearing up his little camp. He picked up the pot and his cup along with the stand he used to place them on in the fire and put them back into the saddle bags hanging from Guinevere's back. He replaced the de-caffeinated coffee from his pack and pulled a small tin of different coffee. Luther intended to have a cup of full strength caffeine in him before heading off and hoped its nice aroma and warmth may help to allay the saddening thoughts that swirled around his head.

He reached for a few of the small twigs he hadn't used the night before and created a small fire from the embers of the old along with the help of a match or two. He realised he still needed use of the little cooking platform which he just placed back in his bags so stepped back over to Guinevere and pulled it out again. He rested it across the fire as before and put his steel mug on top, filled with water.

While his coffee was brewing, he picked up any other lose ends he could see and placed them back in their homes in his bags. He looked around, beyond the perimeter of trees surrounding his camp, to see what he could see and noticed the same swathe of trees and flora as he saw before. For some, small reason he wondered that perhaps there might be something else out there. Perhaps some small little furry thing just on the edge of sight, but to he could see nothing of the sort.

He became lost in thought as he pottered, again striving against this sadness within him, trying to focus on the task at hand, making his coffee and readying himself for the off. He could hear the sounds of birds up in the upper croft of the trees high above him, chirping and singing away along with a few other miscellaneous sounds coming from deeper within the forest. He wished that he could be so joyful in the morning, enough to wake up with the hint of a smile at least.

Once the water was to a boil, he poured in some granules he had in his pack and, with a stir, his coffee was brewed. He sat down once more by the fire and quietly drank it while drive aside the despair he was experiencing. He tried as he could to let the thoughts pass through him, like water passing under a bridge, rather than them sitting and stewing inside of him. He drank from his cup. The hot coffee smelt good as it wafted down his nostrils and its warmth and bitter taste helped to brace his inner spirit.

He felt less assailed by hopelessness and just well enough make an attempt at the day. He packed up the steel platform and put back the rest of his things, including the bowl he had lodged into the tree for Guinevere and then poured some water onto the fire from it. He moved the drenched remains with his foot to ensure it was definitely out - not to reignite again once he had set off. He then untied the loose rope from the tree that held her too and climbed up onto the saddle.

"Right Gwen," he said. "Let's set off again, shall we?" Luther hoped that she was in agreement and gently tapped her sides with the heels of his boots, encouraging her into a steady walk on their way back towards the track making its way through the forest.

Within a minute or two they were back to the track heading south-west. As they turned onto it, Luther looked right and left to see whether any other travellers were making their own way along the path, their own destinations in mind, but could see the way was clear.

Luther felt relieved and glad that he would not have to push himself into conversing with anybody, forcing a conversation. Not that he would be rude, but when feeling as he was this morning, it would take great effort and energy to be social in any way. He needed that energy to keep himself on this road and not turn round and head home or slump down against a tree on the side of it.

Again, he gently tapped Guinevere's sides and she begun to walk in a casual pace. Although it was most likely a wise idea to get to his destination as quickly as possible, increasing the chances of locating Celeste Ignophenen, Luther was once again in no rush to do so. As before he wished to enjoy the journey, having not been this way before, the sounds and sights of the wood were pleasant and endearing to his senses. This morning he hoped he could go for a period of seclusion with only Guinevere as his company, as they travelled through the Dell Wood. Perhaps then he may be able to pull himself out of this pool of misery he once again found himself in.

Chapter 12

The path, as Luther found it, was very similar to what it had been the previous day; pillars of the wood on either side of the track, which itself was no more than a simple path, clear of any obstructions and its surface somewhat trodden and broken from the comings and goings of the travellers through and denizens of, the forest.

Onwards further down the track, for as far as Luther could see was the onset of yet more of the road making its way through the wood. At the very edge of his vision, he thought he could perhaps make out a turn to the left and southwards as trees from that side seemed to snake round and become straight on, suggesting a turn was present. Behind him was the track of the previous day; the same broken path going long off in the distance in a straight line for quite some distance.

While looking about him as he did, he wondered about Agatha, whether she managed to find something to eat on her thundering stomp through the wood. He hoped that even if by just a little bit, his words to her and offer of comfort may have lifted her spirits somewhat. As he thought about it, he wondered just how he ended up talking to a real-life troll, sitting in the woods. Most stories he heard around town and from certain tails in print, tended to paint a picture of, if not a heaving monster, but something you should give quite a wide berth to and be prepared to fight or preferably run from, at a moment's notice. Perhaps as with many things in life, Luther thought, once a greater understanding of a thing had been had, one may well look at it in a different and more enlightened view than before. Indeed, he was hopeful that anyone who had had some reservation about his own condition, either through word of mouth or far away observation, may have it reduced by simply meeting with him and getting to know him.

He felt that this was hopefully the case with Deven. During their meeting weeks ago, he seemed to struggle somewhat in appreciating just how afflicted Luther felt by this sadness within him. Further, he thought, it seemed Deven had difficulty understanding how there was no cause for the effect of which Luther was describing to him. Then again, he thought, it was not in the realms of ridiculous – far from it, to question why something was happening with no real reason for doing so. Luther didn't understand all the ways of magic and mysticism but thought even then there must be a cause for such sorcery to occur.

After several more miles, Luther, atop Guinevere, found himself approaching the bend in the road that he had spied earlier, veering round to the left. There was a thick border of trees straight in front of him which swept round from the line to his right and ushered the track accordingly into a southern facing. To his left the ground crept down gradually, forming a slight and gentle sloping bank starting a hundred yards or so from the corner itself. The bank was perhaps twelve feet in distance from the road and flattened out thereafter. It looked to be a natural feature of some kind, like a feint and casual hill rather than something artificial. In fact, it served no real purpose other than the natural contour of the earth. Perhaps there was softer material on that side, Luther thought, which had been eroded by wind and rain. Maybe some subterranean crater had caused the earth above to fill in the sink below. There were few trees on the bank itself, but where the ground levelled out there featured a similar press of columns, but not as tightly packed together as those to Luther's right. The gap in the trees to the south side of the path meant this part of the road was not covered by any canopy, exposing it to the sky above.

As Luther came to the bank, he could see the sky above him more clearly. He looked up and felt the light upon his face. It was not a particularly sunny day - being in the middle of the autumn season - but, having been used to just the scattering of light filling the wood rather than a blanket of sunshine, it felt all the more bright as he was bathed in the full brightness of the sun. Luther was akin to a hermit, an introvert, who was fond of staying put inside his home, only leaving for places that he felt quite safe. But, this didn't mean that he was opposed to the nurturing power of the star in the sky and the open air. He preferred the darkness, warm clothes and hot coffee, but being outside, even for a short while, taking in the air around him was something he knew could have a positive effect on him. Regardless, he thought, he was going to be outside for quite a while on this journey so should try to abide it as much as he could and perhaps even try enjoying it.

They had reached the corner now and followed it as it turned left moving south. Once they had finished the turn and were facing a southerly direction, Luther looked forward down this new stretch of road to see what lay ahead. It stretched out ahead as before, with just the most trivial of swerves, generally keeping in a straight line as it made off into the distance.

The bank to his left evened out again gradually in the opposite fashion to which he had previously, ending up with both sides of the track on an even footing. The density of trees gradually crept back again after a few hundred yards; the roof of branches with the warm colours of the autumn leaves still clinging on, resisting their fate, mixed with the needles of the evergreens, creating a roof once again. The light dimmed as it found only fewer ways to reach down into the undergrowth of the forest. Luther made way just as the day before - slow and steady - with no great rush to pass through the forest.

After an hour of heading south, the road began to ever so gradually steer round to the right over the course of a few hundred feet. This ended with the road travelling in a south-westerly direction.

For a few hours more they travelled onwards, under the arms of the forest, with Luther regularly patting Guinevere and giving her words of encouragement. She seemed to appreciate it and Luther hoped she would do the same for him if she could.

At several points in this time there appeared other travellers on the road of which Luther had some interaction with. Two human men on horseback heading the opposite direction than his, were the first to be encountered, shortly after Luther and Guinevere had passed a simple crossroads: a path leading south with a wooden sign saying, 'Southern Reaches'; one in the easterly direction stating 'Lightlorne Foothills' and a final road heading southwest with the words 'Bramstone'.

Of the two men, one looked older than the other with

quite the likeness between them, suggesting to Luther they were most likely father and son. Both were dressed quite casually; leather boots and dark trousers with the father wearing a long coat of a muddied green colour over a thick brown jumper topped with a woollen hat over greyed hair. The son - as Luther assumed he was - appeared similarly dressed but wore a blue woollen jumper and short brown hair. Both rode horses of patchwork colours; brown and white blotches mixed all across them and again both carried heavy looking saddle bags with a sword sheathed and strapped above - easy access should they need to defend themselves. Luther thought they may have been traveling to obtain some supplies, now on their return journey or perhaps sell some goods at a store or market nearby.

Quite the conversation was being had between the two which looked to be a common father and son exchange as Luther had experienced with his own father back in Erstwhile. He wondered whether the elder was schooling the younger on something he felt he definitely knew more about; the son feeling slightly condescended to and wishing his father would trust in him more. At least this was a usual occurrence with his own.

As the pair passed by on Luther's right - the path wide enough to accommodate their passing without deviation - they seemed engrossed in their conversation to the degree that they barely seemed to take much notice of him. He gave them a smile and a nod when they were almost at their closest which was casually returned, before quickly returning to their heated conversation.

Further along Luther, having relaxed in his saddle, feeling the best he had in the day after a gloominous start, heard a faint thunder in the distance behind him. He turned quizzically to see what it was or where it may have come from and saw some object coming up the track. This was not a thunderstorm above, but something traveling the land below. Although it was still far from him at this moment, it appeared to be making ground quickly towards him. It looked to be kicking up a lot of dust as it made its way as if a great snorting beast was snarling and sprinting in his direction. Luckily for

Luther, as it came larger into view, he saw that it wasn't some raging behemoth, hell bent on destruction, but instead three horses making a fuss of the earth beneath them as they galloped into view.

The horses all looked to be of a dark tan or near black in complexion, though Luther could not completely confirm it from that distance. He could make out a carriage which the horses were pulling behind and as it came closer towards him, Luther could see a driver sitting atop, animatedly encouraging them to never falter from their breakneck speed. The sound of the carriage, though a lower rumble at first, was quickly graduating into a riotous applause as it grew ever closer to Luther's position.

Guinevere had come to a halt as Luther became quite lax on the reins, even more so than he had been, while also somewhat more interested in the commotion coming swiftly up behind them than the road ahead. He watched for a time as its great pace drew it closer and closer before deciding that perhaps it would be a wise move to pull Guinevere to the side and off of the path. Although there was quite a width of space on the road which would allow the carriage to come by them without collision, Luther had the sense that the driver was more concerned with speed than avoidance of obstacles. Additionally, for Guinevere's sake and – he had to admit - his own, he feared that all the commotion may cause unneeded duress, so he decided that making way for the incoming force of steed, wood and steel was most likely a wise decision. There was ample space in between the trees closest to the track and so he encouraged Guinevere to pull over and wait which she seemed only too happy to oblige.

They pulled over to the right on the north side of the track facing it at ninety degrees so they could see easily in both directions. There was ten yards or so of free space between them and the track, which was mostly tufts of grass, earth and some wildflowers in spots here and there. The flora behind them was the familiar sea of columns of various species with Luther and Guinevere flanked by a Sycamore to their left and a Chestnut to their right. They sat and waited for the carriage to arrive which, was not to be a long one as it had already made serious ground while they were manoeuvring into position.

The carriage was clearer in view now and looked to be quite dark in colour, mostly of painted wood, but with metal pillars and bracings. It looked to have some fanciful fittings which glinted in what light was streaming through the ever growth, though Luther could not make any details as the carriage was moving at such a speed. Its doors were of a usual size and position, at least on the side of which he could see and at the speed it was going. Along the top, Luther caught glimpse of a metal bar running around the edge of the squared roof which looked to have luggage or provisions tied down to it. The horses were almost upon Luther's position in the road.

With a great thunderous rush, the three horses – which Luther could see now were all of a dark chestnut colour - came galloping past at a most stirring speed. The carriage they hauled behind them hurtled by with its wheels skipping the ground at any rock or stone they encountered. At the front of the carriage the driver looked to be wearing a dark red suite and a matching bowler hat. Luther could make out few other details other than the stern look on his face which paid no attention to the man quietly sitting on his horse, at the side of the road; the driver seemed wholly occupied with the task at hand and had no time for pleasantries with other travellers on the road.

The occupants of the carriage itself were unknown as Luther could make out nothing from the brief glimpse he managed. The windows seemed slightly blackened, and Luther thought he could make out perhaps curtains, closed, to provide privacy for its occupants. Even if it were clear as day, Luther reckoned to himself he would have been unable to make out anything but the blurry outline of whomever sat inside.

Just as quickly as the horses and carriage had come blasting up the track, past Luther and Guinevere, had it similarly made its way off into the distance and then gone from view entirely. Luther waited a couple of minutes quietly by the side of the road to see if there was any follow up traffic. While doing so he attempted to calm himself and relax, before heading on. He took in a slow deep inhale of air, focusing just on the breaths themselves, letting any silly thoughts just pass on by as best he could. It seemed that this was just a lone coach in a rush to get somewhere fast, not the first of many clattering monsters, so Luther, feeling well enough, encouraged Guinevere back onto the path.

Again, their casual walk resumed, happy to creep along, not too concerned with pressing on with any great speed. They were back to being alone again on the road; only the sounds of the birds and the swaying of the great ones as they caught a grasp of wind upon them. The stretch of road before them once again wandered off into the distance in an uninterrupted fashion; barely a notable twist or turn could Luther lay his eyes upon.

They walked on in this fashion for what felt to Luther like a couple of hours. He wondered to himself what information Celeste Ignophenen may reveal to him. Would she give some simple and benign explanation? 'The universe is simply an odd place, and some people are born with an inert leaning towards sadness and misery', or perhaps something more grand he wondered, some great being maybe deemed those of some greatness down the road in life must first suffer a great deal to keep a balance within them. He supposed as was his wont that it was most likely the former; he was not anything special and nor did he deserved to be. He thought maybe he could deal with things more easily if he was at least given some more concrete explanation rather than, 'you just feel sad for some reason'. Then he might feel a little better, knowing his lot in life. This was of course once he had managed to find Ms Ignophenen. Would there be a trace, a clue to her whereabouts in Bramstone? He hoped there would be as he had little other to go on. It would be unfortunate to venture so far from his place of safety and comfort to no better fortune, to avail himself of some insight into his condition. He had to concede, he thought, that it was a good thing for him to do, this journey of his, even if he failed to get the result he was looking for. Going outside of his comfort zone, pushing himself occasionally, helped to combat the onset of a crippling fear of the outside world that may otherwise take hold.

He pondered the possibility that he was successful in finding her and she did indeed have some great insight into his disposition but didn't wish to meet with him to discuss the

A GRIM JOURNEY

matter. It was clear from Golon that she would not be easy to find and perhaps that was intentional. Perhaps she didn't wish to be interrupted in whatever ends she was pursuing. He could only wonder what she might make of this odd man having travelled a non-trivial distance to find her. Hopefully, that and her history with Golon would be enough to gain her confidence enough to take seriously his request for knowledge. Perhaps - as was often the case - he was worrying about something that he had no control over and more so, something which may not come to pass. He would focus as well as he could on locating the good lady first before worrying about thereafter.

After what felt to him to be an hour or so with little change to the scenery, Luther made out what looked like another crossroads in the road with a large post bedecked with numerous pointed signs motioning in various directions. This time there were paths leading both left and right as well as proceeding through the forest as he had been doing until now. The trees had given way at four points to allow for the paths to be trodden and were set back slightly, allowing quite a gap in the wood which one could easily identify if flying over-head.

Sitting to the left of the sign sat a trough which Luther could only assume was filled with water for horses to tend to their thirst. The right side looked to have a pipe perhaps reaching the waist height of a human, coming up from the ground. Luther guessed this was most likely a water tap, used to both fill up the water trough for horses and other steeds along with filling the water containers of any weary travellers. The cross-roads seemed to Luther like an important junction in the Dell Wood; it no doubt saw a lot of traffic so provided good reason to have some amenities present.

Once Luther had made way and arrived at the crossroads, criss-crossing the woods, he could make out more clearly the likeness of the signpost and its neighbours. It was a large wooden trunk perhaps a foot and a half in diameter, staked into the ground, mostly brown, but with smearing's of green moss in certain places. It sat in the north-west corner of the junction and featured several signs for the same direction with the similar information, which were arranged so that from any direction of approach to would bear useful insight into where each direction might take you. The signs, nailed on rather than through any kind of joinery were all of slightly different shades of brown with greater amounts of simple moss upon them. Luther assumed this was due to signs being replaced over a period with the older ones being more tested by the vigour's of time. The signpost certainly looked solid and stoic; proudly showing the way for any travellers that sought its wisdom.

At first glance, it seemed quite confusing; covered in signs nailed up and down it; a chaotic gather of useful instruction. But, with a more focused study he could see that all of the signs for each direction all stated the same information. He thought how easily someone could make mischief and move some of them around, but that didn't appear to be the case. This seemed to be quite a major junction in the road leading through the forest and no doubt was tended to, keeping it in good and correct condition.

Guinevere pulled up roughly six feet from the post standing just off the path itself; not to be in the way should anyone need to get by. Luther dismounted and gingerly threw her reigns around part of the frame for the water trough. Guinevere immediately lowered her head into the trough for a revitalising drink while he went to her saddle bags and pulled out a water container. He then walked over to the water tap to refill it and take a cup of water to satiate his own thirst.

The tap was little more than a standing steel pipe, raising up from the ground, bringing with it that most vital of fluids for all living creatures. Luther supposed there must be a well system under the crossroads. Perhaps this was the reason - at least in part - for why this location was used as such. The tap sitting on top of the pipe was of similar steel and presided over a large slab of granite perhaps a foot in length and several feet wide. Placed on this was a bent and battered metal bowl half filled with water. The bowl was most likely used for dogs or wolves or similar animals that found drinking from the water trough slightly more challenging than those of Guinevere's size and greater. He pulled the battered and bruised looking water receptacle to one side and placed his own water container under the tap. He turned it anti-clockwise and after a moment the water was flowing.

    Luther, holding the handle of his water container in one hand and tap in the other, suddenly realised how exposed a traveller such as himself was when stopped here at this crossing. It seemed like a ripe place for an ambush by a group of rogues looking for their next score from an unsuspecting rover.

    He looked up and quickly scanned the tree lines all about the crossroads to see if he could see the trace of anything sinister hiding there, but on first look all seemed to be fine. Perhaps this place was well patrolled he thought. The upkeep of the signpost and the importance of such a crossing may instil the need to keep it safe by the council of the borough.

    He looked around him again, eyes to the ground. He couldn't see any obvious damage to the trough, the signpost or the tap which may suggest signs of struggle or violence. There were no patches of blood, no strewn weapons or effects around the place. The only real signs of damage came in the form of the battered and bruised metal bowl that was perched upon the granite slab. He supposed this was more from being picked up and filled and knocked about by hounds and such rather than from anything more insidious.

    Of the signs pointing left and south, all stated: 'Umber Plain - Southern Reaches', where the right signs pointing north stated: 'Inner Forest: Take Care'. Motioning in the direction he was following, the signs read: 'Bramstone and Southern Reaches'. Lastly the sign pointing towards him and the direction he came, read 'Lonefield and Eastern Boroughs'. It appeared that Luther and Guinevere had at some point crossed over from their own Lonefield Borough and into the Valeworn.

    He had not travelled to the Borough of Valeworn before or to the Umber Plain beyond. The Valeworn was the gateway from the south through to The Boroughs proper. This was due to its position in the land between the Lightlorne Mountains to the northwest and the Border Crags to the southeast. This meant that any army or host of evil things wishing to assail The Boroughs would find it easiest to march across the umber plane of the southern reaches and into the Valeworn. Time proved this true, with this location the engagement point of many of the battles in the war between the invading Conclave to the south and The Boroughs of Old Briton. It was for this reason that the fortress town of Bramstone existed; a bastion of defence and deterrence against those who wished to wage war against the denizens of The Boroughs.

Luther looked across to the signs stating, 'Inner Forest: take care'. He wondered what was in the inner forest and what might one need to be careful of. He imagined most likely that roving bands of bandits prowled the roads, looking for an easy stick up or perhaps here were monsters or predators of some description, looking for their next meal or enforcing the sovereignty of their territory. He thought that it could simply just mean that the track leading into the inner forest may be unkempt and in disrepair, suggesting any traveller take care for potholes, fallen trees or any other such thing that might hinder their journey. An errant pothole could cause great mischief to a wheel of a carriage or wagon if not seen in time. His curiosity was nonetheless stirred, but Luther thought it best to keep course for Bramstone rather than detour and lose any more time than he intended with his casual pace, in his search for Celeste Ignophenen.

As he was preparing to strike out again in the direction of Bramstone, he saw off in the distance, making way from his intended direction, the outline of a horse drawn cart. He thought it was still a ways off, allowing plenty of time for him to pull Guinevere into position on the left side of the track, so he did so and they were once again back into their casual walk. Unlike the previous carriage he had seen earlier, this one seemed to be travelling at a much gentler pace, similar to his own.

After a few minutes, the cart came clear into sight; it looked to be a closed wagon, somewhat like a carriage, but with a curved wooden roof. Its appearance to Luther was like a traveling caravan; a wagon which doubled as both a home and a means of transport. The base and wooden sides and roof of it were all painted in a burgundy with floral designs in several shades of blue, yellow and green. At the front, was a wooden door allowing access into the wagon itself. The curved roof stretched out over this by several feet with the walls doing the same, creating something akin to a porch for a house. The door was painted in much the same way as the rest of the caravan with some additional flourishes of colour and design.

There featured a step from the base of the door below which sat an elven woman holding the reigns of two black horses pulling the carriage. Luther assumed the lady to be a traveling gypsy or perhaps a witch or shaman of some sort as he heard they tended to live in such a way; in a home on wheels, not lingering too long. He decided that he would pause when they came by and introduce himself, hoping they would do the same. A few minutes more and Guinevere had pulled up beside the wagon, whose horses had come to a stop.

"Hello there," said Luther, to the Elf sitting on a cushioned seat at the head of the wagon. It was a dark blue velvet and seemed quite plump and comfortable to be sat on. The elf was wearing a long dark green dress with inlaid patterns of brown round the hem and sleeves. Her hair was a hazel brown featuring several strands strung together and tied with natural looking bands and rings. Her skin was of a tanned brown which Luther thought perhaps meant she had originally come from a more temperate and warmer climate than The Boroughs. Luther noticed that her hands bore several rings of silver on each with a gathering of leather and woven materials on each wrist. Her nails had dark green colouring upon them which, even from where he sat Luther could see was quite chipped and worn as if she liked the colour but wasn't too worried of keeping things immaculate.

"Hello there!" said the elf in quite a jovial tone.

This immediately helped set Luther's heart at ease. If she was a magician or some such, it was good to know they were at least initially, friendly and wasn't about to turn him into a newt if he lost her fancy. "My name is Luther, what brings you on the road today?"

"Hello Luther," she replied "I am Lorel. We're travelling through to Inwood in the inner forest. How about yourself?"

Luther was intrigued and curious to know more of the inner forest and so hoped him not too rude to enquire some about it at the right time in their conversation. "I am heading through to Bramstone myself. I have never been there before, but I think I am heading the right way," he said.

She replied with a smile, "Oh yes, you are on the right track, don't worry. Just keep heading as you are, you'll be there in a day or two."

Luther felt relieved he was heading in the right direction. "Oh, that's great," he said, "I wasn't completely sure of it myself."

"Could I be as bold as to ask about your journey?" he said. "I have never been into the forest - other than a brief visit to its outskirts - let alone to the inner part." Just as he was saying these words a door from the front of the wagon suddenly swung open almost simultaneously.

"I thought I could hear you talking to someone Lorel!" Luther's gaze switched over to the open door and initially, he couldn't see who was talking. But after lowering his gaze his eyes settled on a female gnome standing in the doorway. The first thing that struck Luther about her was her quite eccentric looking hair; it was the colour of electric blue, raised up and swung back like candy floss. He wondered if the air of eccentricity was a common feature of gnomes. He had only known a few and all seemed rather quirky.

She wore a blue blouse with two interesting looking necklaces hanging from her neck; one of plain wooden beads interlaced with the odd carved bead of a different colour – Luther could not make out for sure from this distance, the other, a chain of silver with a medallion hanging from it – again it was difficult to make out exactly what it was, but it looked to be the head of a stag or moose or something similar. Below she wore a blue skirt which matched her top and hair and was made of a simple cotton with the hem looking slightly tattered.

Before Luther could raise up and introduce himself, the gnome beat him to it and said, "Hello there! I am Susan, I see you have met my sister." Luther seemed a little puzzled by this, He had never known of elf and gnome siblings before.

Seeing the puzzled look on his face Lorel ventured, "Not by birth of course, we are half-sisters," she gave a sideways look with a hint of a smile back at Susan which she returned in kind, as if this wasn't the first time they had been greeted with a look of puzzlement on description of their sisterhood.

"Are you off to Bramstone or further South?" Susan enquired.

"Yes, I am, I was just telling your sister about it," Luther replied. "I must say I was quite curious about the inner wood, which Lorel was just telling me was your destination. Could I ask, is it a town, a camp site or literally just the inner part of this great forest?"

"The inner wood is the more esoteric part of the Dell Wood. It isn't patrolled by any militia of the borough or any other and is more attuned to the magical side of things," Lorel replied with a smile.

This further peaked Luther's interest. He wondered what that meant, 'attuned to the magical side of things. He pulled his cardigan around him more and decided to press further - as much as was polite.

"Beasties of the more magical and wonderful variety? Such as Trolls, Satyrs and the like?" he said.

Susan came and leant up against the cushioned seat that Lorel was sitting on and the two again exchanged glances. "Yes indeed! You might find all kinds of things in there, though we are not seeking anything quite so exciting," said Susan.

"We are herbalists and purveyors of home-made trinkets and jewellery," Lorel continued, "My sister and I are looking for some particular herbs, of the sorceress kind, which can be found all around the Dell Wood but are rather denser in the less travelled and secluded parts."

Luther knew a little bit of herbalism from his wanderings locating ingredients for warding powder and was always eager to expand on his knowledge, so he asked what the two women were searching for in particular.

"Candle Flower mostly," Susan replied.

"Shimmer Leaf also," Lorel added.

Luther had seen Shimmer leaf in Gwithen and Lilly's shop, back in Overton. It was quite rare itself, but Candle Flower he had only heard of, never having seen a specimen himself. "They are quite rare herbs, indeed," he said. "I know a little of foraging herbs and plants but have never seen those out in the wild."

"And nor are you likely to," Lorel responded. "They only grow in special places in any kind of large numbers. You have to be careful and only take a few sparingly, you don't want to discourage their regrowth."

"I am sure you don't," Luther said. "Best to work with nature and not exploit it, I feel."

"We very much agree Luther!" Susan responded with a smile upon her face. Luther replied with his own and was happy they shared similar thoughts on the matter.

"What of yourself Luther?" Lorel questioned. "What brings you along the forest road to Bramstone?"

Luther was hoping not to talk too much of his own journey - still feeling unhappy as he was - but felt it was rude not to divulge something at least, considering the sisters had explained details of the own journey. "It is the last known location of someone I seek to gain an audience with," he said, slightly sheepishly. "They supposedly have knowledge concerning certain things which I wish to become enlightened of."

"That is quite cryptic, Luther!" Susan said. "But don't worry, we won't pry if it is of a personal matter." Both of the women smiled.

"It's ok. She may have insight into a malady of which I suffer. Not a physical one, but of the mind. I am prone to a terrible sadness and wish to understand why I suffer so." With these words his gaze had moved from the two ladies on the wagon to the floor beneath it.

"Well," said Lorel seeing him lower his gaze, "I am sorry to hear of your troubles you have Luther. We wish you luck in finding this person and may they bring you some comfort in their words."

"Indeed!" said Susan.

Luther again raised his gaze to meet them and managed to raise a small smile. There was a short pause, after which Luther said, "Well, I have taken up enough of your time. I best be on my way. Very nice to meet sisters such as yourselves. Good luck with your foraging, I hope you find all you need."

"Thank you," they both said, in unison.

"Good luck with your journey too, Luther, we hope you find this person you are looking for," Lorel Followed.

"Yes indeed!" Susan chimed in.

With that Lorel gently rattled the reins of the horses and they pulled off back on their way while Susan opened the door to which she had come and went back into the wagon, closing it behind her. Luther urged Guinevere forward giving Lorel a quiet smile.

After a few minutes Luther could make out the wagon turning at the junction just on the edge of his vision. He wondered what else might be up there and thought to himself that if he could manage it, he would one day like to come back through the Dell Wood and venture there himself. Perhaps with company that time.

He hoped to find an inn or other lodging on the road this day so he could take a rest in a bed and perhaps a bath, so directed to Guinevere to change speeds to a more determined walk than before.

Chapter 13

Guinevere, with a quiet and sombre man, Luther, sitting atop her, was travelling at a quickened pace on the road through the Dell Wood Forest in hope of finding her ride an inn for the evening, a warm meal, a soft bed and something similar for herself on this late and calm afternoon in the sway of autumn.

The forest road carried on very much the same as it had done for the last day or so; a path of dirt and scattered stones flanked on either side by rows of trees: many ferns, some oaks and a smattering of chestnut. Between the track and the brace of pillars was a lane of grass and shrubs which travellers could make use of to pull aside should they have need for a pause or to make way for other traffic. It was on this lane to the right of him that Luther saw a slumped figure, looking to be in some kind of distress.

There was a person up ahead that, from the current distance Luther could see, was covered in a dark hooded cloak. He couldn't make out much more except that they appeared to be kneeling, facing away from him. At least he assumed it was a kneeling person and not someone of shorter stature such as a gnome, as the feint line of a torso was not small enough to confirm.

This situation caused a stir in Luther; the noble soul within him wished to come to the aid of this person, but simultaneously he was weary and unsure. Anything out of the norm; an unusual event that altered the status quo, was unnerving to Luther and not something he enjoyed happening.

'Why today when I am not nearly at my best. But, when am I ever?' he thought to himself. He really hoped for a simple and boring day this day, but nevertheless he planned to pull aside as he came closer, assess the situation and see if there was anything he could do to help.

It was not long before Luther had come close enough for him to call out and ask if this slumped figure was ok or in in need of any assistance. "Hello," he said. "Are you ok? Do you need any help?" Luther had said this from his saddle upon Guinevere and still couldn't make out the face of this figure before him. It looked to be someone of the height of a human adult at least, but were kneeling down, crouched over as if in pain. They were covered by a dark hooded cloak that was ragged and frayed, with some large rips and tears along with dirt and stains all across it. He wondered how this person came to be here in such dishevelled and dissonant a state.

No reply came forth from the hooded and sullen individual. They seemed to be breathing, but not much else from what he could see, so Luther decided to pull Guinevere forward to try and get a look at them from the front and if need be, dismount and offer any aid.

Luther directed Guinevere to pull up slightly and come to a few yards away from this kneeling figure, making sure not to come so close so as to startle them. He pulled round so he was at a right angle and able to get a better look at them. From this direction he could see long hair sticking out from the hood which covered much of the head and face of this person before him. The rest of the cloak was pulled about their body to so give little away as to what they were wearing beneath or more importantly, their physical state. Even their arms were hunched beneath it.

Luther called out again: "Hello, are you ok? Are you in need of some assistance?" He gave pause for a reply, but still the figure slunk down and failed to make any audible sign towards him. They appeared to be breathing; their body raising ever so slightly as they took in breath, but not as regularly or as with as much force as one would hope.

Luther thought that clearly this person was struggling and most likely required some aid, but why were they not replying, he wondered? He called out one last time to them, "Can you hear me? Are you hurt?"

Still no reply was forthcoming. This was quite odd indeed and not the least concerning to Luther. This person could be seriously hurt and not able to respond. Why were they here though, he wondered? He looked around this crumpled figure before him. There wasn't anything in view that could give an inkling to what had happened to this person; no signs of an incident; nothing destroyed; nothing upon the ground such as debris or blood from wounds suffered - it was very odd.

Despite the strangeness of the situation, with no obvious reason for the state of this person, which should instil caution and thoughts of unease, he decided to dismount and get a close-up appraisal of what was happening. Perhaps he could take this person to safety and aid or at least identify what the problem was and decide from there. Before doing so, he looked around him. He felt somewhat uneasy about the situation, but the desire to ease this person's suffering overpowered this caution and he swung his right leg over and slid off of Guinevere's back.

As he stood on the ground, he was several yards away from the hunched figure in front of him, still knelt down and still with no hint of reply. Again, he called out to this morose looking figure in the road and again there was no reply coming forth. What was the matter here, he thought? What was wrong with this person and why would they not reply to him, if they could at all? This situation made him most uncomfortable, but he was still buoyed by his want not to see people in distress and leave them without first trying to offer any help that he could. Luther could not simply get up and abandon this person. He stilled himself and stepped closer towards the hooded figure, looking around him as he did so to looking to avoid any surprise.

As he edged closer, he said, "I am coming closer to take a look at you. I hope this is ok." With still no reply, Luther edged closer still, towards the still shadow of a being with just their slow and awkward breathing showing any signs of life. He stepped nearer and found himself kneeling down. He stooped to see the persons, face if he could, in hope it may divulge something about the state of them. He moved down to an angle in which he was able to then look across and slightly up at the face before him.

He could see now that the long and bedraggled hair and cloak belonged to a female human, but with distinctive elven qualities. Even in this state, Luther realised she was half human, half elf – a rare thing in the world. Her hair was a dark brown almost black hanging down partially covering her face and down either side of her, lost in the darkness of the cloak behind. She appeared to be looking down at the ground, struggling to hold a steady breath. Perhaps this was why she hadn't replied to his words, he thought? All her focus was perhaps narrowed onto breathing and staying alive. Her skin was quite pale and slightly gaunt as if she hadn't eaten all that much, all that often. As dishevelled as she was, Luther could see that the woman before him had an ephemeral beauty to her.

He spoke more softly, trying to catch the gaze of this person. "Hello there, I am Luther. I won't hurt you, don't worry. I am just concerned. Are you ok?" He rested there for a moment, hoping she may this time reply to him, He laid his hands down either side of him, hoping to portray an unaggressive posture with the intent that they would not see him as a threat.

After a silence that lasted perhaps a minute the woman, without raising her gaze up to him; still with her eyes fixed on the ground, said, "You don't want to help me." Her voice was quiet and lathered in a despondent and pathetic tone.

"Why ever not? You seem to be in some distress knelt down here by the roadside without mount or carriage or any effects that I can see?"

Still with eyes down and still with no change in her position she said, "You don't want to help me."

Luther was perplexed, but nonetheless still reserved to help this person - even if they seemed to be against the idea. "I do want to help you," he said again, with a tender voice. "I can't leave you here, alone on this road. Not like this. You look to be struggling and I cannot just walk past without at least knowing you are in safety or have the intention of becoming so." He wondered of the blathering that took hold of him, the rambling of words at this woman.

He was not feeling too greatly comfortable in his kneeling, sat down on the ground opposite this solemn lady with his legs crossed and with his hands still at his sides.

"False words and feigned interest will get you nowhere. Regardless, you don't want to help, trust me."

This seemed to have the opposite effect on Luther; he

was more determined than ever to discover how she came to be here and to help in any way that he could. "I tell no lies, I wish only to help you if I can, even if just to your feet so you may find somewhere to rest for the night and seek medical aid. You look to be in pain."

She moved her head slightly from side to side, but still refused to make eye contact with Luther.

"Would you at least tell me your name?" he said in a gentle voice, still hoping to find an in road somewhere, trying to understand what had happened to her. She coughed and wheezed some as she breathed, clearly, she was in some discomfort. Luther wondered why this was so. Had she been attacked and beaten? Had she been in some kind of accident? The chances of this seemed low considering the lack of any kind of debris around her, although she may have been dragged or crawled her way here from somewhere in the forest off of the road itself.

Perhaps she was simply travelling on foot while unwell, but this seemed quite implausible to Luther; how would she have made it this far and, in this state, with no aid, provision or supplies with her? The state of her was a dilapidated one; her ragged and dirty cloak pocketed as it was with rips and tears held around her, and her shoes - which Luther could now see the ends of - sticking out from under the cloak looked worn and beaten as if their user had dragged them across the ground.

This woman crouched down before him looked to have been beaten and mistreated and this is the assumption that Luther made when attempting to encourage her to disclose what happened to her. "Have you been attacked? Were you traveling the road or the forest perhaps? Were you robbed?" Luther enquired, with his own solemn and dour look upon his face.

With eyes still gazing low upon the ground, avoiding the view of Luther or maybe just not interested in doing so, she said, "Will you not leave me be. You do not want to be involved. I can look after myself."

"Involved in what exactly?" Luther replied.

She let out a groan as if breathing itself was a trying

endeavour. Clearly, she was in pain and distress and Luther felt he must do something to aid her. He was not going to leave her by the roadside.

"I can look after myself." With every word she seemed to wince in pain.

"I am sure you could," he said. "Under normal circumstances, but you seem to be quite hurt, I could perhaps put you on my horse and walk you to the next tavern I am expecting up ahead?" With this she finally raised her head and looked Luther in the eyes.

"Such noble words, but with what intent? You may appear to be…" she paused as she experienced another surge of pain in her mid-rift that she appeared to be clutching under her cloak. Her head lowered again in a natural response to the pain like a contracting spring having been recalled to a position of least strain and exertion.

Luther felt the sudden urge to stretch out his hand and place it upon her shoulder in an attempt to reassure her or offer comfort, but he felt the better of it; this woman seemed mistrustful of others he thought and perhaps, from the look of the condition she was in, was right to do so.

There was a pause that hung in the air for a time that felt to Luther as much longer than it most certainly was.

"You may on the outward look appear to be someone with good intentions," she continued, "Wishing merely to help a stranded traveller, but for how long before your true intentions come rising to the surface, at the most devious of times. Like a shark surging towards their innocent prey."

Luther was quite taken aback; the desire to help her was certainly not in any way a pretence to some sinister plan he had concocted. He wished only to provide any assistance he could to this fallen fellow and couldn't walk by, leaving them in such a condition. He thought to himself what he might say to convince her of his honest and benevolent intentions. "I give you my word," he said, "I wish only to help you if I can. You are clearly suffering there. Please let me help you."

She raised her head back up and met her eyes with his. They were of an almost jade green with red streaks from the iris – a sign of the strain and pain she was under. She stared into his eyes and continued so without muttering a word. He felt perhaps she was assessing him, sizing him up as to whether his words were trustworthy - laying judgement upon him. All he could do was stare back at her and hope his intentions were seen to be sincere. It felt like a decade had passed as she stared into his eyes, hardly blinking, peering into his soul and estimating the worth of him.

She turned her head to her left looking off and away, breaking the stare she held with Luther and muttered a single word, "fine."

Luther raised his own head up, still with his eyes resting on the woman in front of him. "Are you able to stand up?" he said, instinctively holding out both hands to aid her.

"You understand if you offer your help, you take on the consequences of your actions? I don't want anything on my conscience," she said.

It occurred to Luther that perhaps he should enquire about what exactly she meant by this. Perhaps she wasn't refusing his help solely out of a sense of pride, but rather that by offering assistance to her and her accepting it, he was putting his lot in with hers, forfeiting his chance to avoid whatever malice that had been set upon her, his well-being an unwanted load on her mind.

"What consequences do you speak of? I assume you were attacked in the forest somewhere off of the track here. Are your assailants still abroad looking for you?" he enquired, his voice one of concern, but he was resolute to do the right thing regardless of her answer.

"Something like that," she said. "I escaped from those who took me captive, after quite a beating they had laid upon me. Let's just say, I left a bad impression on their leader when he let his guard down. I can only assume they will be looking to take retribution."

"Well then," Luther said. "We had better get going, whoever your pursuers are, and I imagine they will assume you are most likely on foot and not travelling particularly fast with the injury you have suffered. Therefore, with you on horseback we will keep a good distance in front of them, at least until we find save haven."

"You are quite optimistic, aren't you?" she said.

"If only you knew me, you wouldn't say that" he replied with a quiet upon his face.

"I don't know whether to take that as a good thing or not. You are suggesting you are not normally one of a positive ilk, but you think we can escape my pursuers. Perhaps we might then."

She raised her hands above her and Luther took hold of them. She then uncrossed her legs and begun to pull herself up slowly. She leaned heavily into the support from him and with a string of pain in her eyes managed to rise onto her feet, but still bent over in pain. With another movement she pulled herself up gently, close to her full height, but slightly hunched over. With this action her cloak had opened slightly, and Luther could not help but see what lay beneath. She wore black jeans that were mud stained and ripped with the odd patch of blood. On her top she had a platted shirt of red and black that was faded and again featured streaks of mud and tears; it seemed to Luther that she must have been thrown to the ground and handled roughly by these people, whoever they were.

She clearly had been through quite some torment. On her feet she wore some black padded boots which, considering the state of the rest of her clothing were in quite good condition; other than being stained with mud they didn't appear to be ripped or feature any holes that Luther could make out from this angle.

"Come," Luther said. "Let's get you to my horse." He turned and put his left arm on her left shoulder and his right on her right shoulder, gently as he could while hoping to provide support. Slowly they began to move the short distance towards Guinevere.

She paused briefly after each step; each one making her pay in throbbing pain, mostly centred on her midriff. Luther, trying to match her rhythm and anticipating her surges of pain, thought she must have taken a forceful blow to the stomach, perhaps in retaliation for whatever she had done to this person leading, what he could only assume was a group of bandits. Perhaps they thought beating a person was good sport. Perhaps she was someone of value they could ransom. That anyone could do such a thing both dismayed and angered Luther in equal measure. How could anyone kidnap a person, hold them hostage and beat them like this? Why would anyone act this way, to mistreat another person? He hoped once he had made it to some form of civilisation, he could contact the local constabulary of the borough to search out these bandits and bring them swiftly to justice. For now, though, he focused on the pressing task of getting this woman on to Guinevere and away to safety as quickly as he could.

With some patience they made their way to Guinevere, who was standing patiently where Luther had left her. In his haste he hadn't tied her reigns to any would-be anchor, but she hadn't decided to stray anywhere, which was good luck. To get this woman up and onto Guinevere was going to be no easy task; with her injury causing just the simplest of steps to cause her great pain, the motion of lifting herself up and swinging her leg over onto the saddle was most likely going to be quite excruciating.

"We need to get you up and into the saddle," Luther said tenderly. "I am sorry, but there will be no way to do this without you experiencing pain, but once you're up there it won't hurt quite nearly as much."

"Well then, let's just get it over with," she replied, bracing herself. He helped her place her left boot into Guinevere's left stirrup and then clasped his hands together which she then placed her right foot with her body flush against Guinevere's.

"Shall we go on the count of three?" he said.

"Ok."

So, with the count of three, ascending with a scathing hiss of pain, the hooded woman was hoisted up into the saddle.

"I am sorry," Luther said gingerly. He could only imagine how much hurt it was causing her, but with her now in the saddle he should be able to get her to help as quickly as he could. She didn't respond to this remark and instead slunk over and down onto Guinevere's neck, her battered and bruised cloak hanging either side of her and her hood covering most of her face. It seemed she had accepted the situation and therefore Luther's help and was now hanging on to Guinevere ready for the off. Luther took hold of her reins and noticing that the hooded lady was bracing herself against the sides of Guinevere, gently took hold of them and motioned her into a walk.

Chapter 14

Through the Dell Wood in the early hours of the evening, a lonesome, reserved man lead the reins of a noble horse as she carried the bruised and battered body of a lady, in hope of finding her help and safety, somewhere within the confines of the expansive forest.

Luther, leading the way, was determined to find some shelter and was sure there must be a tavern or similar coming up soon along the forest road; it had been quite some time since the last and he assumed that surely some tavern, outpost or other outstretch of sanctuary may soon be discovered. Hopefully whomever they encountered would be able to provide some aid to his charge or at least send for a doctor or healer. Perhaps a good place to rest in the warmth with some food and ointment upon her bruises would help with her recovery from her injuries, if nothing else.

He led Guinevere as quickly as he could, but without causing too much discomfort to her rider - which took a few winces and cries of pain to discover. The pace set was one of a brisk walk, faster than he had been traveling previously, but not enough for Guinevere to break into a strong trot which might cause a lot of thudding or jerk of movement. It felt to Luther almost as if she was aware of the injured and vulnerable person she was carrying on her back and was at pains to avoid causing her any additional discomfort.

Luther had become somewhat used to horseback in the last few days and was now having to keep pace with his steed rather than simply sitting on her back. He felt drained from the day, but also determined to find a place of safety and rest for them all.

For her part, the hooded lady, who Luther had found on the ground, huddled on her knees and in thrall of her pain, was mostly quiet, with the intermittent puncture of the relative calm and silence of their journey by muffled whimpers or sudden in-takes of breath.

A GRIM JOURNEY

Luther thought best not to attempt too much conversation unless she herself instigated it. She looked to be somewhat stable and reticent as she was, and he didn't want to do anything that might change it. Anyway, he thought, he had managed to convince her to let him accompany her to safety which was the most important thing right now so having some sort of meaningful conversation was not particularly urgent. The only thought he had concerning this was how it would be nice to at least know the name of this person, if only so he could address her properly or inform some authority of her condition, rather than awkwardly trying to gain her attention should the need arise. He thought best to just stay quiet and focus on the task of finding refuge.

Before long, confirming Luther's assumption, a building crept into view. In fact, it looked as though there were several of them. Perhaps it was a small village or way station for weary travellers – he would seek to find out. This immediately put him at some ease to know there was in fact somewhere he could seek refuge for the night or at the very least some shelter and perhaps a warm fire for the lady traveling aboard good Guinevere. He supposed that one amongst these buildings was a tavern and perhaps, maybe a guard house that would have access to a healer or some medicinal remedies for his wounded charge. He imagined that such a gathering would provide enough deterrence and security should whomever this woman's captors were, wished to make their presence known.

He decided now might be the time to once again strike up a conversation with the woman being carried by Guinevere, while she held onto her neck, intrusting her care to her.

"So," he said, as he slowed up slightly. "It looks like there is a village or something up ahead. When we get there, we should be able to find some care for you. At the very least we can find you a bed and some warm blankets."

The hooded woman had been resting her head to the left side of Guinevere's neck with both arms slung around her. She raised her head up ever so slightly, but not enough to take in the view ahead of them. Luther supposed this was probably too much of a strain for her or perhaps she was not interested in seeing where they were heading to and more the moment-to-moment pain she was suffering was her only concern.

"Good," she said. A singular word was perhaps all she could muster.

Luther could see that this simple acknowledgement was enough to trouble her physically, so he decided against pressing her any further. He still hoped he might discover her name at least, but it seemed that wasn't to be. The most important thing he felt was to make way as fast as possible, to seek aid and avoid any nasty confrontations with an angry band of highwaymen that were seeking to harm them. Luther raised the pace as he thought manageable, and they pressed on towards the buildings.

As they drew closer to the little settlement, Luther could make out a number of buildings to the left of the road with one singular and prominent among them to the right. He supposed that this must be a guard tower of some sort; it featured a tall, rectangular tower, crested by battlements and a flagpole. From this distance he could not make out whose flag it was but assumed it must be that of the Valeworn Borough. Attached to the tower's right-hand side was a ground floor building perhaps as long as the tower was tall. It had an angular roof that looked to be tiled and windows on the sides with open shutters, letting creep in the little sunlight that was left of the day. Luther imagined this must be the bunk house for the officers of the guard house; somewhere for them to sleep and rest if not on duty.

To the left of the road, which seemed to pass straight through this little settlement, Luther could make out three buildings: The one closest to his view and set back from the road roughly twenty feet was a large based single storey building with a full thatched roof. It might have gone further in length, but from this angle he could only see the width of it, which seemed large enough to suppose it might be a tavern. Indeed, he could make out the outline of a sign hanging from the exterior wall of the roadside of the building. This was probably the sign for the tavern, displaying its name and a fitting artwork. He was quite convinced this was a tavern, and along with the guard house, instilled hope in him that he would find aid for the woman slunk on his horse. All he could do was hope for the best, something that didn't come naturally to him, but he would do what he could.

To the left of this was a smaller building - at least in the width that Luther could see from this angle. It too had a thatched roof and a single chimney stack situated in the middle. It wasn't particularly clear what this building was for as he couldn't see a sign for a shop or similar. There could be one on the side of the building that he could not see denoting it was a shop or service like a blacksmith, though he thought it unlikely to be a smith due to there being just a singular chimney in its centre and the lack of an extended section housing the forge and anvil. He thought perhaps it was merely a dwelling for some of the residents of this small cluster of buildings in the woods. Somewhere nice and warm and cosy.

Behind the tavern and the smaller building, was another, which again seemed ambiguous in its nature. It was roughly the same size as the building to the left, but this time with a tiled roof rather than a thatched one, but with the same centrally placed brick chimney. Perhaps this was also a home for a resident of the little outcrop of civilisation, tucked away in the majesty of the Dell Wood. There were two further buildings that both mirrored the size and shape of these both of which Luther assumed the same.

Though it was already getting dark as the day was transitioning into evening, due to the space cleared in the canopy above from the erected buildings, it became slightly brighter as the last vestiges of light from the sun crept through across the horizon, allied with the moon now ascendant in the sky. Luther could make things out a little clearer at least and noticed a townsman was abroad, lighting lamps on the outside of the assumed guard tower and then proceeding to those outside what Luther supposed to be the tavern. This filled him with resolve and warmed his heart; he was quite tired from the walk and the energy spent earlier in the day just dealing with his own mental disposition that he cherished the thought of lying in a nice comfortable bed, perhaps after something warm to eat and a good cup of coffee.

They moved into the perimeter of the little town stead

and with-it Luther looked up at the sign of the tavern now within sight to read what it said. "The Speckled Plough" were the words along the top line of it, below which was an image of a plough being pulled by a horse with blotches of dark blue upon its long blade. Speckled indeed, Luther thought to himself with a little smile. He decided that he would be calling in at the tavern as soon as he had spoken to whomever was in charge at the guard house. This still being his assumption that it was indeed a guard house.

His mind suddenly darted to an anxious thought; those who had captured this poor woman and beaten her dearly, they would not have associates that worked and live here in this isolated little village in the forest, would they? He assured himself that this was probably not the case. Bandits and thugs were not likely so lucky to count on the treachery of anyone working for the local constabulary. His own dealings with those in Overton gave him no cause to think otherwise.

He looked across and saw a signpost which he hadn't noticed before, sticking up from the ground outside the guard house. He motioned Guinevere to follow him so he could better read it. 'Valeworn Constabulary', it read. Luther was correct, this was a guard house. In front of him, as he stood facing north and directly at the constabulary office, he saw the signpost to his right and roughly twelve feet behind this, a set of doors at the bottom of the tower. They were of thick oak wood, rectangular in fashion of which when closed as they currently were, formed a square. Each had painted black steel struts, up and down their height, roughly six inches apart with two large, twisted steel rings on each door as they met in the middle. In the dead centre of the left-hand door was a large slit which Luther assumed was an opening in the door to be slid aside so the guardsman could see who had come knocking. Below this was a black steel knocker, no doubt to gain attention of the officers behind the door.

Luther gently pulled Guinevere's reins and they walked over to the double doors of the guard tower. As they did so the figure lighting the torches crossed their path. Luther noticed that it was an elven man. He was wearing a dark green cloak over a dark tunic and dark brown studded jacket that bore a silver broach with the Initials V.C. upon it. Around his waist was a sword hanging, sheathed from his right-hand side, which Luther could see the end of poking out below the cape. On his head, under the cloak hood, he wore a studded leather cap with flaps on either side that came down, mostly covering the man's ears. This person was no doubt an officer of the constabulary office, making his evening rounds of lighting the streetlights of this small township.

"Hello there," said Luther, addressing the guardsman as he grew nearer.

"Hello there," rang the reply.

"Are you an officer of the constabulary?" Luther asked. "I am in need of some assistance."

The elf looked at Luther and then to woman hanging onto the horse behind him. "You have an injured person there?"

"Yes, I do," Luther replied. He intended not to divulge too much information as of yet while still out in the open, with no real knowledge of this place.

"Right, ok. You had better bring them to the station and we can send for the doctor. Follow me."

The man walked to the door of the guard tower and thudded the knocker several times. After a brief moment the slit slid open and upon seeing the officer standing there, several noises as of those made when unlocking a door were heard and the right door swung open. Behind the door was another person, this time a male human dressed in similar garb to the elven man knocking the door.

"Thendel," said the man. "Any problem?"

Thendel, the Elven officer stood back slightly from the door. "We have an injured traveller, Gibbins. Will most likely need the doctor's attention." He then stood to the side to reveal Luther holding the reins of Guinevere, carrying the hooded lady upon her back. Gibbins looked at Luther and then the woman clinging to the horse in front of him. He looked down and noticed the hand axe hanging from Luther's side. "You best leave that with me. Visitors can't come into the station armed," said Gibbins. Luther unsheathed his axe and handed it to the Officer.

"Right," said the officer. "We had better get her down

and I'll take your horse round the back. Don't worry she'll be alright."

Luther was a little apprehensive at the idea of leaving Guinevere in the hands of a stranger but was buoyed by the fact it was an officer of the law, of which he had no reason to believe would mistreat or neglect her.

"Right, ok," he said in response.

The hooded woman on top of Guinevere's back, holding onto her neck, had begun to stir, seemingly aware of what was happening. Taking in a draught of pain that showed desperately upon her face as she did so, she hauled herself up in the saddle until she was sitting straight and begun to swing her right leg over and across in preparation to slide down off Guinevere's back. Luther was not prepared for this and was caught slightly off guard by her sudden movements and scrambled to aid her as she slid down. He was in time to take some of her weight as she did so, seeing the streaks of pain in her eyes. He stood there to the left of the hooded lady, bracing her as best he could and motioned officer Thendel to come round to her right.

"I think's its most likely best we carry her rather than aiding her walk, if that's ok with you of course," said Luther. He looked at her, but her face was partially covered by her hood from this angle. He noticed her head nodding in agreement. Luther thought perhaps she may well had liked to try and enter the building on her own steam but had accepted the situation and let them carry her through into the guard house. Officer Gibbins took Guinevere's reins and lead her off round the back of the building and out of Luther's view. Luther and officer Thendel then proceeded to carry the hooded lady into the guard house.

As Luther crossed the threshold of the constabulary building, he was greeted with a bathing of light from a room radiated in the brightness of lamps that were hanging from the walls roughly at shoulder height to a human. As the room was so very well lit, Luther could make out the contents of it quite clearly; it was quite large and filled the entire floor space of the base of the tower. There was a prominent U-shaped wooden desk to the left and westerly wall, behind which was a staircase leading up to the second floor and the battlements above. The desk looked to be made of solid oak and was braced along its front with steel which Luther supposed was to protect it from damage should they bring in a particular rowdy or angry individual, flailing themselves around the place. Standing tall against the back wall, either side of the stairway were two sturdy looking filing cabinets, each with two large draws that in height came up just below the line of lamps surrounding the room. Luther supposed these were for files pertaining to the different cases or incidents of which the constabulary office had to deal with.

Behind the desk sat another officer, another human male dressed in the now familiar outfit of this place. He had a slightly different looking broach upon his breast which Luther thought most likely denoted him a superior office to the constables here. In front of him was a blue logbook, opened up roughly at its centre with writing upon its pages that Luther could not make out from this distance though he imagined it was recorded information of the goings on at the station and events of that day.

To Luther's right, along the south-easterly wall was a row of wooden chairs, facing the desk. They looked to have all initially been the same style, perhaps being part of the same set, but time and use had worn each of their frames in different ways giving each its own unique character. The body of the chairs were all wooden, manufactured from chestnut Luther thought, and had a slight shine to them. This shine had worn away along the arm rests from the years of use; the friction of the hands and arms slowing wearing it away. They had leather cushioned seats of a dark old Briton style racing green that had impressions of different shapes in each; the weight of various sized people creating differing concaved imprints. Luther supposed that these chairs were made use of while people lingered, waiting to either be booked by the clerk officer at the desk opposite or waiting to see be seen for some other purpose.

Up from the chairs was a wooden table on high legs upon which sat a large metal jug and some glass cups stacked up. Luther supposed that this jug, full of water, was available should one require a drink.

A GRIM JOURNEY

Along the southern wall, directly to Luther's left was a small table with a chair either side, facing into the room. Upon the desk was a pack of playing cards, some of which were laid out in a pattern to suggest that a game of solitaire was in motion.

On the north-easterly wall, facing Luther was a line of steel bars stretching from the south-eastern wall breaking briefly in the centre and then continuing to the north-western wall. The gap in this stretch of steel had walls either side of it forming a corridor leading to a door on the back wall. Luther thought this must lead to the other section of the guard house that he had seen from the road.

The walls of this corridor formed one of three for each of the rooms either side of it creating two jail cells. This meant when occupied, those housed within would not be able to see who may be coming through from the back room; they could only see and be seen from the gaps in the bars facing out which was the booking officer and those waiting in the seats. Both had a bed that looked comfortable enough with a firm looking mattress some blankets and a pillow. At the side of each there was a small opening in the wall allowing light in and braced with steel bars which discouraged the drive to escape. At present both cells were absent of any residents.

"Sergeant," said Thendel.

"Yes Thendel. What's happening here?" said the officer seated at the desk. He looked at the officer in front of him, then to Luther and finally the hooded lady, carried between them before returning his gaze back to officer Thendel.

"Injured traveller Sir," said Thendel. "This gentleman found her. They came in on the north-east road."

"Right," said the Sergeant. "When Gibbins reappears, you two get the gurney and take her over to the tavern. Carry her to the back door and tell Louise the situation. She'll put her in a comfortable room. Then you go over to the doctor's house and request that she go and tend to her. In the meantime, I'll speak to this gentleman and detail the incident."

"Yes sir," said Thendel. "Let's put her in a seat for a moment while I get the gurney," he said to Luther and the two

A GRIM JOURNEY

of them gently lowered her down into a one of the chairs. Luther sat in one to her right and Thendel walked off down the corridor between the two cells and disappeared into the back room.

Shortly, officer Gibbins came back into the guardhouse and the sergeant instructed him to assist officer Thendel in taking the injured lady over to inn. Thendel then returned holding a gurney. It looked of quite a simple design; two wooden poles placed in sheathes sown into either side of a length of brown leather with a small stuffed pillow stitched onto one end. There was definitely nothing fancy about it with it firmly built for function over aesthetics. Luther hoped it wouldn't cause too much discomfort for the hooded lady and hopefully the journey over to the tavern would be only brief.

He stood up and away from the hooded lady as she sat hunched in her seat. Thendel and Gibbins then stood either side of her and gently lifted her up with no little exhortation on her part and laid her on top of the gurney which Thendel had laid out on the floor in front of the chairs. They then each took one end of it and lifted the gurney up gently. Luther moved quickly round and past them to the door in which he had entered and held it open for them as they passed through. He watched as they walked slowly with care - not to cause too much discomfort to their charge - across the path Luther had come just minutes ago and then up to and around the tavern across the road and out of sight. He assumed this must be the back entrance and once they were fully out of sight, let the door close again. He walked back towards the desk and sat down in one of the chairs opposite, waiting for the sergeant to address him.

"So," said the Sergeant after a few moments, taking a notebook from somewhere under the desk and a pen from on top, "I am Sergeant Burrow, second in command of this little village of Forestead in the Dell Wood of the Valeworn Constabulary. And who might you be sir?" He looked at Luther and awaited a reply.

"My name is Luther, Luther Dothmeer. I come from the village of Overton in the Lonefield Borough."

"I see," said the sergeant noting down in the notebook

what Luther was saying. "And can I ask what you are doing, travelling the Dell Wood this evening?"

"Yes of course," replied Luther. He was quite nervous speaking with the sergeant. He was anxious of having to explain himself to an officer of the law. He was anxious that the good sergeant would think he was somehow responsible for the injuries that the lady had suffered. He was in a new place that he had never been before, and all of this was quite a lot for him to take in.

"I am on my way from Overton village in the Lonefield Borough to Bramstone. I am looking to meet with someone there concerning a personal matter." Luther hoped this was enough information for the sergeant as he didn't feel like divulging everything concerning his journey.

"I see," said the sergeant writing down all that was said. "And how did you come across this injured woman?"

The sergeant's tone was a stern one which impressed upon Luther that he should be clear in his response. He thought it best to be as descriptive as possible in regard to him encountering the woman, not leave anything out which he thought would be relevant. "I would say about four miles back down the road heading north-east I found her. She was knelt down on the right side of the road and looked to be in need of assistance. I pulled aside and hailed her but received no reply. I proceeded to dismount my horse and check on her. She was not very communicative and looked to be in quite some pain. I managed to ascertain from her that she was being held against her will by a gang of bandits and had found the opportunity to escape. They looked to have beaten her quite heavily, especially around the chest and stomach."

"I see," said the sergeant, again, looking up from his notebook. "Please go on."

"Do you mind if I have a cup of water?" Luther responded. He wished to take a pause and was becoming anxious by all this. He had gone from a quiet lonely ride through the woods to becoming embroiled in the kidnapping of a woman he had never met before. It was all quite a lot to process and Luther, a man used to keeping to himself; shying away from attention, now had it sat squarely on his person.

"Yes of course," said the sergeant, "Please pour yourself a cup." He raised his left hand and made reference to the jug of water and cups Luther had seen earlier.

"Thank you," said Luther, as he stood up and walked over to the table with the jug of water and poured himself a glass. He took a deep gulp of it and then refilled it before walking back and sitting in the same chair as before, in front of the sergeant. This pause in the recounting of the story seemed quite amenable to the sergeant as he used it to write down the remainder of what Luther had just said.

"Are you ok Mr Dothmeer?" Asked the sergeant.

"Yes, I am fine. Sorry, my life is usually a lot more benign than this. All the events of today are quite a lot to take in. I am prone to worry you see."

"I see," said the sergeant yet again, turning the page on his notebook. "Please do not take this as an interrogation sir, I merely wish to know the facts as they lie, and you are the only person that can give them to me. From the way she didn't seem in any way distressed by you carrying her or being fearful in your presence - along with you even bringing her here in the first place of course - leads me to err that you are not her assailant or captor." This revelation helped to calm the nerves of Luther immensely; he no longer felt that he was the subject of an interrogation or that the man was sizing him up quite so much as before, though he was sure the good sergeant would still be assessing the facts of his story. "Now sir, if you could please go on with your story," said the sergeant.

Luther took another sip of his water and continued with his account of what happened. "Well, as I said, she didn't wish to speak too much, through either fear, pain or anything else I am not sure. I managed to convince her that I was not going to cause her any harm and also that regardless of what she may say about my own safety in helping her that I would do so nonetheless."

The sergeant interjected, "She said you may come to harm yourself if you helped her?"

"Yes. She suggested that whoever held her captive and subsequently escaped from, would look to find her again, especially - as she had told me - she had managed to injure their leader in the process. I guess these people will be out searching for her and will not take too well to those who offer her any assistance. Regardless, I couldn't leave her there like that. Not out of some notion of gallantry or saving a damsel in distress, but of the good and right thing to do of offering help and assistance to one in need of it." He paused and looked sullenly at the floor, avoiding eye contact with the sergeant.

"You managed to convince her to let you help her then sir?"

Luther took another sip from the cup. "Yes. I think she understood I wasn't going to leave her there and so accepted my offer of help. I managed to get her onto my horse… my horse, is she ok?" He raised his head back up and glanced at the sergeant.

"Oh yes," said the sergeant. "Don't worry, we have a small stable out back for our own horses and there is plenty of space to accommodate an extra one. Feel free to go and check on her after we are done here."

Luther felt relieved, though he had to admit he wasn't immensely concerned as he couldn't imagine an officer of the law mistreating or stealing his horse. "I will do. Thank you," he said. "So, yes, I managed to convince her to let me help. I assisted her in mounting my horse and then lead them on foot. She didn't say anything from that point and the only audible sounds she made was those of pain from her injuries. I had assumed there would be some place to seek refuge and help and soon enough we came upon this village. Just in the nick of time really."

The sergeant while still looking down at his notebook, quickly writing down the conversation said, "Did the lady divulge any information regarding her background or who she is?" he enquired.

"Sadly not," said Luther, "I don't even know her name. All I know is that she was kidnapped by some gang of vandals and miscreants. It saddens me that anyone would do such a thing." Luther could feel himself getting a little worked up. He was already in a heightened state of anxiety and thinking about how cruel and evil some people could be, wound him up further.

"Indeed sir, terrible business," said the sergeant. "Well, I guess we will have to speak to her after she has had time to rest and heal. Thank you for the information sir. We can keep your horse overnight or if you wish, feel free to obtain stabling over at the tavern. They have good soft beds over there for yourself too. There will be no need to hold you here sir, so feel free to make way on your journey when you please. I would suggest checking in with us before leaving though, should we have need of any extra information before you go."

Luther stood up from his seat and drank the last of the water from the cup and placed it on the desk. "Thank you for the water sergeant and I do hope you can find these dastardly people." The anger at the thought of such villainy had risen to the top.

"We endeavour to do so sir. Do not worry about them coming here and assailing this place. We are more than capable of keeping the town secure. If you go out the front and round the back, you will find your horse in one of the stables. Thank you, sir."

"Right, thank for your time Sergeant, I will of course pop back tomorrow morning and check in before I head off." He turned and walked out of the office. The sergeant turned back to writing in his notebook.

Chapter 15

Luther walked around to the back of the building to find the stables that the sergeant had described. It was a simple wooden walled shed with a wooden roof at an angle with corrugated steel sitting on top. Inside it was split up into several separate bays by wooden walls that rose to roughly the shoulder height of a human adult. The entrance to each faced out and south-east with a rear wall up to the roof. There was a wooden door slightly lower than the height of the separating walls allowing a horse to hang its head over, which was the case now as Luther could see four horses stabled, each with their heads sticking out.

The horse on the far left of these four Luther recognised as Guinevere. She, like the others was looking out across the stables while eating some feed of some kind that was hanging from the outside of each door.

Tending to the horses was an older looking human woman. She had fairly long scraggly hair and wore a coat over a green woollen jumper featuring a few holes and lightly covered with straw and other stable detritus. Below her waist she wore some black jeans that seemed similarly bedecked with holes and a dusting of straw along with some brown leather boots. On her fingers Luther could see woollen gloves with the ends cut off allowing the tips of her fingers to poke out. Her skin was quite pale and worn from age, but still with life inside it. She was busily feeding each horse as she noticed Luther enter.

"Hello there, I assume you are the owner of this horse?" she enquired.

"Yes," said Luther. "Her name is Guinevere and mine Luther," he said with a smile.

"Good to meet both of you," she said. She seems like a good lady your Gwen," said the woman.

"Yes, she is indeed. I have only had her a few days, but I feel quite attached to her already," Luther replied, walking over and stroking Guinevere's neck as she hungrily ate some of the feed that had been provided for her.

"May I ask your name?" said Luther.

"My name is Olive," she said. "I keep the horses for the constabulary office as well as keeping the guard house in good order."

"Ah, right," said Luther, "Must be nice working with animals."

"Yes, it is," she replied, smiling." They keep me busy along with those messy buggers in the guard house."

Luther laughed, "I am sure they do. Is it ok to leave her here in your care for the night? She seems happy enough here and it looks like you are taking good care of her."

"Yes, that's fine, it's no trouble," said Olive.

Luther felt more at ease knowing that Guinevere was in good hands so, feeling quite tired from the day's travel and goings on of the evening, decided to go and obtain a room for the night at the tavern.

"If you would excuse me, I will leave her with you and make way to the Inn over the road. I have had quite a long day and would love a nice warm bed." he hoped that she was ok with him cutting short their brief conversation.

"Yes, that's fine Luther, we are used to weary travellers around here," she said.

"I am sure you must get a steady stream of us through the wood," he replied.

She nodded in agreement.

"Well thank you for looking after her and I wish you a good evening Olive."

"You too," she said, turning back to her duties.

Luther exited the stables and made his way over to the tavern. As he stood outside, he realised he had left his pack and other gear inside Guinevere's saddlebags. He promptly returned into the stables and with apologies to Olive for disturbing her, retrieved them and exited the stables once again.

The day was now into the evening with the lamps previously lit, providing all the light. He checked to see if there was any traffic making its way along the road leading from both north-east and south-west and found the path to be quiet.

He walked across it and covered the short distance to the tavern. He noticed a beaten path leading up from the main track that made a fairly straight line to the cusp of the tavern itself. Below the sign for the speckled plough, which he had seen previously, there was a single wooden door looking solid and proud. It had a thick black doorknob protruding from the middle and right, which Luther grasped hold of and pushed. The door, slowly at first and then with a quicker movement opened into the tavern. Luther stepped into the building and closed the door behind.

The Inside of the tavern was noticeably quiet and laid back with only a low murmuring from the few patrons currently occupying the room. Luther's entrance had disturbed this enough that they mostly turned round to gaze upon whomever it was that had breached the tavern entrance this evening. Luther felt it was though they were half expecting someone to be opening that door any minute and then he remembered that the two officers bringing the hooded lady to the back entrance most likely caused some disturbance. Perhaps, he thought, they had seen this before; some traveller wounded or incapacitated, brought to the rear entrance of the inn causing some stretch of commotion, followed by the rest of their party, to break the docile atmosphere of the hushed inn, filled only with the local people of this small outpost nestled in the great Dell Wood.

The room in which Luther had found himself was the familiar sight one might describe when entering a tavern or pub of a borough. There was a bar, beginning at the right-hand wall almost stretching the entire length of the room, but stopping short enough before the left way to allow a door in the back wall. This was most likely the way through to the rooms beyond, of which, one was hopefully occupied by the injured lady he had found knelt upon the ground. At the right, behind the bar, looked to be an entrance filled not by a door, but by hangings of wooden beads. This must be a small kitchen, Luther thought to himself, as he could smell a whiff of something tasty emanating from that direction. It instantly perked up his appetite that had been somewhat sedated by his urgency to get to get the hooded lady to safety. He now was eager to enquire about something to eat at the first opportunity.

A GRIM JOURNEY

There were six tables arranged around the room, two of which were currently occupied with people. He wasn't sure if they were locals or fellow travellers and wasn't much in the mood for finding out. He did on the other hand wish to discover the situation regarding the hooded lady; to know if they had got her here ok and whether the doctor that was mentioned had come to see her.

Behind the bar was an older gentleman, perhaps in his sixties, who was looking directly at Luther. He imagined the two officers had briefed him of Luther's eventual arrival at the inn this evening upon knocking at the back door to this place with the injured woman in tow. He gave a re-assuring smile to Luther who proceeded to walk over to the bar. This made him feel more at ease and once he had done so the quiet murmur of chatter at the tables had resumed.

"Hello there, we were expecting you shortly," said the man. He wore a brown apron over a white shirt that had been rolled up to above the elbows. His hair was on the turn of grey and was generously thinned on his head.

"Hello," said Luther somewhat meekly. "My name is Luther. I guess you have met the woman I came in with?" He wasn't really sure whether he should divulge too much information. He assumed that the sergeant back at the constabulary office wouldn't want him to speak in too detail of the situation and indeed, he thought, he didn't know who might be listening in; he didn't know the people here and didn't know what connections they had to the people of this area, namely those rogues in the forest, kidnapping people.

"Yes, my wife is out back seeing to her. Will you be wanting a room too? We have a couple of spares if you'd like one," said the man.

"Yes, I suppose I would like a room too, if that's ok?" replied Luther.

"That's no problem at all Luther. You can call me Graham, by the way. My wife's name is Louise. Only the two of us here this evening so if that's alright with you, could you grab a seat and I'll fix you a drink until my wife is back and can show you to your room." Graham, the barman motioned with his left hand to one of the empty tables situated on the north wall near the bar, under a window.

"Yes, right," said Luther. "Could I trouble you for a cup of coffee - decaf? I think I need one after a long day," he said, feeling the exhaustion upon him of a physically and emotionally tiring day.

"That's no problem at all Luther!" came a softened bellow from the man behind the bar. "You fancy some stew as well? We have some lovely beef and mushroom simmering on the stove if you'd like some?"

It seemed that Graham had beaten him to the punch as Luther was about to ask if they were serving anything to eat and was delighted that this was indeed the case. "Yes, yes I think I will. I think that will hit the spot brilliantly. Thank you."

He went over to an empty table and sat down his pack and other items he had pulled from his saddlebags onto an empty chair and then sat in one opposite. The chair was wooden, with a cushioned bottom and a curved wood back which Luther sat back into as he let out a huge sigh. Not one of anguish, but of relief, relief that he made it to safety that the hooded woman he found suffering on the road, was now in the care of a doctor and not out alone in the wilderness. He wondered at the long day and how much had happened in the last few of them. He only wished for a quiet journey to Bramstone, to find this Celeste Ignophenen and beseech her for some clarity. He hoped he could locate her and hoped that she might unfurl the blind to see beyond and understand, even if rudimentarily, why he felt like he did for as long as he had memory to recall it. He felt it was not even an option to consider leaving that woman by the roadside in the state she was in, so worrying about how it could have waylaid the progress of his journey was a pointless endeavour. Even Luther and his penchant for incessant worry and anxiety over a great many things, decided to just let this be. He did the right thing, he thought to himself, and that was what mattered.

Just as he had relaxed into his chair and was teeming on the edge of calm for but a moment, Graham, the bartender approached his table with a tray containing a pot of hot coffee, a white cup on a saucer and a little clay jug of sugar with a silver spoon.

A GRIM JOURNEY

"There you go Luther, some nice hot coffee to warm your innards," said the barkeeper.

"Thank you, Graham, much obliged," replied Luther, looking up at the man with a relieved smile.

"That's no problem, I'll sort you a bowl of stew momentarily and bring it over. Its good stuff." He wandered off back round to the bar and out the back for a minute before returning with a greenish grey bowl bellowing steam from the hot stew. Luther could smell it before it arrived at his table and upon it being placed before him, he looked up to Graham, "It smells wonderful, indeed! I am sure it will taste just as good."

"Oh, it will," replied the barman. "My wife is a fine cook, if I say so myself."

"Well, my compliments to her," said Luther.

"You can give 'em to her yourself when she is back. I am sure she would like to hear it." Graham put down a tablespoon on the table and returned to his duties behind the bar.

Luther looked down at the bowl of stew before him. Just the smell and its warm embrace upon his face was enough to make him feel a measure of contentment, and he was happy for it. He then picked up the spoon and gathered some stew before bringing it to his mouth. It did taste as good as it smelt and fired Luther's hunger more than ever.

Before long he had made short work of his meal and was sitting drinking his coffee and staring across at his belongings trying to keep a clear mind and relax in the moment.

As he sat there, avoiding the urge to dwell on anything in particular for too long, he noticed in his periphery someone coming round the bar and over to his table. It was a middle-aged woman with shoulder length ashen hair in a dark blue skirt down to her ankles and a frilly blouse of a similar colour. Upon both of her wrists she had several bracelets of leather and string and a necklace of a single wooden carving, of which Luther couldn't really make out too well without staring intently upon it.

As she approached him, she said in a hushed tone, "Hello, Luther, is it? I am Louise."

Luther stood up from the table. "Hello Louise, I must

congratulate you on a wonderful stew. I don't think I could have asked for a more perfect meal after such a day."

"Thank you very much!" she replied, clearly happy to hear of the enjoyment of her cooking. "Now," she said. "Shall I show you to your room?"

Luther reached down and drank the last of the coffee in his cup. "Yes sure, that would be great," he said. He picked up his things and promptly followed her as she walked past the bar, through the doorway to the rooms beyond. The other patrons of the tavern took little notice.

"Your friend is now in one of our rooms with the doctor currently," she said as they walked through the corridor.

Along his right side was a long brick wall which Luther noted must be the back wall of the bar and kitchen beyond. To the left was another wall, but with four doors. The doors to the guest rooms, he thought. Directly ahead, at the end of the corridor, was another door.

Just as he was wondering which one she might be staying in, Louise continued, "She administered some healing balm which should help with that terrible bruising that she suffered and luckily she doesn't believe she has any internal damage. She will need to be in bed for a good few days to recover and several weeks after she won't be able to do too much. The poor dear, she took quite a walloping. Who would do such a thing I ask you?" The tone of her voice became sterner at these last words along with her brow furrowing.

"Indeed," said Luther. "I don't understand either. There are some terrible people in the world."

Louise came to a stop outside the third door on their left. "This is you," she said with a smile, her right hand on the doorknob.

All the doors here were similar; solid oak with some panelling in each of the corners; simple yet pleasing to the eye. The doorknob, on the right-hand side of the door Louise was holding was a sphere of solid brass leading to a baseplate on the door of wrinkled lines. It had become worn - most likely from years of use - being turned back and forth as guests entered the room or closed behind them; a worn blotch upon it which had lost the shine it once had.

A GRIM JOURNEY

The door opened inwards; Louise entered the room. She beckoned Luther to follow, which he gladly did. The door had opened to meet the right, north-eastern wall of the room which featured several hanging paintings. There was a common woodland feel among them; one of a peaceful, serene forest another a wintered take with the trees without their leaves and one on the verge of spring with trees and other plants starting to bud with the leaves and flowers of the coming year.

To the left, up against the south wall was a bed which to Luther looked roughly queen size. It had nice, warm looking blankets and several pillows which were very appealing to Luther, as tired as he was. He could imagine himself dropping all his gear on the floor right now, slumping into the bed and drifting off into a deep sleep.

Straight ahead and dead in front of Luther as he stood there, was the back wall of the room. There was a window sitting off centre to the left through which he could see the rest of this little village. To the right of the window was a stand-up wardrobe standing proudly up against the wall. It was of solid wood and looked very sturdy with most of its body comprising of hanging space behind two wooden doors that were currently half open, below which was a long draw with two wooden knobs.

Below the window and close by the bed sat a bedside table with a lamp, lit and glowing. It provided the only light in the room but was more than enough for Luther to see in and it fit his current mood anyway; he cared not for a surge of glaring light upon his tired brow and this radiance was more than ample for his current disposition of quiet and tired emotions, ready for some rest after a most interesting day.

"I hope it is all to your liking," said Louise.

Luther could feel the sense of pride she took and not wishing to disappoint her said, "Oh yes indeed, the room looks great."

"Thank you," came the reply. "Your friend next door is most likely going to be off and asleep for the night, so I would recommend checking on her tomorrow. She could do with a long uninterrupted sleep."

Luther could feel she was quite the motherly figure,

taking good care of those under her roof. He couldn't disagree with her. The hooded lady he had found on the road was quite injured and no doubt needed rest. He himself was in need of it too and so for all concerned it seemed best to adhere to her words.

"Yes, I quite agree," he said "Best to leave the poor woman. I am glad she is now safe and in good care. I think I might myself have an early night too, if that's ok."

"That is no problem at all!" said Louise. "If you need anything just let us know." With those words she exited the room and closed the door behind her.

Luther sat down on the bed. He felt himself sink down onto the mattress; the heavy weight of the day felt acutely through his body. He was both emotionally and physically drained; the events of the last few days had taken a toll on his mind and his body, and he had little energy left. The strain of his mind and that of his body from the day's journey had caused a great lethargy in him and didn't have the energy for much. And still he was worried for the lady he had met out on the road. He hoped she would be ok. He was worried about the people that had accosted her. Would they now be looking for her and perhaps him as well? Did the good sergeant think he had something to do with her kidnapping, regardless of what he had told him to the contrary?

He felt a deep tiredness and with it came a sense of sadness. It took a constant measure of will to keep the depression in check, to keep it from welling up and bearing down upon him, holding dominion over him. That will was becoming depleted; the last couple of days had been draining with yet another morning filled of despair and the events of the day requiring more energy and strength of mind to cope with. He decided, rather than hold a last-ditch attempt to stay awake and challenge the oncoming sadness that he would leave today where it was and turn in for the night.

He took off his shoes and jacket, unsheathed his axe, and took off his cardigan and other clothes until he was in just his under shorts and t-shirt. He then pulled out the closest edge of the several layers of blankets that had been tucked in, under the grey mattress and pulled them back. He climbed into bed and replaced the blankets over him. After turning off the lamp he lay asleep within minutes, drifting off into a deep slumber.

Closer now

With longer pause and strain the Grim Lady pulled herself up from the ground. She had stumbled and fallen more flatly than before, requiring great effort to recover again. She leaned heavily on her sturdy staff, lifting herself back to her feet. The mist, ever in attendance, had fallen with her and kept a watch around her, empathetic of her fall and of the strain upon her eyes as she winced in pain. She was reluctant to stay herself too long from her journey so rising up and onward she headed.

The theatre of night was once again in full motion. The only light tepidly approaching the sky was the glint of the moon as it waxed ever so in its fullness of the tide. Its midnight glow fell gently upon the Grim Lady, showing the bruises and scuffings upon her hands as she grasped her staff within her right hand. Her left hand hung down by her side, edging out from under her long cloak. The greyed brown of her skin was just visible as she seemingly faded into view, reluctant to let her presence be known to the world around her.

But her presence was felt; the flora, around her lit as it was by the quiet glow from the moon, had greyed and become sullen in tandem with her passing. As it had before, it had become downtrodden and meek, but returning to its previous form after her passing; slowly brought back to its colour and character when no longer within reach of her saddening aura.

She was on the verge of transitioning away from the dark canyon, with its darkened and smooth rocks, shining from the moon light. Ahead of her was a steeper and more mountainous climb up the Forlorn Mountains proper. Her progress began to slow even more as the ground below her feet became uneven and unhelpful, causing her to stagger more and often go for the stable support of her whittled staff.

The mountain, which had loomed in the distance previously, was now coming forth to make itself known to her. It would now be a struggle and a testing climb should she wish to make her way up its unforgiving paths and ways. There was a track to be followed, snaking up to and around the waist and then to the top of the mountain's peaks. They were not mortal made, beaten or otherwise, but softly described upon the earth and enough to guide a weary traveller through the pitfalls and trying climbs of the bastion of rock and earth. The Grim Lady had just trodden the beginning of one such path and was slowly creeping up it as it searched off and round a turning up ahead. She moved forward, leaving the canyon behind her. If she even noticed the transition, she made no obvious recognition of it, shuffling and struggling forward, still leaning on her staff for support.

She seemed to make little impression on the ground around her. The earth beneath her feet hardly gave any indication of her footsteps. The odd plant or grass that managed to eke out a living here didn't appear to move as she brushed past it, as if it was refusing to allow any commotion from the grim lady brushing by. It was as if the terrain itself wished to let her pass as quietly and respectfully as it could.

Her presence was barely noticeable to the common eye, but not just from the absence of the sun in the sky and with the silver glimmer from the moon above. It was as though the world was remiss to allow her presence be known; a respectful acknowledgement and silent veneration as she travelled the tracks of old Briton. Without the dulling, grey effect she had upon it, the ground and sparse foliage around her would give little impression of her passing.

The mist, her ever present and only companion, still swept around her perimeter. It's blackish, grey hue sometimes caught a glint from the moon that gave it away ever so briefly. It was as her, not wholly acknowledged by the environment, but always close to the grim lady, all about her, never leaving her. It was patient as she traversed the terrain; slow and steady as she could, her pace affected as it was by her stumbles and falls. When she did so the quiet fog gently moved down with her and when she pulled herself back up with great effort, it softly rose again.

The lower crags above the foothills of the Lightlorne Mountains were populated by rocks and boulders that had become displeased with their higher perches further up the mountain face and decided to hurl themselves down to the lower reaches. These were scattered around the rock underfoot, the base of the mountain itself. Some looked as though they had cast themselves many years previously featuring moss growth and other flora that had grasped footholds in their rough exteriors. Others, were absent of such growth upon them, perhaps only recently making their journey down the mountain, though they seemed noticeably smaller than the older residents of the area.

There were some small bush growths in numerous patches of earth amongst the rocky floor along with resting rocks and noticeably few small trees growing tentatively as they could. Further ahead the boulders and rocks made up more and more of the landscape with the sparse growth of trees falling away completely with just a small number of low scrubs and smotherings of moss here and there.

All of the rock and stone were already quite a muted grey, but as the Grim Lady passed, they took on a more reserved kind of grey. A more sombre grey. If someone were present to witness it, they would most likely tell when this aura had come and passed by any feature of the land, perhaps feeling it upon themselves too.

The turning, seen up ahead, perhaps by the Grim Lady herself, though with no indication she had noticed, was sign posted by two large rocks sitting either side of the simple path she was following. There was a third boulder - slightly rectangular shaped - that was resting mostly on the left-hand boulder beside the path. It reached out across and was greeting the right-hand rock, making a makeshift gateway, beyond which was the turn of the path that followed up and round the mountain. It looked as though this boulder could have simply fallen from the mountain and come to rest on at it was merely a coincidence or perhaps it could have been placed there by a great number of people or just the work of one large and powerful being.

The grim lady hauled herself along the steady path, passed the rocks and the boulders, passed the lonely trees and after a while had come to this stone doorway on the mountain

A GRIM JOURNEY

path. As she reached it, she paused and raised her free left hand, placing it upon the left hand boulderous pillar of the entrance way. Her hand - normally of someone of heritage from the Indian Homelands - was not of brown alone. While still reminiscent of that tone, it had become greyed and muted by the same force that affected her surroundings.

 The doorway of rock became engulfed in the humble and sullen aura that emanated from her. It was as though the stone was empathetic of her and wished to shoulder some of her burden, if just for a moment.

 After some a minute, she removed her hand from the rock, lowered it back down to her side and walked through the stone doorway.

Chapter 16

"So, it seems you are right Vespera, these Peons of Overton Village are too foolish to acknowledge greatness when they see it. Too blinded and naïve to accept the truth... as I tell it to them!"

The well-dressed man, Fabian sat back in the coach he was occupying opposite his two quiet and large warders along with Vespera, the hidden lady, at his side. It was travelling at a great pace, away from the village of Overton in the Lonefield Borough.

"I did suggest this was perhaps not the best idea dear Fabian," said Vespera. "Our control of the Drearom Borough is tentative at best. Branching out to another so soon and one in which conditions are the greater for the common civilian, was always going to be an uphill struggle." There was a twinge of satisfaction in the woman's voice. She enjoyed having one up on the well-dressed man and was if just a little happy to see him fail to succeed on this occasion, so she may bask in the failure of his short comings.

Fabian, looking frustrated and angry in equal measure said, "Yes thank you Vespera. I know you take no small amount of joy from our failings here this evening. Perhaps if you had provided me with some greater insight to their disposition or just how entrenched they were in their own beliefs then maybe I wouldn't have made such a fool of myself!" He refused to look at her and instead took to looking outside, pulling back the fanciful, dark red curtains and leering out with eyes outstretched and full of malice.

"Look at this cretinous place," he said, after a pause, seething in tone. "These fields look like the toil of troglodytes who prefer nothing better than wallowing in their own pointlessness!" He continued with no let-up in aggression, "I am not at fault, no, my performance was impeccable. They were just too stupid to understand. Too set in their ways. They have mingled too much with riff raff of other races and supped from the chalice of mediocrity. Bah!" He turned and looked at the two gentleman sat quietly in front of him, both heavy set and stern looking. "Will you tell Malakai to get us out of here post haste?!"

The large man sitting opposite and, on his right, reached out his right hand and pulled aside a wood slide which exposed the outside of the coach. Through it one could see the coachman, lithe and wiry, in all black and a top hat, sitting casually upon his driver's seat. The other large gentleman to Fabian's left then reached over and spoke into the square hole with a deep, gruff voice, "The boss wants out of here quick."

The coachman, Malakai, turned round and met eyes with the burly man before nodding and turning back to the road ahead, followed by a large whip of his hands. The reigns of the horses began whipping themselves up and down without obviously being held by any corporal being. Regardless, the horses felt the lash of the reigns as they slapped down upon them and drove the carriage on at a greater speed than ever. The large man then took up his former position in the carriage with his fellow sliding shut the small hatch.

Malakai, the wiry coachman, was sat in the driver's position on top of the coach. He wore a long dark black coat almost the length of his body and his top hat perched on his head at a slight angle. He sat back into his leathered seat and watched the road ahead. The immediate area in front of the carriage - and a great deal of the three white horses pulling it - was lit up by two lanterns attached to the chassis of the coach on either side of him. The light was quite orange and bright from the fire dust that was at the centre of each of the lanterns, which were designed in such a way that the light emanating from it was directed forward in whichever way the carriage was heading.

"The sooner we are gone from this place the better," said Fabian, his tone still laced with anger. "Nothing is lost Vespera. We are under no obligation to sway that place under our control, yet. Nothing has been lost. Nothing, but my precious time wasted on those who are too unintelligent and malodorous to appreciate me."

Verspera nodded in agreement. "Yes, nothing is lost."

A GRIM JOURNEY

She seemed almost about to offer up some sardonic remark about the situation, but thought better of it, lest she feel his angry wrath. She sat quietly as the coach roared along the dirt track from Overton, heading east and then southwest back to the Drearom Borough. Fabian pulled out a pocketbook and made some notes within, while muttering to himself intermittently.

Vespera pulled across the curtains of her own window and stared out into the night. She could see the fields of the local lands and the lights of Overton Village quickly fading off into the distance. The carriage took a course southeast from Overton, skirting round the edge of the Dell Wood Forest, taking their journey briefly across the southwestern fringe of the East Borough. The Panifery River ran almost parallel before heading east.

Immediately around the carriage Vespera could see a long line of hedge rows running parallel with the road on which the coach was thundering through. They looked to be kept well enough she thought, though not overly so, allowing them to feel wild and rugged. There featured trees intermittently too, looming from behind the hedges as the coach whizzed by. They were various sizes and types such as chestnuts, ferns and willows. Some of them seemed quite old and addled by time and age as they loomed over the hedges below. She wondered what sights they might have seen over the years; coaches such as hers, streams of soldiers, travelling fairs or lonely wanderers walking the road at night.

Vespera's view was of the southwest. Beyond the hedges, which were only occasionally high enough to block out much of the view, she could see the farmlands whose edge were rimmed by the line of trees of the outmost part of the Dell Wood. She could see several farmhouses, barns and an assortment of sheds and shacks spread across. The fields themselves had recently been harvested on the outset of autumn and now looked quite bare and barren; the bounty of vegetables or corn or wheat or some other arable produce having been taken away and the earth turned over and prepared to be sown anew.

Light shone from most of the farmhouses along with

A GRIM JOURNEY

smoke that flowed from the stacks perched on their roofs, which could be seen against the clear night sky; alight by the moon, shining near full. She wondered what they might be doing, the residents of these places. Enjoying a simple life perhaps, she thought. Just happy to spend their days working their farms and their nights by the fire enjoying a supper and a read of a book or the company of their fellows. She wondered how that would be enough for some people. How such a simple life could provide any kind of excitement or interest. She thought to herself that such a way wouldn't be to her liking. She was meant for greater things than that. She was not meant for such menialities no, hers was a life meant for the finer things: of a fine outfit; of fine dining and luxurious surroundings. She wouldn't be touching a spade or a fork, a cooking tray or anything of the like, not while there were others more suited to such lowly tasks. Let them enjoy it.

The coach rumbled on the road for some time, swiftly making its way through the very edge of the East Borough, turning directly south and into Drearom. Once inside his home borough, Fabian's coach turned south and with no less speed travelled for a short while before reaching the outskirts of a town named Chesterpool.

Fabian swung open the window on his side of the carriage and said with heightened voice, "Ah, the sweet sounds and smell of a town that knows what's right! And who knows best for them!" The smell was a cocktail of smoke from churning chimneys - even at this hour - from large brick buildings that filled the eye scape. The town itself was built on the side of a large sweeping hill facing west with factories and workshops featuring prominently down at its base.

The carriage travelled the road leading east and into the town. It skirted through different roads, this way and that at its unrelenting pace. As the carriage made way into the town, the road beneath it transitioned from the common dirt road to a cobbled street; the hooves of the horses immediately kicking up a great sound as they transitioned to a stone surface.

Lining the streets on either side of the coach were tall streetlights. These lamp posts stretched up straight and were topped with two diamond shaped lamps on either side housing pedestals which were most likely to house some kind of filament or source of illumination. They looked to have once functioned well at lighting the area around them, but now nearly all seemed dark as if no-one had thought or care to light them. This might well have been the case were it not for the odd lit lamp, producing a beacon of light in the otherwise dark and dismal streets. This seemed a rare occurrence though and Vespera not once saw a lamp with two full lights.

There were different sized buildings, all from various forms of industry. Weave works featured on one corner, still with lights inside; work still very much ongoing. There was another building with slated roof top and several chimneys and a sign reading: 'Sutherton's Forgesmiths'. Across from there was another sturdy building again featuring numerous chimneys, but this time there was a sign reading: 'Holts Brickworks', hanging outside. Another, smaller building read 'Crobes Cobblers', though it had no lights on inside. Down another road was a taller bricked building with paint written on the side simply saying: 'Glass Works', which Vespera could make out by the light of one of the few streetlights still in at least half good order.

The Avenues of this lowest part of town, the industrial, manufacturing quarter, as Vespera knew it, were littered with rubbish and refuge strewn about its sides and up against buildings. Vespera thought to herself what a wretched piece of Chesterpool this was. She thought like worker ants, the people that lived and worked here were needed to carry out the menial and labouress work that was required. They themselves were not particularly valuable or inferred much passing thought from those who were more important. They deserved to live here, she thought. They had accommodation at least and they should be lucky for it. They were not cast aside out into the wilderness, out onto the road and forest to fend for themselves and should be thankful for it.

All of the buildings had a common aesthetic theme of a bedraggling of dirt and grime upon their walls. The soot and muck from the different manufacturing buildings formed a layer of dark black grime, the majority of which gathered around the bottom of each building, before spreading upwards.

Amongst these and other buildings were smaller, brick houses, some several stories tall. There were no signs of placards on their exterior suggesting their purpose, but a majority had light emanating from their windows and smoke coming from their chimneys. As the carriage sped by and seemingly at no slower pace than the open road, Vespera could make out various figures in them: a man looking to be cooking something over a stove; a woman quietly reading a book by the window under the moon above and an oil lamp by her side; a couple sitting at a table having dinner and conversing over something or the other. She again wondered what it would be like to live in such a simple way, in such a simple life in this smoky and dirty neighbourhood. She had little time to ponder as the carriage continued with its breakneck speed and before long had passed up from the lower part up to a smaller, less smoke clogged and haughtier part of the town.

This quarter featured smaller buildings that looked mostly free of the caking of black grime upon their walls that was the hallmark of the lower, industrial part. This section was home to mostly cleaner service and crafting businesses rather than those of whose production had caused more filthy by-products such as thick smoke or slick oil and streams of heat.

Contrasting with the lack of working streetlamps in the lowest part of the Chesterpool, the standing lights of this part of town all looked to be in working order. They were the same design, but each had a glowing core of fire dust at its centre bathing the pavement below with glowing orange light. This illuminated each street quite gleefully with each store front brightly ablaze in their warm glow. The streets and buildings here seemed to have more care and attention to its upkeep with a notable absence of detritus littered around.

There was a straight looking building with timbered wood and clean looking glass windows. It had a front wooden door that was painted a burgundy colour with a bright brass door handle to its right centre. On a board across the top of its ground floor there read a sign that said: 'Keenlee's Cloth and Culture'. The floor above was perhaps the residence for whomever ran the shop below. It had a tiled roof with a chimney sat to one side. The tiles themselves looked quite straight and all snuggly in place encompassing a brickwork chimney that breathed smoke into the night. The shop was all dark inside with no visible lights on or people to attend, but the front had several torso mannequins that were dressed up in fine suits of different shades of which now were still quite vibrant from the streetlights outside. Vespera remembered some time previous of Fabian buying several suits from such a tailor and would only accept the best and most extravagantly expensive, which they were only too happy to provide.

Another shop, 'Barrow Street Barbers', whizzed by with the familiar red and white pole hanging, instead of a sign. This place, like the others, was closed for the day, but Vespera could make out several black leather looking chairs in which patrons sat in while receiving their hair cut, shave or other service.

A further shop front grabbed Vespera's attention. It was one that was twice the size of that of those around it. Upon a sign sitting centrally across the top of it read the words: 'Chesterpool Antiques'. The entrance was a set of double doors again centrally situated and made from heavy looking wood featuring a long brass bar handle so that both would open outwards on their hinges allowing quite a wide object to be brought in or out of the store. Vespera briefly caught a glimpse of a couple of items in the store window which would no doubt require the opening in such a way: On the left-hand shop window was a white grand piano that reflected the light brightly from the streetlights outside and looked impeccably expensive she thought; the other, right side had several large pieces of furniture such as a bureau close to the window or a large dark wooden wardrobe sitting up against the wall. She could remember this place delivering several items of furniture to Fabian's residence and wondered what extravagant price he must have paid for some of them. She enjoyed such fine things as well but was loath to pay for them.

The carriage swept through these lit streets and within no time had come upon a third and final section of the town. The coachman, with little exertion, waved his hands towards the horses and the reigns, which seemed to be held up and above the horses all by themselves. The free flying reigns

A GRIM JOURNEY

suddenly raised and lurched backwards exerting a great pressure on the three white horses to come to a stop. All three gave out a neighing grunt as they collapsed their pace down to zero and the coach came to a halt in front of a large set of wrought iron gates. The light from the lamps either side of the coachman lit up the gate in all its glory. The two gates, each one half of the large arch, were double the size of a full-grown human. They were constructed of iron bars that grew from a base horizontal bar just above the ground, each raising up and meeting a curved bar that made up the shape of the arch itself. They looked as if they had been cleaned recently this day and perhaps often as they were stainless and free from the onset of rust.

Each side of this impeccable set of gates was hinged to a steel pillar which itself was connected to a steel fence that stretched off in either direction. Of what the light from the coach uncovered, this fence too was very well maintained and look as close as new as that of the gates themselves. The fencing was simply wrought iron poles stacked vertically with each piercing through both a top and bottom guiding rail. The top of each bar through the top rail, splayed out into a three leaved clover like shape; a larger central leaf flanked by two smaller leaves. This went on for as far as the light could show.

Just to the left, in line with the steel pillar to which the left-hand gate was attached, sat a small pillar box with a neat little lead lined roof. It was mostly lit up from the light of the carriage though there was some light emanating from within. It looked to be guard or porter post where those who allowed or denied entry through the gate were stationed. As the coach approached and came to a halt a human male dressed in a dark red gambeson, black trousers and stern looking black boots stepped out from the guard house and approached the left side of the coach of which Fabian's window was facing. The man had a sheathed sword hanging from his waist and padded leather helmet upon his head. All about him was clean and ironed and well-kept, in keeping with the aesthetic of their surroundings.

"Evening, Mr Elgard sir," said the man as the window opened, showing Fabian, the well-dressed man a, he looked down on the man.

"Yes," said Fabian with a look of contempt. "Open the gate will you, I am in no mood to dawdle." Fabian pulled closed the window, abruptly ending the conversation. The man walked over to the gates and pulled them open one at a time before standing back. The coachman, without even a passing glance at the man, gave a flick of his right hand and the reigns once again jumped up and smacked the top of the horses, encouraging them to once again set the coach into motion. Within a few moments the coach had passed whole through the gates and was into the topmost section of the town, at the highest point of the hill. The gateman then closed each gate in turn and returned to his post.

This section of town was the grandest of the three and featured but a single large mansion house placed centrally from the gateway of which the carriage was now racing to. Surrounding the mansion was a small moat that looked more man made than a natural feature of the land. It was filled with a low level of water and its intention looked more of an aesthetic endeavour rather than providing any real protection from assailment.

It was constructed of dark red brick and consisted of a large central section set back from a forward courtyard and a flanking wing on either side. There were two floors, filled with large and extravagantly featured windows that looked out onto the forecourt before the house.

In front of the main section of the mansion was a drawbridge attached to an outward gatehouse that stood before the abode proper. When lowered this would broach the gap of the moat separating the courtyard and the house to the outside.

There were motifs along the edges of the rooftops with gargoyles perched on every corner. Vespera sometimes flittingly attempted a count of them but grew bored with that exercise rather quickly.

It had even further extravagances, including turrets at the ends of each wing along with two sprouting out from the main, themselves also looking over the forecourt. To Vespera, this house took on the appearance more of a castle than a stately home, even featuring battlements atop the roofs which featured several people armed with crossbows, patrolling backwards and forwards menacingly.

Fabian's coach quickly came up the road leading from the gate, thundering along the paved road leading up to his residence. The draw bridge had begun to lower once the coach had entered this quarter of the city and reached its resting position, ready to allow entry, just before the carriage arrived to cross it. The coach, still moving at quite a speed, passed over the draw bridge with the wheels and hooves clapping loudly upon it as if announcing their arrival. Once it had entered the central court, the chains and pulleys of the gatehouse holding the draw bridge once again sprang into action and it was raised back to its vertical position.

The coach pulled up in front of the building and halted under a porch like jutting that allowed a coach or other form of transport to disgorge its contents without them being battered by the elements.

Malakai, the coachman, still laid back in his position, motioned in the direction of the door on Fabian's side of the coach at which it quickly opened. Fabian then turned and stepped out of the vehicle followed by the two ever present and imposingly large gentlemen.

"It's good to be back in familiar and assuredly deserved surroundings," said Fabian, the well-dressed man.

Vespera opened her own door and slipped out of the right side of the carriage. They were all now standing in the central court when the butler, Jacob walked out from two impressive large wooden doors on the west side facing east. He approached Fabian and then by his side while his employer rambled still angrily about his trip and the group disappeared back through the doors and into the manor.

Chapter 17

Luther opened his eyes to find himself laying in a warm bead, staring up at the ceiling of a quiet room. It was mid-morning and the light from the day was peering through a gap in the curtains of the window.

He was greeted, not just by sunlight and the stillness of the room, but also that familiar and ever-present sadness that welled up inside him. Still though, he thought, he felt better to have slept in a nice warm bed than out in the forest – there was certainly less chance of finding oneself in clear danger from beasties, bandits or otherwise. For once, in a while, he didn't have that feeling as though he was just having a strange dream which, upon waking had caused him some distress. He didn't awake, eyes open, trying to recall what on earth he was dreaming about just moments earlier. What did this mean, he thought? Perhaps it meant nothing at all, and he was just lucky for once; the vagaries of his slumbering mind were never to be fathomed by his waking one. He felt still that waking melancholy. It seemed apart from the odd dreams that he suffered; not completely a side effect of that which he experienced while under the sway of a deep sleep.

Although the sorrow lay about him, he was still appreciative of his surroundings - the snuggly warmth under the reassuring blankets - as much that he felt he would like to just lay there a while. His mind wandered, and for a while he simply took in the surrounding of the room; the pictures on the wall; the window; the closed door; until finally his mind passed away from the room and to the events of the day before. This woman he found out on the road. This woman that he hoped would be on the road to recovery now that she was had reached safety.

Who were these villains that had accosted and imprisoned her anyway? Why would they do such a thing? The idea felt alien to him, that someone would wish to cause suffering on another person, to hold someone captive like that was wretched. It felt so devilish and evil. He hoped sergeant Burrow was willing to seek them out and arrest them, but such was the case sometimes, people might get away with their miss-deeds. The good sergeant might be eager to catch them, but a large group of miscreants out in the woods would be quite the task to apprehend. He wondered perhaps, if the sergeant would seek reinforcements from Bramstone or elsewhere should he wish to go after them and go after them Luther hoped he would. Regardless, Luther in the least, thought he had done all he could and would leave the task of upholding the law of the land to those who best knew how to do so. She was safe and that was what was most important.

His thoughts then turned to the task of himself. He had to raise up and out from his secure and reassuring position here, in this warm and cosy bed. He stared at the gap in the curtains and the light shining through. I must will myself up and out, he thought. I must carry on with the day and make progress in discovering the whereabouts of Celeste Ignophenen.

He pulled his arms from under the covers and took hold of layers of blankets before pulling them across his side, uncovering his body. He immediately felt colder and less protected, but laid there, focusing on the act of sitting up and swinging himself round on the bed. He could not manage it. He saw his arms pulling the blanket back across himself and with it he felt the warmth again. He laid there now, looking up at the ceiling, losing himself in far off thoughts; his journey and where it may take him; his condition and how it might lessen or become worse in time. He wondered why he was so incapable at times.

Why do I struggle with life so bitterly? Why do I not just cope as others do? He thought to himself. He did not know the answer, but he was told there was somewhere out there that perhaps might. He must find her.

Again, he pulled the blankets aside. Again, he laid there, but this time he willed himself on and pulled his body up into a sitting position. He then swung out his legs and sat on the edge of the bed. He rubbed his eyes with his hands and smudged the sleep from them.

Halfway up, he thought. He now needed to stand up

and fully remove himself from the bed, leaving its protection behind. Come on Luther, come on. The urge to lay back down in bed, pull the covers back once again and refuse to face the day, laying snug in his misery, was a strong one. He sat there in quiet contemplation, at war with himself, until suddenly and with great effort he stood straight up and walked over to where he had placed his clothes the night before.

He put on his trousers and boots and his warm purple cardigan. He thought it might be useful to enquire about the opportunity of a shower as he hadn't washed properly in a couple of days. He walked to the door and opened it. He looked out into the corridor and could not see anyone standing there or much noise from the bar beyond. He supposed it was probably too early for too many patrons at this time, but he assumed that the owners of the establishment were probably up and awake.

He stepped out into the hallway and closed the door behind him. He walked down the corridor and rounded the doorway into the bar. He was right in his earlier assumption, with all the tables currently empty. Standing behind the bar though was Graham who was busily wiping up some teacups.

"Hello Luther!" said Graham cheerfully.

Luther envied anyone that could be so positive so early. "Hello Graham", Luther replied.

"Did you have a good night's rest?" Graham enquired.

"I did, yes, thank you. The bed was most comfortable."

Graham gave a nodding smile.

"I was wondering," continued Luther, "Would it be possible to have a wash somewhere?"

"Yes of course!" said Graham with a smile. "The first door on the left behind you there is the bathroom. We have a shower in there and the water pump is ready to go."

Luther turned round at these words to look at the door behind him before turning back. "Oh, brilliant, thank you very much."

"No problem Luther," Replied Graham.

Luther turned back again and went to his room for some fresh clothes from his pack including a black long sleeve cotton shirt and black trousers, before heading to the bathroom for a shower.

Once he was done and dressed, wrapping his warm purple cardigan around him once again, he dropped off his dirty clothes to his room and came back through to the bar. Graham was no longer behind it, but Luther could hear his voice from beyond the hanging beads of the doorway. He waited patiently and after a minute or so before Graham reappeared back through to the Bar.

"Hello again Luther!" he said as his hands parted the beads at their middle. "I hope you haven't been waiting there too long."

Luther shook his head and said, "Oh no, don't worry, I just got here."

Graham smiled and said, "Oh good, good. Now what can I help you with? I can imagine you wouldn't mind something to eat before you head off? I assume you will be heading?"

Luther was a little caught off guard by these words, wondering why the good man assumed he would only be staying the one night, but then he thought of why would he be staying any longer anyway? This village was a small township in the Dell Wood, with few facilities, no doubt nearly all travellers were simply that; travelling and were nothing more than passing through on their way to some other final destination.

"Yes, I will be, quite soon," said Luther. "I was hoping to catch a bite to eat before I go."

"Yes indeed!" Graham quickly responded. "We can whip you something up no problems. We've got all sorts: eggs, bacon, sausages, and slices of toast, hash browns; what'll be?"

Luther thought for a moment, he wasn't overly hungry, but did like the thought of some eggs on toast with bacon and so asked Graham as well as a cup of coffee. The Barman fixed him a cup before disappearing again beyond the hanging beads. Luther sat down back at the table from the night before.

Luther, sitting at the table with his cup of coffee, added a spoonful of sugar from the pot sitting there and wondered about what the day ahead might bring. He should go and check on the woman lying in the room next to his. He wished to know of her condition and be assured she is doing well. He would worry otherwise without some knowledge of how her condition was. He would go and check on her after his breakfast and then pack his things, pay his bill and go see the sergeant over at the guard house. He doubted he would have discovered anything new in the few hours since their last conversation, but he promised to see him before he departed.

Shortly, Graham came through with Luther's breakfast which he could smell before even laying eyes on. He saw to it quickly, perhaps being hungrier than he had first thought and before long he was finished and making way back to his room. He packed up all his things into his pack, put on his long leather coat, sheathed his axe and went back to the bar. Louise was standing there this time of which Luther was glad as he wished to ask her about seeing the hooded lady.

"Hello Louise," he said.

"Hello Luther, sleep well?" she replied.

"I did indeed, thank you very much and the breakfast was just what I needed too. I'd like to settle my bill if that's ok and further, would it be ok if I checked in on the lady I brought in last night?"

She gave a smile and said, "Yes of course to both questions!" He reached for his pouch of money he had taken from his pack and paid Louise for the board and meals before thanking her gratefully for the service.

"She was awake when I checked on her last so she might be amiable to a visitor," Louise said.

"Ok great," replied Luther. "I'll just go knock on her door before I head over to the constabulary office." He thanked Louise again and walked back through the doorway to the rooms beyond.

He came to the room in which Louise had said she was staying and proceeded to knock on the door - it was closed, and he didn't wish to simply walk into her room uninvited - and waited for a reply. He paused for a few moments but didn't hear any anything. He knocked again, listening intently for any sound coming from within. He was about to knock one last time when he heard a voice from the other side of the door. It was not very loud, but he could make out the words:

"Who is it?"

"Luther," he said, against the door. "I am the one who brought you in last night. I was hoping to say goodbye before I carry on with my journey." He waited again for a reply; straining his ears so as not to miss a voice through the door.

"Come in," were the two words he made out amongst the silence. With his pack on his shoulder and some apprehension on his mind, Luther turned the brass doorknob and entered the room.

He was greeted with the woman he had found by the roadside the night before, sitting up in a warm looking bed. Her head was no longer covered, showing her ashen brown hair that slunk down to just below her shoulders. She was wearing a dark blue nightdress which Louise must have dressed her in the night before, Luther thought. She seemed roughly the same age as Luther, though with her elven blood he really had no idea as to how old she really might be.

The room itself was similar to his, with a warm and homely feel to it. There were pictures of serene and picturesque looking scenes hanging from the walls. A long shelf with numerous leather-bound books of stories and myths of old Briton and beyond ran along the right-hand side wall. The bed - in which the woman was sitting up - sat perpendicular to the left wall. Just like his own there was a window in the wall opposite that would have looked out to a similar view if not for the curtains that were draw closed. There was a side table on either side of the bed; one with an oil lamp which was still lit and the other with a jug of water and a glass beside it. On the south-east wall, which housed the door through which he had entered, was a light brown chest of drawers on top of which was another oil lamp which itself was smiling bright into the room.

"Hello," said Luther to the woman, laying in the bed. "I hope you don't mind me checking in on you. I will be carrying on with my journey shortly and wanted to see how you were doing and say goodbye, before I made my way."

She moved slightly in the bed with her back up against the solid board behind with a pillow tucked in between.

Performing even such a small motion gave a noticeable twinge of pain that Luther could see evident in her eyes.

"I am sorry," said Luther. "Are you ok?"

She looked up at him, standing at the end of her bed. "I am doing as well as I could."

"Yes," said Luther "Of course. You have been through a lot. I am just glad you are being looked after and provided with care."

"They are looking after me, yes," she said. "I suppose I should be thanking you for what you did. Perhaps I would have found my own way here eventually, but you made sure of it at least." She looked at him with something of a begrudging smile.

Luther smiled back. "I did what I would hope anyone would." He thought perhaps she might have trouble accepting help from others, especially after she had been treated recently by those of his own gender. "Yes, perhaps you could, I guess I just hastened you to safety, nothing more." She gave him a knowing look.

"So, Luther," she said. "Where are you headed to?"

"I am headed to Bramstone, on a personal matter," Luther replied. "You remember my name from when we met on the road I see."

"Yes," she said, "Louise used your name several times, so I couldn't forget anyway."

"Oh, right," Luther said. "Could I be so bold as to ask you yours?" He briefly looked away from her, aware that perhaps she might not wish to divulge much of her person.

"Magena," she said, meeting his eyes with hers as he looked back to her.

"Well, good to meet you Magena. I won't push any further regarding your business. I wished only to know your name." He gave a small smile and clasped his hands together in a nervous manner.

There was a pause for a moment. Luther felt as though she waited for him to speak again and so he ventured forth, "Right, well," looking down and around him, not quite sure where to rest his gaze. "I had better head of to the constabulary office. The sergeant wished to see me before I set off."

"About that," she said. Again, they looked at each other.

"Yes?" he replied.

"I will not be said to have left you bereft of knowledge of my captors. I will tell the officers in good time so worry not about speaking yourself. There was at least ten of them. All male, except two women. They wore no uniforms or unifying colours. Vagabonds and bandits, nothing more." She gave steely eyes to Luther as if she lamented greatly that she was ever accosted by such people.

"And why did they capture you. If you don't mind me asking?" said Luther.

"They know of my standing and would most likely wish to ransom me."

"Ok," said Luther. He didn't wish to pry too much and was content to hear anything she wished to say freely. "I will make sure to keep my eyes open for them." he said.

"Yes, you should," she said. "They caught me unawares and you they might do you too. I would make to break from the forest in one day; no need to linger should they still be at large. Their Leader, be weary. He had long ginger hair and a scraggly beard. Fierce, but not altogether stupid he is. I would feign ignorance of any knowledge of me should you find yourself confronted."

He nodded his head and said, "Ok, yes. I guess that is probably the best thing to do. Well, thank you for the information, I will do my best to avoid them and see about taking leave of the forest quickly. I guess I had better be off. I am glad to see you safe and sound here and I wish you a full recovery."

He smiled and before turning away she said, "Thanks. Goodbye."

Luther turned and slipped through the doorway with his pack on his back, out into the bar area. After saying goodbye to Graham and Louise, he exited the tavern and crossed the road to the Constabulary office.

As he crossed the road that ran from whence he came the night before, though this place and back into the forest beyond, he looked both left and then right for traffic. As his eyes left the view to his left, something poked his attention. He thought he saw some small little object, on the edge of his vision, leading south-west out of the outpost. He quickly swung his head back to his left to see what it was but couldn't see anything other than the buildings around him and the path leading out. He wondered what it was. Was it the black little critter that he had not seen since that night, two nights ago in the forest with Agatha? Was it back again to test his sanity or was it merely some trick of the mind? He looked around him, searching dearly for any sign of the little thing, but also anything else that he might have mistaken for the small creature. He could make out neither.

What did this mean if anything at all?' He wondered to himself. Was this little critter back again to confuse and confound him? To make him wonder if he was slipping into a madness or was it just simply a trick of the light of day and the shadows it created? He shivered in worry. He had been so caught up in the events of the day before that he had all but forgotten the little mite that happened upon him at the most random of times.

Well, he thought. I can't see it anywhere now. I will just have to accept it must have been simply a figment of my imagination. He crossed the road and proceeded to knock on the door of the constabulary office. The hatch slid open and upon seeing that it was Luther, the door was opened, and he was ushered inside.

Luther was greeted by officer Gibbins, who had unlocked the door. He looked around the office but saw that the chair behind the desk was currently empty.

"Is the sergeant here?" enquired Luther.

"Yes, he is. Just upstairs at the moment, talking with the inspector."

"Oh, right I see," said Luther. "Shall I take a seat?" he asked.

"Yes, if you could sir," replied officer Gibbins, who then went and sat down behind the small table to Luther's left. Evidently, he was in the midst of another game of solitaire as the cards were again laid out on the table in front of him.

Luther sat down in one of the central chairs facing the

desk and placed his pack in one beside him. He looked over to officer Gibbins who seemed immersed in his card game.

"Playing a little Solitaire?" Luther said, enquiringly.

The officer looked over to Luther with a relaxed look and replied, "Yes sir. Feeling good about this one."

"Played a little myself everyone once in a while. Good luck with it," Luther responded.

The officer nodded and turned back to it

Luther turned his gaze back to the vacant chair, awaiting the sergeant to appear from somewhere up in the tower.

After several minutes Luther could hear two muffled voices coming from the direction of the stairway behind the desk in front of him. One was of a human male who he assumed to be sergeant Burrow and another, perhaps female voice too, which he hadn't heard before. He assumed this to be the voice of the inspector who the sergeant was conversing with.

Two figures eventually emerged from the staircase and into the room: sergeant Burrow himself, who was still exchanging words with another person in similar uniform and an elven woman, wearing similar garb to the sergeant and officer Gibbins. Her studded jacket, rather than simply being dark brown and laced with studs, had some additional flourish of silver patterns embroidered into it. She too had a silver broach with the initials V.C. upon them, but again with additional detail. These extra ostentations no doubt signalled her station as the inspector of this constabulary office, Luther thought.

She was just slightly shorter than the sergeant and had light brown hair tied back under a cap, similar to those of her officers, but again with additional little highlights upon it - in keeping with the rest of her uniform.

As they entered the room the Inspector looked up and towards Luther. Officer Gibbins stood and turned towards them. Both the inspector and the sergeant walked around the desk and towards the chair in which Luther was sitting. This caused Luther himself to stand up as well; ready to greet them as they approached.

"Hello, Luther, is it?" said the inspector as they came near.

"Hello, yes I am Luther, good to meet you," he replied.

"Indeed sir. I am Inspector Faithworthy. I understand you have met sergeant Burrow and some of my other officers already."

"Yes, I have," he replied, courteously.

"Good, good. Now, with regards to Magena Strewth, did you know she was the daughter a powerful druid of the forest?"

Luther looked up at her with a curious look. "No, I didn't. I knew and still know next to nothing about her other than her first name being Magena - which I only discovered minutes ago when I bid her farewell."

"I see," she said in a similar manner to sergeant Burrow. "Well done for bringing her here. The last thing we need is an arch-druid rampaging the forest in search of her daughter. You did well in this. I will send word to the inner forest that we have found her. Sergeant Burrow tells me you are headed to Bramstone. You should be there soon enough. Good luck with the rest of your journey sir. Now if you will excuse me, I have other matters to attend to." With that she turned to the sergeant and nodded, who responded with the words "ma'am" followed by Gibbins in turn.

"Right Mr Dothmeer," said sergeant Burrow. "You are free to be on your way. We have all that we need from you unless there is anything you wish to add? She is in good care now and we will have her reunited with her mother as soon as soon as she is recovered."

"Ok, right well, thank you sergeant. I have nothing additional to add to my statement no. I will head off then. Is my horse all, ok?" he asked.

"Yes, she is ready to go. She was fed and watered this morning already." The sergeant reached out his right hand towards Luther who reached out his and shook. "Fare well sir."

"Fare well sergeant," said Luther. "Goodbye officer," he said, looking over to officer Gibbins who gave a nod. Luther picked up his pack and walked over to the door and let himself out.

Once outside, he walked round to the back of the guardhouse and into the small stables where Guinevere was being kept. He found her in the same stable as the night before, just finishing something to eat from a metal bucket on the floor.

Olive the stable master was busy brushing one of the other horses in the stables and when she saw Luther enter, gave him a wave with brush in hand. "Hello again Luther. Come to get your Gwen?" she said.

"Yes," said Luther. "How is she doing?"

"She is doing well. Doing well," said Olive "She is just finishing eating then feel free to take her as you will."

Luther walked to the door of the stable currently housing Guinevere and looked over her. He could see that she was about to finish her food. He opened the door and entered. She already had her saddle on. He gave her shoulders a pat and said hello to her. He then attached his pack to her saddle bags.

By the time he was done, she had finished and raised her head up and around slightly to look at him. He gave her a stroke on her black neck and then led her out of the stable.

"Thank you very much for looking after her, Olive. She seems very happy," he said turning to face her from the edge of the stable shed.

She looked over to him and said, "No problem Luther. Good luck on your journey!" She then turned back to the horse she was brushing.

Luther - once he had Guinevere clear of the stables - pulled himself up onto her saddle and they set out on the road away from Forestead.

Chapter 18

Luther wished to gain as much ground as he could on his destination this day, so he encouraged Guinevere to a sprightly canter on their exit from the outpost. Before long it had shrunk from view in the rear distance behind them and they found themselves once again under the darkened light of the underbrush of the Dell Wood Forest. The trees crept back around and above him as he re-entered the sway of the woodland, reducing the light from the sun above to the dim and darkened hue that they had been used to the days previous.

He travelled for at least an hour before encountering another soul upon the road; two figures on horse-back coming up from the horizon as the road kept to as straight a line as it could. As they came closer Luther saw they appeared to be in some sort of uniform, and he could make out a stick like appendage protruding from each of their waists; a sword sheathed and hanging at the ready no doubt.

They came closer and closer before Luther could make out what they were wearing in a clearer manner. It was same uniform as the officers of the constabulary from the outpost of which he had just came from.

They must be outriders, he thought to himself. He wondered if they had been dispatched from the station in search of any clues or information regarding the hooded lady's abduction. After momentarily pondering this thought he then wondered why they would have come from this direction and not from the east path out of town on which he had discovered the lady at the side of the road. They must simply be out on patrol, he thought. Within several minutes he had met up with the two officers, all three sat astride their horses.

"Hello there," said Luther to the two gentlemen, hoping for a cordial conversation with the officers. He didn't recognise either of them from the guard house. He wondered perhaps if they were asleep in the bunkhouse or otherwise preoccupied for him to have seen them. He even wondered if perhaps they had started off from some other town. Perhaps where he was headed. He would endeavour to find out if he could without prying too much into the business. Both of them appeared to be human: one male and one female. Both wore those familiar studded jackets and leather caps with green cloaks and silver broaches upon their chests of the uniform of Valeworn

"Good morning sir," said the female officer to Luther's right. "Heading out from the Forestead sir?"

Luther looked across to her and replied: "Yes indeed I come from there not too long ago." His hands clasped somewhat together with a nervousness. He was always anxious of meeting new people, and he had done a lot of that in the last few days. He also felt slight unease as he didn't recognise either officer. He doubted these were imposters; the bandits that had kidnapped Magena masquerading as officers of the law. He took in a deep breath.

"Right sir. You must be Mr Dothmeer?" This caught Luther somewhat off guard, but also disarming his worry somewhat as no bandits impersonating a member of the local police force was going to know he would be travelling the road at this time and importantly, what his name was.

"Yes, that's me," he said tentatively. "I am on my way to Bramstone. I was hoping to make good progress today and leave the Dell Wood."

"If you kick up a good canter sir, you should make clear of the forest by late afternoon. Just be careful on your way. As you are well aware there are bandits and other unfriendly things that can wander these woods," said the male officer to the Luther's left.

"Yes indeed," said Luther. "So, you yourselves started off from Forestead today? I was wondering if you had come from Bramstone and might tell me of how far from the forests edge it was."

"We started out at dawn this morning, on patrol, but with an eye for clues on the whereabouts of those hoodlums that kidnapped the lady you brought in last night. We came up out through the forest, but to no avail," the male officer replied.

"Ah, right. I was wondering that," Luther replied. "I

don't know these woods at all and most likely would get lost if I strayed off the track."

"That you would," said the female officer. "You can easily find yourself stuck with no idea where you are if you don't know the paths well."

"Or even find yourself in front a beastie that isn't particularly happy to make your acquaintance," broached the other.

Luther gave a smile and thought of Agatha and how he stumbled into her literal clutches.

"Yes, I can imagine," he said in response. He thanked them for the advice, followed by a goodbye and a nod from them both, before bringing Guinevere back up to a brisk walk.

They had been making good time and it was not before the mid-afternoon before Luther found cause to pull up Guinevere by the side of the road. He spied a trough of water next to what looked like a small sign post a hundred yards up ahead, so he gently slowed Guinevere before they slowly walked up to it. It was a long steel trough filled with water in front of a wooden post with two signs on it; one facing south-west, reading: 'Bramstone' and one facing north-east with the words: 'Forestead Village', written in black paint. Luther was glad he was on the right track to Bramstone, though he was quite sure it was difficult not to be, at this point as there was just one road leading out of the village and he hadn't come across any crossing since he had left.

Guinevere headed to the water trough and upon arriving, Luther dismounted to stretch his legs while he let her take a brief rest and drink. He raised his arms above him diagonally and gave a low yawning noise as he stretched himself out. Beyond that ever-present melancholy that seemed never to fully release him from its grip, he was feeling relaxed and content enough with his own existence. For now, at least.

This in itself to him was a cause of anxiety and worry. Feeling close to that elusive happiness or joy could also instil a sense of foreboding within his soul. He would often think of how great feelings of happiness or a stolen glimpse at gaiety meant he was due the touch of a more extreme sadness and depression; a price must be paid for the luxury of experiencing a modicum of mirth or happiness. And the scales, they were scales that had been rigged by some hitherto force in the favour of those of misery; even when idle and at rest they didn't sit evenly, but with a great strain to the side of anguish.

I must take care, he thought, suddenly. He looked all around him, aware of his vulnerable position.

There are bandits and vagabonds abroad with a mind to do harm should they be suspicious of me helping that woman by the side of road or simply because they felt like it, he said to himself. All seemed quite quiet though; the usual ambient sounds of the forest were present, but no sound that might fill him with alarm was piercing the air. The road was empty in both directions, and he stood alone at the crossing, with no-one else within sight. With no obvious sense of danger, he decided to let Guinevere take a good gulp at the water trough while he sat down on the grass by the wayside of the road, with legs stretched out, thinking to himself.

Once she no longer seemed interested in the water trough, Luther stood up and climbed back onto Guinevere's saddle. He leaned down from his sitting position and gave her a pat on the left side of her neck. "Good girl, Gwen, I hope you had a nice drink there," he said to her. He then turned her back towards the road heading south-west and they were once again back on the road leading through the Dell Wood Forest.

He saw several more travellers on the road at this time, including a merchant caravan of several carts pulled up from a crossroads from the south. They ventured across the road, heading on a northern route through the forest as Luther pulled Guinevere to a halt. This crossroads was similar to the previous with a bemusing yet insightful number of road signs along with a small water trough - Guinevere didn't seem too interested in it this time having already had her fill previously.

The carts and coaches of the caravan numbered four in total of each and were laden with crates of goods and manned by several people each: some sitting at the coachman's position, some on top, looking all around and some sitting at the rear - their view of whence they came. These people were mostly elven men and women dressed in earthly coloured tunics and trousers with capes swept round them and firm boots upon their feet. Among their number was a couple of flarfen folk; a pair sitting together at the front of a cart; one male and one female. They were dressed in the same dark earthly colours as their companions.

As they all crossed in front of him, seeing him standing there, they each in turn gave a nod or a gingerly wave in his direction with the male Flarfen tipping the flat cap on his brow upon spying Luther at the roadside, waiting for them to pass. Luther returned in kind; giving a nod as the convoy of carts crossed his path while accompanying it with a smile as best, he could. After they had passed by, Luther prompted Guinevere to carry on to their own.

Several hours pressed through with passing just a few more travellers on the road while the dim light of the Dell Wood pressed in around him with passing every hour of the day. Luther supposed that he must be getting close to the edge of the forest by now as he had willed Guinevere on with expediency. They had kept this way for those last several hours while making good ground, he thought, as the endless trees on either side of them swept past faster than ever.

His mind had become a wonder of thoughts of his destination again: would there be signs of Celeste Ignophenen at Bramstone? Perhaps she was still there? Would she see him if she was? The thought of the hooded woman, Magena Strewth, how was she doing? Would her mother come soon to claim her? Would she seek vengeance on those who had harmed her daughter? What was she even like, this Arch Druid? Luther had never met a druid, let alone one of such a high position. He had heard of them of course, casters of the woods, adept at natural magics. Far less concerned with the crowds of others in their brick houses and their streetlights and more interested in the mystical and primal ways of the world.

His thoughts had wandered off, with only a vague thread of the road amongst the tapestries of musings and ideas, clambering for his attention. That thought of the track ahead and what may lay upon it had become a lesser priority for the whirring cogs in his overly ponderous mind. He had become too engrossed in the mix of worry and speculation, too concerned with what might yet be, to focus on the movements and scenery of what was occurring in the here and now.

Surely, he would find this woman that he sought, he wondered to himself. It may only be a simple task of enquiry once he had reached the town of Bramstone and then following the directions to her location. But this line of thought, of wishful thinking, of optimism in an outcome so splendidly in his favour, would only lead to his downfall, he thought. His luck and perhaps more vitally, what he deserved, was not to find her so easily with so little paid in return. Why should he be so bold and so flagrant in his wish of good things to come? He shouldn't attempt to upset that languid and utterly skewed balance of hope. He would be made to pay for it, was that final thought in his mind.

Chapter 19

An abrupt and sudden stop. Guinevere had pulled up by herself and in doing so, jerked Luther back into focus on the close surroundings, away from his incessant worry. Suddenly pulled back into the present, he held to her reigns and looked to the road in front of them to see the cause of her abrupt standstill.

Standing in the road were several humans in dirty looking clothes, not lately washed, with mean looks in their eyes, all staring up at Luther. There looked to be roughly a dozen of them, mostly men, but there were two women amongst their number that Luther could make out. All present had unkempt, long hair of different shades of brown and dirty blonde, wearing various coloured hoods, atop dark leather, beaten breastplates and boots and trousers, covered in old mud. Each carried a weapon of some kind: a spear in several hands, short swords, clubs and several different sized shields were spread amongst them, all unsheathed and menacing,

At the front and to Luther's left - roughly eleven 'o clock on the face of one - was a man that stuck out from the rest. He had long ginger hair and a scraggly beard. He wore a dark brown leather chest plate with brass studding along the front with a black cloak draped around his shoulders and held too by a brass broach. Unlike the others in his retinue, his weapon was not in hand; remaining quiet in its sheath, hanging from his belt that was tied in a knot at the front. His trousers and boots of similar hue and material of his fellows was not as dirty and ragged as those around which helped to single him out from them. Luther knew then that this man was their leader, and this man was almost certainly he whom Magena had escaped from.

Luther's hand instinctively went to his side, to the hand axe in its sheath, but quickly thought the better of it. He couldn't possibly overcome all these people and threatening them was almost certainly out of the question if he wanted to

come away from this with his life.
　　　He would have begun berating himself for failing to see these people standing in the road or waiting close by eliminating any chance of simple escape, had it not been for the leader and addressing him.
　　　"So," said the man staring up at Luther. "A traveller out on the road in the forest. Making quite the pace as well hey. I wonder why someone would be anxious to leave the Dell Wood on such a lovely day as this." He flashed a grin at the men around him and all in unison their black and beaten teeth glinted from their sinister smiles.
　　　Luther thought of making a break for it; quickly kicking Guinevere into action and bolting through them, catching them unawares. Could he clear them and make an escape, he wondered? They had no horses, but he might be skewered from his saddle by an errant spear as he flew past them. He decided that the best course of action was to attempt to somehow talk himself out of this situation.
　　　"Hello there," Luther said. "I have quite urgent business in Bramstone and wish to break the forest by nightfall if I can. What can I help you with?" He kept eye contact with the leader of this group through most of this, but with those final words his gaze swept across the group surrounding him, as he held his nerve.
　　　"Yes?" said the man with long ginger hair, his right hand perched on the hilt of his sword. "You wouldn't be making a quick run for it for other reasons? Such as a roving band of scallywags, at large in the woods?" He gave another generous grin to those around him. A woman stood behind gave a quiet chuckle which seemed to please him.
　　　"I know inhabitants of the Dell Wood are not to be underestimated but, I am simply in a hurry to make my destination. Are you looking for someone?" Luther tried to make these words seem as genuine as he could. Hopefully, they would buy his naivety and allow him to pass. He thought they may not wish to bring further attention to themselves by attacking another person out on the open forest road.
　　　"You could say we are looking for someone, yeah," said the man with the scraggly beard. "One of our own, yeah.

She turned on us in the night and now we looking to get her back. Haven't seen a woman in a hood out on the road have you by any chance?" He gave yet another smile and then looked on at Luther fixatedly; eager to hear and judge the content of his reply.

"No," said Luther. "I haven't seen anyone of that description out on the roadside. Were they on horseback or on foot?" Luther hoped to fan the flames of ignorance and did not want to be caught knowing she had no horse or other form of transport with her. "I have seen others of course, on the road. Travellers such as myself, but no-one by themselves which you say they were?" He tried to keep his voice firm but was quite anxious in this situation. He was fearing the worst but was determined to try and keep calm and carry this through.

"She was all alone," came the response from the man who spoke for and must be leading this group, Luther thought. "She didn't have a horse neither. On the other side of the Village back there." He pointed in the direction of which Luther had come, towards the village of Forestead. "She was most likely on the road east of the village, so if you were travelling the day before you might have seen her. I bet she had gotten to the road by then. She hurt herself you see. Fell over." He looked again at those around him with a sly smile. "She was probably in some pain." The words sneered from his mouth with a sense of satisfaction that if Luther had not known for sure she hadn't met with a fall, then he would surely have guessed as so.

Luther, holding his anger in check at the man, shook his head and said "No, sorry. I haven't seen anyone like that. I imagine I would recall seeing a lonely figure, travelling the road, wounded. I can't help you with that." He looked around at the gathering of people, looking for a sympathetic face amongst them, but all he could see were grins and prying eyes staring back at him.

"That is a shame," said the man. "A shame you didn't see her and a shame that if you did you don't want to tell us."

Luther looked him in the eyes. "I have no reason to lie because I haven't seen anyone as you describe. Now if you will stand aside, I need to continue with my journey." He gripped

Guinevere's reins and made to pull away, but the gang of people standing in the road stood firm raising their weapons up in defiance.

"You see, you might not have seen her, but you have seen us, and we have seen you. There is a price to be paid for that." The others around him moved in to form a more tightly knit wall of bodies around Guinevere. If Luther tried to make a break for it, he would no doubt be removed from the saddle by those spears or Guinevere's legs cut to shreds as they made a break for it. It didn't seem to Luther that he was going to get out of this without a scratch.

The man with the scraggy beard, pulled the sword from its sheath with his left hand and pointed it directly at Luther.

"Now if you please, come down from this fine horse of yours so you can address us proper." Luther knew by doing so, he would be in even more danger than he already was. The exact people he had hoped to miss while on his travels in the woods, now had him surrounded. "You don't want to keep me waiting," said their leader. Luther, with little other option, accepted the situation and dismounted from Guinevere.

"That's better," said their leader, now with his sword pointing directly at Luther's chest. "There's a price to be paid for seeing our faces. What have you got that will cover your tab?"

Knowing full well that that he was being robbed Luther felt the need to stall for time not for any reason other than to delay the inevitable violence that was lingering over him. "I am sorry, but I have nothing I can give you. I travel alone and have nothing of great value to others. All I have is that which I need for this journey."

The ginger haired man looked him up and down and just then one of the women at the back of the group holding a spear said, "I bet he has some gold on 'im boss. No-one travels without something in their pockets!"

The leader of the bandits paused while he heard these words and said to Luther, "My compatriot here says wise words indeed. You don't have but a few coins to cover the cost of passing through my forest?"

A GRIM JOURNEY

Luther knew he would have to give something to these people that had confronted him, but if he reached for his pouch of gold pieces, he would likely never see it again.

"As I said, I have only a few gold as needed for my travels. If I give you any, I will have nothing left."

The sword pointed at him was now pressed up against his ribs. "I'll make this simple," said the man with the scraggy beard. "You give us all you have, or you will never make it out of the forest." He gave yet another grin which was followed by another round of snickers and dark grins

"I see," said Luther as he reached into his pack and managed to pull enough coins from his pouch without pulling it out itself. "Here, this is nearly all I have." He handed over several gold and silver pieces.

"Just enough for your travels, heh?" said the scraggy bearded man. "Looks like quite a bit more than just that. I don't like people lying to me." He drew back his sword and replaced it with a stiff right-handed blow from the pommel to Luther's chest.

Half expecting some sort of violent response, Luther was somewhat ready for a strike heading his way, but still wasn't prepared for the ferocity of the thump which caused him to sink to his knees from the impact. He winced in pain and struggled for breath. A part of him wanted to lash out at this man, but this would no doubt lead to his fellows piling in. He knew full well he had little to no chance against this gang when stood up straight and uninjured, so making any attempt to take these people on from a position of such weakness would be tantamount to suicide.

The bandit leader placed his hand into the pack where Luther had reached just moments before and pulled out the pouch of coins. "Yes indeed, much more than expected." Two of his men then grabbed Luther by either arm and pulled him up to his feet. The scraggy bearded man then turned back to him. "So, still not seen that good for nothing woman? Don't lie to me again!"

Luther looked up at the man, still feeling the effects of the blow to his stomach. "I have not seen them," he replied.

"Well," said their leader. "Don't let them say we don't

take nothing for nothing." And with that he hit Luther with a right cross punch across his right side of his head. This bloodied Luther's nose and lip and set the scene for some large bruising. Luther let out a groan as the blow landed but was still filled with some desire to strike out at the man, but that was shortly dissolved by a blow from the other side by one of the men holding him, at the direction of the scraggy bearded man. They let go of Luther and he fell again to his knees with blood coming from his nose and a cut on his cheek. He began coughing, spitting up some blood as he did so.

     The leader of the bandits then said "Perhaps you don't know anything. Thanks for the coin, will serve us nicely." He walked to Guinevere's rear and slapped her rightly accompanied by "Yaah!" which sent a fright, causing her to bolt off into the woodland north of the road. With a smile on the face of the scraggy bearded man, he motioned to the members of his entourage, and they all walked away laughing, down the road in the direction of the village, leaving Luther crouched over in pain with Guinevere nowhere to be seen. As they walked past him several snickered and muttered things under their breaths. Luther couldn't make out much with the pain surging through him but caught the words of one mentioning how lucky he was to get away with just a beating, which was then followed by a stiff boot to Luther's side, knocking him over to his left.

     After several minutes, the group of bandits were beginning to disappear over the horizon; mingling in with the ever-present columns of the earth as they stood on either side of the road. Luther lay there on his side, his face bleeding and his midriff racked in pain.

     All he could think of was how stupid he had been to have not seen them out on the road. How moronic he was to have walked right into an ambush.

     It was no ambush at all, he thought to himself. You are just a fool, who blindly blundered into the arms of rogues. You only have yourself to blame for the situation you find yourself in. He berated himself for not seeing them earlier, for not spying this group of people clearly standing out in the road. He spat out some more blood onto the ground. This was certainly a rebalancing of things for his earlier, more positive attitude.

Laying there, battered and bruised, dismayed at his own stupidity, he wondered what he was to do. All his money had been taken. He had no means to pay for anything. He was injured and on foot, stranded almost. Had Guinevere still been at his side, he thought, perhaps he may have been able to pull himself up onto her and made as best he could for Bramstone. But where was she now, he wondered? Had she darted off through the woods, never to be seen by him again? Was she scared and alone in the forest somewhere, unsure herself what to do?

Sorry Guinevere, he thought. I am sorry I lead us into that avoidable situation. I am sorry you are now alone, much as I am now.

He rested his head down on the road and stared outwards across to the south wood, cursing himself and wallowing in sadness. He could see the columns standing there, stretching out. He wondered what they made of the events unfolding in front of them. Did they take pity, he wondered, or were they indifferent to his situation; not concerned with the trials of a mortal man, on the road through their forest, especially not one as stupid and hopeless as he.

He stared past them, and past those past them and on into the gloom and darkness of the inner wood. He lost himself in his own misery and as before that gang of criminals, he lost himself to his thoughts, barely taking notice around him. Glad to do so.

There was simply darkness and incomprehensible shadows that played at the edge of his line of sight as it traced through the forest. He spat out another mouthful of blood, feeling the crimson in his mouth. He looked out at the shadows and darkness and stared there for eternity. He didn't wish to return to the present, to take in the events as they had happened. His only desire was to forget his pain and stare, becoming lost in blackness.

The darkness he could see was all a gloom of nothing. There was just a sea of black, unwavering. No comprehensible shapes within, flitting out from his view. He closed his eyes and felt a judder of pain in his face and chest as he did so. Now all was completely dark, but with the echoes of shapes in his vision and the sadness in his heart. Nothing of them seemed a likeness of anything, rather arbitrary curves and clumps swimming in his mind, all he could see. Time seemed to stand still but exist in the eternity as he stared out with eyes closed. A formless shape here a passing outline there; his attention fleeting and non-committal. The shapes of anything, but nothing and nothing of worth – just like him.

But, then there was a shape in the darkness. A familiar shape. A shape that was small and round and dark. Luther lingered his attention upon it, for he felt acquainted with its form and feeling. A little circular, spherical ball of fur. A ball of nothing but blackness. His focus was now squarely fixated on it as it washed around his closed eyes. He knew of this creature. He had encountered it before he thought. The lament in his mind and gloom within him observed the creature and wondered what it was and why it was so familiar.

He opened his eyes. The haze of misery and oblivion somewhat subsided for now. The formless shapes had dispersed. But that which he had seen with his eyes firmly shut had not disappeared once opened. It had stayed resolute and refused to leave with the other dark things, for what reason he couldn't give.

Chapter 20

So, there it is again, he said to himself, still lying on his side, still aching from the blows he received, but lit with curiosity of the thing in front of him. When he had seen this dark mass before, he had been met with copious anxiety, but also a calm and relaxed demeanour; two quite opposing forces swirling up within him. This time he didn't feel anxious. Perhaps, he thought, he was too battered and bruised for any anxiety to well up and wash over him - as was usually the case. All he felt now was relaxed and unstrained. Not stressed. Not by that creature which he saw, at least. A sedate and composed feeling overcame him to a muddied background of aching pain.

He stared at this little creature. Just as those times he had seen it before, it was a little ball with no apparent arms, legs head or any other kind of appendages; simply a round critter of jet-black fur that both confused Luther and filled him with an easiness.

How did it get here he thought to himself? And if there is an answer to that then where did it come from?

He wondered if it somehow followed him and kept itself hidden all this time. Perhaps, he thought, perhaps it was hidden in plain sight, in the recesses of his mind; brought forth by great strain on his mind and body when he had little energy left to fortify his own sanity. Whatever the reason, whether conjured from his mind or simply an inquisitive little fellow that liked to follow him around, it was back again and standing or sitting, he thought, right in front of him as he lay slumped and injured upon the ground.

He had little energy for much else other than to stare at the strange furry creature. With eyes still glaring at it and with what energy he did have he moved his right hand up to his face and felt the beginnings of a swelling. Their strikes had hit him hard and although he had mostly expected a violent outcome, it did little to temper the force of the hits from the bandits as they struck him.

He again wondered how the little critter, stationary and maybe calm, he thought, managed to do anything without any obvious way in which to interact with the world around it, other – of course - than simply rolling around. Perhaps it simply didn't require those obvious and simple things which one would expect from any inhabitant of this world. Was it facing him, he wondered? Was it staring at him as intently as he was at it? Was it even aware of this bruised and beaten man of misery, lying there as he was or was it oblivious to his very existence?

As another wave of pain swept over the muscles in his face and chest, he thought perhaps the small creeper in front of him must know something of him. It must be conscious of him; otherwise, why would it continue to show up nearby at the strangest of times? It had appeared too often now for it to be a mere coincidence. And if this was the case that it indeed mean to appear by Luther, that it was somehow planned, it did little to explain whether it existed in just his mind or was some creature of the world that was heretofore unknown, until now.

Luther thought it could literally keep appearing because he had willed it into a being through strain and stress upon his soul; conjured into existence just as his mind was at its most vulnerable. It could be some strange and magical beastie that had shown some interest in Luther for whatever reason and now chose to appear before him at seemingly random points in his life.

It might not, he thought, be the same creature; perhaps there were numerous numbers of these little things. For surely if one exists, there must be more. This small, round creeper must have come from something, and conventional wisdom would suggest that this thing, if it was indeed a product of the natural world, must have been birthed or spawned from some parent, nurturing or not. He wondered again on the probability of that being true and then his brain came upon the thought of how long he had been laying here staring at this little critter, ignoring the immediate situation he was in.

He began to wonder what was to happen now, but before he could begin to explore the idea the small circular lump of fur, clad in blackest night, began to move. It slowly rolled in that way in which Luther had seen it do before; all of its own volition with no obvious means of propulsion; no kick-off from some unseen limb or flap of a wing or some contortion of the body; it simply set out rolling. And it rolled gently across Luther's path. Across the road to the edge of the trees north of it, before suddenly coming to a stop. Luther wondered if it paused there for a reason of its own or whether it waited for Luther to acknowledge it, as if it was aware in any way of his presence and wished for him to follow.

He laid there, still on his side, in bitter pain with his neck stretched upwards; eyes firmly pressed on the strange being that had yet again appeared in life.

Where is it going, he wondered? Is it waiting for me to follow?

Something, somewhere in him, a melding of curiosity and preservation urged him to press the muscles in his body into movement and make his own way after it, wherever it was heading.

With eyes still perched on the creature, he rolled onto his front while reaching out his right arm onto the ground. He let out a silent wail of pain. He was now facing forwards and towards the thing, his arm forming a triangle with his angled shoulder line. He spat out some more blood and pushed up his left arm, so he was now in a kneeling position, all the while looking at the small black furred creature in front of him, at the edge of the road.

Luther now on his knees with his hands on the rough track that travelled the forest, let out several audible coughs. He was in a lot of pain from the blows to his head and chest, but his desire to follow the round and black-haired beast - as he had done before - was enough to ignore it, for now.

Luther rasped for breath, prolonged for an age with each breath-taking great strain upon his chest. His exhales seemed to time with the waves of pain from his injuries like bitter waves upon a beaten shore.

He moved into a slow crawl across the road in roughly the same line as the creature had taken. After several pauses, taking in deep breaths, he had crawled to where it was currently standing or sitting - he was never sure. When he had reached that far, the creature began to slowly roll once again, this time at no great pace, as if it were aware of the speed in which its follower was able to handle. Luther imagined this could be the case or simply it had paused for its own reasons, with nothing other than coincidence to explain it.

It rolled over from the road and into the greenery before the columns that lay beyond. Luther followed after as best he could. This surreal moment in which he crawled after this odd little thing was an escape from the broiling of anxiety and worry in his maddening mind. It pushed back the thoughts and the acknowledgement of the situation; he didn't have to concern himself with acceptance of losing both his horse, his health and all of his money. He would focus purely on the task at hand; only on following the furry critter that had once again rolled into his life. He would see if it led him somewhere of intrigue - as it had before - or if only to his doom and oblivion. He wouldn't mind either.

Luther kept crawling across the green edge before the tree line north of the road and continued into the forest. Once again, he was beholden to a black little creature of ambiguity and mystery whom he had no idea even existed in the real world or simply conjured through the gaps in his troubled mind. The columns of the earth rose up either side of him as he came about them: there were great ferns and oaks, wide and strong as they raised themselves up to the sky above with gatherings of smaller plants sitting between them. Luther took no notice of any of them, for he had little enough energy just to pull himself along the forest floor to have any left to take in his other surroundings. All that was in him was concerned with keeping up with the odd little creature that was once again leading him on some unknown trail through the forest to some unknown destination, if there was one at all.

His main view was of the creature he was following, with little care for what laid ahead of it. All he could manage between coughs and the occasional wipe of his face - whose cuts were beginning to clot - was the area in and around that of which he pursued, a narrowed and singular vision. Had there been any other living being in close proximity, he would not have realised its existence and cared not for it regardless even if he did. For all his interest was placed on that which was leading him, whether it was aware of it or not.

He dragged himself through the undergrowth made up of dead leaves, dead wood and muddy soil which was covering his hands and knees as he placed and moved them across the ground. Normally he wouldn't be completely happy to dirty himself so much by crawling on the carpet beneath these old columns, but he really no longer cared. He was already battered and bruised with stains of blood upon his shirt and cardigan. His trousers were dark and therefore didn't show up much dirt leaving little to worry of even if he was inclined to.

There isn't much lower I can be, he thought to himself, so getting mud and dirt all over himself was not worthy of consideration.

He had crawled, while the creature had rolled, roughly two hundred yards into the forest before the gloom began to really set in around them. There was even less light coming through into the forest proper; away from the gap in the tree line created by the road leading through it. There was the smallest of glows to be had from the sun above, but it was less constant and missed several features of the forest floor as the great columns stretched out their arms to reach one another, high above in the canopy of the wood.

Luther, still in a daze, again took little notice of the gradual dimming of light around him; still with a focus squarely on the little creature as it passed through the Dell Wood; all other things irrelevant and meaningless.

Further they went. Further into the forest. Further away from where he was punched and kicked to the ground in smarting pain. Luther's eyes were firmly set on the critter in front of him. This strange little thing with nothing to belie the features of its being. Just a ball of striking black fur that rolled on through the forest. He was so indeed focused on his pursuit of the creature that he failed to notice a few subtle things such as the fact that this critter, perhaps slightly bigger than a football appeared to not attract any dirt or detritus from the forest floor. Luther, conversely, was getting dirty from the ground, but the creature itself was completely clean. Each time it completed a revolution of its round body, driving through the forest, no mud, dead leaves, twigs, or other bits of the woodland carpet seemed to stick to it. All its fur was spotless, as if it were bathed in some protective coating that repelled anything that wished to cling to it. It was as though the world around it had no impact on the state of the thing. In fact, if Luther had been interested in looking so, he would have noticed that the hair itself wasn't becoming flattened or squashed so the beastie's body rolled over it. It was a most peculiar thing and not how something should behave in the natural world, unless of course this was simply a figment of his imagination.

Luther cared not at this time to question the reality of this entity and thought only of following it across the forest floor. It gave him a straight and simple purpose which is all he wanted. He didn't wish to think of how unfortunate his situation had become. He wanted to ignore the fact he was battered and bruised, without any coin to pay his way and most sadly, the loss of his horse Guinevere. All that mattered now was to follow the creature and to come what may.

They travelled even further into the wood, half a mile from the roadside. With Luther still travelling on his hands and knees, suffering from cuts and bruises that stayed his hands sometimes due to a sting of throbbing reality, meant this had taken some time and the day had shifted by several hour. He had to stop several times to catch his breath and feel the tenderness of his face before continuing after the small creature. Oddly enough the thing itself was somehow aware when he did so. It would move out several yards from where he had stopped and wait patiently for him to continue. It was though it wished for him to follow it, that there was purpose for him to be doing so. At the very least it was not afraid or concerned with his pursuit of it and seemed content enough to let him follow.

The rolling ball of fur absent of the mark of the undergrowth appeared to be taking a course through it that afforded Luther the most amount of room to crawl. Instead of passing easily between the gaps in a bush that lay in the middle of line they were treading, it paused and then rolled sideways around it before carrying on past where there was ample room for Luther to follow unmolested.

And then it suddenly came to a stop. Not to wait for Luther this time - who was still in tow, not to change direction having come to some obstacle in their way, but for some other, different reason it would seem. It appeared it had come across some creature in the woods, standing directly in front of them. Luther looked on at the little ball of fur that had come to a halt and recovered somewhat from the malaise that had overcome him on his travel across the forest floor. The sound of breathing came to him, heavy breathing in fact, he thought. Not from himself, though he was suddenly more aware of his own course and rough inhalation of breath, but some other creature entirely. He looked at the small sphere of black fur and felt it wasn't coming from the creeper of which was his whole focus for this entire time, but something else besides them.

The breaths seemed to come from above his head somewhere, from something standing tall above him. He was still on all fours on the ground, a low position to begin which meant there was quite a few number of different creatures that could be towering over him, he thought, now with his consciousness pulling away from the stupor he was in; taking in the environment with the awareness similar to his usual self.

Luther looked ahead and past the black furry thing to see two legs from some creature standing in their way. They were black and begun from the ground as hooves with some sort of metal rim at their base. He looked further and saw behind these two legs another pair of black hooved pinions. He leant back and up on his knees to take a better look, his sight somewhat reduced not only from the gloom, but the strike to his face, and he saw that the legs belonged to a large black body that had a saddle sitting in its middle and what looked to be some bags hanging near its rear. Looking back at Luther, breathing heavily with eyes of distress was the head of a horse. All its hair was jet black except for white around its eyes. He had found Guinevere.

Luther, with some difficulty from his own injuries stood up from his knees to see her proper. He was immediately happy to see her and for a moment forgot about the pain in his face and chest to walk around the other creature which, he assumed hadn't moved, to swing his arms around her neck to give her a hug. As he did so he could feel her breathing begin to slow as he reassured her and gave her a pat.

"Thank goodness you are alright Gwen. I thought you lost. I don't know how you would have fared out here alone, perhaps better than I, but I am glad to see you are safe," he said.

He looked down towards the creature he was following, or to where he thought it was standing or sitting or whatever position it was in, to find that it was missing.

He looked around him, the light was dim, and the creature was black, which made it quite difficult to locate if it was still somewhere around. He looked in front of Guinevere, either side of her and behind to no avail. Maybe, he thought, it had simply rolled away somewhere off into the forest, carrying on to wherever it was headed, if indeed it was headed anywhere at all. Or, he had to concede, it was conjured up by his weird mind as it lay in a delicate way after the bruising he had sustained from his confrontation with the bandits. Perhaps it was just the madness in his mind finding a way to get him moving through the situation, but as ever the thing seemed so real and its awareness of him felt so acute that it was difficult to simply dismiss as the conjured phantom of a crazy person.

He was too injured and tired from trawling through the forest on his hands and knees to raise himself to any full height of anxious pondering on the subject and just accepted the strangeness of the situation he found himself in. Better that, he thought, than slip ever further into the depths of lunacy. He accepted that the beastie was gone again. To reappear perhaps at some other juncture in his life on the edge of the veil of sanity.

"We may not know what that thing was Gwen, but I am glad it led me to you, and I find you unharmed. That lifts my spirits no end!" Luther said.

He momentarily wondered, had Guinevere seen the creature? Had she noticed this man on his hands and knees crawling along the floor, led by some ball of fur? Regardless, there was no way for her to tell him so, so little point in wondering.

Looking around his vicinity he began to take in the grandness of the forest he had just recently been crawling through. It must have just still been the afternoon with still some couple of daylight hours left in the day, but the forest was murky and dimmed of light from above. Luther decided that if he started now, he could make for Bramstone and be out of the forest before the full dark of the evening was upon them.

He heard that it was a fortress town, a bastion against encroaching evildoers that wished to extend villainy to The Boroughs. Luther thought this most likely meant there were clerics, tending to the spiritual and physical wounds of soldiers stationed there. He could beseech their help for his own wounds and perhaps find a place to rest before setting about finding Ms Celeste Ignophenen.

He gave a cough and felt both cheeks with his hands; they were tender and sore, but the cuts seemed to have clotted some.

"Ok Gwen," he said to his steed "Let's get out of here and make for Bramstone."

He placed his foot on her left stirrup and hoisted himself up into the saddle with no simple surge of pain. He looked behind him with a creak of smarting from his chest and noted that the contents of his saddle bags all seemed to be intact. This was good news, he thought, as he still had provisions and warm clothes should he need them and hopefully his bag of warding powder was still present at the bottom of one of them.

Upward

From this height there was a view to be seen: of the steppes of the mountains as they stretched up; the boulders below that had made great journeys downward, perhaps setting off from this lofty position; the edges of The Boroughs in the distance; the mass of columns that formed the sprawled grasp of the Dell Wood Forest. It was approaching dusk, but there was still enough light to make out the features as they were, up from the mountainside.

The grim lady had climbed slowly and steadily up to the altitude where this view was now to be seen. If she was aware of the inspiring view from this elevation, then she wasn't showing it; her gaze had only stayed forwards and down on the path ahead, not turning in either direction to behold the view below.

She had travelled up from the foothills, past the initial crags and through the make-shift doorway of wayward boulders to the side of one of the Lightlorne Mountains. She followed a path that ran alongside a steep rock wall to her left with her right being a steep drop accompanied by the wondrous view she seemed to have no interest in taking in.

The steep rock wall to her left was a huge, sheer, solid rock that raised up to the higher echelons of this particular member of the mountain range. It was, like the rocks and boulders below, quite dark in colour to begin with; mostly of darkened slate and it too like all others that had come into contact with her and the mist that surrounded her, become greyed and muted as she shuffled past as if in reverence of her passing.

There was little in the way of plant growth or moss or any other such things, even though there were small inlets and notches in the otherwise uniformly smooth mountain face that would prove useful to flora looking for an anchor in this place. No shrub or grasping vine had managed to etch out a living on the almost barren mountain side. The only sign of life around the Grim Lady, as she slowly walked with the aid of her whittled staff, was a pair of farrel birds. They had created a nest in one of the larger outlets some fifty feet upwards from the hooded head of the grim lady. They were both currently in the nest, their heads tucked under the edges of their wings, half asleep in the dusk of the day looking forlorn and melancholy as the Grim Lady passed below. Their feathers, usually of a tan brown colour had become dulled and grey - a result of close enough proximity to the lady as she ambled along the path under their nest, affecting them as she did.

The path itself that the Grim Lady travelled was clear of any great obstruction with only some small juts from the rock face or stony outcrop sticking out from the edge, facing out into the steppes below. The floor beneath her feet was lightly dusted with exceedingly small, gravely rocks that had been thrown out by the cliff side above and wandering boulders that had slipped down the mountainside. The base of it was formed of sheer rock, similar to that of the wall face to the Grim Ladies left, with the same dark greyish black of familiar slate.

She didn't make much for a figure, walking slowly and surely as she did along the mountain way and that haze that was always about her, kept her obscured from view from any onlookers; only visible to those who really meant to look for her, otherwise absent from and remiss to be taken as a part of that which meant be seen.

She slowed her steady, shuffling walk and gradually came to a stop. There was no particular feature on the mountain pass that may have grabbed her attention, no point of interest that encouraged a passer-by to stop and inspect it. She simply came to a halt on the lonesome mountain pass all for her own reason and that reason soon became apparent. She lifted herself up to her full height, which was only somewhat taller than the hunched over posture she travelled in as she went about her journey. When she had reached her highest height, she let out a great sighing breath. It was a great sorrowful and gloominous exhalation that sent forth through her body a ripple that came from her lungs and mouth and travelled all through her mid rift through her lower body and away through her feet. As she let

A GRIM JOURNEY

out this sigh her torso slumped back down and her hand, holding onto her sturdy staff, slid down it's shaft as she herself came down to one knee. She took the staff with both hands and put her faith in its stature as she leant heavily upon it.

The mist, that fog that hung around her like a cluster of orbiting moons of a planet, seemed to react to her great sigh, scattering downwards and out as if somehow it too was exhaling with some unknown force, aping her actions as if an echo of her will. It was almost like a mirror of her, reflecting her mood and actions much like it did as she stumbled or fell to a knee on her steady walk through the mountain pass.

The greying effect that diminished the area in her proximity; to become dull and sullen, seemed to expand at this great exhale, effecting an increased perimeter of mountain-scape as it did so. The very exhalation was as though a great force of energy had pulsed out and away from the grim lady, like that from a stone that dropped into a quiet lake. It was as if it was all too much for her, as though she had to lighten some of that which weighed heavy upon her.

She stayed in this position, slunk down for some time, holding onto her resolute staff. The world around her appeared to slow down as if to take in the deep sigh, trying to absorb it; an attempt to lighten some of the load that lay upon her shoulders. She paused there for some long seconds, gathering herself perhaps or simply taking in some respite from that which hung heavy on her. The mist that had pushed out around her stayed in that position, mimicking that of the Grim Lady. Surrounding them, the sheer rocky face of the mountain, the path below her feet and even the view from that height all seemed in pause, as though the world was allowing time for her to rest for just a mere moment, as though it felt sympathy for her struggle.

Then slowly, with no great haste, she raised her chest and breathed back in, beginning to gradually pull herself up from her resting state - still leaning on her staff. Her legs sluggishly began to straighten, pulling her back up to that hunched position that she had held for so long before. Her face sheltered by her hood and the enveloping mist, came briefly into view, showing a morose but thankful look. It was as if though still strung by an unenviable weight upon her, she was glad to have this moment's respite.

The mist, in reaction to her inhalation of breath and ascension back to her feet, slunk back in to meet her and was once again close by. In parallel, the scope of the dulling of the earth and those features, pulled back as well, affecting that usual distance orbiting her.

Again, she stood hunched, leaning on her staff with the ever-attending fog close by her side. Her legs began to move; right and left, right and left with her wooden support clasped tightly in her right hand, aiding her as she went. She continued with her roam through the Lightlorne Mountains.

Chapter 21

Luther travelled the road leading out from the Dell Wood now for what felt like an hour before finally arriving at the mouth of the forest as it gave up on its claim to the land. He pulled up the reins of Guinevere for a moment to observe what lay in front of him.

The bleeding on his face had slowed and begun to clot and the pain from his wounds was beginning to subside - if just a little. He raised his right hand to his face and felt the swelling that was now forming. He didn't have a mirror or any such thing with him which left his thoughts to wonder how he might look. He must appear a mess, he thought. He imagined he most likely would have at least one black eye and the bloody and bruising might look quite the sight to onlookers.

He had pulled a dark purple cloak from his saddlebags that thankfully still had all their contents besides the pouch of coins that had be stolen. The cloak was thick material, ideal to keep one warm in cold weather. It was pulled all about him with the hood raised up over his head, providing comfort and protection from both the elements and perhaps prying eyes, should they find themselves coming to rest upon him. Along with the cloak he had grabbed some grey fingerless gloves which he slid his hands into. He had been feeling quite exposed to the world after his encounter with the group of vagabonds. Having a warm cloak on his shoulders, fastened at the front with several toggles gave him both physical and spiritual warmth as he focused back to the task of making it to Bramstone before nightfall.

There was a signpost here, indicating the direction to Bramstone or back into the Dell Wood, complete with a water trough. Guinevere seemed interested in having a drink and Luther couldn't blame her after her start through the forest. She wandered over and begun to take her fill. With her head lowered Luther looked out from the forest road and saw that it still travelled in a gingerly south and west direction. He could make out something in the far distance at the edge of his line of sight that looked to perhaps be a line of buildings, buildings that were no doubt part of Bramstone and the destination he sought.

To his right and north-west of the road - it headed straight for that town - was the body of mostly flat and grassy plains. They were wild and unkempt; clearly not used for any kind of farming, arable or otherwise with no fencing, hedges or anything else to keep in animals of which a farmer might rely upon. There seemed to be no sign of any buildings at all, no matter how small, to his left or his right. He wondered why this might be the case. Were these lands deliberately kept this way should the line at Bramstone be broken, tempering the damage that may be caused from some rampaging army? Perhaps there were creatures here not seen by his beaten eyes, which were of great ecological importance that the local authorities did not wish to disturb? Perhaps it was just the whim of some landowners to keep them as they were - wild and free. Perhaps they wished to be kept secluded from the pesterings of man and other races of the world. Luther pictured perhaps some grandiose sage or warlock up above somewhere surveying the ground from some unseen tower, eager to keep watch for intruders in their untamed land.

Of what was present in the plains, Luther could see trees spattered around; a gradual decrease had occurred as he reached the edge of the forest and now, they were strewn scantily across his view. There were tracks from animals present in the soil close to where Guinevere stood that went off into the fields to his right. The ground was covered in a sea of grass, relatively short in stature. Luther thought there must be roving herds of animals of some kind that wandered these plains feeding on it, keeping it down to a shallow level - the thought of it refusing to grow for any other reason seemed a silly one.

Past the landscape, on the edge of his vision to the west he, could make out the juttings of the Lightlorne Mountains, raising up to their peaks. He wondered what it would be like to climb even one of its lower echelons; reaching its apex after what must be a long and arduous journey; no mere feat of endurance, but worth the effort in doing so.

He could see rocky outcrops break up the monotony of the view of grass: A collection of large stone here, a lonely boulder there; they were strewn randomly about the place with little sense of intention. Luther wondered how some of these rocks came here. Had they come down the mountains some years past, thrown up by the ground below or simply formed right here as they stood, somehow It was interesting to ponder such things, but for now he had other pressing matters on his mind that rendered such thoughts superfluous.

To the south-west, past more outcrops, random boulders and trees looking lonely, there were the faint outlines of perhaps the edge of The Border Crags to meet the horizon.

Turning left and south-east laid the edge of the Drearom Borough and he imagined there must be towns and villages that way that he just couldn't make out from this distance.

Luther turned away from the sight of the wilderness to that of the road which had now broken free of the forest and made an almost straight run south-west towards Bramstone. He could not see a bend or turn in the track before it was lost in the distance. Beside the straightness in the direction of the road, he couldn't see any other travellers either and wondered why that was the case. Did the town not expect many visitors? Perhaps, he thought. Perhaps not many people wished to visit a frontier town, a town whose sole function was to be a buttress of security for The Boroughs; to provide bastion against any oncoming dangers from the south, in whatever form that might take. Perhaps the only traffic on this road was that of supplies for the barracks or soldiers or tradesmen perhaps, but the odd traveller with no reason to visit other than naïve interest in that place was most likely seldom seen.

After she had drunk enough to meet her thirst, Luther gently coaxed Guinevere back from the water trough. He thought she seemed happy enough and they set off again following the road south-west towards Bramstone.

Guinevere's footsteps created a gentle rhythm that passed up through the saddle and felt by Luther. It caused some discomfort from the blow to his stomach, but he also led into it with his mind, following the gentle bob as they walked, letting his thoughts wander off again.

His mind floated back to the search for Celeste Ignophenen. Again, he wondered whether she would meet with him if he found her and what, if anything, would she be able to tell him. He couldn't help himself but think of these things; the nature of his mind seemed to amplify both his worry and his ponderings as a natural course of action. As he worried and hoped of finding her, he was also mindful enough to avoid letting his brain wander too far off from the reality around him; he didn't wish to be caught out once again and find himself in another unenviable position at the end of a sharp weapon.

They crept along the road for some time, but not in any particularly great haste. He was eager to arrive in Bramstone, but worried at the same time. Along with the business of locating Ms Ignophenen was the other pressing matter on his mind of being made penniless by a roving band of ill intent – at least on this journey away from his hometown and his meagre holdings.

He would have to find some way of gaining accommodation for the evening. Perhaps, he thought, he could sell what warding powder he had to pay his way in Bramstone. He decided he would also enquire about the existence of any clerics in the town that may be able to provide some aid to him; to point him in the right direction for his needs and maybe some tending to the wounds on his face and chest. He would also make a point to report what had happened to him on the road through the forest. He imagined that the local authorities would be interested in the information of a local band of bandits that may well cause problems to their supply lines and the general law and order of the area. Perhaps, he thought, they might get word back to Forestead Village of his encounter with them. They would no doubt wish to know of that gang's rovings on the village road and to be made aware that they were indeed seeking the woman who had escaped their clutches.

After what felt like to Luther roughly an hour, he had come in full view of the town of Bramstone, now standing out clear in front. Closest to him on the road was a guard post that he presumed must be the first point of contact when entering the town from The Dell Wood direction. Either side of the pathway were two identical looking stone towers, square in construction and made of thick dark grey granite stone. They were two floors high and crested by battlements of which were both manned by what looked to be soldiers carrying some kind of ranged weaponry – most likely crossbows. There were slits lower down in each that Luther figured were used both for observation and firing such bolts and arrows and other missiles should the need arise.

Sitting atop each was some steel framing, crested with metal roofs, angled slightly to let rain drip off the edges with a cutting in the middle allowing for a brick chimney to come through and stick out into the sky. Luther imagined that each one must have a burner of some kind sitting beneath that provided heat on cold nights and perhaps a stove or means to cook something warm to eat.

On the left side tower next to the framing was a wooden winch and pulley that had a wooden platform roughly four-foot square that hung down from its outstretched arm. From each corner of the platform was a length of rope that met those from the others above and in the middle of the platform, forming the outline of a pyramid. This was lashed round and tight with a further length of rope that hung from the winch itself. Luther thought this was most likely used to hoist supplies up to the top of the tower; forgoing carrying it up through the building itself - which might prove quite cumbersome.

Flying from each tower was a flag that Luther recognised as the colours of The Boroughs United; a stag rearing up on its hind legs, coloured white, on a background of very dark brown.

Between the towers was a long stone bridge like structure that spanned from one to the other along the line of the battlements that formed the square frame of a gatehouse. In that space between them was the large steel gate; two imposing steel looking doors forming a square shape with rounded corners reinforced around its borders with strips of steel featuring large angular studs. Both doors were currently closed shut.

Stretching from the towers in both east and westerly directions was a curtain wall that spanned his field of view before disappearing into the distance. It was made of similar stone blocks as the towers themselves but was only one floor high with battlements all along. He couldn't make out any other protruding buildings from the line of stone other than the two standing here on either side of the road. To Luther it didn't seem like it would provide a great deal of protection should it come under attack, but he then thought it probably wouldn't need to. Those in charge would not be expecting to be sieged from a force coming from within The Boroughs themselves, so only moderate defences would be sufficient. He imagined that the perimeter facing the Southern Reaches was most heavily defended with manned towers, barbicans, batters and other such defensive fortifications in place to repel invaders.

Luther stirred himself and they moved off towards the gate house. He would need to gain entry into the town, and he was hoping that doing so would not be too difficult a task. He couldn't spy anyone standing by at the gate itself but assumed once he got close enough the guardsman at the top of one of the towers would be able to assist him.

He hoped the protocol was to hail those that approached the gate with the intention of enquiring what business they have in the town. He certainly didn't want to be fired upon as soon as he was sighted, but he didn't think this would be the case; why would they open fire on someone merely approaching the gate, especially from within the borough side?

It didn't take too long to make the approach to the gate and the towers that minded it, although the day was now waned with the onset of the evening fast approaching. He stopped perhaps twenty yards from it before which both guards on either position had already trained their crossbows upon him; watching his every move.

"Hello there!" Luther shouted up to the men. As he did so a third person down somewhere out of sight, suddenly came into view and stuck their head between the battlements.

"Hello!" was the shout that came back down. The voice was a feminine one and sounded elf like in tone. From what Luther could see from this angle she was wearing a leather cap with a guard across the nose and a studded brigandine of dark brown; very similar to that of the crossbowmen to her flanks.

"Can we help you?" said the Elf.

"I hope so," replied Luther. "My name is Luther, Luther Dothmeer. I come from the town of Overton in the Lonefield Borough. I have come to Bramstone, for some personal business. My journey took me through the Dell Wood and unfortunately, I was set upon by a group of bandits shortly before leaving the forest. You may be able to see for yourselves from the state of me." He tried to give a smile as he spoke, but it pained him to do so from the bruises upon his face and the pain in his chest.

The woman looked down at him for a moment. "Right, I see. I am sorry to hear of your trouble sir. What is the nature of your business in Bramstone?"

"I am seeking an audience with a certain person that was last reported to be in the area. A Celeste Ignophenen," Luther replied.

The lead soldier looked back at the guardsman in her tower with the crossbow and over to the other in the tower opposite.

"Yes, we know Ms Ignophenen. Quite well known to the town. Not one to be left waiting if you don't want an earful." The guards all let out a laugh.

"Oh, that's brilliant," Luther said, "Would you happen to know whether she is in the town currently or abroad elsewhere?"

"She came by here a few weeks ago, not sure if she stayed long in town or went off somewhere into the Southern Reaches. She comes and goes a lot, but she didn't come back through this way at least," she shouted down in response. This was good to hear, Luther thought. She had at least been seen in the last few weeks and if she hadn't come back this way, perhaps she was busy in the town somewhere. Golon had mentioned she was a seeker of knowledge and perhaps she was engrossed in tomes and books in the Library of Bramstone. All it would require would be to simply locate it and try to engage her attention. He did think to himself that such a simple and tellingly, easy, situation would most likely not be the one he would find himself in. He could only hope.

"Thank you for the information!" Luther shouted up. It still pained to exhale and shouting with the weight of his lungs was certainly not very comfortable. "Am I granted access?" he continued.

"Yes sir. That's fine," replied the woman. She turned back out of view and Luther thought he could hear her shouting down somewhere. After a brief pause Luther could hear some noises coming from behind the gate which he attributed to those of some large bar or brace being raised or slid out of the way before the left door of the gate slowly opened inwards into the gatehouse.

Behind the gate was a portcullis of latticed steel that blocked the entrance to the gatehouse from the other side. With the opening of the gate came another soldier, this time a male human. He stood there with his back up against the large door and beckoned for Luther to come past him. Luther was able to pass through without dismounting from Guinevere - it seemed designed to accommodate such a passing. He then stopped short of the portcullis.

Luther could see inside the gatehouse now. He thought this intermediate area between the outside walls and the sanctuary of the town of Bramstome must be a holding area of sorts. Along with its obvious defensive qualities, providing a secondary defensive gate to be contended with after breaching the first one, it also gave a means to inspect those that wished to enter or leave the town itself.

It was a simple space with the same stone bricks forming the walls of the inner section of the gate house. There was heraldry hanging from the walls; the same image of the stag on a brown background displayed clearly from the banners that hung from a horizontal wooden pole. On either side of him was a set of stairs that spiralled up and out of view. Luther thought these must lead up to the other sections of the gate house, spanning the height of them. On either side of the heraldry, in the middle of both south-east and north-west walls were racks holding various weapons: armaments such as half swords, hand axes and the odd shield. To his right, in the southwest corner was a small inlet holding a more robust rack of greater height which held large weapons such as full-length spears and various pole arms. To his left in the southeast corner in an identical inlet across from the other was a modest fireplace with several stools close by. There was a spit hanging over the fire itself with a pot hang from it currently and the warming smell of a hearty stew of some kind on the go.

Looking behind him briefly he saw a large cross beam in an upright position to the east side of the gate. It must have been what he had heard being raised before entering, he thought, as he saw another winch mechanism attached to it.

The guard that had opened the gate now stood looking at him. It seemed to Luther that he was inspecting him; deciding whether he would be any threat or looking to cause any trouble or perhaps, Luther wondered if he was merely staring at the cuts and bruises on this dishevelled looking person on a horse in front of him. He had indeed paused on Luther's face, the cuts evident as they were and the bruising already forming. He then looked about Luther's person; he saw the hand axe down at his side, still in its sheath; the slight hunch over pose of the man on the horse, still feeling the effects of the day's events upon his body. He looked at Guinevere's face and the saddlebags on her back and then paused.

"Alright," he said. "Raise the gate!" he shouted up towards one of the flights of stairs. After a brief pause Luther heard several clanking and clunking noises as the portcullis began to rise. He thought it must go straight up into a gap in the wall somewhere out of sight.

Once it had raised high enough for him to pass through - while still astride Guinevere - he said thank you to the guardsman who gave a nod and Luther moved off into the town. When he was clear through the portcullis it slowly descended down again behind him. Luther had made it to Bramstone.

Chapter 22

As Luther exited the gatehouse, he was met with the view of the outskirts of the town of Bramstone. This outer part of the town consisted of small houses and farm buildings surrounded by small plots of land for growing.

The road from the gatehouse took on more of a solid track of stone, travelling first past the small farm holdings and then through some brick houses before meeting another stone curtain wall blocking the view beyond.

The farmhouses looked to be mostly constructed of some a sort of brownish red brick with slated tile roofs. They were accompanied by different sized wooden barns and sheds. Several lined the track as it kept quite a straight line past them. It had turn offs at several points, spawning new roads that went in both directions creating rows of buildings one after another. At first these roads were very sparsely populated featuring only farm holdings accompanied by crop land, but as Luther's sight drove into the distance, he noticed a sudden change as the farms turned into industrial buildings featuring several chimney stacks or large wooden barn like structures that Luther wondered must be used for some sort of storage. He imagined that these buildings processed some of the produce from the farms alongside making other goods and supplies that were required by the large garrison of soldiers that surely were present here; such an important strategic position would require significant support.

Luther thought to himself that some of these must be the homes to the numerous workman and craftsman of the surrounding buildings along with some stores which may be interested in purchasing what warding powder he had left. He hoped he could get enough for a bed for the night at least and perhaps some other supplies he might be in need of.

He would do his best to seek out a cleric of which there must be at least one, he thought, in such a sprawling place. They would hopefully provide some respite, perhaps having something for his wounds and the swelling upon his face. He didn't wish to find the doctor of the garrison; they were most likely busy with the needs of those stationed here and it would require a great stress to approach where they were located - most likely with lots of busyness and coming and going that would not bode well for his anxiety.

No, he thought. I will enquire about the local cleric and beseech their aid.

The pair of them, Luther and Guinevere, started along the road, past the farms that lay there. On his right he saw a human couple out in the fields, driving a plough through the earth at their feet. It was being drawn by two large and strong looking horses. They were dragging the metal plough effortlessly through the soil.

Further along they saw another farmhouse connected by a large barn that was filled with bales of hay. Along its eastern wall struck out a roof supported by two wooden supports. Out in the field by its side was grazing land of a crowd of cows that were quietly chewing on grass; too busy eating to take much notice of the tired looking man, creeping by on his horse, looking solemn and forlorn.

They passed several more farms, some arable some pastoral. On his right, to the west of the road where mostly the ground was flat and level, there was a hill that arose from the ground with quite a prominence, roughly half a mile away. Sitting on top of it was a tall building, several floors high with four large vanes protruding from a central spindle, facing north. Luther recognised it as a windmill. It was most likely, he thought, used to mill flour and perhaps some other goods. It no doubt caught some wind up there as he could see the vanes spinning round in a clockwise direction.

Before long they had passed through the collection of farms and other buildings to where the rows of roads became more tightly packed together; the need for great space between them now diminished as the farmland gave way to urban neighbourhoods. At this point, the streets had become more cobble like with Guinevere's hooves clip clopping as she walked over them. There were lamp posts too, though it was

A GRIM JOURNEY

still early enough in the evening for them to remain unlit.

There were also people there, wandering around, busy with their own business. Luther thought maybe they were making their way home, or to an inn or similar for the evening. He walked past several such buildings: 'The timid Knight', 'The Half Moon', 'The Old Minstrel' among them. They were of mixed construction with some being of the wooden kind; large beams and uprights for walls and thatched roofs, while several were of brick and mortar topped with slate tile. All had patrons present, including what Luther recognised as soldiers, most likely on leave and requiring a pint or two. He could see them, looking in through their windows as Guinevere walked past, not particularly full of people. They were most likely yet to fill up with evening goers.

Besides the inns, Luther noted several industrial buildings, nestled in between terraced houses and other structures. There was the odd blacksmith, still working away at the anvil; the clangs rising out above the din of the pulse of the town. There was a bakers, closed now, but still with some produce in the windows, under glass covers. Luther could see lights on up in the next floor, the Baker most likely readying something to eat for the evening. Luther felt the tinge in his stomach at this thought, not of the painful blow he had received earlier, but of the draw of hunger upon him. He would like to find something to eat, if he could. He still had supplies enough in his bag he thought, if he could only find an open fire, he could make himself a simple meal; the thought of a tin of beans was easily enough to whet his appetite.

Luther noticed several stores such as a herbalist's which he might have to visit could he not find aid from a cleric. He spied a general store to his left aptly named 'General Store' on the sign hanging down. He thought this was as better place than any to stop so he pulled Guinevere over to one side and tied her reins loosely to a lamp just outside. He went to his saddle bags and searched with his hands for the bag of warding powder. He grabbed hold of something which felt like the bag he was looking for and pulled it out. Luckily, it was indeed the item he was looking for. Luther felt a sigh of relief. He hadn't actually checked since his encounter with the forest bandits if any of his other belongings were missing; he wasn't aware of them taking anything else besides his coin bag, but he wouldn't know for sure until he looked.

The store front was a simple one with the door to the left side of a large glass window. Beyond this was a tiered wooden, window display stand that featured different items for sale including: canned food; several general survival items such as matches, pots and pans; a row of camping knives of different shapes and sizes and some warm looking boots. There was a sign on the door hanging from the other side that read 'open'. Luther took a breath and pushed it open, entering the shop.

Inside there was what Luther expected from a general store; shelves and racks full of general items that one might require. The walls on both sides of him were lined with shelves of such goods. On his left side were more food items, more tinned goods, some alcohol for drinking and several racks of clothes. On his right was a cabinet of hunting and survival knives, surrounded by even more shelves carrying household items.

In front of him was the shop counter, behind which was another great array of different items, sitting happily on their shelves. Standing behind the counter was a man with dark, tan like skin; Luther wondered if he had heritage in the old Indian homelands. Around his waist and hanging from his neck was a leather apron over the top of a black t-shirt with some form of print on it. The man had a black goatee beard and short, hair. He looked up with a smile when he noticed Luther opening the door and entering the shop.

"Hello there, I am Arjun," said the shop owner.

"Hello there Arjun, nice to meet you. I am Luther." He hoped the look of him; bruised and battered, would not put off the shopkeep.

"Looking for anything specific or just having a browse?" Arjun said. Luther had noted from his brief look at the many shelves around him that he couldn't make out at least, any sign of any warding powder. He thought perhaps his luck had changed slightly though didn't dwell on that thought for too long lest he jinx himself.

"Well, on my journey here through the Dell Wood, I

met with some trouble. You can probably tell by the cuts and bruises on my face."

Arjun looked at Luther and replied "Yes, I didn't want to bring it up. Are you alright? It looks rather sore."

Luther winced a little, but gave a determined look, "I should be ok, I was hoping to find a cleric in town that might be able to provide something to ease the pain and tend the wounds."

"Right," said Arjun. "There is a cleric here in town, as well as an infirmary, but they are usually busy looking after soldiers and the like."

"I thought as much," said Luther. "You couldn't point me in the direction of the cleric's location please?"

"Yes sure, they are not too far. There are two clerics in fact, a married couple. They live in and maintain a small chapel just before the gatehouse into the garrison. If you turn right out of the shop and follow the road, then you will come across it no problem. Just a short walk," Arjun said from behind the counter.

"That's brilliant, thank you," replied Luther.

"Now," said Arjun, "Is there anything you were looking for in the store?"

Luther had another brief glance around the shop and still could not see anything that he might recognise as warding powder. "Well, when I was accosted in the forest, they traded my coin purse for blows to my face, so I am now without any way to pay for anything. But, when I look around, I see you don't seem to have any warding powder." He paused briefly for the man behind the counter to respond.

"No," came the reply. "I am actually all out at the moment. The ingredients are tricky to come by round here and a great many of the shipments are bound straight for the garrison".

"I see," said Luther. He raised up the bag of warding powder in his possession. "I have a knack for finding the ingredients. In fact, it is my profession, I guess you could say. I have some here if you would be interested in purchasing it?"

Luther walked over to the counter and placed the leather pouch upon its worn greying surface. He pulled it open to show the warding powder inside. Arjun came over from his side of the counter and looked at it.

"Well," said Arjun. "Let's have a look. Do you mind if I pick up the bag?"

"No, please, go ahead," Luther said.

Arjun picked up the bag and bringing it closer to his face, looked in on the dust. True warding powder had a distinctive green glow to it, something akin to the colour of leaves from the trees lit up by the sun, which was difficult to replicate. Arjun was experienced with discerning the authenticity of warding powder and so, after examining it for a few moments turned to Luther. "This looks to be genuine and good stuff. You selling it all?" he said.

Luther nodded and said, "Yes if you are interested. I am of course not very well placed to haggle a price, with you knowing my situation so I will take whatever you think is a good amount for it." Luther knew he was at the mercy of Arjun's good nature; he had no coin at all, so whatever he was offered he would have to accept.

"Well," said Arjun, "I can offer you six gold pieces for what you have here. That is the usual price I pay relative to the amount, so I offer you the same."

Luther looked happy and gave a smile; this was more than he expected and was grateful for the offer. "Yes, I will take it. Thank you very much." He let Arjun take the powder and place it somewhere under the counter before pulling out another pouch and counting out six gold pieces which he then slid across it to Luther, who gratefully accepted it and placed it in his pocket.

There are still decent people in the world, Luther thought to himself. He knew that Arjun could have easily offered a lower amount for the dust, and he would have had no choice but to accept, but he had offered a fair price - much to Luther's joy. This restored an inkling of hope he had lost after his run in with the bandits in the forest.

After thanking Arjun and wishing him a good day, he exited the store. He walked over to and untied Guinevere from the lamp post. He didn't climb onto her saddle, instead deciding to simply lead her by the reins and press along the street on foot. He gave her a pat on her neck. "You have been carrying me all day I think you need a rest, girl." Her eyes turned towards him, and he wondered if she understood his words or appreciated the sentiment.

They walked in the direction towards to the inner wall separating this part of town from the most fortified section beyond. The road turned slightly to the left, directing the road in a southerly direction. He hoped to come by that which Arjun said should be the cleric's chapel. Luther thought to himself how back in Overton they didn't have a resident doctor or cleric that might tend to those in need.

Deven or the elven sisters – with their herbal knowledge - were generally able to take care of most problems people might have, though a cleric would be versed in a great many more remedies and healing spells and a doctor would have thorough knowledge of the human body and its capabilities.

They passed by yet more buildings, sitting on either side of the road. They walked by an inn on the west side of the road named 'The Cat and Anchor'. It looked quite quiet inside from what he could see; roughly half the tables being vacant. There was a butchers on his right, of which, Luther saw a man at the counter making up some sausages. The majority of the other buildings looked to be housing for the local populace smattered with the other odd shop between them.

Luther was becoming quite tired, narrowing his view and desire to take much else in from his surroundings as they walked further on the cobbled street. The pain in his chest and face was aching more and he felt only for the need of a bed and some rest. He was struggling with all the things that had happened on his journey. It went against the hope he had of a quiet and uneventful one and he wondered how much of a toll it took upon him both physically and mentally. There was a thought in him though, a thought that was at least a little grateful for some of his experiences: he had a conversation with a troll which was something he never thought he would do; he had met some interesting and good people and managed to help someone in need; his presence upon the road had provided some good for the world and that was comforting to him.

A GRIM JOURNEY

His mind slunk again into deep thought concerning what he was to do next and what had already happened. He could hear the clip clop of Guinevere's hooves upon the cobble stone like a metronome that provided a steady back beat to the thoughts inside his head. His vision lay solely on what was in front of him; his peripherals were lost while he pondered recent events. He was still aware enough that he noticed the inner curtain wall of the town that lead to the barracks and battlements beyond which, was the umber plain and the southern reaches, looming up ahead.

This inner wall that separated the outer part of the town from the inner more fortified one, was tough looking and robust. It was noticeably taller with battlements stretching up higher to form a better protection for anyone up there upon them.

The road lead through another gatehouse, again, similar to that he had previously encountered, with two large towers on either side of the gate itself. There was another bridge between the pair of towers, similarly with a gate below. On this side though was the portcullis. Luther assumed the sturdier front gate must be on the other side, providing a bastion for a second line of defence should an enemy manage to breach the main battlements beyond.

Before the gatehouse was a crossroads with the street going both easterly and westerly directions; parallel to the great wall with the road passing south through the gatehouse itself.

Just before the crossroads on the right at the end of the line of buildings was one that looked like a small chapel. It had wooden walls of vertical, wide planks of wood with windows cut out on either side. There were wooden flower boxes hanging down beneath each of them with an assortment of different flowers and herbs. By each of the windows, on both their left and right were clumps of huddle moss doing exactly as their name's sake suggested. There was certainly magic going on inside.

There were wooden shutters flanking each window on the outside which were currently closed except for those in the front of the building, facing Luther, that appeared only partially shut. These sat on either side a humble looking wooden front door. He could see a light glow coming through from inside the building, perhaps from a fire or lamp light. The warmth emanating from within; seeping out from the gaps in the shutters appealed to Luther and he was instinctively drawn to it.

This must be the cleric chapel, he thought to himself. Indeed, when he had walked closer, he could see a symbol of one of the clerical orders sitting above the door. It was of a crescent moon. That rang a bell in his mind; he had heard of a clerical order of that name before in some of his books from the guild of Mage Scribes. It must be the order of the Crescent Moon, he thought to himself.

Luther swung Guinevere's reins around another lamp post just near the front of the building and approached the entrance doors. There was a large iron knocker sitting in the centre of it. He pulled it up and knocked on it twice before stepping back slightly and waiting for a reply. He waited for a minute or so but couldn't hear any kind of movement or action coming from behind it. He stepped forward and was about to knock again when he heard some movement through the slightly open windows on either side of the door.

"Hello, hello, just one moment please!" came the words of a husky male voice beyond the door.

Luther heard the man come up to the door, the sound of a lock being undone and perhaps that of a wooden bar being removed from the other side. He stood back again as not to be upon the man as he opened it and moments later it swung inwards to reveal a middle-aged looking man standing in the doorway. He was wearing dark blue robes, lined with a light grey, with grey crescent moons woven into the body of it. It looked to Luther of doing the job well of keeping someone warm while also belying the station of its owner. There was a hood to it that was slung back allowing Luther to see the dark brown head of slightly receding hair upon his head. The man's face was slightly worn with the onset of wrinkles and a smile from a short haired, bearded face.

"Hello there," said the man. His voice was gentle and warm which worked well to put Luther at ease. Knocking on the doors of strange buildings in strange towns he had never been to before was not something Luther particularly liked to make a habit of. The thoughts that raced through his mind were of approaching the wrong door and finding himself in some awkward situation where he would have to explain his mistake and walk away flushed red in embarrassment. He was worried that whoever opened the door might question his reason for doing; telling him to be gone and again finding himself filled with awkwardness. Luckily this didn't happen, and Luther felt relieved.

"Hello," said Luther. "I am Luther, Luther Dothmeer. Is this the cleric chapel?"

The man smiled at Luther with an earthly and gentle smile. "Yes, indeed it is. My name's Edgar, Edgar Cragswood. My wife and I maintain this little chapel here for the Crescent Order," - Luther felt right in in his assumption. The cleric looked to have noticed the cuts and bruises on Luther's face but didn't immediately draw attention to them. "Do you need some help, Luther?" he continued.

"Yes, I imagine you have noticed the state of me. I was set upon by a gang of bandits on the edge of the Dell Wood. They beat me and stole my coin purse. I was wondering if I might seek some help for my wounds. I didn't want to trouble the Doctor at the barracks." He looked a little glum and fretted slightly at the thought of intruding upon the good Cleric. He thought they most likely were quite busy with other members of the town's problems if the only doctor was kept busy by the soldiers stationed here. "Only if it is no trouble and you are not busy elsewhere of course. I don't want to trouble you," Luther continued.

Edgar, the cleric, looked at Luther's face with a focused eye now and after a few moments he said, "It does look like you ran into a fair amount of trouble indeed. We can have a look at it yes. Did you come on horseback?"

"Yes, I did. I have my horse, Guinevere, tied to the lamppost outside," Luther replied.

"Ok that's fine," replied the cleric. "If you come with me, we can have a look at you. We'll get your horse into the stables down the way." He stood aside from the door and beckoned Luther to come through, closing it after he had done so.

A GRIM JOURNEY

Luther couldn't make out much beyond the older cleric from where he first stood, but he could now take the surroundings quite clearly. He had entered a small hall of wooden walls and flooring with the windows now from the other side. Along the back wall was a fireplace with an armchair on either side, both sat on a thick, dark looking rug. The fireplace was of large bare brick and topped with a thick wooden beam across it that had seen the wear of time - even in an enclosed place, spared from the weather. Luther wondered how old this place must be. There were pictures on the wall above the fireplace. They were of serene settings: in the woods on a fresh morning, on a hillside in the middle of the day; a quiet riverbank with trees hanging over, and others. There was a dark wooden door to the right of the fireplace that was currently closed. Luther imagined this must be the private quarters of the couple that lived here.

There were six beds, three on each side of the room. They had warm looking patchwork blankets that appeared to be hand made with love and care along with fluffy looking pillows. Luther almost had the urge to simply dive under those warm blankets right now and sleep off some of the misery of the day past. Of the six, four were currently empty with two occupied by what Luther assumed were injured or sick people. To his right, close to the door was a human man - at least Luther thought it was a man, as he could only make out a short head of hair of someone laying on their side under a blanket and fast asleep. The bed to the right of this was empty with the next bed along the right and north wall was filled with an elderly looking human lady, currently sat up and eating a bowl of soup. At her side, sitting in a cushioned chair facing her, was another woman in similar dress to Edgar. She was in conversation with the woman as she ate. Luther supposed that this must be Edgar's wife whom he said he ran this small chapel with.

"You are welcome to stay the night Luther," Edgar said, drawing Luther's focus back to him. At these words, the other lady dressed in similar garb had turned round and gave a welcoming smile before turning back to her conversation.

"Thank you," said Luther. "I think that might be

good."

"Well," said Edgar "This one ok?" He pointed to a bed on the left side of the room, across from the man lying on his side.

"Yes, that's great, thank you. I must get my things from my horse though first and make sure she is ok if that's alright?"

Edgar smiled and said, "Yes no problem at all! I can come help if you wish or otherwise feel free to go yourself."

"I should be fine. I just want to grab my pack and lighten the load on her." Luther walked back to the door and to Guinevere. He pulled out his pack as well as a few other things and then after giving her a gentle stroke and pat, returned inside the chapel.

"Once we've had a look at you, you take some rest and I'll take your horse over to the stables. Don't worry, as I said it isn't far," said Edgar, once Luther was back inside.

Luther was glad at the sight of the bed. It awakened the need in him to rest before he could do much else. "If that is not too much bother then I thank you," he said.

"That's no problem, Luther. You're a bit worse for the wear today. Now, you have a sit on the bed, and I'll have a look at your cuts and bruises."

Luther placed his pack by the bed and sat down. Edgar pulled over a chair that was sat up against the wall and pulled out some glasses from a pocket in his robes. He looked through them to the cuts and bruises on Luther's face. He asked him to turn his face slightly so he could get a good look.

"You look quite sore, Luther," said Edgar. "Luckily the cuts don't look too deep, but you're going to bruise quite a bit." He pulled out a round metal tin from a pocket in his robes and gently unscrewed the top to reveal a greenish white looking substance. He dabbed his fingers into the tub which looked to be some sort of ointment and went to rub it into Luther's face, stopping just short of doing so before saying, "Now, this is going to sting quite a lot, but it will heal you up just fine. Shall I continue?"

Luther was eager to feel a little less sore and having heard of the properties of such substances he motioned for

Edgar to continue. The cleric gently spread the healing balm onto the wounds on Luther's face. "You can rub it more yourself Luther, work it in some, but not too much." He pulled Luther's hands up to where he had applied the cream and let him rub it in more himself.

Almost immediately Luther could feel the aching in his cheeks start to subside to a more manageable level.

"This cream," said Luther. "It is magical in some way?"

Edgar, with a smile upon his face said, "Yes, it is indeed Luther. By itself this is an antiseptic cream and would have some effect regardless, but it has been infused with a healing magic that can sooth and restore living beings from great harm."

The balm seemed to be working at a preternatural rate as he could feel the pain and the soreness subsiding.

"This is fascinating stuff," Luther said. "I feel the pain reducing already". He placed his hand back up to his face and felt the swelling. It too seemed to have reduced noticeably. "And the swelling too," he said.

Edgar smiled through his glasses a knowing smile. "Now, Luther, are you hurt anywhere else? I saw you feel your chest as you walked over. Were you hurt there?"

Luther felt the place in his chest where he was viciously kicked by one of the bandits. "Yes," he said. "One of those villains booted me in the side at full whack. I think they might have cracked a rib." His hand felt the area again and he gave a wince.

"Right," said Edgar. "Take some from the pot here, not too much, and rub it on the area where it hurts. It will take care of the rest." Luther reached over and took a small amount of the stuff from the tin and pulled to the side his cardigan and shirt before rubbing it on the affected area. Almost instantly he felt a warmth pass over his chest and the pain subsiding.

"Thank you so much," Luther said, with a sigh of relief. "We don't have a cleric, or a doctor in fact, back in Overton where I live. We would have to travel further afield for help from one such as yourself. Though we have a local mage that can work some wonders," he said, looking around the room.

"We try to be wherever we can be of help," replied Edgar. "I have heard of Overton village, passed through there a fear years ago even. I imagine should a cleric feel it is needed they might one day take up residence."

Luther recalled from his books on the clerical orders of how once initiated, a cleric was free to choose a parish in which to care for. This was not limited in any way by population, density or proximity to towns, cities or otherwise.

He had heard how various clerical orders differed in training and initiation rituals, with the only constant among them being the requirement that an individual be gifted in some way magically, with the way of healing.

Conversely, a medical student attended one of the prestigious schools of medicine, learning the anatomy of the body of each the races - though usually focusing on one. It was not a requirement - with their focus on practical medicine - but nearly all doctors and nurses were gifted magically in the art of healing, though perhaps not as much so as a cleric.

He imagined Edgar and his wife cast some sort of spell upon the healing cream which gave it these wonderful properties that were working so fast on relinquishing the pain and damage upon him. Perhaps even, some sort of magical cantrip was cast upon the tin as the cleric picked it up and took off the lid.

"Now," said Edgar. "Please make yourself comfortable. We have some soup on the go, I can serve you some up and then I'll walk your horse round to the stables."

"Only if it's not too much trouble to do that, Edgar. I am imposing on you too much as it is," Luther quickly replied. He felt a sudden guilt at taking up the man's time, helping someone as unimportant as himself.

"It's no bother Luther, I need to stretch my legs anyway. Thank you for the concern, but it is fine. You just get yourself comfortable and let the healing take effect." With that he patted Luther on the shoulder and stood up before walking over to the fireplace. There was a pot on the fire to one side which Luther had no noticed before. Edgar removed the lid and Luther was met with the aroma of a creamy mushroom soup.

A GRIM JOURNEY

Edgar took a bowl from a nearby cupboard and scooped some warm soup into it. He then took a spoon from the same cupboard and walked back over and handed it to Luther. "That should help set you straight," Edgar said. "Sometimes a good warm meal can work wonders!"

"It can indeed," said Luther, taking the bowl from him. Luther had taken off his boots and sat up on the bed with his back to the backboard.

Edgar, seeing that his charge was comfortable enough and about to tuck into the warm bowl of soup said, "Right well, you get that down you and get some rest. With a good night's sleep, you should be up and ready to go where you will tomorrow."

"Thank you, Edgar," Luther said quickly, seeing his opportunity to thank the man quickly closing as he moved away. "Thanks for your kindness, taking me in and seeing to my wounds. I greatly appreciate it."

Edgar turned back around and said, "It's no problem at all Luther," before turning away again.

He walked to the cleric sitting in a chair by the other bed and placed his hand upon her shoulder. She turned her head briefly, away from the conversation she was having with the elderly woman. Luther saw him whisper something into her ear and she looked over briefly to Luther who she met with a smile. Edgar then walked to the front door and slipped on a dark blue, hooded cloak that was hanging from a peg on the wall next to the door. He then opened it and stood their briefly, before walking through to meet the evening, the door closing behind him.

Chapter 23

"Are you sure this is a prudent idea, Fabian?" said Vespera, her voice betraying a slight concern in her otherwise indifferent demeanour.

"What ails you Vespera? When the righteous must take action, do you shy away from what must be done?" said Fabian.

It was late evening and Fabian the well-dressed man, alongside Vespera, the hidden lady, were standing on the bank of the Panifery River looking on to Overton Village to the west. There were trees all along the riverbank itself with high grass between them and the fields before Overton, all hiding the two figures well from view.

"I do not mean to question your judgement of course, dear Fabian. I am just your lowly servant; not vested with the same wisdom and insight as one such as yourself." She thickly laid on the compliments in an effort to see her words through to him unmolested.

"Indeed, you don't Vespera. Trust that my judgement is supreme in this," he boasted.

"Oh of course," replied Vespera, the hidden lady. "I merely wished to remind you of perhaps how this might be seen by some of our benefactors. From my own experience, they wish to stay hidden and not be so openly malevolent." At that final word she knew as soon as it left her lips that it would be taken up with.

"Malevolent you say?!" said Fabian. "This is no act of evil! If anything, we are doing the work of the incorrupt and good! These fools met the truth as I told it, with indignation and contempt. This elf that leads them a pin up for the belligerent! They will know soon enough the folly of their actions and they will rue the day they believed themselves better than me!"

Vespera seemed to acknowledge that her words would do little to sway him from his current course of action.

"Then perhaps may I suggest we act soon and act quickly before they are alerted to our presence. It will only be a matter of time," she ventured.

"You worry too much Vespera. These small people have already shown their stupidity at rebuffing my golden words and wisdom. They would be simply too stupid to ever see what is to come, much less do anything about it!" His voice raised up and above its usual volume as if goading the cluster of buildings making up the body of Overton Village - standing not far from where they were standing.

Vespera, feeling she had said all she could to temper the wrath of Fabian's wounded ego said, "Yes, I shall of course give way to your higher intellect."

Usually, he would be more aware of the obvious twinge of sarcasm in her voice, but he was still too full of besmirched pride to be aware, or care if he did. "Good," he said.

"Signal our men, Malakai, will you?" Fabian looked over and nodded to Malakai the coachman, who was standing several yards along the riverbank to his right. Malakai returned with his own nod and a wry smile upon his face before turning and with a flick of a wrist a small flare of light seemed to emanate from his hand, shooting up the riverside and then high enough into the sky to be known for those who wished to see it and no further, before disappearing in a blink of an eye.

Among the trees, standing, waiting for the command, was a troop of men and women clad in leather armour with steel rimmed, leather helmets and their faces covered by bandit style masks. There was no heraldry, marks or symbols denoting their identity; each shorn of any features that might suggest who they were or who they represented. All were armed with wooden clubs or maces of some description. Some held a shield either on their back or in their other hand. They were mostly covered by the dark and the trees and the high grass they were hiding in, but all looked to be awaiting this very signal.

There were several, among those gathered, mounted upon horseback. They looked to be officers of some sort or at least leaders of those present. The colour of their horses was difficult to distinguish in the darkness of the evening but were most certainly of some dark hue as not to attract much attention from the moon light. Their riders each carried a similar club that was either in hand ready for action or hanging from their belt.

All of them were clad in a measure of quiet and stillness until this moment and had now begun to move quietly from their positions, towards Overton village.

After a good few strides, the gathering of mercenaries had begun to emerge from the protection of the trees and the undergrowth before stalking through the high grass and then across the crop fields just outside the village proper. At their forefront were the lieutenants on their horses, now more visible in the moonlight. They were clad in similar garb to their compatriots on foot; leather armour and helmets upon their heads their faces covered by masks. Again, similarly their outfits were absent of any markings that may describe their identity. They looked just as eager as their charges for what was about to unfold but were all quietly barking orders for those present to stay themselves, as if they were waiting for a final command from the riverbank from whence the flare had just originated.

They crept quietly across the crop fields until they were mere yards from the closest buildings on the edge of Overton before halting and looking around them for some final signal to begin. It was not long before this signal was made clear for them to see as another spark of bright flame shot out from the riverbank and the night was on.

They began to move again at a quickened pace towards the buildings in front of them on the east side of the village. To their left, in the south of the town was the Duck Feather Inn, whose windows were aglow with the light emanating from inside.

Up from the tavern lay the Tailors and Tannery. The lower floor was all dark, having closed for the day, but the floor above had lights on and the chimney breathing from the stack on the roof.

To their right as they continued the quiet stalk, was the blacksmiths. Toby was working later than usual, and his forge was still lit with his arm hammering away at a sword, freshly forged and bright red in colour from the heat of the flame.

North of the blacksmiths, set back, stood the herbalists of the Gwithen and Lilly, the elven sisters. Again, the lower floor of this building was dark and quiet, having been shut for the day. The upper floor though was also dark and absent of any activity, the owners clearly not present and away for the evening.

The brigade of mercenaries had now reached the very edge of the town, almost within touching distance of the closest buildings. Riders atop their mounts nodded to each other and then to those around them on foot.

Several of the mercenary soldiers pulled out wooden torches they had been carrying in a free hand or slung over their shoulders. A smaller number pulled out a flint and tinder from a pocket and begun to light their torches. Once they were up and roaring enough with flame, they lit their closest fellows' torches who in turn lit their neighbours as if the flames were eager to have company. The soldiers then surged forward, carrying forth their insidious light into the village proper.

Whether they saw the blacksmith in his forge or just decided on a different route, then band funnelled through the space between the tannery and the inn. If anyone had been looking outside at this time, they would have seen a host of men and woman quietly moving into position, their masked faces lit by the blazing torches in hand.

Any question as to their intent was quickly answered as all at once the brigade split off into several groups surrounding the tavern, the town hall to the south-west, the guard house - standing in the centre of the village, the store, Golon's shop and some straight north to the blacksmiths and the village green.

The door of the tavern flew open with a loud bang as if someone had given it a large strike with the flat of their boot, almost ripping off the door latch. In came several of the mercenary outfit to the startled and confused faces of those inside.

Several tables were occupied with people who were, up until now, quietly enjoying a drink with friends or in the middle of a game of some sorts: Gwithin and Lilly were sat at a table to the left; the general store owners Gareth and Kate were at another table with Thelia the leader of the village council; the flarfen, Throven was at a table near a window with another, female flarfen, playing some sort of game with young Steve Lodson; Golon was sitting on a tall stool by the bar and was up until this moment in conversation with Nathanael; sitting round another table just by them was a group of four: Delia, her husband Marcus, Harold and his sister Alma, all residents of the village and until now were in a joyous mood enjoying each other's company.

All had looked up towards the group of intruders as they filed violently into the room, looking intimidating and keen to pounce like a pack of wolves kept chained and starved of a good meal. Nathanael, looked to the men and momentarily over to Thelia who had turned ever so briefly to meet his eyes before turning back to the band of mercenaries.

"Can I help you?" said Nathanael, as he gave them his now full attention.

One of them stepped forward. It was the woman who had been at the inn the night Luther first saw the ball of black fur - deep in some conversation with the group of men. "Your village has been found wanting by those greater than yourselves. You spurn that which is for your own benefit. You are not pure," she said, as her gaze, that had until now been centred on Nathanael, turned to Thraven and his wife and then round to Lilly and Gwithen and on to Golon, before returning to the old mage as he stood behind the bar. "You have rejected a truth and you will now pay for that rejection." She gave a nod to those people either side of her, with clubs and maces raised and fires in hand who then passed by her. The group of men and women, clad for battle set upon all those present.

Several of the armed brutes surged towards the table of Gareth, Thelia and Kate. The villagers raised from their chairs and tried to put them between themselves and the aggressors: Gareth picked his up and used it to try and fend them off; Kate stood behind him, both hands on his back; Thelia came round to Gareth's left, having grabbed another chair.

"Be gone from hear you filthy toe rags! You have no

business being here!" Thelia shouted at the assailants who had now all entered the room and fanned themselves out to face the patrons of the tavern. "Go back to your holes," she yelled again.

Several of the intruders cracked their clubs on the table by Thelia, Gareth and Kate, smashing it aside, grimacing intently at them. One to Gareth's left swung his club in such a way as to attempt to disarm him of the chair, whose legs were pointed in their direction. This didn't quite do as intended, with Gareth having a heavy grip upon it; his work at the store lifting and carrying so much as he did, enabling him to hold it firmly by the back rest. It did, however, cause him to stagger slightly as he did so, turning him clockwise and opening his guard to a blow from another of the men with his club, hitting Gareth on the shoulder and upper arm. This caused him to let out a shout of pain as it connected and almost made him fall to one knee. He pulled himself up again, but not before being dealt another blow to his face from his first assailant. This blow he managed to absorb some with the wood of the chair, but it was not enough to temper the power of the strike completely as the wooden club contacted his jaw, sending him reeling backwards and bleeding from his mouth and nose.

Kate, now screaming at the men to leave them alone, dropped to hold her husband in her hands, his shoulders and head resting on her knees. Thelia, who had until now been standing somewhat behind Gareth, stepped forward over her downed friend with the legs of her own chair pointing in their attacker's direction hoping to dissuade them from any further attacks on the man on the ground.

Thraven, his wife, Camlin, and Steven had stood up from their table. The two flarfen, rather than picking up a chair as some sort of defensive weapon, bared their sharp teeth and claws on their hands - a flarfen may be shorter in stature than a typical human or elf, but they more than capable of causing an injury when confronted. Steven, seeing the actions of those around him, picked up a chair and raised it threateningly as he could with a look on his face of worry and uncertainty.

Several of the assailants, including the woman who led them, lunged towards the trio with clubs raised. Thraven, with quite a speed, slipped to the side of them and swiped at one man with his claws causing him to drop his club while letting out a shout of pain. The other mercenaries swung at Camlin, who was as quick as her husband, dodging the blow from a woman to her right, the swing missing by a good margin. This dodge though took the Flarfen woman closer in range to the leader of the group who had just addressed them. The leader made a sideways swing with her own wooden club and managed to catch Camlin with a hit to her midriff which caused her to wince in pain but keep her poise as she then ducked away again.

Steven impressed by his fellow's agility and spurred on by their gusto, attempted to press back their attackers; he stepped forward with his left leg, holding the chair by the back rest, facing up and legs facing away. He motioned towards the woman who had missed Camlin along with another man to her right that had a grin of angry aggression on his face. Both swung at him with their clubs from either side. Steven was unsure which way to turn and awkwardly raising the chair in some vein attempt to block both, surprisingly with some success, but ultimately not enough to deflect the blows convincingly. Both struck either side of him at the top of each arm. This damage caused him to drop the chair as he grimaced in pain. Seizing the advantage, he received a jab from one of the aggressors to his belly, sharp and sudden, which caused him to bend forward, unfortunately opening up for a knee to his head which drove him to the floor.

Lilly and Gwithen were approached by two more men. "Look here, two elf witches," said one to the other who replied with a toothy grin and a slap of his club on the table between them, his other holding a flaming torch that lit up the foul look in his eyes.

"Why are you here?!" shouted Gwithen. "Be gone from here and take your wickedness with you!"

The man replied with his club in hand, resting on the table. "We're here to teach a lesson. You need to learn the way of things, yeah. We aren't going anywhere!" With that he pulled up his club from the table and swung from left to right in an attempt to catch Gwithen in the ribs. Elves, not known for their sloth like reactions proved true and she sprung backwards, pulling his sister with her to create some distance between them and the ruffians. The men split up and advanced on the two elves round either side of the circular table.

"Stay back you wretches!" Lilly shouted. Still the men came forward, each seemingly intent to continue their attack. Gwithen stood back from the table to the left as the men stood, with Lilly to the right, both keenly aware of the danger they were in. They were not fighting people and not trained in any particular combat, but still had their natural elven finesse to aid them.

Both men looked at each other and with a very subtle nod between them, begun to swing at their targets. They swung up with the intention to come arcing down on the two women but were never to hit their mark.

The man to the right suddenly dropped his weapon arm down almost letting go of both it and the torch that was in his left but managed to keep them clasped desperately in his hands. He simultaneously was moved whole in body to his left as if something unexpected had impacted into the right side of him. The other man made more progress with his swing, but similarly stopped short of hitting Gwithen, letting his club drop to the floor as he fell over to his left as if something had struck him suddenly and violently.

Gwithen and Lilly raised desperate smiles on their faces as they realised what was happening. Both men had been struck by the hand of a single person, Toby the blacksmith. He had evidently seen the band of mercenaries skulking on the edge of town and followed the group that split off towards the tavern where his wife was enjoying an evening. He had come through the door struck wide open and proceeded to strike both of the men attacking Lilly and her sister in the ribs from behind with his smith's hammer in short order. He then stood with the sisters and prepared to strike the man still on his feet.

"Lilly, are you ok?!" He said. "Gwithen?"

"Toby! What is going on? I am so glad to see you, my love!" said Lilly, happy in the knowledge her husband was unharmed.

"I don't know who these blaggards are, but I saw them

on the edge of town just minutes ago," he said. "Get back and be gone with you, scum!" He shouted angrily at the man still on his feet.

This thug that had advanced on Lilly, stepped back, still in pain from the blow he had taken from the hammer and moved over to the man on the floor while throwing the torch at Toby who swatted it to the ground and stamped it out. He dragged up the other to his feet and they slowly recoiled from the angry Blacksmith.

Those of the mercenaries that were assailing Thelia, Gareth and Kate, seeing the wrathful blacksmith smite the two men to their left, paused in surprise and themselves took several steps back, all except the leader who had heralded their arrival. She gave a steeled and spiteful look to Toby and swung her club at Thelia who too had looked over at the commotion to her right. She was struck in the chest which had become exposed after she lowered the chair in her hands having momentarily taken her eyes of the people in front of her. She let out not a sound of pain, though it was clearly shown on her face. She stepped back and dropped the chair before pulling herself up straight again and sticking out her arms to put up some defence to her attackers.

Yet another group of assailants - three gruff looking men - had set upon Delia, Marcus, Harold and Alma who were all caught as unawares as everyone else. They had managed to stand themselves up, but not quite with the wherewithal to arm themselves with anything at hand. The three men jumped on this and swung their maces towards them, seemingly with no specific target in mind. Two of the three connected with something: one landing square in the chest of Marcus, who immediately fell to one knee and the other catching Alma on the back of the head. She fell to the ground unconscious. Harold let out a shout for his sister that echoed around the tavern and threw himself at the man who had just knocked her to the floor. This brute was not prepared for such a furious reaction and was caught off the front foot as the maddened sibling threw himself with all his might and tackled him to the ground.

Harold began punching the man repeatedly on either

side of his head before being interrupted by one of his compatriots kicking Marcus in the head, still on one knee, causing him to fall to his left. Seeing his friend take another blow to his head nudged Harold back to his senses somewhat, getting up from the man he was flailing at and moving to put himself between Marcus, his sister and their aggressors. Before he could do so Marcus was then sharply punted again for good measure, coughing and spluttering as a result.

Several more mercenaries came through the open door of the tavern, two women and a man, perhaps having followed Toby from his forge. There was an imposing number of them now and the beleaguered defenders had no chance of repelling them. Having seen more of their comrade's funnel through the doors, those that he been shaken by the blacksmiths arrival now redoubled their efforts and advanced again on their prey.

At least they would have. From the direction of the bar suddenly came numerous projectiles of some kind. Not physical bolts, or arrows or rock from a sling, but something else entirely. These things seemed not to have form as such rather, their very existence betrayed by the shimmering of the air around them. They were the shape and curvature perhaps of a circular pan, but their edges softened and known only from the way they displaced the light around them.

They shot out from the direction of the bar and hit six of the assailants as they stood, in the middle of the tavern. The force of each sent the individuals off their feet and back several yards with some hitting the back wall and one particularly unlucky woman flying out of the wide-open space of the doorway.

All involved looked over towards the bar from where these barely seen missiles had emanated. Standing on top of it was Golon, a knife in one hand, looking out at the intruders with a stern look on his face that was unusual for such jovial individual. He appeared to be standing guard. Standing guard over someone behind the bar. Nathanael, the wizened old mage whose tavern had just been breached by a gang of hoodlums looked to be channelling some sort of spell. He stood with one hand held high above his head and the other planted on the surface of the bar, bracing himself as he summoned such magical forces. He had evidently been using his soulful strength and energy to summon up such projectiles of force and sorcerous power to hurl at the unwanted guests.

"Go back to whence you came you baleful miscreants!" Golon shouted, from his position on the bar, staring a hole through the woman that led this band of thugs. "There is more where that came from, he's just getting started and he could use the practice on your bunch of dummies!"

The woman grimaced and looked around her, at the empty spaces where her fellows were just standing and back and to the ground where they currently resided. She gave a grimaced nod them all, as if an order. Those still on their feet began to edge away, towards the door. They slowly moved from the bar, pulling up those of them from the ground and dragged them with them as they slunk out of the tavern. These were the first to leave followed by those injured by the blacksmith and the flarfen and lastly the woman that led them. She backtracked slowly and lastly of the lot, sharing her angry eyes and hateful intentions between both Thelia and Golon, who followed her every move as she made way back outside. Her steps took her further and further away, the last of her band leaving the tavern and with one final scathing look at Thelia, stepped out and away from view.

As they left, Thelia turned and looked straight to Nathanael who still had his hand raised, eyes focused on the door, but somewhat slightly glazed; still in a state of readiness to unleash more magic upon those that wished to cause harm. He seemed to notice her looking at him as his steeled face turned towards her and immediately lightened upon doing so. He gave her a small smile before turning back to the blown-out entrance of the inn. She in turn turned to Gareth beside her who lay on the ground in Kate's arms.

"Gareth!" she said kneeling down next to Kate. "How is he?" she continued.

"I am ok," Gareth said, looking up to her with a bloodied face. Kate had pulled out a handkerchief from her pocket and was dabbing at a wound.

"Who were these people and how many more are they?! In fact, what about the others. They could be attacking the whole village!" Kate said passionately to Thelia, but with eyes looking desperately at her husband's face.

"I am not sure," Thelia said. She looked briefly at Kate and Gareth and then around the room, seeing the damage caused to her fellow villagers of Overton. "That woman said something about the village rejecting something or other. I wonder if it had anything to do with that man that gave that bigoted speech the other day. He went off in a fury when it was evident, he wouldn't get his way." Her eyes went across to Steven, Thraven and Camlin. The two flarfen had knelt down to tend to Steven who lay injured on the ground.

"How is he?" She said to Camlin whose hands were placed gently on his chest.

"He is ok. He took a good few blows with some blood spilled, but he will pull through I am sure of it," replied Camlin.

Gwithen walked over to them, staring at Gareth and Steven, both on the ground, faces crimson with blood.

"I can get some healing herbs and make something for their wounds. I don't know what is going on outside though; it might be difficult to make it there and back without encountering more trouble."

Toby, after embracing his wife said, "I can go with you Gwithen. If any more of these scoundrels are around. I will give them what for."

"We may all have to leave this place," Golon suddenly interrupted, "I can smell kindling. I think they might be setting fire to the Tavern." His voice was surprisingly calm while conveying such a revelation to the danger they were in.

Nathanael dropped his gaze from the door seemingly having snapped out of the concentration he had previously been in. "I don't think they are finished with us just yet and I am not sure what state the rest of the town will be in." He looked across the room, to Golon and then to Thelia. "We need to get out of here," he continued, "Perhaps that is what they want. I imagine more of those toe rags are outside waiting for us. I suggest we go out the back and see what awaits us?"

Thelia nodded and said, "Right, let's get everyone to their feet and make for the back door."

Thraven and Camlin pulled Steven to his feet while Toby helped Gareth get to his. Harold pulled up Marcus from the floor who was still coughing and spluttering, but with his gaze firmly set on Alma who was lying prone on the floor. Delia, aided by Gwithen picked her up between them before the group as one, moved towards the bar and the back exit of the tavern.

Nathanael reached below the bar and picked up a wooden staff. He nodded to Golon who then climbed down from his position.

Chapter 24

Nathanael was the first through the door with his staff in his right hand while his left hand was raised up as if ready to throw something from it. There was nothing tangible in his hand, but rather a glow that seemed to rest upon his palm.

After Nathanael came Golon. His usual brightness and positive demeanour replaced by a steeled look of determination. He still had his knife in hand, raised and ready whilst he looked around both left and right, assessing the surroundings for any potential foes or allies. He motioned for the others to follow him out of the door and outside.

Toby came through the doorway, Gareth's right arm slung over his shoulder, carrying a good deal of the injured man's weight. After this came Kate, with anxious eyes on her injured husband; too pre-occupied to look at or think of anything else. They were quickly followed by the two flarfen, propping up Steven. Being shorter in stature than a human he was slightly more hunched over, but the two of them carried his weight with no issue. Behind them came the others: Gwithen and Delia carrying a still unconscious, but breathing Alma followed by Lilly and then Harold, with his arm around Marcus, who was still coughing, but managing to walk. Lastly came Thelia who was staring all around her as she came, watching over the others as they shuffled through the door at the rear of the tavern.

They found themselves outside and to the east facing of the tavern. North of them was the tannery and opposite the road leading south, out of the village. Above the coughing and groans of pain from the variously injured members of their party, they could hear commotion coming from the centre of the town, though none could see what was causing it from where they currently stood, hidden by the wall of the buildings close by.

Nathanael edged forwards, intending to take a look around the northern wall of his tavern. He stuck his head round the corner of the wall with his staff held low and still his left hand held high with the glow, still making its presence known. He paused there for a few moments before quickly pulling back to the group.

"Well, it's not good. I can say that much," he said. "I can see the flicker of flame and smoke which most likely accounts for the burning we can smell. I fear I will be left without a home after tonight. But it matters not for such things, we must get to safety and see if the others in town are ok," he continued, with eyes set across to Thelia, who stared back at him. "We must try and make for the guard house, if we can. I saw some men outside I didn't recognise, but I don't think they have gained entry."

"Well, it's either a straight run for the front entrance of the guard tower or we try and make it around the back way," Thelia replied. "I imagine they are waiting for us to do something. Though I guess there is a chance they were not expecting the prowess of an old mage to be so deterring to their efforts." For a moment she lowered her usual stern look and smiled a sincere smile at Nathanael who may well have blushed had it been under other circumstances.

"I think its best we try and go around if we can," said Golon. "We can't manage much speed carrying the injured so perhaps a sharp dash to the front, past who knows how many of them, might be a rash decision."

"I agree," said Gwithen. I can try and get to our shop and grab some things. Along the way".

"Gwithen we should stay together!" said Lilly to her sister.

"I know Lilly, but we will need to tend to the injured," said Gwithen.

"Well, let me go with Toby instead," replied Lilly.

"Ok, Toby, you go with her when we move, I will help Gareth," said Nathanael. "Let's get to the Tannery first though and assess the situation."

Toby who was looking around and beyond the tavern, looked to Nathanael and then to Lilly. "Yes, that sounds good. I am not going to leave your side," he said.

"Ok," said Nathanael. "Let us keep to the east of the

village and round the tannery. Hopefully, we can make it to the rear of the guard house unhindered. Though we must be prepared for a fight."

They began moving towards the tannery which lay sixty yards in front of them but staying close to the field edge to the right with the intention of attracting the least attention as possible.

As they made some way towards the tannery, they looked to their left as a sudden bout of flame flared off from the side of the tavern; their assailants had set a fire with the eager flames anxious to consume the building whole.

Nathanael held up briefly and stared at his inn, alive with fire. A saddened look crept onto his face as his home burned in front of him, but he then re-doubled himself, remembering the still imminently dangerous situation they were in.

The others had stopped behind him, themselves enthralled by the sudden thundering of fire as it caught itself upon the thatched roof of the building. They all noticed Nathanael standing there staring at the inevitable desolation of all he owned and instinctively turned and followed him as he pulled himself away from the fiery scene, towards the next building.

They crept across to the tannery and turning their eyes west, towards the centre of the village, they could all see now the group of mercenaries that had invaded the town: there were several outside the front of the guard house as it faced the square in the middle of the village; several standing at the general store, directly across the square; the town hall to the southwest assailed at its front doors.

Thelia, looking towards the town hall, hoped that if anyone had sought refuge behind those sturdy doors that they held long enough for help to arrive. She kept her stride though, moving with the rest of the group.

There were people crowded outside of the Duck Feather Inn as its roof was ablaze, sending forth tendril like flames, searching to find something to burn amongst the brickwork of the outer walls, though it would inevitably engulf the innards of Nathanael's beloved home.

Those standing outside the tavern - had they made the effort to - would have seen the bedraggled group making their way from the rear of the inn, but all seemed quite enthralled by the act of arson before them. Nathanael wondered if it was more than this; they seemed if anything, quite uninterested in searching for him and his party; surely, they expected those inside to escape through some other way besides the main entrance, but they seemed content to watch the place become engulfed in flames.

The injured group of villagers ambled as best they could towards the eastern side of the tannery building. They saw the lights were on above, but the store below was all closed up for the evening as they would normally expect. They could not see if there were more of the mercenaries on the northern or north-west side of the building due to the direction. The group approached it, but pressed on, nonetheless. They reached the east wall of the Tailors and Tannery and paused for a breath. The air was starting to become bedecked with smoke from the burning building which wasn't pleasant, but those carrying the injured were glad for the break regardless.

"Wait here," said Nathanael, intending to move around the north-east corner of the building to assess the situation before they moved on towards the guard house that now lay west of them. He was interrupted by Thelia who was bringing up the rear.

"Nathanael," she said. "Be careful please," before giving a muted smile which he returned in kind before turning away and disappearing around the corner, still with his left hand held up, still glowing with some sort of weird otherworldly energy.

Within less than a minute he had returned with a look of concern upon his brow. "Well, it's not as bad as one would think," he said, addressing them all. "There are several people on horseback on the village green. They appear to be directing this attack but seem preoccupied with barking orders at those around them. Still, they may well notice us making a break for the rear of the guard house." He paused momentarily and then continued, "It seems as though the way is clear past Toby's and up to your place." He looked to Gwithen and Lilly as he said so. "It is most probably best if you go and get what you need and meet us back here before we go. They may well see us as we break for the guard house making it more difficult for anyone else to follow suit. We will wait here for your return, and all go together."

"Yes, I think that's a good idea, replied Gwithen. "I would be too worried about Lilly and Toby should we reach safety without them."

"I agree," said Harold, still holding up Marcus.

"Ok then. Lilly and I will make for their place and get what we need to tend to some of the wounds. Hopefully, we will not be long," said Toby. He uncoupled his arm from Gareth with Nathanael moving into his place, his staff arm somewhat awkwardly around him. Lilly walked over to Toby and placed her hand on his back, before turning to Gwithen with a smile and then moving off north, towards their shop together.

The group of them waited by the wall of the tannery facing east, all with eyes and ears alive to sense any incoming danger. They stared out towards the fields to the east. Perhaps they might have seen the small gathering on the riverbank: a well-dressed man in a dark red suit, looking intently at the unravelling mayhem; a woman in long black leather, seemingly apathetic to the situation; a wiry looking man with a top hat, rubbing his hands together in enjoyment of the situation; behind them almost hidden, two men large in stature - imposing and quiet.

They were not seen though. Hidden by the reach of the trees of the riverbank and the high grass between them or perhaps, by some more esoteric sorcery. All that the bruised group, hunched against the wall, could discern were the quiet fields and the steady river as it quietly journeyed southeast before turning straight due east. All except Nathanael. He had been scanning the riverbank and the long grass for any signs of movement or the onset of yet more invaders to their village.

"Golon," he said.

"Yes Nathanael?" Golon had been following by Nathanael and too was staring out across to the east of the village.

"Hmm, I thought I could see someone out there across the field. Though I am not really sure." He tried to motion with his left hand still held high, in the direction in which he thought he may have caught the glimpse of several figures.

"I am not sure I can see much, especially from down hear Nathanael," replied Golon.

"Yes, of course, Golon. Never mind," said Nathanael before turning his head away.

"Nathanael" said Golon. "What do we do about Reginald and Carrey? The lights are on up there" They both looked up to the floor above the ground, light glowing out from the windows.

"Buggering Hell!" Nathanael shouted before looking around. "Sorry, I had forgotten about them. I hope they are alright! If they had some sort of backdoor, we could somehow check on them, but the only entrance is through the front, right in full sight of any who wished to see. Once we reach the guard house, we will see about checking on them and whoever else," he said.

"Yes indeed, we must get who we have to safety," said Golon. Hopefully Deven will have made his way here by them. Perhaps we could dissuade them from continuing with this attack once he does so."

The fire from the inn had fully engulfed its roof and begun to spread to the inside. The blaze was in full roaring motion and the night air was filling with smoke.

Lilly and Toby had snuck quietly from the tannery, across the edge of the field to their east and up to Toby's forge. They both paused momentarily on the east wall of the building. Their home was attached to the smithy on the floor above and behind the forge itself.

"Are you ok my love?" said Toby, turning to Lilly as they rested against the wall.

"I am ok dearest. I am just worried and concerned. Who are these people and why are they doing this?"

"I wish I knew," replied Toby, looking around him. He turned back and snuck his head ever so much round the corner to see what he could see. He quickly turned back and grabbed Lilly by the hand. "We need to go now," he said.

"Why? What's happening?" she replied.

His face turned back to her with an embittered look upon it. "Those bastards are setting fire to our home Lilly. They are using the forge to light kindling. It won't be long now before it too goes up in flames."

She looked into his eyes and squeezed his hand as he held hers. "It doesn't matter my love. We are safe and that's all that matters." Toby tried to give a smile but struggled to contain his anger rising once more at the thought of his livelihood and their home too, going up in flames.

Still hands clasped together they turned and set off again, running as quickly as they could north to Lilly and Gwithen's Herbalist shop. The building was dark; they had shut up shop earlier in the evening and Gwithen, who lived above had come to the tavern. There didn't appear to be any of the intruders around, although Lilly could still see the men on horseback on the village green, behind the guard tower and the outlines further south. She quickly pulled her husband with her as she dashed to the front of her store and opened it before the two of them filed in. She decided not to light any lamps and kept it in darkness. She quickly went behind the counter and grabbed several pouches of various herbs and a cream in a small round, metal tin while Toby stood guard by the door, hammer in hand. Once Lilly had all she came for, she quickly looked around - even in the darkness - and hoped that it wouldn't be the last time that she saw it, before rushing over to Toby and they both exited the shop.

The couple ran back to the easterly wall of the herbalist building with the blacksmiths roughly sixty yards away, now ridden with the invasion of flame all about it. Toby stared intently at his smithy as Lilly held his hand, pulling him ever onward, refusing to have him stand and watch the destruction unfold.

They made their way as quickly and quietly as they could, back to the rest of the group who were still waiting against the Tannery building.

"Lilly!" Gwithen exclaimed as she saw her sister approach. "You are both ok? I am so sorry about your home! We could see the smoke from here."

"It's ok," said Toby "We are ok and that's all that matters," echoing Lilly's words to him. There was still a hint of anger in his eyes, and he may well have liked to run out and swing for these people that had set his home ablaze, but he refrained from doing so, guessing how that would most likely end.

"Ok," said Nathanael. "It's time we made a run for the guard house." He still had his left hand held high as he said this, his other with staff grasped tightly was around Gareth's shoulders, propping him up.

"It seems they are determined to cause as much mayhem as possible," said Thelia.

"Yes indeed" said Golon, looking up at her. "The safest place for us right now is the guard house," he continued.

"Yes," said Kate, taking her attention away from her husband. "But even if they aren't aware of our intention, it seems they will surely catch us before we make it."

Golon looked over to her and said "Well, I think Nathanael is aware. I have the feeling that he his has something in mind to ease our passage there." He looked over to Nathanael, still with his hand held high and they both nodded at each other.

"Yes," Nathanael said. "Everyone, get ready. We are going to make a dash across for the back entrance to the guard house. It has yet to be set on attacked with fire and once we get there, we should be able to prevent them from ever doing so."

As they were readying for the off, Toby came and relieved Nathanael, putting his arm back around Gareth, allowing Nathanael to co-ordinate things as best he could. Harold stood holding Marcus from his left. He was a man in his early forties, clean shaven with dark brown hair that that ran down the side of his face, wearing a platted shirt of dark reds and browns with dark grey trousers and leather boots. His sister Alma, who was carried by Delia and Gwithen, had similarly brown hair, down to her shoulders and wore an off-white cotton dress with a dark blue cardigan button up at the front. She was still unconscious as Harold looked over to her.

"How is she doing?" Harold said to Delia, a woman in her thirties with short dark hair, wearing a thick material blue dress and long boots.

"She is ok Harold. She still breathes. Don't worry we will take care of her as we go," she replied.

"Thank you, Delia. Those cowards. How could they strike my dear sister?" His teeth gritted as he recalled the violence in the tavern that now stood all consumed in a fiery embrace, casting shadows across the village square.

"How is Marcus?" she said of her husband who was hung low upon the shoulder of his friend, his face cut and bleeding, though still somewhat aware of the situation.

"I am ok my dear," he said looking up to her from blood shot eyes. "Take more than that to keep me down." He gave a well-intended smile at these words but caused his wife to tear up at the sight of it.

"Is everyone good to go?" said Golon, as Nathanael peered around the wall, observing the path they were about to take towards the rear of the guard house. His left arm had never left that raised position with the feint glow emanating from the palm of his hand. He could see the smoke from blacksmiths to the north, perhaps sixty yards away, fiercely churning flames of destruction that was gutting the building with unrepentant force.

There were several people there along their path; not anyone that he recognised, but rather wearing the same uniform as those that had come crashing into his tavern. They were revelling in the havoc they were causing, with several holding torches which they were using to ignite anything they could find that was as yet untouched by the flame.

South, Nathanael saw his own home, his tavern; the Duck Feather Inn, where he had enjoyed many days and nights serving the local residents and visitors to the village; exchanging stories and advice with those that came to taste his famous Husky Honey Mead. Now it was all but consumed by a raging fire that cared not for the possessions and memories of an old wizard. He held his beard and stroked it earnestly as he stared and lost himself in the moment; the shadow of melancholy sat over him. Lastly and straight ahead, he could see the guard tower, that place the townspeople would seek for protection whenever it was needed.

A GRIM JOURNEY

The Lonefield Borough Constabulary building, as it was known, now stood stoic and solid in the face of the commotion. Behind in the village green were those captains in charge of this menace of men and women, their mouths barking orders and with satisfied looks on each of their faces. Around them were the foot soldiers that had snuck into the town, several of which the group of townspeople held up behind the tannery building, had already had the misfortune of dealing with. The building itself seemed to be holding up and there were several guardsman standing in the turret with crossbows trained on anyone that good too close. This created a perimeter around it which the invaders were reluctant to cross and instead were moving around the other buildings of the village, occupying the village green and the outer edge of the square, south of it. Nathanael took note of this before turning his eyes to what else he could see.

The store straight ahead of him, run by Gareth and Kate was at the moment still standing and still bereft of the interest of a passing flame. Nathanael did notice a small group of the mercenary soldiers converging on it, several with torches in hand. It seemed as though they had every intention of adding it to the list of buildings making up the inferno.

To the south-west of his view, he could just make out the shape of the town hall; its outline and stature had become somewhat obscured from the smoke and fire of the Duck Feather inn. Nathanael couldn't confirm if it was burning, but of what he could see of it, it seemed not to have been tampered with.

Of the houses and the stables to the north-east, including Luther's beyond, he could not tell as the guard house lay square in his line of sight. The gathering cloud of smoke from the burning embers of the buildings around the village was also hampering his view quite substantially; he knew little of what lay past it.

"On my call," said Nathanael "We will make a break for the rear of the guard house. Do not worry about those which may wish to do us more harm!" He looked over to the still upraised palm of his hand before looking back to the group. He motioned all to move and the group of villagers, huddled and beaten by a band of ferocious vagabonds, ventured out in roughly single file from around their hiding place behind the Tailors and Tannery. They made their way towards the guard house building, standing in the centre of the village.

At the off they were at least somewhat shielded from view by the smoke of the buildings that now roared of flame in the night. They moved as quickly as they could, but sticking together, which meant they moved at the slowest pace of the group - those being carried or supported by the others.

Nathanael took the lead followed right behind by Golon. He still had his hand held high while Golon, skulked along with his dagger at hand. Next in line was Marcus, propped up by Harold; held up by the right shoulder as his arm was slung around Harold.

Alma was still unconscious from the blow to the back of the head she took in the bar, but Delia, holding her from her left side could see her still breathing as they carried her. To her right was Gwithen, whose gaze was busy looking out for incoming danger; watchful for anything that might approach with malignant intent. Behind them came Steven, flanked on either side by the flarfen couple of Thraven and Camlin. Their noses were twitching here and there as their heightened sense of smell took in the odour of the smoke, the burning wood and smell of angry evildoers.

Behind them came Gareth, bloodied from his wounds, looking ahead to the guard house whilst wincing in pain from the injuries done. Toby walked on his right, his left arm around just below Gareth's shoulder. Toby's right arm was held free with his hand firmly grasping his smith's hammer. He held a fierce look on his face, it taking only the slightest provocation for him to use it on any who got to close.

Lastly came Thelia, bringing up the rear. She was extremely observant of all the goings on around them, even with the obscuring smoke and fire in the air. She watched for any more of their attackers. She thought to herself it only a matter of time before they were noticed, this bedraggled party of battered and bruised patrons of the once renowned Duck Feather Inn. She briefly looked to Nathanael - as she often was want to do - but her eyes shifted to his upright hand with his palm facing the sky. She knew of his abilities as a mage. She knew there was still power left in those wizened hands; retired or not he was still a mage and mages didn't rightly forget all knowledge of the power they once wielded.

The assembled villagers, cast as they were as refugees, looking for safety from the violence around them, had made thirty or forty yards of the hundred distance to the rear of the guard house before they were noticed by several of the mounted captains on the green.

"There is more!" One shouted, pointing to them from his lofted position.

Another shouted, "Are they from the tavern?" to one of his men standing close. It was one of those that had charged into the inn previously and retreated at the show of magical prowess from Nathanael.

"Yes sir, that's them!" he replied.

"Well!" said the captain "Get after them!" He swung his head round to address several of the mercenaries that stood around them, several with torches held close, lighting their faces in the dark.

Roughly a dozen of those on foot turned and moved to intercept the party with one of the captains breaking from the others on the green and making his way over. He hung back, intending to let the foot soldiers carry out his whims, instead of getting involved personally. Those on foot moved quickly to meet the party who was unable to accelerate their pace in any way in response to the threat that was now upon them. They were bound by the slowest among them and were not interested at splitting up.

"Here they come!" Golon shouted to Nathanael.

"Yes," Nathanael responded. "Everyone, keep moving towards the guard house! Don't stop or turn back, even if they get close!" he said, turning to the rest of the group, still with his left hand held high. It seemed to be glowing brighter than before. Thelia thought he must be intending to cast some sort of spell, but what specifically, she was unsure. She wouldn't have to wait long. None of the group pulled to a stop. All heeding Nathanael's words, they focused on the guard house ahead while doing the best they could to ignore those that approached them with bad intentions in mind.

There mercenaries came closer, and closer still to the band of villagers, the look of malice ever clearer on their faces with every threatening step. There were mostly men, but several women in the troop and besides the violent intent the one common thread among them was the race they belonged to; they were all human.

The villagers kept moving; the shuffle and drag as they helped the injured in an uneven step evident in their stride. But they kept moving. There were a few stops and starts here and there; Toby set a foot wrong and had to steady himself - he was grimacing at the mercenaries and not focused on where he was walking; Gwithen and Delia came out of step with each other which lead to a brief pause as they realigned themselves, clutching Alma from either side. But they kept moving.

Golon, due to his smaller stature had to exert more energy to keep up but was quick on his feet. He weaved to and fro between them as they went, urging all to not give into fright. He suddenly heard another voice, besides those from the north of them that were bearing down upon them. It was the voice of the woman that had led the charge through the doors of the tavern. She was leading them now to prey upon the villagers from the south. Golon thought they must have stood outside, enjoying their act of arson. Now though, they were after him and his band of fellows who were now caught in a pincer between the two angry groups of malicious mercenaries.

"Keep going everyone!" Nathanael suddenly shouted, his voice rising out above the crackle of burning ember, of determined steps and calls of anger aimed in their direction. He took a step aside from the group and paused in his position until he was in the middle of the line and begun moving again. His upraised hand he now raised even further until it was stretched out to its full length above his head. "Yo-Bandi!" came the call from his lips and he paused for a moment and in that moment the glow from his palm grew inexorably in strength. Whereas before it had been a subtle glow, like that of a candle laying low, it had now grown in intensity many times over; glowing wide and bright from his palm in all directions. Its colour was a bright orangey red and somehow otherworldly as if not quite in phase with reality.

The moment was brief, but its powerful beaming glow managed to pull attention from all those that were aiming to prey upon the villagers like a struggling herd of deer on an open plain. Of the villagers themselves, either they were all uninterested in it or somehow couldn't see the resplendent show of radiance for all pressed on regardless. Nathanael's arm then slammed down with a sudden and forceful movement with the palm of his hand out flat, facing the ground.

With this striking action the brightness expanded exponentially in all directions in almost a blink of an eye. It reached out to the sight of the mercenary soldiers on both sides of the villagers. And all stopped in their tracks. Every man and woman, both mounted and on foot stood, staring at the light that burst out from Nathanael's hand. They stood transfixed by it, dazzled by it, either unable to or unwilling to take a step closer towards the villagers. Their focus was now completely on the bright light all around them. They stood as if enchanted, just staring.

The villagers all slowed in unison, but not to stare at the explosion of brightness. To them, the soldiers abruptly and for no apparent reason came to a sudden stop and now all seem somehow stupefied. Golon's voice raised up from below.

"Keep moving everyone! Don't stop!"

They looked around to their fellows and with a few shrugged shoulders and simple acceptance, kept moving to the guard house.

They crossed the distance and arrived at the back gate of the building. Nathanael had pulled up the rear with the aid of Thelia. He looked somewhat drained and tired as if he had just spent a great deal of energy.

The guardsman up in the battlement had shouted down to open the gate which greeted them as they arrived. They all staggered through with Nathanael and Thelia lastly followed by Golon who had been keeping a keen eye on their would-be assailants should they break free of the trance they were grasped by. With all through the gate and into the building he gave one last glance back and then stepped through the doorway.

Chapter 25

Eyes open, straight up in bed. Here sat Luther. He was momentarily confused and unsure as to where he was and what he was doing. This wasn't the bedroom of his home in Overton Village; there was no poster of Randolph Montgomery Henceforth; he didn't recognise the surroundings of this place and he was fairly sure his was the only bed in his room, but now he could see five others.

He wasn't out on the road either. There was no soil beneath him, but rather a mattress firm and warm. There were no columns of the earth or other flora in the vicinity and when he looked up there was no idle sky or sun that he could see, but rather the rafters of a building.

The realisation came to him. He was not at home or out on the road alone. He was in the chapel of the cleric couple that he had found the night before. He looked around him further. The windows had their shutters open slightly, letting in the morning sunlight. He could see the man in the bed opposite who was awake, and sitting up in bed, enjoying a round of toast. Luther looked across to the other bed of the older woman and saw that she too was awake, drinking a cup of tea. When their eyes met, Luther gave each a smile to each before looking around the room once more.

He wasn't uncomfortable, but he was not particularly sure what to do in the situation; should he strike up a conversation with them both or perhaps just a friendly nod or better to leave them to their own devices and not make a fool of himself trying to do either. The smile seemed to be enough. He could not see Edgar or his wife anywhere in the room and wondered where they might be. Perhaps they were busy away somewhere doing some good, he thought.

He sat there for a while, pondering the events of the day before. After a few minutes the front door opened and in came Edgar's wife. He noticed the crescent moons on her Dark blue robes before raising his gaze to her face to see a welcoming smile upon it.

"Good morning, Luther," said the woman.

"Good morning," replied Luther.

"I don't think we have properly met," she said.

"No, I don't believe we have."

"My name is Agnes," said the cleric, entering the room proper and closing the door behind her. "How are you feeling this morning, Luther?"

Luther sat himself up straighter in the bend and said, "I am feeling quite good, yes. The pain in my face body has subsided, to the point where it feels almost gone. That healing salve your husband applied is fantastic stuff!"

She gave a knowing smile at this remark, almost as if she knew his condition before he even mentioned it. "Well, I am glad to hear it. You seemed a bit worse for wear when you came in," she said.

Luther suddenly thought back to the encounter with the bandits out on the forest road. Had they been apprehended?' he thought. Or would they slink into the forest and evade capture, free to accost and attack other travellers through the Dell Wood? He had no idea.

"Yes," he said. "It turned out not to be particularly safe on the forest road. Though admittedly I was aware of some trouble roaming the place, I had hoped to avoid it, but sadly that wasn't the case." He didn't want to be too explicit in details of how he knew there might be trouble. Perhaps the woman, Magena Strewth, whom he had found on the road leading into Forestead would appreciate some discretion as to what had befallen her. Pre-empting the inevitable question of how he knew this he said, "I had heard at the village of Forestead, of bandits roaming the woods lately. I had hoped not to make their acquaintance and I regret that wasn't so."

Her brow lowered in a soothing way and with reassurance in her eyes said, "Well, don't worry about that. You are past that and safely in Bramstone now. We'll let the barracks know there are bandits skulking this side of the forest road. I imagine they might send out a patrol to look for them. We can't be having people being assaulted while making their way here! Heavens no!" She turned the conversation away to more immediate concerns, "Are you hungry? I could make you up some toast or perhaps some scrambled eggs?"

Luther's belly had already decided the answer before his mind could decide on the matter with a rumble of his stomach: "Yes please some scrambled eggs would be lovely. But only if it is no trouble."

She smiled and nodded adding, "It is no trouble. Ok, I'll just be a minute and then I'll get them going for you," said Agnes.

Luther thanked her and she turned away before exiting out to the back before re-appearing a few minutes later. She got out a pan and some eggs and got them cooking over the fire along with some sliced breath for some toasting. Before long Luther was happily sitting up in bed, hungrily wolfing down breakfast along with a warming cup of tea that from a pot that was sitting to one side under a cosy.

And then from nowhere, like a bolt from the middle of blue, but in slow and silent motion, it fell upon him. He had managed to be free of it upon waking, which was unusual, but wonderful for him. He nearly always awoke in the midst of it caressing his soul, but today he had been spared; given a brief respite, at least for a while.

He went from a mood of contentment and at least, quiet hopefulness to one of bleakness, of ill feeling and sadness. What had gone before, that had brought some joy or optimism; waking up in a nice warm bed, wounds healed, and body recuperated; hope of finding the woman he sought, all gone now. It mattered not how joyous or happy things might be before, how positive the outlook seemed or how warm and comforting the surroundings were, when he was feeling as he did now, all paled away, grey and bleak, his defences pushed back and in remission.

He finished the breakfast as best he could though it was slow going; each mouthful felt so much longer and laboured as his appetite was stealing away. He then placed it on the little bed side table to his left. He felt for nothing other than to pull the covers right back over himself and to go back to the sanctity of sleep. At least then, if he was not awake, unconscious and unknowing of the waking world, he might find peace. Sleep was closer to oblivion he thought.

    He waited quietly until he could get Agnes' attention; she was busy now seeing to the other guests of the chapel. When she got up from the chair sitting by the older woman, he managed to catch her eye and she walked over to him.

    "Hi Luther," she said, standing at the end of his bed. "Are you ok? Has something happened?" She had obviously noted the melancholy on his face and his sudden reluctance to now look her in the eyes past getting her attention.

    "I have struggles with myself, internally," Muttered Luther, looking down at the patterned covers under which he was sitting. "I get feelings of sadness. I am sorry I am not much to talk to right now." Agnes smiled a friendly smile and briefly managed to make eye contact with Luther long enough for him to take note.

    "I see," she said. "No need to be sorry though, Luther. It's not your fault if you are feeling unwell of the body or the soul."

    Luther raised his head as she said that last part. Was it a problem of the soul, he wondered? Was it more than simply the case of a malfunctioning brain, inclined to certain ways of being? He began to lose himself to the thoughts of this, but he saw Agnes, still standing at the foot of his bed and he pulled himself up out of it enough to continue conversing with her.

    "Sorry, again, Agnes. I kind of wandered off a bit there." He forced himself to look her straight in the eyes as he said this. "My mind has a habit of doing that," he said.

    "It's completely fine Luther, don't worry." As if she was reading his whim, she said, "If you wish to have a bit more sleep, I can wake you up in a few hours. It's no trouble."

    "Yes, I think I will, if that's ok," Luther replied. She nodded a reassuring nod with a quiet smile and then turned away to check on the man opposite.

    Luther was relieved by the prospect of slipping back down into the bed and sleeping for a little while longer. The feeling was not lost on him concerning his withdrawal from the world, for a little while longer. Perhaps it was better to get up, eyes open and awake and make some attempt at meeting the day head on; not letting himself be overcome by the misery that was upon him. He wished he were capable of that, but today he was reticent of the struggle to overcome and wished only to sleep. At least if he were not conscious, he wouldn't need to deal with such sadness. It was times like this, with his mood in such a way, that he understood the embrace of oblivion; putting an end to it would no doubt put a stop to the misery he could feel, forever. He slunk back down and pulled the blanket over him, turned his head to the side, on the pillow and after a few minutes had fallen asleep again.

Chapter 26

He awoke for the second time in the day, several hours later. He opened his eyes to the warm surroundings of the little chapel of the crescent moon. He had something of a headache, probably because of the extra sleep, he thought to himself. He stared around him; at the decorations of the room and of the rafters above him. It took some time to gather himself and his wayward thoughts. He felt better from the additional time sleeping; not quite as miserable as several hours ago, but at the same time he felt a guilt at his surrender to his disposition and perhaps the time lost in his search for Celeste Ignophenen.

Right, he thought to himself. I must push myself up and out of this bed. I must get up, get myself ready and resume my search.

He pulled himself up to a sitting position and looked around the room again. Neither of the clerics were in the room. The woman across looked at him and gave a welcoming smile while the other man in his bed was reading a paper of some kind. It must be the local borough paper, Luther thought to himself.

After some mental urging, he pulled across the blankets and managed to swing his legs round so that his feet were planted flat on the floor.

The woman across from him, suddenly said, "They made a bath for you in the other room. Said to tell you so when you woke up. I imagine it's still warm. First door on the left."

"Oh right," said Luther. "Thank you. I will surely take them up on it."

He pulled some clothes from his pack and went into the next room. He was greeted by a thin corridor with two doors on the left. He took the first on the left as instructed and was greeted by a bathroom with a bath already filled with hot water from taps sitting over its rim. It was a free-standing old Steel bath with pipes coming up from below somewhere that fed water into it. Luther was happy at the thought of a nice warm bath, but again he couldn't help but think of the consequences: This is too much good all at once.

He struggled to just accept good fortune as he was ever concerned with paying for it later, even to the point of ignoring perhaps what he had already paid for in misadventure already. He turned and slid across the bar on the door, locking it. He then took off his clothes and got into the bath.

After what seemed a good part of an hour of thoughts and wonderings and reassuring warmth of the water, he had finished his bath and got himself dressed. He put on a new, black shirt that had the print of a local band in his home borough: 'Zyllah'. He had seen them perform several times at the town hall in Overton.

He put on a grey woollen cardigan, replacing his purple one he had been wearing thus far on his journey. He wondered if he could find a place to wash some of his clothes with the hope of removing the dirt and blood from the blows to his face. Lastly, he put on some black jeans and boots and then walked back out to the main room to find Edgar sitting at the fireplace with a cup of tea.

"Hello Luther," he said.

"Hi Edgar. Thank you for the bath and thank you for all you have done for me. I am feeling a lot better physically than when I came in last night."

"That's good to hear," replied Edgar after taking a sip of his tea. "And how are you feeling mentally? Agnes mentioned you were not feeling too well earlier? If you would rather not speak of it, I understand of course."

"Well," Luther replied. "It is a long story really, but the crux of the matter is that I am susceptible to sadness and anxiety. I worry and I am sad and then I worry that I am sad and then sad because of it. It just strikes me like a bolt sometimes. No matter how I might be feeling at the time or the night before, I can suddenly turn to the slave of misery in the shortest of time."

Luther was relieved to have finished this description of his condition. He felt it was sometimes difficult to explain, but this time at least he was content with how he had conveyed that which afflicted him.

"It must be hard dealing with something like that Luther," Edgar said. "You are stronger than you think though. You made it here by yourself after a right thumping from a right band of thugs. There is strength there."

"Thank you," said Luther. He gave a glum smile as best he could. He appreciated the sentiment.

"I think I will grab my things and be on my way if that's alright?" Luther said.

"Of course, it is," Edgar responded. "I am glad we could help you."

Luther walked over to his pack and took out a gold coin. "Here, please take this. I am sorry it's not much."

He handed the coin to Edgar who said, "You don't need to give us anything Luther, it is our duty and our want to help those in need,"

"I know," Luther replied, "Please take it as a donation to the cause and all the good work you an Agnes are doing here."

"Ok," said Edgar. "Thank you for the donation."

He took the gold from Luther and then said, "So, where are you headed from here?"

"I think I will head over to the main barracks and see if I can get some information as to the whereabouts of the person I am looking for."

"I see," said Edgar. "Are you happy to tell me who you seek? I might be able to point to the right person."

"Yes of course," replied Luther. "I am seeking a woman named Celeste Ignophenen. Apparently, she frequents these parts fairly often."

"Ahh," said Edgar. "Ms Ignophenen. Yes, she comes to the town often. Seeker of esoteric knowledge that one. Always bothering the archivist at the library about some book or another."

"Oh right," said Luther. "So, you know her?"

Edgar smiled. "Yes, we know her. She has been in here several times after one mishap or another. She is a good sort, but she can be quite bossy and knows what she wants, that one. We last saw her a few months back. She came in with cuts and bruises after a brush with someone or something,"

A GRIM JOURNEY

"Right, ok," Luther replied. "Where would be the best place to ask or person to talk to about her whereabouts?"

"I would go through the gate at the inner wall, just outside and make for the library, which isn't too far from there. If anyone has had any news of her it will be the archivist as it's her, she speaks to most."

"Ok. That's great. I will make for the library immediately. Is it ok if I leave Guinevere here while I go? You have done so much already so I understand if not."

"Yes, that's fine Luther don't worry. Take your time," said Edgar.

"Brilliant. I will gather my things and then be on my way. Thank you for your kindness Edgar. I will not forget it." He reached over and put out his hand. Edgar set his tea to one side, stood up and shook it with his own.

"No problem Luther at all," he said.

"Please give my regards to Agnes too," Luther said.

"I will do," replied Edgar.

Luther pulled on his jacket and before taking up his pack, made the bed back to what it had been the night before. He took hold of his axe and placing in it sheath, exited the temple.

He was greeted outside by the early afternoon of a cold day. Not too cold, he felt, but enough to make its presence known. There were few people walking hither and the sky above was overcast with clouds.

He turned right and walked towards the gate, through to the inner curtain wall. He came to the portcullis of the gatehouse. Standing there were two guards of similar garb to the soldiers he had seen previously. They were both human males with swords sheathed in their belts and were currently staring at the man approaching them.

"Hello there," said Luther, vaguely addressing them both.

"Hello sir," said the soldier on the left. "Can we help you?" It was a stern, but not completely cold tone.

"Yes, I hope so," said Luther. "I am in town looking for a certain individual for personal business and I have been told that the archivist of the library may know of their whereabouts."

This was quite nerve wracking for Luther. Not only because of approaching two random soldiers, people - he had never met before - but the very real possibility of being permitted entry, was not a given, perhaps making his entire journey pointless.

"Can I ask who this person is that you are seeking sir?", said the same soldier. Luther was slightly hesitant at first. Would the identity of this person make or break his chances of making it through? Regardless, he had to disclose it. "I am looking for a Celeste Ignophenen", he said after a pause. Before they had a chance for a verbal response Luther continued, "It's of a personal matter that I believe she might be able to help me with."

The two guards looked at each other with a knowing look and a wry looking smile on both before turning back to Luther. The soldier on the right now replied: "Yes, Ms Ignophenen. Don't let her catch you not pronouncing her name improper!" They looked at one another again.

"We know her yes," said the soldier on the left.

"It's difficult not to," said the right.

"Yeah, you had better be on top form when speaking with her or she'll eat you for breakfast." Uttered the soldier to the left.

"I see" replied Luther. "So, she is quite a stern lady?"

"You could say that sir yes," said the soldier to the right.

"Does she come by here often, then?" Luther enquired.

"Often enough that most of the town knows who she is sir, yes," was the reply from the right soldier.

"The archivist at the library is the person to talk to for sure," said the left.

"Ok, yes. That is what I have been told" Luther replied. He then pulled up some courage and said: "So, could I please pass through?"

"Yes, that's fine sir. Don't be causing any commotion though as we won't hear the end of it."

The soldier on the left turned and shouted something

through the portcullis gate and after a moment it began to rise. Luther thanked both of the guards and passed through.

He now found himself in a similar middle hall like the one he had passed through previously the day before. There were weapon racks and benches and heraldry around the walls and several soldiers stood inside. Luther tried to keep his gaze to the large gate opposite, smiling as best he could if he caught the eye of any of the soldiers.

The gate ahead consisted not of a lattice of wood, but two large rectangular metal looking doors crossed by two large wooden beams connected to pulleys. Luther thought it was no doubt meant to hold under duress from the outside should the very outer walls of Bramstone be breached.

He walked over to it and waited patiently. Two guards, one on either side of him began winding the winches attached to the large timber pieces, sitting stoic across the doors. Slowly both timbers raised up ninety degrees with their pivot points set back along the wall. The doors were then pulled open by another two soldiers and Luther passed through after receiving a nod from one of them to do so.

Once Luther had crossed over from the guardhouse and beyond, the doors were quickly closed again behind him. Luther had made it to the heart of the military stronghold of Bramstone. The bastion that stood strong against any encroaching evil from the south. The first line of defence.

To greet him were two more soldiers standing guard outside the gate with several more up above the gate armed with crossbows.

The area directly outside the gatehouse was clear of any building or construct in a roughly one-hundred-yard radius. Luther imagined that this must be, should the gatehouse become besieged, and the soldiers therein could see assailants coming from a good distance. The ground under Luther's feet was cobbled and stretched out for all he could see. Several hundred yards ahead he caught a glimpse of the outward facing wall; that which must stand firm and resolute against all who intended to invade The Boroughs.

Beyond the clearing surrounding the gate there were buildings with narrow alleys running between them which spread out like the roots of a tree. Luther wondered what these buildings were for. Perhaps they were living quarters for soldiers, perhaps clerical buildings for bureaucracy and administration, perhaps more supply buildings or store buildings, armouries and whatever else a functioning army might require.

Luther, realising that he didn't actually know where the library might be in this sprawl of bricks and alleys, turned round and ventured to ask one of the soldiers standing guard.

"Hello there," he said, addressing them both as best he could.

"Hello sir," again came the reply, but this time coming from the right-hand soldier.

"Could I ask?" Luther paused a moment. "Could you please tell me where I might find the library?"

The soldier looked at him for a moment as if sizing up his intentions before saying, "Yes sir. Can I ask what business you might have with the library and/or persons therein?" said the soldier on the left.

"Oh, yeah of course, sorry," said Luther. "I am looking to find a certain person that, may currently be at the library or at least the archivist may know of their whereabouts."

"And who is that sir?" said the soldier on the right.

"An Ms Celeste Ignophenen. I have heard she is quite well known around the town."

As before, both soldiers turned their heads towards each other and gave a knowing smile.

"Yes, most of the soldiery and civilians know of or have met in person, Ms Ignophenen," said the left soldier.

"Yes," laughed the right.

Luther wondered by asking his business or who it was with that they were somehow sizing him up; deciding if he was a malevolent force intending to cause harm. Perhaps, he thought, with his knowledge of Ms Ignophenen this may prove he was not. He hoped anyway.

"If you pass through the gate here, take the right-hand street and follow to its final turn, you will see the library on the right. The last building," said the soldier on the left.

"Thank you very much," said Luther. He gave a nod to

A GRIM JOURNEY

them both and passed through the gate making his way towards the very right street that stretched off to the north-west.

The street was quite a narrow width between the wall on his right and the rows of buildings on his left. These buildings though, seemed somewhat raggedy, as if they had been hastily constructed or at least the builder was not too concerned in keeping everything square and straight. There were slate roofs that jutted out slightly wonkily at odd angles, walls that were not quite straight with mixed colour and sized brick and door frames that were skew. The buildings themselves were different sizes too, as if they were constructed with no sense in mind of the aesthetics of the neighbourhood – if there were any; a short run of terraced buildings, all the same size; a smattering of singular, detached buildings all with mismatched brickwork; a lone warehouse or barn stuck randomly in between as those slung in arbitrarily without cause or reason.

Luther wondered if all this randomness and haphazard design was actually intentional. Perhaps it didn't matter how they were constructed; they were most likely all used for military purposes. He imagined their construction was not concerned with worry about the exacticies or aesthetics of a proud homeowner.

The street was mostly quiet, with Luther only very occasionally seeing anyone else. Any time he did see others it was military personnel such as guards standing outside a particular building or on patrol walking past him. All would give him a slight look of suspicion with a nod as he passed straight by.

He wondered of the narrowness of the streets; was this all on purpose he thought? The buildings were all close together, so should some ordinance or vicious spell come flying over the wall it would cause widespread destruction. Maybe that was the point, he thought. If the outer wall were breached then an invading force would need to fight through the narrow streets, bottlenecking their advance. Clambering over swathes of rubble and debris would surely slow them further, providing time to rally defences at the next line of battlements and ample practice for the archers and other ranged military units - both physical and magical - to harry them and slow them further.

He walked for roughly thirty minutes with several turn offs snaking south amongst other lines of buildings. He remembered the guard's words though: 'Follow to its final turn.' And so, he kept walking, finally coming to a last turn in the street. Ahead of him was now a rock face. This must be the beginning of the outcrops of the Lightlorne Mountains, he thought.

He wondered that this bastion city must stretch right across the breadth of land between the Lightlorne Mountains to the west and north, and the Border Crags to the south. To his right, just before the wall jutted up against the rocks was a small stone building – the only one to be seen on this side of the road. It looked quite unassuming and was little bigger than an outhouse or shed. He wondered, could this be the library? But it was so small. It could barely house several people, let alone reams of scrolls and shelves of books. The guard said clearly that it was the last building on the right. It turned out to be the only building on the right that he had come across with everything else being the wall separating the two parts of the city. Here it was, the last one in the row. It must be this.

He approached the little brick shelter and noticed a wooden door. It was a simple looking thing of old and worn wood - nothing fancy or grand in its demeanour - sitting in the doorway with an iron handle on the right side. There was no sign or indication to convey the purpose of this small and unassuming building. Luther was expecting something much grander or formally pronounced as was perhaps expected for such a place as a great library.

He stood there for a moment and finally decided to knock on the door. What did he have to lose, he thought? The only worry he had was of someone angrily opening the door, asking why they were being bothered.

He stood there for a while and waited. There was no answer. He knocked a second time and again there was no answer. Either there was no-one there or this place was abandoned. How could this be a library? He thought. He hadn't miss-heard the guard. Of this, he was sure.

Against his worrisome nature, his hand reached for the

door handle and made to turn it anti-clockwise. He pushed it gently and to his surprise the door started to open inwards. He followed it in.

Inside, all he could see was a small space lit on either side by a single lantern light. Directly ahead, perhaps ten feet in front of him was another door. This one looked grander and more substantial than the plain one he had just opened with Luther noticing square panelling and a large brass door knocker in its centre. At roughly shoulder height below this, to the left was an ornate door handle that curved out from the door in the way of a teapot handle. He wondered; this door looked quite thick and quite airtight in its frame. Perhaps as it stood here resolute and stern against the outside, it would be most difficult for anyone beyond it to hear the knocks on the outer door. Maybe, they might hear knocks on this inner one. He decided to test this idea and raised the knocker on the new door and then hit it against with no small amount of force. He wasn't prepared however, for the power in which its own weight would provide to the swing and it landed on the door with quite a resounding thud.

Oh dear, he thought. He worried that should it be heard by those yonder; they might become annoyed at someone loudly banging on the library door. Libraries after all, he thought, were places known for their appreciation of being quiet.

He waited. This time longer than the previous door; he was remiss to use the door knocker once again. He waited still but could hear nothing. He decided to put his ear up against the door in an attempt to focus his hearing on any movement that might be happening on the other side of it. Nothing at first, but then shortly he thought he could hear something - steps coming closer. There were feint thuds and the odd scrape as if someone was walking closer to the door. It seemed to Luther there must be a set of stairs behind this door or somewhere close as the noises seemed reminiscent of a stride up a set.

The sound crept closer, and he didn't have to strain his ears quite so much to hear it. Closer it came before suddenly cutting off.

Hmm that's odd, Luther though, before being

presented with the fact that this person behind this large wooden door must have come to a halt, most likely because they might be about to open it.

He suddenly pulled himself back and away from the door and stood up straight, in an attempt to look at ease and presentable to whoever he was about to encounter.

Luther could hear a creaking, scraping sound from the other side of the door. Noises perhaps, of a bolt and a latch then and then the twisting of a handle. The door then breathed a breath as though it were pulled from a happy resting sleep, before slowly opening inwards.

Luther waited patiently for the door to open and reveal that which it guarded. It was in no hurry and cautiously it swung inwards at a steady pace. Eventually it had moved close to ninety degrees from its starting position and standing with a hand pressed against it, bracing it open, was a flarfen female. Immediately Luther thought of the scraping to have been the claws of her feet as she approached.

She was under five foot in height - a common size for a flarfen - which allowed Luther to look over her to spy what was beyond. What he could see were more lanterns lighting a staircase. He could see only a few of them as they veered off to the left; the beginnings of a spiral, leading down.

He thought of his rudeness at gazing past the woman in front of him rather than addressing her directly and turned back his view to correct this. He looked down at the flarfen female; she was wearing a cardigan of blue cotton, pale shirt and thin dark trousers. Her feet were bare as was usual for one of her people. Upon her feminine features she wore a pair of small circular glasses, through which she was looking up at Luther staring down at her.

"Sorry, hello," said Luther. "Nice to meet you. I am Luther. Is this the library?"

The woman twitched her nose as if sizing him up by the scent of him and said, "Hello Luther. I am Ethel the archivist of Bramstone Library."

"Oh right," he replied. "I was told it was the last building on the right in the corner there, but I was expecting something larger, I suppose, rather than the small building here." He hoped his words and had not caused any offense. "I am sorry, I didn't mean suggest that I was disappointed of course. Just not what I expected."

Before he could berate himself too much she replied, "Yes, that's fine. Don't worry. Most people are confused when they first visit here. You probably wish to know why it is the way it is and that is a fairly straight forward answer; this library contains a great many books and scrolls concerning threats to The Boroughs. A great many books indeed of the Mage Scribes – as well as many others - are housed here concerning all sorts of knowledge on all sorts of things. Should the outer walls ever be breached and the town over run, this inconsequential looking little building will be lost amongst all the others. This in turn provides us time to deal with our libraries contents as we will, before being discovered."

This seemed reasonable enough to Luther. Such a wealth of information as she had described to him would be unfortunate to fall into the wrong hands.

"I hadn't thought of that," he said "But now I have, it makes a lot of sense. No use being overt about the location of such an important place for all to see."

Ethel gave a smile before saying, "So Luther, what can I help you with? Are you looking for some information?"

"Yes right, sorry yes," the words blundered from Luther's mouth. "Not exactly, no. I am looking for a person actually or perhaps information to that person's whereabouts."

"I see," said Ethel. "And who might that be?"

Luther was busy looking at the ground, anxious of the situation, but pulled himself up and said, "I am looking for a Ms Celeste Ignophenen. I was told by a friend and the guards here that you may know of her whereabouts?"

The flarfen's smile went slightly coy as she replied, "Ah, you are after Celeste, are you? What do you want with her if you don't mind my asking?"

Luther, having managed to keep eye contact with her said, "I am told by my friend back in Overton – who is an old friend of hers - that she may be able to help me with a personal matter." He then looked around the small shelter, breaking contact with her bespectacled eyes.

"Ok," she said, "What's your friend's name?"

Luther was catching on that he was being scrutinised by the archivist. It seemed she wouldn't let just anyone into her charge and was prepared to inspect all that tried to. "My friend's name is Golon. He is one of the Gnome folk and lives in Overton Village in the Lonefield Borough, as do I," he said.

"Ah, Golon, I have heard his name mentioned one or twice by Celeste."

Luther perked up at this and immediately gave in to his earnest desire for knowledge about his condition.

"So, you know her quite well?" he said quickly.

"Oh yes, I know her very well. She frequents here often. After all we do have quite an extensive body of information here on the unusual and more esoteric way of things; books on beasts, on magic and spells, histories of the land and volumes on the happenings of the ragged knights." She had puffed her chest slightly, clearly proud of her station. "Would you care to have a look?" she said.

Luther was interested both by his love of books, but also perhaps he might be better in the graces of the archivist graces so he said, "Yes of course, I would love to. Thank you."

"Right! Follow me!" she said, happy to have a visitor to the library.

She stepped to one side and made an ushering motion for Luther to pass by her. He stepped through the doorway, past Ethel and down a few steps before turning and awaiting more instruction. Ethel then closed the door and locked it once again. She went to make her way past Luther as he stood to the side allowing her to pass. "Follow me," she said, before setting off down the stairs with Luther in tow.

He followed behind the Flarfen woman who, rather than walking each step, performed a skip or jump down two at a time, before pausing briefly to allow Luther to catch up with her. He was always impressed by the lithe agility of the Flarfen folk.

The walls framing the staircase were close to a dark brown which were brightened to a hazel in proximity to the lanterns that hung in a staggered fashion on either side. They looked to be of fire dust which Luther noted from their distinctive red glow; more solidly and purely red as opposed to the natural flame of a more conventional oil lamp.

Luther began to think of what the sight might be when they had descended to the library itself. Would it be rows upon rows of wooden shelves lined up and down a low hall? Maybe tall stretches of cases leading high to the roof, accessed by stairs on rails of which he had heard of some grand Libraries employing. Perhaps it was set out hither and thither, as wants needed - he would soon find out.

Between watching Ethel swiftly skip from step to step and wondering of the grandness of the library itself, he had momentarily misplaced the goal of coming here, that of locating Celeste Ignophenen. After one final turn the staircase had reached its bottom. They had reached the library.

The stairs entered in a gap in between two huge bookcases standing on either side of the pair. Luther could see the room open into a massive cavern that looked to have originally been a natural cave of some kind. There were stalactites of different sizes hanging from the roof some forty yards above his head as Luther stood looking up. Besides these, dotted all around, were large pillars that looked to be natural occurrences; perhaps all that remained from rock that had been eroded away over many years, creating this hollow cavern. Some were larger and thicker than others and some looked to have been added to with stone bases that may be helping to shore up the weight upon them.

Below and filling the large floor of the cave were cobblestones, similar to that of the surface above. Luther imagined these must have been placed here rather than somehow appearing naturally; they formed a fairly even surface for shelves and other furnishings to be placed on happily.

In the middle of this large cavern was a large round wooden desk with a hollow centre. He assumed this must be the archivist's desk and workspace where she conducted her duties. From this, spreading out from either side, were large wooden bookcases, curved in nature, close to a semi-circle, but with a gap on the north and south ends, straight ahead of Luther. They were roughly the height of a grown human; perhaps six feet tall, ending with impressive large wooden statues of various beasties. These inner bookcases – as Luther assumed they were from this distance - were surrounded by longer shelves that stretched around them, giving way only for the occasional pillar of rock, this time taller by half than the previous. These were then in turn surrounded by larger cases and so on until they reached close to the sides of the cave, each with a gap at the east and west edges. The effect was like a ripple from a stone, thrown into a quiet pond, echoing outwards.

Hanging from spots dotted all along the roof of the cavern high above, nestled in between stalactites were long lanterns that hung low from long, thin steel chains. Because they were attached to the roof wherever there was an absence of stalactites the light emanating from them was not particularly ordered or evenly spread out. Rather, the lamps and their light were placed where they were able instead of what provided the optimal light for every part of the library. The end effect was of somewhat patchy illumination throughout the cavern with some isles resplendent in glow while others were quite dim, but still, mostly enough for someone to see their way through. The form in the lamps looked to be of fire dust set in the lanterns, enough for a firm glow and enough heat to provide some warmth to the cavern.

Beyond the alleys of books, on the other side of the outer and tallest row, Luther could not tell what lay beyond; perhaps more books, perhaps desks and tables for study, maybe sleeping quarters for the archivist herself.

The archivist, Ethel, stood patiently and proudly as Luther took in the sight around him. After he had gazed, taking in the grandness of what he saw, he turned to her and said, "This is very impressive, Ethel. Who would have known from such a small little shelter above what greatness lay below?"

"Exactly!" she said, smiling robustly with pride.

"I guess that is indeed exactly the point," he said. "No-one would ever know what lies on the other side of these great rows of books?"

"There are some desks for study and my quarters of course. Nothing too exciting," she replied.

"I see," said Luther.

She beckoned Luther to follow her as she walked

through the middle of the bookcases and towards her desk. When they arrived, she stopped and said, "Now. You were looking for Celeste Ignophenen?"

Luther snapped back to point in hand and quickly replied, "Yes, indeed I am. Would you have any idea of her current whereabouts?"

The archivist smiled and said, "I would hope so as she currently sits under this very roof."

"She does?!" Luther exclaimed excitedly.

"She does yes, she sits at one of the desks beyond, poring over several of our older manuscripts."

"Oh, that is great news. Great news indeed!" Luther said, barely holding onto his excitement. "Can I meet her?"

"I will go and ask for an audience. But know this. She is not fond of being disturbed in her work. What shall I say as your reason for being here?"

Luther suddenly thought for a moment. The excitement came to a stop. He had perhaps one chance and one chance only to make an impression upon this woman. If she thought his reasoning folly and refuse to meet him then all would be for naught; his journey here ending in failure.

"Tell her, I am Luther Dothmeer. I come from the Lonefield Borough to the northeast, and I come seeking an audience with her on the suggestion of my good friend Golon of Overton Village. Tell her, that I have a condition that she may have some insight upon," he said, as calmly and as earnestly as he could. "Please though, it is nothing dangerous or infectious and I am fine. Her wisdom may help to put my mind at rest that is all. I have travelled quite far and not without some trepidation. If she would see me, if only for a few minutes, then I would be eternally grateful." Luther's face had turned stern and serious. He knew what was at stake; he must speak with Ms Ignophenen. He must.

"Ok Luther, I will go speak to her. Please look as you like at our boundless volumes but take care. All are precious."

She turned and proceeded forward and north, through the centre line in the middle of the cavern that divided the circular rows of tomes in two. It was a fair walk, after which she turned left and out of view.

A GRIM JOURNEY

Luther himself, ventured down the nearest isle to his left. The bookcases raised up either side of him; the right side, closest to the middle desk, stood lower than the left, but well above the height of him. Ahead of him he could see a wooden ladder almost like a staircase which was attached to a square base with a small wheel in each corner underneath. Luther imagined this was for locating books in the upper reaches of the library.

In several places, protruding from one of the intervals of vertical timber in the bookcases were dark, varnished wooden signs featuring names of different genres and subjects. The writing was chiselled into the sign and painted white which made for a prominent point of information. He could see several others protruding out, disappearing off into the distance with the closest reading: 'Beasts of The Boroughs'. To his right was a similar sign that read: 'Magical Substances'. He looked over the books concerning 'Beasts of The Boroughs'. There were rows of books of different sizes and colours, all neatly sitting one after the other, shelf after shelf.

It was quite an impressive store of knowledge and yet Luther seemed absent of engagement with what would usually interest him greatly; his eyes scanned over and over again the titles of the tomes in front of him without ever absorbing theirs or their author's names. He was not really present in this moment, but rather his mind had wandered away, concerned with worry and anxiety. He had found the woman he sought so earnestly and was terribly grateful for this, but the thoughts now whipped round in his mind of what he was to say to her. How would he go about persuading her to impart her knowledge? How would she react to his questioning? Would he accidently offend her somehow? All these thoughts and more were at the forefront of his mind.

But there was another pervasive thought that wallowed at the back of his mind: He had managed to find Ms Ignophenen quite easily. Yes, it was by suffering violence and kept thoroughly out of his comfort, he thought, but was it enough? He felt that for such a good turn of fate he must have to bear misfortune. It was something he struggled with greatly; good luck and joy must be paid for with sadness and misery.

A GRIM JOURNEY

He scrolled over more books here and there staring at their titles: 'The life of Trolls', 'Creatures of the Dell Wood', 'Ware Badgers: A Thorough Understanding', amongst others. He rested his view upon a row of books at his eye level, lost in those swirling thoughts. All around him lost as he stared through and past the collection of tomes sitting quietly on their shelves.

His grip of time was lost as he stared out unknowingly, wondering of what he may say to this Celeste Ignophenen. What would he say to her if she indeed would give him the chance to? He was shipped away, riding his own thoughts so much so that he didn't notice the figure of the archivist approaching from the other side of the cavern.

"Luther?" said the archivist.

He snapped out of his thoughts and arrived back in the room. "Hello Ethel, sorry, my mind wandered off there," he said.

"That's ok. I have spoken with Ms Ignophenen, and she has agreed to meet with you."

"That's brilliant, thank you," replied Luther. "Right now?"

"Yes, right now. She luckily wishes to have a small break in her study – usually she is quite against being interrupted, but she seems amiable."

"Right, ok." His thoughts quickly raced to concern; more good news, more luck that will need to be paid for. He pulled himself out of it. I will not dwell on it. Not now, not when I am so close to answers, he thought. "Ok, right. I shall go over now then," he said.

"Ok, I will leave you to it, but don't keep her waiting. Just head straight up from here and then to the left at the end of the row of books. She is at one of the desks there." The archivist said, before walking off towards her desk, leaving Luther alone.

Luther sprung into motion. His brain, rather than allow itself to be consumed by emotion and filled with more anxiety, thrust his body forward. He walked the corridor between the walls of bookcases. He strolled hopefully, at a good pace and within a minute or so he had made it across to the other side.

A GRIM JOURNEY

The bookcases, once at the distant side of the library, gave way to the corridor that passed through the equatorial line in the middle of it. Luther paused just before this. He would need to turn left in the next few steps and be in view of the person he had sought these last few days.

'No turning back,' he thought. Again, he found himself driven as though some safety measure had kicked in within him that wouldn't allow his mind to dwell on lingering thoughts of doubt. He stepped forward

Chapter 27

The sky over Overton Village was aghast at the destruction that bellowed into the heavens. Several buildings were little more than burnt out wrecks of once noble structures; their innards offered up to the warm embrace of the open flame. Though nearly all had walls of granite, their insides were propped and decorated with more flammable materials which had all been destroyed by fire; all worldly possessions, furniture and decoration burnt to cinders.

The Duck Feather Inn, long standing and proud member of the village, now lay beaten and burnt out with only it's exterior stone walls remaining of the once great structure. They were scared from lashings of flame, black and burnt, miserable in their existence. The sections of floor that once housed a bar and tables filled with joyous laughter and merriment were all gone; only blackened vestiges of the edges of the timber joists remained. This was the same above; all trace of the rooms upstairs were destroyed by the fire that had raged through the night. The roof, a thick and tight thatching was the first to be consumed, all gone as if never to have existed. The Duck Feather Inn all but ceased to be.

The Blacksmith's joined with the remnants of the tavern, passing dark smoke out into the sky from the carcass that once the home of Toby and Lilly. It had fared slightly better, being a building that dealt with the possibility of a spreading fire every day the forge was lit; the roof was constructed of slate and brick rather than a flame hungry thatching. Several of the timbers stretching across the expanse between the walls had managed to withstand the fierce heat and flames from below but were worst for ware; deeply blackened and scorched from end to end. Several slate tiles had fallen from place, but many had managed to cling to the rafters that still existed. The inside of the building fared not quite so well, with all furnishings and possessions raised to the ground. The forge itself, mostly of brick was still in place, but caked in blackness of soot with the steel of the anvil glowing and burning to the touch. Any of the steel tools that might have had leather or wooden handles such as hammer or chisel had all been burnt away leaving only metal skeletons in their place.

The tannery building lay in a similar state to the tavern; its thatched roof ripe fuel for the fire that had swept through it. It lay as a carcass of a building, all the clothing and leather housed within burnt to a crisp, giving off a less than pleasant smell. The occupants were nowhere to be seen within the blackened mess.

The Town hall, lay differently than those others set aflame the night before. The two large front doors were set ablaze, burnt to ash, leaving an open space where they once resided. Other parts of the building's structure looked to have been recently feeling the licks of flame, but a great part of it was still standing and absent of any of the effects of fire. The inner hallway was half black with the furniture inside looking as though it was on its way to destruction. The wooden panelling on the interior walls and timbers above were scorched out too, but similarly the scaring of fire seemed to come to an abrupt halt further in. It was as if all at once the fire had given up on the idea and spontaneously blew itself out.

Golon's Exciting Emporium of Wonderment and Adventure - a source of joy and innocence - lay smoking in ruins. Its wooden structure was nothing more than hot ashen remains including all that was housed within; all the toys, all the magical displays enjoyed by many. All the whimsical and wonderful signs and show pieces were nothing more than destroyed and meaningless clumps of ash and cinder. There was little to discern that here once stood a proud and beaming centre of happiness.

Several residences, further north of the hall were similar burning wrecks; their roofs and insides all consumed with fire and their brick exteriors scorched and burnt from the roaring furnace of flames from the night before.

The general store of Kate and Gareth too, fared little better from the arson and was now simply a blackened, sooted husk of a building. All the produce and various items for sale were unrecognisable as they had been sacrificed to the embers;

burnt up as fuel for the fire.

Despite the destruction wrought upon the village there were few buildings that had avoided the full embrace of flame. Among them was the herbalists building, north of the Blacksmiths which stood as it had before the night's pandemonium, but with several telling signs of what had transpired. There were singe marks upon the wooden flower boxes that lay below the front windows that faced south towards the smithy. The windows themselves had the presence of soot upon them around their edges and the shutters closed as they were featured a smattering of black ash across them. The roof too had signs of fire with parts of the thatching and vines that crept across it featuring the effects of smoke and heat. The main structure - and luckily nothing inside - had felt the effects of the inferno from the night before.

There were several other homes too, situated further back from the village square that lay unharmed. The house of Luther Dothmeer too, was amongst these. It was left as it was the day Luther had set off on his journey to Bramstone with no indications of fire damage without or within.

The guard house, in the centre of the village, struck out from the debris of the buildings around it. It appeared to have no discernible damage to its exterior. The large double doors of its main entrance were completely intact along with its rear gate that opened out to the green squared behind. It was as though it had been spared the attentions of the evildoers or their attempts to burn its doors and vestiges were repelled by those inside.

Atop the turret on the east of the building stood a guardsman of the constabulary holding a crossbow with eyes trained into the distance to the south and east, keeping close watch for any further incursions. He looked tired and weary, as though he had been on watch for some time after a trying and weary night.

Inside the guard house could be found many of the residents of Overton village. There were several present whose homes and livelihoods had been destroyed, but others also that had fled from the ravages of the flame and violence. They were strewn around the main room of the building; some were slunk up against the walls; some standing, peering from the observation holes, looking for any sign of the attackers from the night before; some sat in the middle of the room in shock. As a whole they were either silent or stern. They even sat silently, perhaps pondering the night's events or in conversation, questioning the motives of their assailants or wondering to each other what they would do in the aftermath.

Amongst the worry ridden present was Nathanael the old mage whose home and business now lay stricken. He was stood up against a back wall in conversation with Deven who held a staff in similar vein to Nathanael's, with a dark cloak about him and pale robe beneath. He too leant against the wall, as though he had spent a great wealth of energy and now stood recuperating.

"It seems they aren't coming back Nathanael," Deven said, looking around the room at the gathering of villagers.

"No, it doesn't seem so," said Nathanael, staring forward. "I am glad you came when you did," he continued.

"Yes, I saw all the commotion and the fire and came as quickly as I could. They had ravaged much of the village already though – I should have gotten here sooner."

"Well," said Nathanael. "It was not something we sit and expect to happen. There is no chance you could be prepared for such a thing. It wasn't like we are on the frontier of the southern reaches, the wilds of the north or a lone settlement in some far-off part of the Lightlorne. This is Overton Village of the Lonefield of The Boroughs. Who would ever think such a thing might happen?"

"Indeed," said Deven. "I wonder who these people were. They took their injured with them and I saw no heraldry upon them. It would seem they were intent on hiding their identities or any sign of their benefactors."

"I don't know Deven," replied Nathanael, "Some rogue band of mercenaries out to raid an unsuspecting village? Though they didn't seem much interested in looting anything. Attacking a village in the middle of The Boroughs, the gall of it."

"Indeed," Deven replied, again. "They seemed more concerned with wanton destruction rather than securing any valuables."

"Perhaps it was the Covenant," came a third voice. It was Thelia, head of Overton's council. She was standing to Nathaniel's left with her back up against the wall with eyes locked on the large doors at the front of the guard house.

Nathanael passed her a look of concern before replying: "Surely not? Their last incursion was twenty years ago at the Great War."

"True," said Thelia, "but we all know of their scheming ways. Perhaps they sent agents into The Boroughs, somehow bypassing Bramstone. Perhaps across the Lightlorne".

"It would be quite the dangerous journey to attempt a crossing over the mountains from west to east. And they would have to come around by sea to the western coast of the mountain range – itself quite an arduous trip," replied Nathanael.

"Perhaps," said Deven. "I have spoken to the Inspector, and he has sent a rider to Cadforf. The Borough parliament needs to be told of this. Riders to Slipping and Earstwhile too."

"That's good," replied Thelia "Other towns must be aware of the potential danger. I hope parliament sends means to combat this threat and find out where they came from."

"Yes, these bastards need to be caught and justice dealt, via several beatings in custody and at every other opportunity!" Toby, the blacksmith was sitting up against the wall to Deven's right, with his wife half asleep, on his shoulder.

"Well, yes Toby. It would be good if they were all caught and I understand your wish for vengeance, really, I do, but we must try and keep ourselves above their level. We are better than that," said Thelia.

Lilly reached and squeezed the arm of her husband reassuringly and he gave a grim nod of acceptance to Thelia.

"I had better go check on Reginald and the others," said Deven.

"I'll come with you," said Thelia.

The two of them walked to a smaller room of the guard house. Inside were several fold out beds, little more than canvas over a thin steel skeleton with a pillow and blanket. Laying on each of them was a villager that had been injured the night before: Marcus lay in one, thick bruising and a streaking cut on his face; Alma lay in another, bruising on the back of her head and still not conscious; Steven occupied another bed across from her, laying on his side, hunched up in pain with several cuts on his face with blood marks being wiped away by Gwithen, sitting on the edge; Gareth unlike the others was up and sitting on the edge of his bed next to his wife Kate, himself with several cuts to the face and swollen and bloody lip. The two of them were talking quietly, broken up by the regular twinge of pain from Gareth which was met with tender touches from Kate. They both repeatedly looked over to yet another bed, in which lay the form of a man unconscious. It was Reginald who ran the Tailors and Tannery with his wife Carrey. She was currently sitting by his side on a small chair that had been provided for her.

     Reginald was covered in bruises and cuts to his face which had caused great swelling; he was barely recognisable from the damage he had sustained. Carrey held his hand and was quietly sobbing to herself.

     "Hello Carrey. How is he doing?" said Thelia tenderly, putting her hand gently on Carrey's shoulder.

     "He still hasn't woken," she said tearfully.

     "I am sure he will," said Deven.

     "Yes of course," added Thelia.

     "I am so sorry I didn't get here in time Carrey," said Deven. "Trust in this though, I have never seen such bravery or will as that of your Reg. He didn't give them an inch."

     "They burnt down our home and our livelihood regardless and now my Reginald lies here on the verge of death," Carrey said tearfully, looking down at her husband as he lay there, breathing slowly.

     "Yes, sorry yes I just meant…" Deven said meekly.

     "It's ok," replied Carrey. "I know you mean well. I just want him to pull through and come back to me. Thank you for coming when you did Deven. I don't know what might have happened had you not driven them off. You look quite exhausted yourself. You should make sure to get some rest."

"I will," said Deven.

There were several other beds, filled by locals that had been caught in the fighting or not made it to the guard house in time. Owen the stable master was sat by one such bed, his white, wispy hair all out of place as though he had been involved in a raucous of some kind. The person in the bed was an older lady of whom Owen seemed quite concerned about, holding her hand in his, staring intently at her.

Deven and Thelia both walked over to him, and she laid her hand on his shoulder. "How is she Owen?" Thelia said.

"Oh, hello Thelia, Hello Deven!" Owen exclaimed with much enthusiasm though noticeably tempered from his usual happy exuberance. "Mary is doing ok. She slips in and out, but she's a Staunton and Staunton's are built to last - you watch!"

"That they are," said Thelia, with half a smile.

Owen turned to Deven and stood up from the stool he was sitting on. Deven had taken to leaning on his staff to keep himself up; exhaustion was getting to him.

"You looked drained Deven," he said. "All that last night, saving us from the fire in the town hall. That terrible fire that blazed all around us and then Poof! All at once it was gone. I have never seen anything like it. I don't think my sister and I would have survived much longer, nor the others should you have not come!" He took Deven's left hand which he wasn't using for support upon his staff and shook it vigorously.

"It's alright," said Deven. "I just wish I had arrived quicker. I was dozing in my chair at home and by the time I had stirred and made my way down to the village proper, so much was already happening. It all transpired so fast."

"It did indeed," said Thelia. "You got here as soon as you could Deven, we all know that. Besides, you aren't our sworn protector. We have the constabulary guard for that. Your help is greatly appreciated regardless, as always."

"Yes, yes, it is!" The old man shook Deven's hand even more enthusiastically. "Whatever you did to get her breathing again Deven, was truly astounding!"

"As I said Owen, it is totally alright," Deven said after a long breath.

"Well,", said Owen. "If you ever need anything Deven, a good horse…" he let out a sigh and stared into the far wall. "The horses. I let them all go and off towards the Dell Wood. I couldn't let those terrible people get their hands on them!"

"Perhaps we can find them Owen," said Thelia. "I think the stables still stand. I don't think they contended with any mages being present, let alone two of them." She looked back to the doorway leading to the main hall of the guard house, where Nathanael stood against a wall.

"I heard of Nathanael's actions. The old man never fails to impress," Deven said, with a sincere smile.

"Less of the old." said Thelia, almost defensively, but jovial in manner. "Anyway, we will leave you alone Owen. Let us know if there is anything you need."

"Thank you, Thelia. I will." Owen turned and sat back down, grasping his sister's hand once again.

Thelia and Deven then turned and went to make their way out of the room, but not before pausing briefly by Gwithen. "How is Steven and the others doing?" said Thelia.

"He is ok, mostly. Everyone should pull through. I have used what healing herbs and tonics I have for the cuts and the bruises. Reginald, we tried our best to tend to his injuries. The poor thing suffered a desperate beating from those evil people, and I have no idea how he was still on his feet when you came, Deven. Owen's sister, Carol," she continued. "Well, she should hopefully pull through. Restarting her heart as you did Deven saved her life. I just hope you look after yourself though. You expended a great deal of energy doing all that last night."

"Yes, thank you, I will be alright. I will take some rest once we know all is ok," said Deven. "Nathanael looks pretty tired too. I am glad he was here, to cover your escape from the Inn. The inn, such a travesty."

"Yes, to both points," said Thelia. "He is tired and spent a great deal of energy himself last night. We would have been caught by those vile people without him. Should they had done so, I would expect many of us to be lying here too." She blushed slightly with her concern for Nathanael all too apparent.

"He has fortitude still," Gwithen said. "He might be retired from the Mage Scribes, but he is still very much the Nathanael Obverick of the battle of Copper Pass those years ago."

"Indeed, he is," said Deven. "Well, if you will excuse me, I will go talk to my fellow mage and perhaps get some sleep myself." He smiled at both and walked outside towards Nathanael, still stood, leaning up against the wall.

Chapter 28

Luther found himself standing out beyond the relative safety of the isle of books and was staring at what lay beyond. There was a large fireplace, up against the end wall of the cave with a chimney breast that scaled the side of the cavern and up to the surface above. The height of the fireplace was just shorter than Luther stood, with a large stone mantle across it, decorated with odds and ends such as little statues of beasts, along with a few books. Set above it a few feet, on the chimney breast were a pair of antlers mounted on a wooden backing. They looked large and proud, and Luther wondered whether they had been shorn by a stag or some other beastie. Below, in the fireplace itself, there was currently a fire roaring mightily, producing a lot of warmth for anyone nearby.

On either side of the fireplace were walls of brick and mortar, three on each side that squared off part of the cavern. There was a doorway into each, beyond which Luther assumed must be the living quarters of the archivist and perhaps a kitchen or something similar in the other.

Between the fireplace and where Luther stood, at the edge of the outer ring of bookcases, were several rectangular desks with books on them sitting piled at different heights. At one particular table, close to the south side wall of the cavernous library was what Luther could only assume was a small bear, fast asleep, who was sitting with its back against a table leg. For some reason he knew somewhat instinctively that this was not the small furry creature that had appeared before him several times now. He could make out the appendages of its arms and legs, sticking out from its body which the black creature most definitely didn't have. This bear had fur that was dark grey, yet not nearly dark and black enough for Luther to be concerned it was that thing he had met several times before. Indeed, the bear had a head and features of the face such as eyes and a snout, again something which the other creature didn't.

Looking up, he saw sitting at the table, a woman of pale skin with long dark hair that was tied back in a ponytail. She looked middle aged and well kempt with a blue blouse and covered by a dark blue, fitted jumper over which she wore short fur coat. Around her neck she had a scarf, below which hung several necklaces, each holding various icons which Luther couldn't make out from this distance.

The lady was not looking at Luther, but rather engrossed in a book that lay in front of her. Luther thought best to wait for her to acknowledge him rather than interrupt her. The only audible noise she gave for the moment was the occasional sniffle of someone who was suffering from a cold. He waited quietly.

"So," said Celeste Ignophenen, not taking her eyes from her book. "Ethel says you wish to talk to me about something or some such." She gave another sniffle, her eyes resting on the book in front of her.

"Umm, yes. Yes, I do, if that's ok?" said Luther. He was nervous and was already beginning to stutter his words a little. He was now standing in front of the woman that he sought, that may shed, if just a little light on why he was how he was.

"Well, the archivist tells me you have travelled from the Lonefield Borough? Overton, was it?" her head still looking over the book in front of her.

"Yes, I have. My friend, my friend Golon told me you may be able to help me understand some problems I am dealing with. Or perhaps provide some insight at least." He felt lucky she was still staring at her book and not at the anxiety addled mess of a man in front of her, trying to keep himself together.

She removed her eyes from the pages and sat back in the chair. She looked Luther up and down before saying: "Golon sent you, did he? I haven't seen him in quite some time. I heard he opened some kind of shop. Golon, a store keep! Who would have thought it?!" she said, followed by another sniffle.

Luther thought to himself what this meant. Golon had been a resident for a few years in Overton having moved there when Luther was in his mid-twenties. He wondered what Golon might have been in another life. He had to admit, he seemed to have knowledge of things Luther wouldn't expect which suggested he was a worldly gnome who may have seen or experienced more than he had ever let on.

"Tell me. Does he still dress like he runs a brothel?" she said, snapping Luther from his thoughts.

"He does dress quite gregariously, if that's what you mean, yes," replied Luther.

"Ha! Yes, that's Golon. A peacock, but a wise one," Celeste said. "So, as you have forced me to break from study earlier than I wished, tell me, why have you come here?" She said this rather sternly as though she hoped that whatever Luther had to say, it had best be worth her time. "Well? Would you like to sit down?"

"Yes, sorry yes," Luther replied rather nervously. He tried to remember how to walk - having suddenly completely forgotten how to do so - and managed to step around the small bear that was still asleep with its back against a table leg and then pulled out a chair from the end opposite and sat down.

She sniffed again and repeated her question, "So, why are you here?"

"Well," said Luther. "Sorry, yes. It's kind of a strange thing I guess, but important to me, nonetheless. I was hoping you may be able to shed light on something and in turn would help me deal with it better."

She looked at him intently and said: "Well if you stop stuttering and let out what you wish to talk about then perhaps, I can help you!" She seemed none too pleased to be interrupted during her study to be met with a man that was fumbling for his words but was short of outright anger.

"Right, sorry," Luther said. "I have this condition you see." He tried to think about the words he was to say out of fear of annoying her further. "I am inflicted by a sadness you see. A sadness that doesn't have any root cause of trauma or some such – I had a good childhood with no traumatising events. The sadness I experience seems to have coalesced from nowhere."

Her look turned slightly less stern. "Go on," she said.

"Well, I wake up in the mornings, and I feel a sadness, misery really that seems to have no point of origin. Sometimes it is delayed, like this very morning I was affected after being offered a brief respite before it fell upon me once again. It is as if the world wishes to me to feel depressed, it wills me to be sad or perhaps in the least, doesn't seem concerned that I am." His tone turned down, as had his mood. He had gone from a quiet excitement and apprehension to a disheartened gloominess as he now sat pondering why he was the way he was. "It doesn't seem to matter what my mood might be from the previous day. It seemingly has no effect on the mood I will be in the next. I have gone to sleep feeling positive and jovial, only to awake the next day feeling upset and despondent,"

"I see" said Celeste, she had turned her gaze fully upon Luther who was finding it difficult to keep eye contact, rather looking around the room in avoidance. "And what of your dreams?" she said.

"My dreams?" replied Luther "Well I know that I have them. Not always, but often. I am unable to ever recall what they were though."

"Not at all?" she said. "Not even a glimpse?"

"I have strong feelings about what may have happened, but it doesn't translate into any kind of recollection. It is frustrating to say the least."

"Ok, ok" she said. "And you say you had no troubles in your childhood? No traumatic events that may have caused you mental anguish. What about further in life? Did something happen, some event that may have some impact?"

"No, not at all", said Luther. "My parents were very good to me and to my brother and sister. They still live where I was brought up, in Earstwhile in The East Borough. I was fortunate to have a quiet an uneventful upbringing; nothing untoward; nothing that could possibly lead to how I feel now." He put his right hand on a book nearby, grey in colour, and fiddled with it nervously, opening and closing it while waiting for her response.

"That is interesting Luther," she said. "So, you have this impeccable sadness that you can't recall having any kind of trigger or cause in your past. This mood is also unaffected by any previous, perhaps happy mood beforehand?"

"Yes, but there is more," he said.

"More? Then go on. You have caught my interest," she said ending, with a sniffle. She stared at him as he fiddled with the book and closed her own. All her focus was upon the main sat in front of her.

"Well," he said, pulling his hands back and placing then on his thighs. He realised his right leg had been desperately moving; rising up and down on the front of his foot He wondered if she noticed.

He had pondered briefly on describing the strange little ball of fur that he had seen, which only ever seemed to appear when there was no-one else present to verify its existence, but he thought better of it for now at least and decided to speak of something else.

"I have this overbearing feeling sometimes, mostly when I am in a very low, feeling particularly sad. I get this feeling that somehow… I don't know it's silly..."

"Nothing is silly!" chimed in Celeste. "Say what you will!"

"Ok," Luther said. "Well, it feels sometimes, I have this deep feeling that for whatever reason the world, the universe, whatever wants me to be this way. It wishes that I have this to deal with. That I am not meant to be a happy person, an overly positive person. Perhaps I am doomed to impeding sadness. In a way though, I would be alright with it if just I had some explanation as to why."

"I see," she said. She had pulled up a cup of tea she had close by, amongst the piles of books around her.

"Not that I am remiss to the idea that I may just be a miserable individual," he continued. "Just the way my brain works. It's just that I have this feeling you know. I know it sounds silly." He looked down at his shaking legs, avoiding eye contact.

"Well," said Celeste Ignophenen. That is an interesting plot you find yourself in. And you think I may have some knowledge to the fact of why you are why you are? Perhaps gleamed from the many tomes of knowledge that I poured over in my time? 'Celeste must know something, must be useful for something.' Golon, the cheek of him!"

"I am sorry," said Luther. "I don't mean to offend you

in anyway. Golon spoke of you sincerely.

Celeste Ignophenen stood up from her chair, which made a creaking noise as she did so, but not enough to wake the slumbering bear leaning against the table. Luther looked down at it.

"Don't worry about him. It takes a lot to wake the lazy thing up. He might even be pretending - the sneaky bugger!" She began pacing back and forth in front of the fireplace, seemingly thinking to herself, punctuated by the occasional sniffle. Luther sat in his chair and waited for her to speak again.

She paused in her pacing briefly. "So yes, you being depressed. Sad. Miserable, even. It's not a rare thing, feelings of sadness. It doesn't make you special." She continued pacing.

"I know," said Luther, avoiding eye contact with her, though she herself was mostly staring at the cobbled floor in thought.

"Yes. Nothing from your past? Be honest!" Her words felt stern to Luther. She was not one to trifle with in a discussion.

Luther chose the words carefully. "No, nothing. I mean the usual things that might upset anyone of course," he said.

"Yes of course, of course," she replied, still pacing. "And how long have you felt like this? Is it recent?"

"It's odd," he replied, "At first it feels like a recent thing, only the last few years, but the more I think about it the more I realise it has been longer than this, perhaps even as far back as my early childhood. Perhaps you may ask why I haven't sought help before and what I can say to that is I didn't think I could be helped or should be. Everyone has their own problems. Best not to trouble them with mine." He looked briefly at her and their eyes met before Luther turned away and she continued her pacing.

"I see," she said again, deep in thought. She kept pacing back and forth for a minute with neither of them saying a word. Luther was patiently awaiting any knowledge she might have to impart to him.

She paused her steady walk in front of the fireplace. "Over my years, I have travelled far," she said. "Travelled around The Boroughs, to the Border Crags, over the Winding Sea to the Antrapan highlands and beyond. You were lucky indeed to have found me here. I will soon be off again through the Southern Reaches and into Covenant territory."

"You would willingly go into their lands?" said Luther, looking somewhat set aback by this revelation.

"I would yes. If you know the right people and who not to get on the wrong side of, then one can happily travel unmolested. Obviously, I know the right people," she replied.

"Oh ok. But still, I know the war was twenty years ago, but I don't think whoever leads them have forgotten about it. Though I can't imagine that all that dwell there share the same feelings of ill will towards or seek war and destruction upon us."

"This is true" she said. "But Like I said, you just need to know the right people. They are not all out to get us and not all angry evil beings wishing to see The Boroughs wiped from the map." She blew her nose into a hanky before continuing pacing.

Luther tried to see the best in people as much as he could. Judging a whole nation on the actions of their leaders was best avoided, he thought. At the same time, it was difficult for him to truly accept this, as all he had heard the last twenty years of his life, and at the time of the war itself was of the villainy of the covenant, of their desire to sow chaos and see the destruction of The Boroughs and all who dwelt within.

"Yes of course. I shouldn't jump to conclusions, all I have is the memories from my youth and tales of those on the front lines," he said.

"Right, anyway" she said. "As I was saying, I have travelled far in my years and read a great many tomes and manuscripts of knowledge and magic. There is much to be learnt you know, from what happened during the Magic Event. Not just from how it happened, but more so of what its implications were. There are those that have conducted research both magical and mundane that need to be preserved and learned from. Further, there is knowledge that preceded the event from both realities that must be learned from and must be kept safe!"

"Would any of it be of help with what I have described to you?" Luther interrupted. He was eager for information and was unable to stop himself from blurting out these words.

She paused for a moment, looking at Luther, then said, "Before you interrupted me, I was about to describe what I know. Right, as I was saying, there exist tomes of knowledge kept secure in great Libraries such as this and more so elsewhere - in less than comfortable surroundings - that describe certain observations of things." She resumed her pacing back and forth with the odd sniffle thrown in. "The fusing of our two worlds of the whimsical and the astute, of humans and fantastical, was not without repercussions. As you most likely know, humans have become capable of casting magic spells. Now a tempered mind might wish to argue the semantics of it. 'It's not magic, but perhaps explained by some other way of manipulating the elements around them, somehow', but regardless Magic is Magic." She stood still and rather than look at Luther, sitting in his chair eagerly gazing around the room with his right leg busily stuttering up and down, she kept her gaze to the fire in front of them.

"Are you alright?" ventured Luther.

"Yes. Yes, I am fine," she said, staring into the flames. "Since the event, those few hundred years ago, all manner of phenomena have been observed. For example, the existence of the warble bears; they originated not from ours or theirs, but seemingly a result of a fusion of both. She stole a look at the little bear sitting asleep against the table and began pacing once again. "There are other things you see, rather more esoteric," she said. "Magic you see, has an interesting way of manifesting, especially in humans who have lived with it only just, compared to the Elves. This is not to say that there isn't members of other races with immense power of course; the weaving of magic is entrenched in them to a degree which we humans have yet to understand. Tell me, have you heard of 'Emotional Energy Congregation?'"

"Emotional Energy Congregation?" said Luther, "Emotions congregating around something or someone?"

"Something like that Luther," she replied. "There are, let us say, beings in the world that are attuned in a way to certain thoughts and feelings. From what I have gathered in my years of learning, - and many they are - this is not a recent development, at least not within the other races. Humans though, have only recently experienced this phenomenon, perhaps only the last fifty years or so. These people or creatures even, find themselves effected in certain ways by emotions of those around them. But more than this. It is as though they feel the emotions in the open air that fills the reality around us. These affected so, draw upon those emotions and act like a focal point for their congregation."

"Do you think I could be suffering something similar?" Luther said.

"Perhaps you could be suffering similarly yes. The tomes of the Mage Scribes and others mention it cryptically, with little description of what to look for or the common traits to be aware of, for someone of that demeanour. So there really isn't any way I can tell without the use of certain magic, to see the ephemeral."

"Sorry, I am not sure I follow," he replied.

"Well," said Celeste after another sniffle. "There is a way to see that which eludes the simple eyes of those such as you and me. There exists a host of things around us that we cannot see or indeed interact with. But by the use of magic, we can pull back that cover that blinds us and see into that other world of energy, and of emotions."

Luther was both intrigued and worried at the same time. Was he somehow a conduit or a focal point for certain emotions? Did he attract them? And what of this hidden veil in the first place? Could he believe this at all? It was certainly interesting if nothing else. He knew of course of magic and how through its application one could control things in the natural world but hadn't ever really thought of what might be present in a different realm of existence. Such things were not a normal subject for anyone to ponder, let alone comprehend. He had hoped perhaps there would be a more simplistic reason for why he was why he was. He thought Celeste Ignophenen might be some kind of student of the mind, able to diagnose a simple problem with how his mind worked the way it did. Then at least he would know for sure. Perhaps even, she could have recommended something to ease the symptoms; some tonic or medicine; mental exercises; some magic to alter how he thought, though he probably wouldn't be comfortable with the latter. Instead of any of that he had been presented with a quite different suggestion - one most fantastical and difficult to grasp.

"You look concerned, Luther," said Celeste Ignophenen looking at him sat in the chair. "It is quite common when confronted with deeper knowledge of things. I of course am no stranger to the esoteric and the deep understanding; it would take something quite dramatic to confound or confuse me!" She puffed her chest a little with these words, clearly proud of her learned ways, before sniffling again.

"Yes of course," said Luther. "I am a little taken aback. I never once considered it would be something like that, something supernatural that was affecting me. And you think it could be something like this?"

"It is plausible," said Celeste. "But we don't know for sure. It is just a simple hypothesis from what you have described to me. It could be, but simply you are just that way inclined. Your mind having decided it wished to be a certain way for some reason. The comings and goings in your brain, twisting themselves up in this way. Indeed, we could discover literally nothing. No emotional energies that are drawn to your person. It would still be interesting to try though, I feel."

Luther was anxious to know if this was the cause, if he was somehow affected by the whims of magic and whatever else from another sphere of being. "Is there a way to find out? Some spell or procedure that may show us what is the case? I am sorry, I am taking up your time. I was so eager for insight that I forgot myself."

Celeste Ignophenen had resumed pacing in front of the fire, holding her chin with her thumb and forefinger. If she had taken in what Luther was saying at this time it was unclear. She seemed lost in thought as she moved back and forth. "Yes, yes," she said. "You have sparked my interest, Luther. Not because you feel sad – though of course that is lamentable – no, it is because of the way you describe it and its apparent lack of cause. Normally you have cause and effect. The cause of me throwing a trifle at you will have the effect of you being covered in trifle and most likely riled up in anger and confusion. But you say there seems nothing that could have caused your condition. This intrigues me you see." She had stopped pacing and was now looking straight into the fire that roared in front of her. "Well," she said. "You ask me if there is some way to find out. There may well be. Yes indeed. Hmm." She trailed off again with more lingering gaze upon the fire with the occasional sniffle.

Luther sat quietly in the chair and waited for her to speak again.

"I believe, through various rights and verses of sorcerous induction that we could create a spell that would lift the veil and allow us to peer into that other side and determine the truth of in our hypothesis."

"I see. Have you ever tried this before?" said Luther, a nervous twinge hanging in his words.

"Have I ever performed such a thing?" she said. "No, I have not. But I have read of similar rituals performed in the past."

"Were they successful?" he asked.

"From what I can tell, they may have been. What I have discovered in their writings is that they lifted the veil or perhaps believe they did, but there have been variable results. I think it depends on the subject of the spell. I have read of one induction where although they were quite confident with what had transpired, i.e., something happened; perhaps a change of light, a swirl of magic winds, a sense of the otherworldly, but on the whole, they were unable to discern a definitive answer."

"Oh, so it has never worked before?"

"It depends on what you define as 'working!'" She snapped a sniffling snap. "In several more recent attempts – perhaps in the last forty years - it worked in the sense that the boundary between existences was breached, but there was nothing to be seen on the other side. Nothing tangible and discreet at least. There do exist though, older scrolls – several hundred years and older, around just after the time of the magic event that slammed together our reality with that of the elves and the gnomes etc. They mention glimpses of otherworldly things, things that seemed drawn to the subject of the spell."

"Ok, I see," said Luther.

"Also, of course, we can't invoke the rights of ritual that will breach the other side at any old place. We must go to a specific place."

"A specific place?" Luther said.

"Yes, a specific place," she replied. "Enacting a spell of such specific characteristics requires a specially selected place. Somewhere there is sufficient friction between spheres of energy that would allow one to move aside that which masks us from sight other worldly things in the universe and lay bare what there is to see."

"Honestly," she said, "I am quite intrigued to see for myself. I have only ever read about these phenomena. And it being a fairly recent thing in terms of long-term history, there isn't a great body of text to read. I have never seen it in person, obviously. In fact, I doubt many people have – that are alive at least."

"So, what will you have me do?" Luther said curiously. He was becoming anxious and filled with worry. Although he was happy to have found the person he sought and that she had provided some form of explanation, it was all a quite a lot to take in. His leg was shaking with anxiety more than ever before.

"It will take energy on both our parts to perform what must be done for the ritual to succeed. It may also cause you some anxiety to see what we will behold; the unknown, but then revealed. I know this is quite the request of you. I can see the worry on your face. It is merely a suggestion and nothing else. If you do not feel you wish to participate then there is nothing lost, but the knowledge and insight we could have gained." She looked towards Luther with these words, as if in encouragement to agree to the proceedings.

"Where must we go? Is there a place you have in mind?" Luther said, now making eye contact with the woman in front of the fireplace.

"I know of such a place," she responded, sniffling. "It would require a small trek into the foothills of the Lightlorne Mountains beyond this fortress town. Will you agree and come with me?"

"Will it take some time?" said Luther.

"Perhaps a couple of hours," said Celeste Ignophenen. "It is an old ritual site just in the early crags. We have no need to scale even the lowest part of the mountains - just venture into its vicinity."

Luther looked into the roaring fireplace and let his mind wander. It seemed this might be quite the ordeal. Did he really want to mess around with such things? It would certainly be easier for him to just thank her for her time and come away with that nugget of knowledge she had bestowed on him. But would that be enough? He wouldn't know for sure unless he agreed to participate. Maybe revealing this to him may cause some epiphany that waylaid the roving thought that thundered around in his mind. He had come this far already, he thought. He must go all in.

"Yes, I am quite anxious, but I must know," he said, looking back to Celeste Ignophenen who had sat back down at the table.

"Good, good! This will be most interesting! Most interesting indeed!" she exclaimed excitedly. "We can make way immediately if you wish? We should be back by nightfall."

"I guess so, sure," said Luther. "I don't wish to detract from your work though. I have already taken up enough of your time."

"Nonsense!" She said pointedly. "My studies and my work are all tied in with learning of new and yet as seen wonders and intrigues. I have plumbed the depths of knowledge of this place and the other, looking for answers and artefacts of interest that could provide some insight into the workings of the universe. Then you walk through the door with great promise to provide me with just that! Oh, the chance of it!"

"I just don't want to waste anybody's time. That's all," Luther said.

"My other work can wait. This takes precedent! We could be the first to actually see clearly to another side and maybe glimpse something there." She seemed quite intent on giving this her fullest attention and Luther was not going to argue with her.

"Ok," he said.

"Brilliant! We shall start immediately!"

"Right. Blimey. ok. We shall set off now?" He looked at her sheepishly, not knowing what to expect.

"Just stay there for a moment" she said. "Before we head anywhere, I must speak with the archivist to arrange what we need for the ritual." She stood up again and walked off towards the central desk of the archivist in the midst of all the bookcases.

Luther sat at the desk and waited patiently for her to return. He tried his best to shake off all the worry and anxiety that had begun to build up inside him. This will all be ok Luther. She is a learned and intelligent woman. She knows what she is doing. His mind wondered again with thoughts not only of worry, but also a little of hope. Though it would only reveal the truth of her suspicions, if indeed they were true, he thought, it would be a relief in a way, giving some insight for feeling how he did.

After what seemed close to half an hour, Celeste Ignophenen appeared again from around the bookcases and stood by the desk with the little bear still asleep up against one of its legs. "I have notes of my own of course but I have sent the archivist to find some other books that details the rites to invoke the spell. Once she returns, we can begin the journey to the ritual site," said Celeste Ignophenen.

Luther thought of saying something about his worries but steeled himself and stood up. He was wearing his jacket over his cardigan so felt warm enough for the journey. His axe was sheathed at his side should he require it.

"I recall reading the book which detailed what must be vocally expressed for the spell but there require motions and otherwise, in certain books that live here in the library," she said

"Are you a mage as well?" Luther asked.

"I am not a mage by the usual definition, but I have enough power within me to cast a few spells when needed. Magic is not the exclusive field of learned and named mages you now." She gave Luther a sly smile.

She was not letting on quite how powerful she might

be he thought, but Luther decided against pressing her further.
"It will take only but a few moments to cast the spell – if my calculations are correct - and create a rift through our reality to another. Enough for us at least, to take a look. Do not be concerned of what we will see. Remember that all we are doing is viewing what is already there. You are in no danger."

Chapter 29

Luther stood up with his pack over his shoulder and waited to follow the two ladies back up the stairs. To his surprise, rather than make their way back through the library and up the staircase – the way in which he came in – they walked to the back of the cavern by the quarters of the archivist in some until now, unseen corner.

When they reached this darkened nook of the cavern, they stopped. Luther could see only the wall of the rock face; a dark brownish grey rock that made up the cavern which housed the library. Luther was a little confused as to why they had come this way.

The archivist, Ethel, seeing the puzzled look on his face said, "Ah you wonder why we have come this way and not the way you came in. Even more so as there seems to be no way forward now?"

"Yes, I am a little confused," replied Luther.

"Things are not always as they seem, Luther," said Ethel.

"You will do well to heed that advice," said Celeste.

"Oh right," Luther said. He was still unsure what was happening, but he trusted the two women did.

Ethel walked up to the rock face and placed her left hand upon it. She uttered a word that Luther could just about make out: 'Reeba'. After several moments part of the rock face near where she was standing began to shudder and then suddenly there appeared an outline in the rock in the shape of a rectangular door. Ethel then placed her left hand in the middle of it and gently pushed. The wall then gave way, opening inwards as if hinged on its right-hand side.

The three of them were met by what looked like a tunnel into the rock. Looking up from where he was standing, Luther could see that this tunnel went straight forward with a steady incline. It was roughly four feet wide and perhaps just over six feet tall; enough for grown humans to walk in single file.

"Wow," said Luther. "I have never seen something like that before. Some sort of secret passage with a password and everything!" It was something out of one of his Randolph Montgomery Henceforth books, he thought.

"What did we say?" said Ethel with a smile on her face before stepping into the tunnel followed by Celeste and then last Luther bringing up the rear.

As Luther broached the tunnel, he could feel something brush against his legs. He looked down and in the light of the library still grasping at the edge of the tunnel, saw the shape of a little bear running by him towards Celeste.

"He finally awakes!" sniffled Celeste. "Lazy bugger!"

It was the warble bear that been, up until now, fast asleep against a chair leg in the library. Luther wondered in what capacity it served Celeste - if any way at all - besides being a pet. Would it be a familiar or some sorts or perhaps simply a small and useful accomplice to her schemes, whatever they may be?

Once all were through, the door behind them appeared to be closing itself as it slowly moved back towards its closed position behind them and with it, the light from the library.

There was no light in the tunnel in the form of torches or lanterns, but Luther was not left to wonder long how they would see their way through it; Celeste pulled something from her bag that looked like a little lantern, brass in construction with a little housing for some fuel of some sort. She clicked her hands while briefly staring at the lantern upon which it suddenly came to life. It was the similar warm flame of fire dust.

Luther looked back briefly to the door and could make out no gaps of light or indication of anything but a solid wall of rock. Curious, he thought, when magic was involved, it is usually best not to try and explain it to oneself and carry on. So, he did.

They walked up through the inclined tunnel in relative silence. Luther was left to his wonderings; where would this tunnel reach the surface? If it did indeed so. Would this lead outside the town itself? Who knew of this secret tunnel? Every now and then his thoughts were jogged by the sudden glimpse of the Warble bear shuffling around their feet; it would keep up with Celeste for a time and then get lost in its own thoughts and lag behind near Luther, before seemingly vanishing and reappearing back by Celeste's side.

Luther supposed they had walked just over half a mile before wondering when this tunnel might come to an end. "Ah there we are," said Ethel, loud enough for Luther to hear it. "Just up there and we will be out!" They had come to another rock face, straight ahead.

In similar fashion as she had done before, when approaching it, Ethel placed her hand upon the rock wall, time saying the word, "Abeer." A moment passed and there now appeared an outline of a door, this time with a something similar to a handle made from the earth itself. She took hold of the handle and opened it inwards on hidden hinges towards the three of them,

With the opening of the door, the tunnel was bathed in light from the sky above. It was still the afternoon with few clouds in the sky allowing for plenty of sun light to rain down upon them.

The three of them - followed by a warble bear - stepped out from the tunnel several feet. When all were clear, the door begun to slowly move back into position as the previous had, and after several moments it had closed completely, behind them. This side of the rock was covered in vines and other climbing plants that before his very eyes seemed to move across the area of the door masking it further. Luther stepped towards it with the intention of discovering the lines or grooves in the rock betraying the outline of the door, but again, he could not find a single thing. He turned back towards Celeste and Ethel.

"So, what was that tunnel for?" he said.

"Ah, well," said the archivist. "As you know, the Library of Bramstone houses many great books, scrolls, manuscripts and other assorted tomes of knowledge. Much of the information is very precious both from an academic and strategic point of view. There are many maps of local lands, spell books of rites and rituals and the locations of important sites that would be of great interest to those with malevolent intent."

"Yes, indeed there is!" added Celeste.

"I see yes," said Luther. "So, this tunnel would be used to ferry away all the scripture from the library in the case that the town was overrun?"

"Yes, exactly," said Ethel. "Though, as you can imagine we couldn't take all with us so we would sadly have to bring just the most vital items."

"I understand," replied Luther. "I suppose you haven't had to do that yet - and hopefully never will of course."

"No, we haven't, and I hope we won't have too either."

Luther turned away from what was the tunnel entrance. Before him was the under croft of several trees and bushes that obscured the location of the door while still allowing ample light through overhead. Ethel gave motion to follow and so he walked after the two ladies and the bear out from behind the bushes and trees.

Once clear, Luther was greeted with the outskirts of the Lightlorne Mountain range. Directly before them was a slow incline of rocky outcrops and grass leading up to the main foothills of the mountains themselves. There were trees too after a while that had huddled together in the form of woodland, obscuring his view.

To Luther's right he saw a tribe of goats grazing on the grass out in the open. To his left he saw more of the same outcrops and behind him to the south he could see the tops of the buildings of Bramstone. The rock of the tunnel seemed to be buttressed against one of the outer walls of the town itself. Luther wondered how any army could come from this direction. Indeed, he thought it unfeasible for an invading force to approach from this direction; they would need to traverse the mountains themselves from the sea beyond and then scale the solid rock leading to the town walls from which they would most likely be felled by well-placed missiles of some description.

Celeste Ignophenen stepped out in front, taking the lead, and said, "Right, follow me. It's only perhaps a mile or so up there." She pointed to the wood north of them and began walking in that direction with her bear, Ethel the archivist and Luther behind her.

Once they made it to the huddled mass of columns of the earth, they then walked further for roughly twenty minutes. The wood was common and filled with chestnut, oak, and other species. They were not too close together to obscure a great deal of light, so the small party was fairly well lit in the later afternoon of the day.

Celeste came to a stop as the rough path through the trees they were taking came to a fork in the road. To the right it seemed to go off deeper into the wood and to the foothills proper. To the left Luther could see off in the distance, a clearing of some sort.

"This way please!" said Celeste sternly with a sniffle.

They followed her as she turned and took the left path towards the clearing. Before long, the woodland had given away enough for it to be seen in full.

The clearing itself was small, Luther thought, perhaps just fifty feet square. There was grass, but it was quite short, only a few inches in growth. In the middle was what Luther thought to be a shrine or alter of some sort; a large grey slab of stone placed vertically and resting on two short, roughly rectangular stones, laying on the ground.

Gathered around the shrine were large rocks, each roughly the length of Luther, but laid flat on the ground. What was curious to him was how flat each one was. It was though they had been purposely filed down to give a smooth and regimented top. They were almost like large stone tablets laying around the central altar, as if some giant creature was organising them to be chiselled with their writings but, for some reason left strewn and unwritten upon the ground.

Celeste motioned for them to continue towards the central shrine, so they all followed her with the bear teleporting back to her side once it had again lagged behind again. Luther had never seen a warble bear let alone witness one disappearing and reappearing somewhere else before his very eyes. He was quite impressed with what he saw.

"Now, here we are," said Celeste.

"What is this place?" asked Luther.

"This is an old ritual site, used by druids, seers and other magical users to perform special rites. It's still used even to this day," replied Ethel.

"And I suppose you will ask why this place and not some other?" said Celeste, pre-empting additional questions from him.

"Yes, I suppose that was my next question," he replied.

"Because this area here, this site, for whatever reason, perhaps the soil, the rocks or even the grass – as short as it is – is conducive to the conjuring of magical energies. Additionally, this place is known to be situated at a point where the boundary between spheres of energy is notably thin. What this means laymen's terms, is that this place is a good place to cast magic," said Celeste looking at Luther.

"Right, that seems fair enough," he said.

"Yes right, well, shall we begin preparations?" continued Celeste.

The archivist, Ethel took the books off her shoulder and handed them to Celeste. There were three in total; the aforementioned 'Incantations Concerning the Veil' – a thick red leather book; a dark brown leather tome that looked to have had an interesting life, titled: 'Other worldly Words' and finally a black book, not as thick as the other two which Luther was unable to see the title of. She handed them to Celeste who placed them down upon the stone altar. She thumbed through each in turn before leaving them open at certain pages.

"Right," said Celeste. "I have found the incantations and movements which will need to be performed for our needs of this spell."

"Oh, right, that's good," replied Luther.

She had put her own bag down on the alter besides the books. She pulled out a small draw-string sack and retrieved a handful of powder. Luther recognised the glowing red of warding powder.

"Warding powder?" he said.

"Yes, well observed," Celeste replied. "You are probably wondering why after saying there is no danger that I then proceed to pull some out of this bag?"

"Yes, the thought had crossed my mind."

"It's best to always playthings on the safe side, don't you think?"

"Yes, of course," replied Luther. This did waylay his immediate concern, but Luther wondered what dangers could arise; perhaps nothing at all, as she had suggested. He would go with this thought, he decided.

"Ok, if you could please stand just in front of me and try not to fidget," said Celeste.

Luther walked over to a spot roughly ten feet in front of her as she stood in front of the altar. She proceeded to hand the powder to Luther who she directed to spread around himself in a tight circle as he stood there. Celeste turned round to the altar and fixed her gazed at the red book. She turned and said some words quietly, which Luther failed to catch, and moved her arms around in some deliberate motion. Then she turned back to the altar and read from the blue book, still with her arms moving. She motioned for the archivist to take a step back from her position observing the ritual and then picked up the small black book and held it in front of her as she faced Luther.

"Now, Luther. Things are going to get a little exciting but stay calm. I will not let any harm befall you." She gave a reassuring smile, followed by a sniffle and then closed her eyes. She began breathing slowly and Luther got the feeling she was welling up energy inside of her. Up and down her chest rose with each deep breath she took in. Luther could feel the air become heavier around him. He felt heavier in himself somehow.

Several times over and over did she breathe, slowly and purposefully, before, with a last deep breath out, she her eyes opened. Reading from the book she said aloud in a strong and echoing voice, "Choo Lee Bookanda! Break the Barrier!" She then repeated: "Choo Lee Bookanda! Break the Barrier!" She repeated this phrase over and over, each time with as much gusto and power as the last.

The air around Luther was becoming heavier, as if he could feel some presence in it. He had a surge of anxiety through his body but managed to stay his fears.

A GRIM JOURNEY

"Choo Lee Bookanda! Break the barrier!" she repeated over and over. As she did so the air felt heavier and heavier.

Luther was now feeling a wave of sadness coming over him, pulsing with every repetition of the verse coming from Celeste's lips. Stronger and stronger it came, riding the crest and colliding with Luther; greater and greater.

"Choo Lee Bookanda! Break the Barrier!" came the words again, and again.

Luther felt a wave pass through him with every call, with each one bringing more and more melancholy, more sadness as if each one carried a ship laden with a bounty of emotion that slammed into him and wrecked upon his shore.

"Choo Lee Bookanda! Breaker the Barrier!"

Luther's eyes welled up. He was filling with despair, but he was desperate to see if Ms Ignophenen's theory was correct, which fed his determination to see it through.

"Choo Lee Bookanda! Break the Barrier!" Luther's eyes were wet, fuelled by waves of sadness. It was as though someone had set a large boulder upon his back, made of sorrow and despair.

"Choo Lee Bookanda! Break the Barrier!" She looked Luther in his tearful eyes and with no word said between them, she knew his wish was to carry on.

He felt the energy in the air around him, like a great blanket that was full of sorrow. He felt as though his spirit was on the verge of collapsing under the weight of it - something had to give.

"Choo Lee Bookanda! Break the Barrier!

His eyes were now streaming with tears; he could no longer control himself. He was filled with sadness. Filled with despair.

"Choo Lee Bookanda! Break the Barrier!"

There was a shudder in the air, felt by both Celeste and the archivist as a pulse that pushed through their bodies. Then there was a shimmer, and as if a lantern suddenly come to life in the depths of the deepest oceans, there was something now present to the simple eye which was hidden before.

Above Luther, as he stood there, appeared something resembling a flowing river. It was not of water though, but something else entirely, an energy of some kind. Its colour was of a reserved grey with hints of blue and black within. These colours swished and swashed within as if beings of some kind that were woven into the fabric of this stream

The source of the river was not clear, as it stretched out upwards into the sky and beyond the range of onlooker's vision. It flowed from above, meandering and weaving its way on route to pool above Luther's head. It was indeed a pool. A pool of something, with the colours intermingling - moving this way and that. Each individual colour of energy seemed its own entity between two to six inches roughly, in length.

Both Celeste Ignophenen and Ethel, stood staring at what had been revealed to them. This distraught man before them was somehow some kind of focal point or destination for these strange energies that emanated from somewhere, away in the sky.

Both were filled with a melancholy of their own, finding themselves in the presence of something strange that perhaps they were not intended to see.

"I feel a sadness creeping over me," said the archivist. Have you ever seen or felt anything like this Celeste?"

"No, never," said Celeste Ignophenen, quietly. "Never anything like this. This... river of some kind seems to be drawn to him. And yes, I feel a dour wave pressing upon me, which seems to have been caused by this scene we see before us."

"And what is it exactly?" quizzed the archivist.

"Well, purely speculation of course..." She paused imminently as she felt a pang of sadness move through her body. "I think this might be a physical manifestation of emotions, perhaps, sad ones?" replied Celeste, staring intently. Pondering around the solemn looking soul in front of them. "They don't seem to be negative in the sense of malignancy. I don't feel in danger in any way, just, weathered by a sorrow, all of a sudden."

"I see," said the archivist, not taking her eyes from Luther. "And why is it here, this stream? Why is Luther seemingly its destination, I wonder? I must say, my mood has turned quite sober."

Celeste with eyes still cast on the sight in front of her

said, "I am not totally sure. It seems as if Luther is some sort of focal point for these roiling... emotions? I wonder, are they here because this man suffers from gloom and despair, or does he feel how he does because they are here? Either could be plausible, that is for sure, or maybe even both, hmm." She went to walk over to Luther who was still standing there, sobbing. She ducked as if not to collide with the stream by some chance. And then a lone colour of bleak blue energy slowly drifted lower than the others and, rather than colliding with her, passed straight through her as if she were not there. It resumed its gentle glide, reaching back up to the pool floating above Luther.

      She placed her hand on Luther's shoulder. He had stopped sobbing, standing there with a quiet look upon on his face with his hands resting by his side, looking down at the floor. To Celeste, his look and his position seemed vacant as if he were someone else entirely.

Chapter 30

Luther stood staring ahead. He could no longer see the clearing outside the town of Bramstone, but rather a different place; a place dark and gloominous.

There were several paths ahead through a darkened wood. The sky and the air were dark. The trees, those columns of the earth that filled this place were not trees at all, but blurred outlines resembling them. Their presence was of something almost like a floating mist or fog, each lingering in position; anchored to the ground. Their colour was of dull greys, near black, and they rose several meters each into the sky, of which itself was darkened, but somehow illuminated by some hidden source, lighting just enough for Luther to see a short distance around him.

He stepped forward, towards one of the trees of mist, several slow and slothful steps. He came close by. Slowly, an arm shaped appendage from the tree quietly seemed to reach out to him. From it, he could feel some force emanating, energy that breezed through it and into him. It was as though something had been passed to Luther. He gave a glum smile and walked to another which, in turn acted in a similar way. He felt some strange affinity with these things, though what they were, he was not really sure. He approached several more and each in turned reached out to Luther with a similar foggy gloom, sending a pulse through his body.

He felt no particular drive to do anything, to feel anything. He just had a need to wander through the forest of strange, hazy, mist like things. Luther walked amongst them with no idea of the time spent; no realisation of the duration of his visit as he strolled in this twilight forest. He didn't care for it either. Nothing mattered anymore; all that was in life was left alone and he cared nothing for it.

Luther strolled through yet more of them, and each in turn reached out to him in a similar fashion. He seemed little concerned with this and even gave a small, brief smile when they did so. He made his way through the woods – whether by design or otherwise - to a crossroads of sorts. There were eight paths reaching out in all directions of a compass, criss-crossing at the centre. It was absent of any sign or direction.

He stood there a while and quietly wondered which way to take. There was no obvious difference in their appearance or what they lead to, each pathway simply a corridor or long enough gap through the trees of the wood. He didn't know what path to take but felt no anxiety that might usually strike him when his decisions were unclear.

They all looked the same; just the floor of the forest laying the way in each direction. These paths appeared not to have been created by some being, but rather, somehow, a natural occurrence, as if the trees of mist themselves had aligned where they stood, allowing for clear passage by them.

He felt remiss to select a direction and instead stood there where he was. He would remain there and wasn't bothered for it. He stood looking at and through the trees of mist and fog and thought nothing of where he was and why he was there. He was simply content to exist in this place.

All present were Luther and the tree like gatherings of mist. He was resigned to stay here with them, awaiting nothing. His head turned left gently, and he viewed the paths that featured there, simply the mist and that void between then. He turned his head to the right and again was met with the rows of mist and fog arranged for the paths to find their way between them.

He turned round and his vision swept gently across more of them, gathered as they were around him. He looked down to the ground and took in nothing of what he saw, instead turning his thoughts to emptiness. He would stay here forever.

But something caught the corner of his eye, creeping at the edge of his peripheral. It seemed different from the grey things that surrounded him. It was small, and decidedly darker, like a round black furry pillow. Luther, nudged by its appearance didn't quite turn his head to see, but rather raised his eyes in admission of its presence. It had appeared in the upper right of his vision having seemingly moved on from outside of his view.

Luther's mind was less empty. His thoughts had

spurred into motion at the sight of this thing and when it begun to move, he turned his head towards it. This blackened round thing of fur and blackness rolled closer, and he watched it come. Slowly it moved, but steady in motion as it rolled towards him. It approached nearly directly in front of him, standing there. It came to a stop. It remained, in silence, perhaps several yards between them. His sole attention was now focused on this thing. He gave a sombre smile and stared through its blackened dark body.

It didn't move further but stayed still before Luther. He didn't say a word, but instead continued to stare into it. Through it. It became all he could see. All he focused on. All he wished to know. Just darkness. Yet comforting.

And then it simply began to move once more. Slowly, as before, but not towards him. It moved away, the round and fury creature revolving slowly beyond him. It moved towards a gap in the trees; one of the paths created by their gathering. Luther looked up to see where it led, but he could not tell.

It paused again, further from him this time. And with this Luther found himself moving his legs, moving himself towards the small round and furry thing that had gathered his attention. As he shuffled himself towards it, slowly and steadily - much like it had done - it in turn began to roll towards and then down the path it had seemingly chosen.

These two beings walked quietly and stoically; one following the other through the parting between the tree-like things which seemed to reach for him as he passed through as though saying goodbye to a loved one. Luther paused briefly, as did that which he followed, and he turned to them. He gave another muted smile and turned back, before once again walking the path after the small black being that lead him through the forest. Yet he could not see where this path lead. It lay hidden and out of sight to him. What obscured it, he couldn't tell; all he knew was to follow the creature and that was all that was needed.

As he took several more steps forward, on the path, after the ball of fur rolling in front, Luther's features became somewhat faded, as though they were beginning to pale back into the background of this place. His extremities, his arms, his legs, all slunk from view, greying from those who might observe him. With each step he took, this effect greatened with his entire body fading more intensely with every stride he took. The look on Luther's face was one of quiet acceptance and tranquillity.

Chapter 31

"Luther? Are you ok?" said Celeste, her hand resting on his shoulder. The air had taken a breath. The strange river of coalesced energies had vanished from view as suddenly as it had appeared.

Luther gave no response for a few moments before nodding gently.

"Were you aware of what was just now flowing above your head?" Celeste said, inquisitively.

"I don't know," came the words from his lips. His tone was quiet and subdued with tears still fresh upon his face. He wiped his them with his hands.

"They must be emotions made manifest," said Celeste. "Though I would suggest they are not particularly happy ones. They seem to be flowing to you Luther - it was most extraordinary. I don't think they are want to cause any harm - if indeed they were capable – but, it seems, these are what lay heavy on your mind. You say you are unsure of seeing them though? They were pretty clear for all to see."

Luther was still quiet. Moments passed with no-one saying a word. "I don't know," he said again. "It was like I wasn't present. It was like I was somewhere else. I did see some things, I think. It's all kind of hazy, hazy and dream like. I was lost, but without the anxiety of it, if that makes any sense."

He was looking mostly straight ahead, thinking of what had just happened. He struggled to recall the events during the spell, as if it were one of his dreams; always forgotten. He knew he was crying, filled with emotion and then something changed. He was aware of being in a different place, somewhere else than this here where he found himself to be.

He thought perhaps he was lost somewhere, but not lost to be found; content with where he was and how he was. There was a feeling though that he did not entirely belong there, at least not for now. He couldn't place his finger on the cause for him to leave that place; what entity or whim of his own that had led to his departure.

As he took further breaths inward, his wits came back to him with the realisation of where he was and why he was there.

"Do you have a thought to where you were Luther, if not here?" said the archivist. She herself had been quite taken aback by what she had seen but was intrigued as her inquisitiveness afforded her.

"I was somehow, somewhere else," Luther replied. "I was moved to a different place than here. It was quiet and peaceful. I think it was anyway, but yes, it was not somewhere I was meant to be maybe." Perhaps not for now, no, he wondered to himself.

"Fascinating! Fascinating indeed!" said Celeste Ignophenen, sniffling, tracing her eyes from him to above his head where those entities were circling. "I have never seen anything like it, though I had read of people that were somehow affected some way by the emotions that ebb and flow within us, I never would have thought to have seen such things made manifest!" She reached into her own bag and pulled out a pencil and a notebook which she began furiously writing down all she had seen, and all that Luther would say.

"I must say I have only ever read passing reference to such things, and I only presumed the description of these individuals were more metaphoric than real life occurrences – certainly not something I would witness in a person," continued Celeste.

"You had doubts of the spell working Celeste?" said Ethel.

"Well, I thought it would be an interesting experiment and on the off chance that it actually worked then it would be most fascinating to behold," Celeste responded.

"Something worked," said Luther, with eyes still forward.

The archivist and Celeste both turned and looked at Luther. "Yes, it did indeed Luther!" said Celeste. "Now, tell me more; how do you feel? Where was this place you said you went to? For us you never left this place!" She was clearly eager to know more.

"I can't really recall too well," said Luther. He rested the palm of his hands down on his legs. "All I can tell you is that for that duration I was somewhere else. Somewhere I had not been to before or seen or heard about. I was lost, I think, in that place, but with little inclination to become found."

"I see," replied Celeste. "Could you describe the place?"

"I can't really, in much detail anyway. It was nowhere I had been before if it was anywhere at all."

"Ok," replied Celeste, slightly frustrated. "That seemed to be quite the ordeal there Luther. Thank you for allowing us to witness it. I will need to write up about what we saw. I will need to discuss with the archivist what we both beheld and send a report to the Mage Scribes for perhaps some form publication. Thrilling stuff! Some evidence for this notion of Emotional Energy Congregation." She continued scribbling into her notebook.

"It was quite the experience to be sure," said Ethel. "What will you do now Luther?"

"I am not sure" he replied. "I feel different though."

"In what way?" Ethel replied.

"I feel a quiet reassurance that perhaps I must bear this burden I feel I have upon me. Perhaps there is reason to this misery and gloom that I feel."

"I see. Well, I am glad for you if that be the case," Ethel said.

"Yes of course!" said Celeste putting down her notebook momentarily to blow her nose. "You looked to be some sort of focal point for these emotions – if that is what they are, of course. It was as if you were a lightning rod perhaps, which pulled to ground these emotions manifest. Where from I wonder?"

"Yes, I think perhaps you are right. I feel, for whatever reason that these things you saw are drawn to me. Well, better I keep them to me, so they don't wander elsewhere. I feel that would be for the best."

"But why would you wish to hold onto these things.

They seem to cause you, not harm at least, but sadness and a fatigue of the spirit," said Celeste intently with a sniffle.

"Yes, I suppose, but I feel as though they are drawn to me and perhaps, I can guide them with me. That way they wouldn't fall on others. Perhaps I was somehow meant to have them as my charge. I don't know really," Luther replied. He tried to give an assuring smile as he finally rose his eyes to meet Celeste's.

"You are a noble soul," said the archivist. "It seems quite the burden."

"Yes, it does," said Celeste. "Well, Luther what will you do now?"

"I feel quite like going home," Luther said, wiping his eyes with his sleeve. "We should make ourselves ready."

"Oh Luther! I still have much to ask. Descriptions! Insight is what I need!"

"I am sure you do, but perhaps you got a better idea of what transpired. I can only recall some vague thoughts and feelings with no vivid recollection of what happened. It's quite a journey ` should you wish to discuss this further and perhaps when I have had time to think it through myself, then I would gladly welcome both of you into my home in Overton."

"I think I may well take you up on that!" Said Ms Ignophenen, still staring at Luther, her eyes full of amazement at what she just saw. She yielded to the reality that no matter how much she wished for more information from Luther at this time, it would not be forthcoming.

Luther came away from where he stood and made motions towards the path back to the tunnel. His mood was a strange one. He felt distant as though he was separate from the world. He felt he was outside of things with no anchor to hold him steady in the present. The one thing he wished for was his home and his bed. He had been in unfamiliar surroundings for long enough and with the revelations of the day fresh in his mind his wish was only to be back home, in Overton village.

"I think I would like to go to the cleric's temple where I left my horse and begin the way home - if that's ok," Luther said.

"Very well," said Celeste. "Let us make way back to

the library."

"Yes, of course," added Ethel.

The three of them gathered their things. Celeste gave a nudge with her foot to the warble bear - having seemingly fallen asleep again though all that happened - and they made their way back towards the tunnel.

Luther led them this time, seemingly intent on finding his way back to his horse as quickly as he could.

They arrived at the tunnel entrance or where at least Luther thought it was. He stood aside and let Ethel come by. Again, she placed her hand upon the rock and uttered the words "Reeba." Luther noted to himself that this was not the same phrase used to come through on the other side. He wondered perhaps it was 'Reeba' for entering the tunnel and 'Abeer' to leave.

Like before, after the utterance of the word, there appeared a line around the edge of a stone door and Ethel pushed it inwards, allowing them access to the tunnel. They all walked through into the darkness and again Celeste lit her lamp as it closed behind them.

The brief journey through the tunnel was a quiet one. Luther's mind was awash with thoughts and wonderings. He struggled to recall what happened in any great detail. The only thing he could grasp was that something had indeed transpired, and it involved entities of some sort. Entities that had something to do with him, with his condition; how his mind was beset with sadness.

"I will make sure to come and visit you. It's been too long since I have seen Golon, so I will have more than enough reason to venture that way," Celeste said, breaking the silence of the walk.

Luther jogged from his thoughts said, "Yes of course and I would be delighted to have you." Luther would normally feel unease at the thought of visitors to his safe place, his home, but his mind was still seafaring in a storm of thoughts and emotions that he had no time for other worry.

They reached the other side of the tunnel and as Luther guessed, Ethel said the other word for exiting: "Abeer." The door in the rock face gently opened in as she pulled some unseen handle, born of the stone itself. They arrived back at the library and found it the same as how they left it.

"Luther, that was most interesting. Most eye opening too. I have never seen such a thing before," said the archivist, as the door closed again just before a little bear ran through the doorway to Celeste Ignophenen's side.

Luther gave a small smile at the bear and said, "It was for sure. Though, I do wish I could recall some more specific details. It was no doubt enlightening though and I thank you both."

"It was all perfectly well Luther!" said Celeste with a sniffle. "I have much to think about and to gather into words for a report. Yes, most interesting stuff." She walked over to the desk at which Luther had found her. She pulled the notebook from her bag and immediately started scribbling some notes down again.

"I had better be off then, if that's ok with you both?" said Luther

"Of course," said Ethel, the archivist.

"Yes, that's fine. That's fine," said Celeste. "I will most certainly be looking for you in the next few weeks. I will need to ask questions and discover what you saw, what you felt. Most fascinating stuff!" She raised her hand and Luther shook it with his own.

"Thank you again," said Luther to Celeste.

"See you soon Luther," she said, before turning back and feverishly writing down all that was in her head.

"I shall walk with you back to the way you came in," said Ethel.

"Sure. Of course," replied Luther.

The two of them walked slowly through the library. Luther wondered intently what had transgressed. Though he struggled to recall any details, he had come away feeling a modicum of reassurance that, perhaps there was some rhyme or reason for feeling like he did. He felt that perhaps he was somehow meant to have these feelings and perhaps he was somehow doing a service by shepherding these thoughts or emotions that were present with him.

"Goodbye Luther," said Ethel as they reached the door

above the stairs. "Have a god trip back."

"Thank you, Ethel. And thank you for not turning me away."

"No problem at all. Be well Luther," said archivist. "It has been quite the day."

"Yes, it has," he replied. They both smiled and Luther turned and exited the inner door, which the archivist locked behind him. He then stepped over to the outer exit and left the library.

It was now on the crest of evening and Luther was met encroaching darkness with just a slight of light. He thought it better anyway as he didn't wish to be greeted by the bright hue of the day; blinding him somewhat after his eyes had become attuned to the dimmer light of the house of books below.

All was still quite as he had left it; there was little to be heard or seen other than the rows of buildings standing as they were. The wonky lines of the architecture still protruded in misshapen angles. He took a breath and pulled himself up before stepping out and making his way to the temple.

The walk back was very similar to the way to the library, a lonely affair. Though this time we wondered not the reason for the strangeness of the buildings around him, but for the event he had just been a part of.

Roughly another forty minutes had passed before he arrived back at the Gatehouse that stood between here and the more populated part of the town that housed the temple where Guinevere was stabled.

The same two guards were standing guard as before and when Luther approached within ear shot, one of them said, "Evening sir. You found what you were looking for?"

Luther was slightly bereft of energy since the day's events and not particularly wishing for much conversation, nevertheless tried to respond as best he could, "Hello, I believe I did find what I was looking for, yes. In more ways than one."

"Very good sir," replied the other guard.

Luther gave both soldiers a muted smile and passed through the gatehouse back to the less fortified part of town.

He walked fairly quickly over to the temple and knocked on the door as he had done the previous evening. It opened and Luther was met by the warm smile of Edgar the Cleric.

"Hello Luther."

"Hello Edgar," said Luther.

"Found it all ok I hope?" he said.

"Yes indeed, thank you."

"All your business taken care of?" said Edgar.

Luther was reluctant to make too much eye contact with the cleric, but with these words he tepidly did so. "All taken care of," Luther replied. He gave a smile as best he could.

"Good, good!" quietly bellowed Edgar. "You will be wanting your horse I assume? She's been fed and in good spirits."

"Thank you, Edgar, I am most thankful for all your kind help."

"It's no problem at all," said Edgar. The cleric rather than inviting Luther in, stepped forward and closed the door behind before leading the way behind the temple building to the small adjoined stable.

Inside was Guinevere, who raised her head upon seeing the two figures enter. Luther walked over to her neck, and she lowered it slightly and gave him a nudging hello.

"Hello Gwen," Luther, said stroking her neck and rubbing her nose. "I hope you have kept well. We have a long trip ahead of us, back home." He turned to Edgar, "She looks happy."

Edgar smiled at Luther and said, "She's been munching away on some feed most the day. She is probably up for a bit of exercise!" He took a step closer and patted her on her side.

Luther said, "Right well, I had better be on my way then. Thank you, Edgar, for all your help and please say thank you to Agnes when you see her. If you ever find yourself near Overton village then please drop in at any time."

"It's no trouble at all, Luther. No trouble at all. I shall convey the thanks to Agnes."

The Cleric took a step back as Luther attached his pack to the saddlebags and then with a swift foot into a stirrup, he hoisted himself up and into the saddle. He adjusted his coat and the axe in his sheath at his side and then looked down at Edgar.

"Thank you again Edgar and I wish you all the best."

"You too Luther." The cleric waved as Luther gently encouraged Guinevere back onto the main street and off through Bramstone.

He wondered if the journey back would be quicker. At least he hoped for a less eventful one as his fingers touched the almost healed cut on his face, reminding him of his run in with the bandits on the forest road.

He felt an urgency to find himself back in familiar surroundings which filled him with a drive to find his way back home as quickly as possible.

Besides this he felt a modicum of hope. He now had some very real proof of what caused him to feel the way he felt. Though the reason was not exactly understood, he now knew that it wasn't just his own overarching emotional state that drove him into a sadness and anxiety. There was some other external thing that caused or were somehow associated with these endeavours of misery upon him. He hoped now he could at least accept this as his lot.

The knowledge he wasn't going crazy was of buoying relief. His thoughts now turned almost fully to the journey home. He wished to share his experiences with Nathanael and Golon, upon his return to Overton. He wished to be back there now, enjoying a hearty Coffee by Nathanael's hand and warming assurance of the fireplace. Yes, he thought to himself. Only good things awaited.

A GRIM JOURNEY

Solace

A peak of the Lightlorne mountain range reached out into the simmering ends of the day - light that was fading past the horizon. The height of the rocky edifice was steep as it leered over the mountainside before it, like some knowing duke, aloof and haughty in expression. Its form was dark and abrupt, this rock face atop the mountain. It's almost black rock stretched out all in one piece like a large slab of darkened ice, but with little to reflect upon its thoughts. It was flat and smooth at the edifice of the body of rock, almost like a plateau from which to stand and look out upon the other great peaks and lands that sprawled amongst the foothills. The edges of it were jagged and rough as if the rock face had become frayed. On all sides it looked craggy and tough, making climbing to this spot dangerous in the least if it were not for the small gap that looked to form the sides of a small path that wound its way between the sharp rocky outcrops.

The path that weaved its way up to the mountain top looked not carved or made by intentional hand, but rather a natural shallow groove carved out from some other mineral that lay against that which now featured on the ascent to the top. It was somewhat smooth and wide enough for travel in single file. It followed the contours of the rock as it slowly crept down the solemn mountain.

Looking down this way, facing south, was the path trodden by a lone figure, slowly approaching. This figure was shrouded, not only by a cloak simply pulled about her, but also some local fog that surrounded her as she walked. It seemed to travel as she did, move with every footfall upon the ground, jutting and staggering with any lose step she might make. It seemed to obscure her to a degree, as though she didn't wish to be seen or observed as she quietly and solemnly crept towards the quiet top of the rock.

She carried with her a staff in hand. It looked gnarled and well used. The figure was leaning heavily upon it with every step she took. It would seem she may well fall to the ground should she lose grip of it. Her movement of slow paces, almost shuffling, suggested she was under some steady strain; some weight that pressed upon her as she walked, lagging her steps, reducing her pace to a crawl.

The figure stumbled. She fell down to a knee and paused. It seemed to have taken on a grey hue beyond the darkness of its base colour; a circular imprint of dark and simple grey that formed a perimeter around her, moving with her. The knuckles of her hands were pressed against the rock beneath. The staff lay horizontally, along its length between her hands.

An observer might think she might stay there, spent of all energy and given up upon her journey. This was eventually answered by gripping it with her left and planting it vertically. She placed both hands upon the staff, the dark skin of her fingers clutching it tightly as though restraining the heavy load she bore. Her face came into focus for a moment, until now nearly hidden from view beneath her hood and the fog like aura. She gave a sturdy wince laced with determination as she pulled herself back to her feet pressing heavily upon the staff.

She was now back to that familiar position; slightly hunched with a steeled grip and a determination to continue her journey. The hood she wore looked forward seemingly as she spied where she must go. She once again began moving at a slow, creeping pace. The ground below now turned grey as she passed over it, taking in a breath as she passed by and returning to its near blackened shade as she passed, exhaling again and continuing to breath.

She walked up the small path between the jagged rocks that lead up to the blunted peak, placing the staff just in front of her with every step. Slowly and tepidly, she pulled herself onwards until she had reached the top of this mountain. Her tired legs paused as she crested it and along with the quiet mist. The dark rock beneath her feet had now turned that muted grey; the ground waited with bated breath.

She raised her hooded head high enough for her to see out and beyond, momentarily looking at that which lay down the sheer mountainside. The drop before her was vast, taking many moments to connect with the ground should something become dislodged and escape the stony face.

She looked left, and looked right, and lowered her head again. She looked at the staff in her left hand and twisted that hand slightly as it grasped the wood of it. She rose each foot in turn, just slightly. Her breathing was slow and steady as if she took time to observe every inhale she took.

She sunk down low, but still on her feet, and paused there for several moments. The dark and quiet mist mimicked her movements and stooped down with her. The rock in proximity, beneath her feet, went from that dark and whole black, laying under the weight of what burden she bore and turned to the solemn and meagre grey emanating out from her like a tired breath. Her view veered down to her shoes perhaps to ponder for a while the journey they had taken her. The lowlands of the moor up to the mountainside and the further reaches before this final stand.

Several more moments passed, but she remained crouched in position. She gave no visual or audible telling as to her mood or intention. A few more moments passed before she finally stirred and pulled herself up slowly to her feet, as she was before. It took several more moments to reach an upright and familiar stance as she laid both hands heavy upon the staff, calling on great effort to drag her body up again.

The greying all around her did not retract as she rose up, but rather kept expanding across the top of the mountain. It reached the edge before the drop down on the sheer sides and at that which contained the path that brought the grim lady here. And further it went, a wave front of greying that travelled down the mountain in all directions. It picked up pace with each metre passed, moving quicker and quicker yet with a slothful and tender caress. All became grey and dimmed and quiet and remiss to speak out as though the earth was in a sorrowful mind that seemed sadly to accept that which passed over it.

It swept down and down, through the passages and pathways and across the great swathes of rock and mineral as they lay. It seemed it would not stop, perhaps destined for the horizon.

The grim lady now stood up as straight as she may and

A GRIM JOURNEY

sturdy as she must. She seemed to take little notice of the roving riff of grey that spread forth from her. The mist had raised up with her and around her like a faithful companion determined to provide comfort. She seemed to move her head in such a way as though she finally acknowledged it. She gave something akin to a knowing, thankful smile.

And then, with a simple step forward, she fell from this platform high upon the mountain.

She fell with her staff in hand and the mist still orbiting her, never leaving her side.

She fell quietly, not with a gasp or scream or shout, but with a contented look up her face that would slip into view beneath the hood that covered her.

She fell with little but her cloak and garb grey as the stony face of cliff and rock glided past with every fathom that she fell.

She fell until falling was no longer able.

She fell until the ground below wished only to envelop her. To take her to its bosom.

She fell until there was nowhere left to fall. Just a sudden stop and what that might entail. But, before she fell with arms stretched out and staff in hand, the mist, faithful as it was, moved itself from around her and rather pulled itself below her. And as she fell these last moments. These last few simple moments. It was as though she fell on a bed of dusky mist that set itself between the ground and its charge as if with every intention to entertain.

She fell. She fell, hit the earth beneath her.

But, a failure in the tragedy of impact; there was something else. The mist reached the climax of the fall before her and as she passed through, it embraced her as if determined to avert that fate. The grey landscape looked on with awe as the grim lady, rather than a final, inevitable end was now no longer; vanished from sight in a simple instant. The mist that valiantly broke the fall had disappeared. All that remained was a gnarled old wooden staff simply laying across the ground. The earth took in a sigh of relief, as the wave of muted grey swept back from the horizon, carefully undoing all it had laid. The grim Lady was gone, the earth had not forgotten.

The End.

Scott Littleton has suffered from mental health issues from a young age. He turned to writing, in his thirties, as a way to express the inner workings of someone who suffers from mental illness and the way in which they interact with the world.
He holds a master's degree in Software Engineering.

Printed in Great Britain
by Amazon